Finn couldn't be left in the dark. He had to know what they were facing. "What's the matter?"

The doctor smiled up at him. "Nothing at all. You're having twins."

"Twins!"

Holly said it at the same time as Finn.

"Yes, see here." The doctor showed them both babies.

It was the most amazing thing Finn had ever witnessed in his life. Twins. Who'd have thought? His vision started to blur, causing him to blink repeatedly. He was going to be a father.

He glanced down at Holly. A tear streamed down her cheek. His gut clenched. Was that a sign of joy or unhappiness? It was hard for him to tell. And then she turned and smiled at him. He released the pent-up breath in his lungs.

"Finn, are you okay?"

He glanced up, finding that he was alone with Holly. "Okay? No."

Her lips formed an O. "Can I say or do anything?"

He shook his head. He should be the one reassuring her, letting her know this was all going to be all right, but he couldn't lie to her. He had no idea how any of this was going to be all right. He was the last person in the world who should be a father. In fact, up until this point, he'd intended to leave all his estate to designated charities.

But now ... Wow, everything had just changed.

HER FESTIVE BABY BOMBSHELL

BY
JENNIFER FAYE

First Published in Great Britain 2016
By Mills & Boon, an imprint of HarperCollins Publishers
1 London Bridge Street, London, SE1 9GF

© Jennifer F. Stroka

ISBN: 978-0-263-92025-3

23-1216

Our policy is to use papers that are natural, renewable and recyclable products and made from wood grown in sustainable forests. The logging and manufacturing processes conform to the legal environmental regulations of the country of origin.

Printed and bound in Spain
by CPI, Barcelona

First Published in Great Britain 2016
By Mills & Boon, an imprint of HarperCollins*Publishers*
1 London Bridge Street, London, SE1 9GF

© 2016 Jennifer F. Stroka

ISBN: 978-0-263-92025-3

23-1016

Award-winning author **Jennifer Faye** pens fun, heart-warming romances. Jennifer has won the RT Reviewers' Choice Best Book Award, is a Top Pick author and has been nominated for numerous awards. Now living her dream, she resides with her patient husband, one amazing daughter—the other remarkable daughter is off chasing her own dreams—and two spoiled cats. She'd love to hear from you via her website: www.jenniferfaye.com.

For Nancy F.
To a wonderful lady that I'm honored to know.
Thanks so much for the encouragement.

PROLOGUE

Lockwood International Offices, New York City

"WHAT ARE YOU doing here?" a rich, deep voice called out from the shadows of the executive suite.

Holly Abrams froze. The breath caught in her throat. The pounding of her heart echoed in her ears. She searched the darkness for the mysterious man.

And then he stepped into the light. She immediately recognized him. It was the CEO of Lockwood International, Finn Lockwood. The air whooshed from her lungs.

This wasn't the first time their paths had crossed, but they weren't by any stretch of the imagination what you would consider friends. And he didn't sound the least bit happy to see her, but then again, why should he?

When her gaze met his, her palms grew damp. "Hi." Why did her voice have to be so soft—so seductive? She swallowed hard.

"Isn't it a bit late for you to be working?"

Overtime was nothing new to Holly. After a failed engagement, she'd sworn off men and instead focused all of her energy on her career. When she was working, she felt confident and driven.

"I…uh, have these papers for you." She held out the large manila envelope to him. "I was told you wanted this contract right away." When he went to retrieve the envelope, their fingers brushed. A jolt of awareness arched between them. The sensation zinged up her arm and settled in her chest.

"Thank you." As the seconds ticked by, he asked, "Is there something else you need?"

Need? Her gaze dipped to his lips—his very kissable lips.

She remembered their last meeting in the elevator. They'd been alone when she'd dropped a slip of paper. They'd simultaneously bent over to retrieve it, bringing their faces so close. When they'd straightened, he'd stared at her as though seeing her as a woman instead of as a paralegal in Lockwood's legal department. She knew when a man was interested in her, but when the elevator dinged and the doors slid open, the moment had passed. It had left her wondering if it'd been a product of wishful thinking on her part.

And now, before she made a further fool of herself, she needed to make a speedy exit. "I'll just let you deal with that." She turned to retrace her footsteps back to the elevator when she remembered her manners. She glanced over her shoulder. "Good night."

"Wait."

With her back to him, she inwardly groaned. Her gaze moved to the elevator at the end of the hallway. Her escape was so close and yet so far away. Suppressing a resigned sigh, she turned.

"Come with me." Without waiting for her response, he strode into his office.

What in the world did he want with her? Her black peep-toe platform pumps echoed as she crossed the marble floor. She couldn't tell which was louder, the *click-click* of her heels or the *thump-thump* of her heart. Most people didn't make her nervous, but Mr. Lockwood was the exception.

When Holly entered the spacious office, she had to admit she was awed. While he read over the document, she took in her surroundings. Behind Mr. Lockwood's desk stood a wall of windows. Being so high up, it provided the most amazing view of Manhattan. She longed to rush over and stare out at the bustling city, but she didn't dare.

The sound of a desk drawer opening distracted her. Mr. Lockwood appeared to be searching for something. While he was preoccupied, she continued her visual tour of his office. It reminded her of a museum with its impressive sculptures as well as a baseball collection ensconced in glass cases. But the bookcases spanning an entire wall were what drew her in.

She struggled not to gape at the large collection of books. He liked to read. They had that in common. She wanted to slip across the room and examine the titles, but when she glanced over at Mr. Lockwood, he pointed to one of the two chairs in front of his desk. Without a word, she complied.

"What do you think of the office?"

"It's very nice." She indicated the floor-to-ceiling bookcases. "Have you read them all?"

"I have. And what about you? Do you like to read?"

"Oh, yes." She laced her fingers together to keep from fidgeting with the hem of her skirt. "I read every chance I get."

"Is that why you're not downstairs at the company's fiftieth anniversary celebration? Would you prefer to be at home reading?"

Was this some sort of test? She hesitated. Was there a right and a wrong answer? Her clasped hands tightened as his gaze probed her. Could he tell how nervous his presence made her?

"I missed the party because I needed to finish the contract." She indicated the document on his desk. "I was just going to leave it for you before I headed home." She wasn't the only one not attending the party. What was his excuse for skipping his own celebration? "I figured you'd be at the party."

"I already made a brief appearance. No one will let their guard down around the boss so I made a quick exit, letting everyone get back to having a good time."

She could totally understand people being nervous around him. He was an intense man, who insisted on only the best from his employees. "That can't be much fun for you."

He shrugged. "I'm fine with it."

She looked at him in a new light, realizing for the first time that the privilege of working up here in this ivory tower was also a sentence of isolation. "It doesn't seem right that you're working instead of celebrating your family's accomplishments."

He shook his head. "This is the way it must be."

Well, now, that was an odd comment. It was on the tip of her tongue to question him about it, but she thought better of it. She had a feeling his pleasantness had its limitations.

Quietness settled over the room as Mr. Lockwood scanned the twenty-one-page document. Holly struggled to sit still—waiting and wondering why he wanted her to remain there. Her index finger repeatedly smoothed over the chipped nail polish on her thumb.

There was something about this man that turned her into a mass of jittery nerves. But what? It wasn't his billions or his power. It was something more intrinsic, but she couldn't quite put her finger on it.

"This exhibit isn't right." He gestured to a page in the contract. "Do you have your source material?"

"Not on me. But I double-checked everything." In actuality, she'd quadruple-checked the figures, but she didn't want to sound like she'd been trying too hard to impress him.

His brows drew together into a formidable line. "You had to have made a mistake. This doesn't make sense."

"Prove it." The words slipped past her lips before she could stop them.

Mr. Lockwood's eyes widened as though unaccustomed to being challenged. She continued to hold his gaze. She wasn't going to back down—not when the one thing she greatly valued was in question—her reputation.

"These exhibits are skewed. I'm positive of it." His eyes darkened. "I'll log in to the system and then you can show me where you pulled your numbers."

For the next hour they worked side by side, going over the figures in the exhibits. In the end the contract was wrong, but to Holly's relief, it hadn't been her fault. The numbers on one of the source files had been transposed. After printing a revised copy, Finn signed it. Holly used his personal assistant's scanner to email the contract to the designated party.

"Thanks for the assistance." Finn slipped the hard copy back into the envelope. "Sorry to take up so much of your evening and for causing you to miss dinner." He glanced at his Rolex. "We'll have to remedy that."

"That's okay. It's not a big deal."

"I insist on dinner." He stood and then moved around the desk. "You did me a big favor tonight by helping with the contract." His gaze dipped to her lips before quickly returning to her face. The corners of his mouth lifted into a sexy smile. "And I'd like to show you how thankful I am for the help with meeting that deadline."

Oh, he definitely had more than dinner on his mind. The thought sent a new wave of nervous tremors through her stomach. She glanced away. Her initial inclination was to turn him down. Her experience with men was less than impressive. But did that mean she had to live in solitude?

What was wrong with a little company? A little laughter and perhaps flirting? And maybe a little more. Her gaze met his once more. It'd all be fine as long as neither of them had any expectations. After all, it wasn't like it would ever happen again.

"Dinner sounds good."

"Great." He made a brief phone call and then turned to her. "It's all arranged. I'll just drop this envelope on Clara's desk and then we'll be off."

A little voice inside Holly said to be cautious. Finn Lockwood wasn't just any man and she knew nothing of his world. But another part of her was drawn to him like a moth to a flame—and boy, was he hot.

The sizzling tension smoldered between them as they quietly rode down in the elevator. When they stepped into the parking garage beneath the building there was a sleek black town car waiting for them. A driver immediately alighted and opened the door for them.

Holly climbed in first, followed by Finn. When he joined her, his muscular leg brushed against hers. Her stomach shivered with excitement. When their hands came to rest side by side on the leather seat, neither pulled away. It felt as though the interior of the car was statically charged. Every nerve ending tingled with anticipation.

As the car eased into the Friday evening traffic, she glanced over at Finn. She was surprised to find him staring back at her. Her heart *thump-thumped*, loud and fast.

"Where to, sir?" the driver asked.

"The penthouse." Finn's darkened gaze returned to Holly. "I thought we would dine in. Unless, of course, you have something else in mind."

She had something on her mind, but it wasn't food. Perhaps she had been spending too much time working these days because there had to be a reasonable explanation for her lack of common sense. Because all she could think about was how much she longed to press her lips to his.

CHAPTER ONE

Seven weeks later...

BAH, HUMBUG...

Finn Lockwood didn't care if the saying was cliché. It was how he felt. Even though this was the first week after Thanksgiving, the holiday festivities were in full swing. He wanted no part of having a holly jolly Christmas. Even though he'd turned off the speakers in his office, the music still crept down the hallway, taunting him with its joyous melody.

He did his utmost to block out the mocking words. Instead, he focused on the stack of papers awaiting his signature. He was so close to being out of here—out of the office—out of New York City.

"I just love this." His longtime assistant, Clara, strode into his office with a hefty stack of papers.

"Love what? The endless phone calls and this mess of paperwork?"

"Um, no." Color filled her cheeks as she placed the papers on his desk. "I meant this song, 'Home for the Holidays.' It puts me in a warm fuzzy mood."

His pen hovered over the document as he paused to listen. The sentimental words about home and family stabbed at his scarred heart. "To each his own."

She swept her dark bobbed hair behind her ear. "Although it never feels like the holiday season until that first snowflake falls. Don't you think so?"

He frowned at her. "How long have you known me?"

"Almost eight years."

"And by now I'd have thought you'd realize I don't do holidays."

"I... I just keep hoping—"

"Don't. It's not going to happen." An awkward silence ensued as he glanced over a disbursement and then signed it.

"Oh. I almost forgot. These came for you." She handed over two tickets for the Mistletoe Ball.

He accepted the tickets. Without bothering to look at them, he slipped them in a side desk drawer with other tickets from years gone by. When he glanced back at his assistant, unspoken questions reflected in her eyes. "What?"

Clara hesitated, fidgeting with the pen in her hand. "Why do you order tickets every year but then never use them?"

"Don't you think it's a worthy cause?" When Clara nodded, he continued. "I want to do my part." His voice grew husky with emotion. "If everyone does their part, maybe they'll find a cure for leukemia. The damn disease steals lives far too soon." His hand tightened around the pen. "It leaves nothing but devastation in its wake."

Clara's eyes widened. "I... I agree. I, um, just can't afford the tickets."

Finn realized he'd said too much. No one knew he was the sole sponsor of the ball and that was the way he intended for it to remain. But he just couldn't attend—couldn't face the guilt. If it wasn't for him and his actions, his mother and father would still be alive. They'd be attending the ball each year just like they'd always done in years past.

Finn pulled open the desk drawer and removed the tickets. "Here. Take them. It'd be better if they were used rather than sitting around gathering dust."

Her gaze moved from the tickets to him. "But I couldn't. You should give them to someone else."

When she rattled off the names of people who headed up his various divisions and departments, he said, "I want you to have them."

"Thank you." She accepted the tickets with a hesitant smile.

"Now back to business. I hope this is the last of what I need to sign because we have a trip to prepare for."

"A trip? When?"

"Tomorrow morning." This wasn't the first time he'd sprung a spur-of-the-moment trip on her. "And I'll need you there—"

"But…" Clara worried her bottom lip.

"But what? Surely you can reschedule anything on my calendar for some time after the first of the year."

"It's not that."

Color stained her cheeks as she glanced down at the tickets. She remained quiet, which was so unlike her. Something was definitely amiss and he didn't like it, not one little bit. They were set to leave in the morning for his private island in the Caribbean for a secret business meeting. When it concluded, Clara would return to New York while he remained in the sun and sand until after the New Year—when life returned to normal and people were no longer gushing with the holiday spirit.

Clara's continued silence worried him. He leaned back in his chair, taking in the worry lines bracketing her eyes. "What's the problem?"

"I got engaged last night." She held up her hand. A sparkly diamond now resided on her ring finger.

"Congratulations."

"Thank you."

"I'm sure you'll have lots of planning to do after our trip—"

"Well, um…that's the thing." Her gaze dipped again. "We're eloping this weekend."

"What?" She couldn't be serious. He had everything worked out. His business associates were meeting them on his private island in two days. "You can't back out on me now."

"I'm really sorry. But Steve, my fiancé, he, um…surprised me with tickets to fly to Vegas."

Finn resisted rolling his eyes. *Could things get any worse?* His plans had already hit a major snag, prompting this emergency meeting, and now his trusted employee was running off to Vegas to get hitched by some Elvis impersonator. *This is just great!*

"You can't bail on me." He raked his fingers through his hair. "I need your assistance for this meeting. It's important."

"Oh. Um…" She wrung her hands together.

He caught the shimmer of unshed tears in Clara's eyes. This was not good—not good at all. He was so used to having Clara at his beck and call that he hadn't anticipated this scenario. He hated being put in this position—choosing between his work and his associate's happiness. There had to be a compromise.

After a bit of thought, he conceded. "If you can find a suitable replacement, you can have the time off. But it'll have to be done pronto. My meeting can't be delayed."

Clara's eyes widened. "I'll get right on it. I'll have someone by this afternoon."

She turned and rushed out the door, leaving him alone to scowl about his plans being upended. Normally he'd have insisted on being involved in the selection of a temporary PA, but these weren't normal circumstances. His private jet was already being fueled up for tomorrow's flight.

He tapped his pen repeatedly on the desk. Why did Clara have to pick now to elope? Not that he wasn't happy for her. He was. He just wasn't happy about the surprise. Okay, so he didn't like surprises and certainly not when they caused his plans to go awry.

Just like his evening with Holly. Talk about everything going sideways—in a mind-blowing way. It'd been weeks since they'd been together and he still couldn't get her out of his system. Though they'd agreed there would be no repeat of the amazing evening, he regretted letting her go more than he thought possible.

* * *

What had she been thinking?

Holly Abrams stood alone in the elevator at Lockwood International. She pressed the button for the top floor—Finn's floor. The last time she'd visited the executive suite things had spiraled totally out of control. One moment they were talking work and the next she'd been in Finn's luxury penthouse. The memory made her stomach dip.

There'd been candles, delicious food, sparkling wine and honeyed compliments. It'd been quite a heady combination. And when at last he'd pressed his lips to hers, she'd have sworn she'd fallen head over heels in love with him. It was though this thing had been building between them since they first met. Love at first sight?

She didn't believe in it. This thing, it had to be infatuation—a great big case of it. And even though they'd mutually agreed to go their separate ways, her oasis at the office had turned stressful with reminders of Finn at every turn.

The elevator dinged and the door slid open. She stepped out. Taking a deep, steadying breath, she started down the hallway toward Clara's desk—toward Finn's office. However, Clara wasn't at her desk. Holly's gaze moved to Finn's closed door. She had a moment of déjà vu and her heart raced.

The door swung open. Who was it? Finn?

And then Clara stepped into the hallway. Holly sighed. She dismissed the disappointment that assailed her as Clara headed toward her.

The young woman's eyes reflected an inner turmoil. "There you are. Thank goodness you came."

"What's the matter?"

"Everything."

"Whoa. It can't be that bad."

"You're right." The frown on Clara's face said otherwise. "I... I need to ask you for a huge favor. And I'll totally understand if you can't do it. I just don't know anyone else who can help. And this just has to work out—"

"Slow down. Tell me what it is." Holly thought of Clara as a friend ever since they met on the charity committee. The woman was always generous in word and deed.

"My boyfriend proposed last night." A smile lifted her lips as she held up her left hand.

"Wow! Congratulations! I'm so happy for you." She gave Clara a brief hug.

Clara pulled back. "Thank you. It really was a surprise. We've been together for over five years now. I'd pretty much given up on him ever proposing. Anyway the plan is we catch a plane tomorrow and elope in Vegas followed by a honeymoon in Napa Valley. I can't postpone it. I don't want him changing his mind."

"Don't worry. Everything will work out." She was happy that Clara was finally getting her happily-ever-after. Holly didn't see such a rosy future for herself, but it didn't mean she didn't believe it could happen for others. "What can I do to help?"

"I know this is a lot to ask, but I need you to fill in for me while I'm off on my honeymoon."

"What?" Clara wanted her to be Finn's assistant? No. Impossible. Finn would never agree. She must have misunderstood. "You want me to be Mr. Lockwood's assistant?"

Clara nodded. "It won't be for long."

Her friend had absolutely no idea what she was asking of her. None whatsoever. She'd given Finn her word that she'd stay clear of him just as he'd agreed to do the same for her.

Now it appeared she had to make a very difficult choice—keep her word to Finn or keep her friendship with Clara. Holly's stomach plummeted into her Louis Vuittons. She desperately wanted to do both.

But that wasn't possible.

CHAPTER TWO

THERE HAD TO be a way out.

But how? Holly couldn't bear to hurt Clara's feelings. But Holly acting as Finn's assistant for even the briefest time would be at the very least awkward. It'd raise too many memories—memories best left alone.

How did she explain that this arrangement would never work? No one knew about that special evening she'd spent with Finn. And it had to remain that way.

Holly smoothed a nonexistent wrinkle from her skirt. "I can't just move up here. What about my work in the legal department?"

Clara sent her a pleading look with her eyes. "If that's all you're worried about, I worked it out with your boss. You are temporarily transferred here. But don't worry. Working for Mr. Lockwood comes with benefits."

She'd already sampled Mr. Lockwood's benefits and they were unforgettable, but she was certain that was not what Clara meant. "Did you talk this over with F…ah, Mr. Lockwood?"

Clara's eyes momentarily widened at Holly's slip of the tongue. "I did and he's on board."

He was? Really? She was running out of excuses about why this wouldn't work. But maybe this was the break she was looking for. If Finn was open to taking her on as his assistant, would it be such a stretch to think he'd consider giving her a personal referral?

It was time she left Lockwood International. And like a sign, there was an opening at another *Fortune 500* company for an assistant to the lead counsel. She'd heard about the position through a friend of a friend. But the attorney was older and wanted someone closer to his age with top qualifications.

The cards were stacked against Holly as she was in her twenties and her experience was so-so, depending on what the position required. But it would be a big boost for her and it would make it possible for her mother to make her time off permanent.

Holly had come up with one thing that just might make gaining the new position a real possibility, a letter of recommendation from Finn—a well-respected businessman. Although she hadn't quite figured out how to approach him. But then again, it appeared he'd taken that problem out of her hands.

After all, she'd only have to be his PA for one week and then he'd be on his annual holiday. She'd have the office to herself. In the meantime, it wasn't like they were going to be working in the same office. He'd be down the hall behind a closed door and she'd be out here. If he could make it work, then so could she.

"I'll do it."

Clara's face lit up like a Christmas tree. "I was hoping you'd say that. I can spend the rest of today going over current projects with you, but first let's go get you introduced to Mr. Lockwood."

On wooden legs, Holly followed Clara down the hallway. Her morning coffee sloshed in her stomach, making her nauseated. *Keep it together. Just act professional.*

Clara knocked on the door and then entered. Holly followed her inside. Her heart picked up its pace as her gaze eagerly sought him out. His hair appeared freshly trimmed. And the blue button-up accentuated his broad, muscular shoulders. Holly swallowed hard.

He glanced up from his computer monitor. Was that surprise reflected in his blue-gray eyes? It couldn't be. He'd approved this scenario. In a blink, the look was gone.

"Mr. Lockwood, I'd like to introduce Holly Abrams." Clara's voice drew Holly from her thoughts. "She's from the legal department."

"We've met." His gaze moved between the two women. "The question is what's she doing in my office?"

Clara sent him a nervous smile. "She's agreed to step up and fill in for me while I'm away on my honeymoon. Her boss in legal gave nothing but rave reviews about her."

"I see." Finn's gaze moved to Holly.

What was she missing here? Hadn't Clara said Finn had approved of this temporary assignment? She forced a smile to her lips as his intense gaze held her captive. Her heart continued to race and her palms grew damp. She should say something, but the jumbled words in her mind refused to form a cohesive sentence.

Clara spoke, breaking the mounting silence. "She'll do a really good job for you."

"I don't know about this." Finn leaned back in the black leather chair. "Why don't you give us a moment to talk?" Clara made a discreet exit. It wasn't until the door snicked shut that Finn spoke again with a serious, no-nonsense tone. "Okay, we're alone now. Please explain to me what happened to our agreement to keep clear of each other."

"Clara said that she okayed this with you. I figured if you were big enough to deal with this awkward situation for Clara's sake then so was I. After all, Clara would do most anything for anyone. And it is her wedding—"

"Enough. I get the point. But this—" he gestured back and forth between them "—it won't work."

"That's fine with me. Do you have someone else who can fill in?"

Finn cleared his throat. "No, I don't."

Holly clasped her hands together to keep from fidgeting and straightened her shoulders. "I know that we've never worked together, but I think I can do the job."

Finn leaned back in his chair and crossed his arms. "Tell me why I should give you a chance."

Holly swallowed hard, not expecting to have to interview for the position, but when she recalled the desperation in her friend's voice, she knew she couldn't let Clara down. "I'm a hard worker. I'm the first through the door in the morning and I'm the last out in the evening."

"Are you sure that's a good thing? Perhaps you just don't get your work done in a timely manner."

Her gaze narrowed. Why exactly was he giving her such a hard time? A smart retort teetered on the tip of her tongue, but she choked it back, refusing to let him provoke her. "No. I like to be punctual. I like to have the coffee brewing and a chance to take off my coat before the phone starts ringing. And I don't rush out the door at the end of the day simply because I can't. I usually have a task or two dropped on my desk by my boss as he's leaving."

Finn nodded as though her answer pleased him. "And you think you're up to the challenges of being my PA?"

"I do."

"You do realize that what happened between us is in the past. It will have no bearing on our working relationship."

"I wouldn't have it any other way."

"Good."

"Does that mean I have the position?" The breath caught in her throat as she waited for his answer.

Seconds ticked by and still he said nothing. What in the world? She thought of all the things she could say to him to sell herself, but she didn't want to look desperate because she wasn't. Oh, maybe she was just a bit. She had a plan and he played a pivotal role.

"Okay. You've convinced me. We'll do this."

The breath rushed from Holly's straining lungs. "Thank you. I'll go catch up on everything I need to know from Clara."

"Holly, remember this is strictly work."

Like she could or would forget. "I understand, Mr. Lockwood."

He frowned. "I don't think we have to be that formal. Finn will do."

"Yes, sir...erm...Finn."

This was it, she was in. She should be inwardly cheering or smiling or something. And yet she stood there transfixed by the man who danced through her dreams each night and left her longing for a glance of him each day. The truth was that she didn't know how to react. It was one of those good news–bad news scenarios.

The best thing she could do was leave. The sooner, the better. She turned for the door.

"Holly, there's one more thing." He waited until she turned around before continuing. "Make sure you aren't late tomorrow morning. Takeoff is at six a.m. sharp."

"Takeoff?"

Finn's brows scrunched together. "Clara didn't tell you?"

"Tell me what?"

"We're leaving first thing in the morning for the Caribbean. I have an extremely important meeting there."

This was not what she'd been expecting at all. How was she supposed to fly to a sunny destination spot with the sexiest guy alive—a man who could heat her blood with just a look? She inwardly groaned. She was in so much trouble here.

Not only was she nervous about being around him—about remembering their first night together in vivid detail—but she was also a nervous flier, as in white-knuckling it through turbulence. Exactly how long was a flight from New York City to the Caribbean?

No matter what, she wasn't about to back out of this arrangement. There was too much riding on it—too many people counting on her. Her mother's pale face flashed in her mind. After her mother's recent stroke, the doctor had warned that with her other medical conditions, if she didn't slow down, her health would be put at greater risk. Holly needed to do whatever she could to further her career in order to support her and her mother.

"Holly? Will that be a problem?"

His voice drew her from her frantic thoughts. "I didn't know. Where will we be staying?"

"On my private island."

Oh, boy! One private island. One sexy guy. And a whole lot of chemistry. What could possibly go wrong with this scenario?

CHAPTER THREE

TWENTY-TWO MINUTES LATE, Holly rushed through the airport early the next morning. Her suitcase *clunk-clunked* as it rolled over the tiled floor.

She hadn't meant to stay up late the night before, talking on the phone, but it'd been a long time since she'd heard her mother so exuberant. Apparently the Sunshine State agreed with her, especially the strolls along the beach while Holly's aunt was off at her waitressing job.

When her mother mentioned returning to New York, Holly readily assured her there was no rush. At the same time, she'd made a mental note to send her aunt some more money to cover her mother's living expenses. Holly proceeded to fill her mother in on the business trip, citing her absence as another reason for her mother to remain in Florida. Her mother actually sounded relieved, confirming Holly's belief that she needed to do everything to ensure her mother didn't have to worry about money. And that hinged on impressing Finn.

But this morning, if anything could have gone wrong, it had. As late as she was, Finn would think she was incompetent or worse that she'd changed her mind and backed out without a word. And because she'd been so rattled yesterday, she'd forgotten to get his cell number.

When she finally reached the prearranged meeting spot, Finn stood there, frowning. She was breathless and feeling totally out of sorts.

His piercing gaze met hers. "I didn't think you were going to show up."

She attempted to catch her breath. "There was an accident."

Immediately his anger morphed into concern. "Are you okay?"

"It wasn't me. It was the vehicle two cars up from my cab." In that moment the horrific events played in her mind. "One second we're moving along the highway and the next a little sports car attempts to cut off a souped-up pickup truck with large knobby tires. The car swerved wildly across the lanes as tires screeched and the driver tried to regain control, but the car lifted and flipped a couple of times." Tears welled up in her eyes. "I never witnessed something so horrific. I… I don't think the driver made it."

Finn reached out to her and pulled her close. Her cheek rested against his shoulder. "Thank God you're safe."

Her emotions bubbled to the surface. The worry. The fear. The shock. She wasn't sure how much time had passed as Finn continued to hold her. Horrific scenes of the accident played in her mind, one after the other. She knew she shouldn't seek comfort in his arms. Although it was innocent enough, it wasn't part of their agreement. And yet, she didn't move.

It was only when she started to gather herself that she noticed the spicy scent of his cologne. It would be so easy to forget about their agreement and turn in his arms, claiming his very kissable lips. Every cell in her body longed to do just that. Just once more.

But she couldn't. Once would not be enough. Frustration balled up inside her. Besides, he was just being nice— a gentleman. She refused to throw herself at him and ruin everything. After all, she was out to prove to him that she was an invaluable asset in the office.

With great regret, she extricated herself from his arms, already missing the warmth of his touch. "I must be such a mess." She swiped her hands over her cheeks. "Sorry about that. I… I'm usually—"

"No apologies necessary." He waved away her words. "I'm just relieved you're safe."

The sincerity in his words had her glancing up at him. In that moment he'd reverted back to Finn Lockwood, the friendly man who'd taken her to his penthouse to thank her for her help with the contract. The man who'd spent the evening wining and dining her with some pasta he'd whipped up himself. The same man who'd entertained her with tales of hilarious fiascos at the office. The man who'd swept her off her feet.

"What are you thinking?"

His voice drew her from her thoughts. Not about to tell him the truth, she said, "That we should get moving. I've already put you behind schedule."

"You're right." He gestured for her to walk ahead of him.

Her insides shivered with nervous tension. She couldn't tell if it was from being held in Finn's arms or the thought of soaring through the air in his jet. Maybe she should mention her fear of flying to Finn. Then again, they'd already shared more than enough for now. She would just lose herself in her work. If all went well, he'd never even know of her phobia of heights.

What had he been thinking?

Finn sat across the aisle from Holly on his private jet. They were in midflight and Holly had been surprisingly quiet. It suited him just fine. He was preparing for his upcoming meeting, or he had been until thoughts of Holly infiltrated his mind. Truth be told, he hadn't been able to let go of the memories of their night together. She was amazing and so easy to be with. Most people wouldn't find that to be a problem, but he did.

He refused to let someone get close to him—he would do nothing but lead them to unhappiness. Because that was what happened to the people he cared about—he let them down. And Holly was too nice to get caught up with the likes of him.

The onboard phone buzzed. Finn took the call from the pilot. After a brief conversation, he turned to Holly, who had her window shade drawn. He presumed it was to cut down on the glare on her digital tablet. He, on the other hand, enjoyed being able to look out at the world around them. However, the overcast day hampered much of his view. "That was the captain. He said we should buckle our seat belts as we're about to hit some rough weather."

Without argument or for that matter a word, Holly did as he asked. She then returned her attention to the tablet as though she hadn't heard him. What in the world had her so absorbed?

He gave a shake of his head and turned back to his laptop. He'd been working on an agenda for his upcoming meeting, but he'd totally lost track of his line of thought. He started reading the last couple of bullet points when his attention meandered back to Holly.

Giving up on his attempt to work, Finn closed his laptop. He glanced over at her, which was a mistake. He was immediately drawn in by her natural beauty. He loved that she didn't wear heavy makeup, only a little bit to accent her own unique qualities.

There was just something so different about Holly, but he couldn't quite put his finger on exactly what made her so much more appealing than the other women who had passed through his life. Maybe it was that she was content with her life—not looking to him for a leg up in her career. Or maybe it was that she treated him like everybody else instead of trying to cater to him. Whatever it was, he was intrigued by her.

Realizing he was staring, he cleared his throat. "What are you reading?"

She glanced up as though completely lost in thought. "What did you say?"

He smiled, liking the sheepish look on her face and the touch of pink in her cheeks. "I was wondering what had you so deep in thought."

She glanced down at her tablet and then back at him. "Um, nothing."

"Must be something to have you so preoccupied."

"Just some work."

"Work? I don't recall giving you anything to do on the way to the island."

She worried her bottom lip. "I was doing a little research."

"Do tell. I'm thoroughly intrigued."

She set aside her tablet. "I downloaded some background on the businessmen that you'll be meeting with."

"Really? I thought you'd prefer to read a book."

"I like to be prepared. Clara gave me their names. I hope you don't mind."

"What else did she tell you about the meeting?"

"Nothing except that it is extremely important and top secret."

He smiled, liking that Clara had emphasized discretion. Of course, Holly would learn all about his plans soon enough. "Let me know if you uncover anything noteworthy."

"I will." She once more picked up her tablet.

Why was she working so hard on this? Surely she wasn't this thorough normally. There had to be something driving her. Was she afraid of disappointing him?

Or more likely, she was doing whatever she could to ignore him.

Just then the plane started to vibrate. Finn glanced over at Holly and noticed that she had the armrests in a death grip. "Don't worry. It's just some turbulence."

She looked at him, her eyes as big as saucers. "Maybe we should land until it passes over."

"You don't fly much, do you?"

She shook her head. "Never had much reason. Anyplace I've ever wanted to go I can get to by train or car."

"Well, relax. Turbulence is common. It's nothing to worry about."

"Easy for you to say," she said in a huff.

He suppressed a chuckle. She did have spirit. Maybe that was what he liked so much about her. Otherwise, why would he have agreed to this completely unorthodox arrangement?

Perhaps if he could get her talking, she'd temporarily forget about the turbulence. "Where are these places you visit by car or train?"

She glanced at him with an *Are you serious*? look. He continued staring at her, prompting her to talk.

"I... I don't go away often."

"But when you do travel, where do you go?"

"The ocean."

It wasn't much, but it was a start. "Which beach is your favorite?"

"Ocean City and..." The plane shook again. Her fingers tightened on the armrests. Her knuckles were white.

"I must admit I've never been to Ocean City. Is there much to do there?" When she didn't respond, he said, "Holly?"

"Um, yes. Ah, there's plenty to do along the boardwalk. But I like to take a book and sit on the beach."

"What do you read?"

"Mysteries. Some thrillers."

He continued talking books and authors with her. He found that she was truly passionate about books. As she talked about a series of suspense novels she was in the process of reading, his attention was drawn to her lips—her tempting lips. It'd be so easy to forget the reason for this trip and the fact she was helping him out.

What would she say if he were to take her in his arms and press his lips to hers?

His phone buzzed again. After a brief conversation with the pilot, he turned to Holly. "The pilot believes we're past the bad weather. You can relax. It should be smooth flying from here on out."

The tension visibly drained from her as her shoulders relaxed and her hands released the armrests. "That's good news. I guess I'm not a very good flyer."

"Oh, trust me, you're doing fine. I've experienced worse. Much worse." He inwardly shuddered, recalling a couple of experiences while flying commercial airlines.

His attention returned to his laptop. He was surprised the break had him feeling refreshed. His fingers flew over the keyboard. Some time had passed when he grew thirsty.

He got up from his seat. "Can I get you something to drink?"

"That sounds good. But I can get it."

She stood up and followed him to the front of the plane where there was a small kitchenette. "I'm surprised you don't have any staff on board."

"Staff? For just me?" He shook his head. "I don't need anyone standing around, waiting for something to do. Besides, I appreciate the time alone."

"Oh."

"Sorry. I didn't mean that the way it sounded. I'm happy having you along."

"You are?" Her eyes widened. And was that a smile playing at the corners of her lips?

"I am. You're doing me a big favor. This meeting can't be rescheduled. It's time sensitive. And I didn't want to ruin Clara's wedding."

"Seems it all worked out."

He arched a brow. "Did it? Are you really okay with being here?"

"I—"

The plane violently shuddered. Then the plane dipped. A gasp tore from Holly's lips. Her body swayed forward. He sprang into action, catching her.

"It'll be okay."

The fear in her eyes said she didn't believe him.

As the pilot guided the plane through a particularly rough patch of airspace, Finn held on to Holly, who in turn held on to him. This was the exact thing he'd told himself that wouldn't occur on this trip, but fate seemed to have other plans.

He looked down at her as she lifted her chin. Their gazes met and held. Even when the plane leveled out, he continued to hold her. The emotions reflected in her eyes were intense. Or was he reading what he wanted to see in them?

He did know one thing—having her this close was doing all sorts of crazy things to his body. He caught a whiff of her soft floral scent and inhaled deeper. The pleasing scent swept him back to that not-so-long-ago night. Maybe playing it safe was overrated.

The plane started to vibrate again. Her wide-eyed gaze reflected fear. He knew how to distract her. His head dipped. His lips swooped in, claiming hers. She didn't move at first as though surprised by his actions. But in seconds her lips moved beneath his.

Holly was amazing. He'd never met a woman who intrigued him both mentally and physically. Her lips parted and his tongue slipped inside. She tasted of mint with a hint of chocolate. A moan swelled in his throat.

His thoughts turned toward the big bed in the back of the plane. Should he even entertain such an idea? But with the heat of their kiss, it wasn't out of bounds. All he had to do was scoop her up in his arms. It wasn't like it'd be their first time. Or even their second.

There was a sound. But he brushed it off, not wanting

anything to ruin this moment. And yet there it was again. He concentrated for a second and realized it was the private line from the cockpit.

With great regret, he pulled back. "I better get that. It's the pilot."

Her lips were rosy and slightly swollen. And her eyes were slightly dilated. He'd never seen a more tempting sight. And yet his mind told him the interruption was exactly what they needed. It would give them time to come to their senses.

CHAPTER FOUR

"THIS IS YOUR PLACE?"

Holly exited the helicopter that had transported them from the airstrip on the big island to Finn's private island. The landing zone sat atop a hill. It was the only place on the small island cleared of greenery except for the white sandy beach.

Finn moved to her side. "Do you like it?"

"I do. I've only ever seen places like this on television or on the internet. I never imagined I would one day step foot in paradise."

"Paradise?"

"Yes. You don't think so?"

"I never really thought about it." He rolled her suitcase to the edge of the helipad. "I'm afraid we have to walk to the house. It isn't far."

"No worries. This jaunt is nothing compared to the hour I spend each day at the gym sweating my butt off." She pressed her lips together, realizing she'd probably shared more than he ever wanted to know about her.

When she reached for her suitcase, their fingers brushed. He looked at her. "I can take it."

She wasn't about to be treated like a helpless woman. She'd been standing on her own two feet since she was ten and her father had walked out on her and her mother. Someone had to pick up the slack. At that point in time, her mother hadn't been in any condition.

Holly's grip tightened around the handle. "I can manage."

"You do know it'll have to be carried over the rough terrain."

"Understood. I'll count it as exercise on my calorie counter."

He shook his head as he stepped back. "By the way,

there's a gym at the house. Please feel free to use it. I certainly don't make it there nearly enough."

"Thanks. I just might take you up on the offer." When he gestured for her to go ahead of him, she said, "I'd rather follow while I get my bearings."

With a shrug, he set off down the stone path surrounded by lush green foliage.

Her gaze followed him and he set a steady pace.

But it wasn't the beautiful setting that held her attention—it was Finn. His shoulders were broad and muscled, while his waist was trim without an ounce of flub. And his backside, well, it was toned. A perfect package.

"See anything in particular you like?"

Heat rushed to her cheeks. Had he just busted her checking him out? Her gaze lifted and she was relieved to see that he was still facing straight ahead. "Lots. You're so lucky to live here."

"Only part-time. When you're done working, please feel free to use all of the facilities including the pool."

He didn't have to give her any more encouragement. She had every intention of checking it all out since she would never be back here again. "I do have to admit that this does feel strange."

"How so?"

"Leaving the snow and Christmas decorations in New York and landing here where there's nothing but a warm breeze and sunshine. Do you decorate a palm tree instead of a pine tree for Christmas?"

He stopped walking and turned to her. "I don't do either. I thought Clara might have mentioned it."

"She didn't say a word."

"Long story short, I don't like Christmas." He turned and continued along the path to the house.

He didn't like Christmas? She really wanted to hear the long version of that story. Was he a real-life Grinch? Impossible. He was friendly—when he wanted to be. Social—again, when he wanted to be. So why did he hate Christmas?

Wait. Who hated Christmas? It was full of heartwarming, sentimental moments. Twinkle lights. Snowflakes. Presents. Shopping. Definitely lots of shopping. And the most delicious food.

Whatever. His reasons for not enjoying the holiday were his problem. They were certainly none of her business. But that wasn't enough to suppress her curiosity.

"Why don't you like Christmas?" she blurted out.

He stopped. His shoulders straightened. When he turned, his forehead was creased with lines and his brows were drawn together. "Does everyone have to enjoy the holidays?"

She shrugged. "I suppose not. But I'm sure they all have a reason. I was just curious about yours."

"And if I don't want to share?"

"It's your right. I just thought after we talked on the plane that we were at the stage where we shared things with each other."

"You mean you equate our talk of books to digging into my life and finding out how my mind ticks? No." He shook his head. "My personal life is off limits." His tone lacked its earlier warmth. In fact, it was distinctly cold and rumbled with agitation. "You might research prospective business associates, but I'd appreciate it if you wouldn't put my life under your microscope."

What is he afraid I'll find?

She gave herself a mental shake. He was right. She was treading on a subject that was none of her business. His dislike of Christmas had nothing to do with her presence on—what was the name of this island? She scanned her mind, but she didn't recall him ever mentioning it.

"What did you say the name of this island is?"

"I didn't."

Surely this wasn't another one of those subjects that was off limits. Even she couldn't be that unlucky.

As though reading her mind, he said, "It's called Lockwood Isle."

Not exactly original, but fitting. "Your own island nation."

He shrugged. "Something like that. It's a place to get away from everything."

Her phone buzzed with a new email. "Not exactly everything. I see there's internet access."

"As much as I'd like to totally escape, I do have an international company to run. I can't cut myself off completely."

Holly was relieved to know that she could keep in contact with her mother. Even though she'd made financial arrangements with her aunt for her mother to make her very first visit to Florida, she still wanted to talk with her daily. Holly needed the reassurance that there weren't any setbacks with her health.

Her gaze strayed back to her host. She might not have to worry too much about her mother right now, but she did have to worry about Finn. That kiss on the plane, it couldn't happen again. He wasn't looking for anything serious and neither was she. Her focus had to be on getting his recommendation for the new job.

Finn stopped walking. "Here we are."

She glanced up at the white house with aqua shutters. The home was raised up on what looked like stilts. Each post was thick like an enormous tree trunk. It certainly looked sturdy enough.

Still staring at the impressive structure, she asked, "Why is the house on pylons? Are there a lot of storms?"

"No. But some of them bring in a high storm surge. I like to be prepared."

She had a feeling it wasn't just storms he liked to be prepared for. He struck her as the type of man who carefully plotted out not only his business but also his whole life, avoiding as many storms as possible.

"Will this do?"

Later that afternoon Finn glanced up from his desk in his study to find Holly standing there in a white sundress, holding a file folder. The bodice hugged her generous curves and tied around her neck, leaving just enough of her cleavage to tempt and tease. He swallowed hard. He should tell her to change clothes because there was no way he could conduct business with her looking so desirable.

Instead, he said, "Thank you." He accepted the file. "By the way, don't forget to pack lots of sunscreen."

"Pack? I never unpacked." Her eyes filled with confusion. "We're leaving?"

"Yes. Tomorrow morning we're setting sail on my yacht."

"Yacht?"

"Did I forget to mention it?" When she nodded, he added, "We'll be cruising around the islands for a couple of days until my business is concluded."

"Sounds great." Her voice lacked conviction.

"Have you been sailing before?"

She hesitated. "No."

Why exactly had he brought her along on this trip? Oh, yes, because her credentials were excellent. But that was when she was in a skyscraper in New York City. She didn't seem to fare so well outside her element. But it was too late to change course now. He just had to hope for the best— definitely not his idea of a good strategy, but the only one he had at this particular moment.

"Don't worry." He hoped to ease the worry lines now marring her face. "The yacht is spacious. You'll have your own stateroom." He took a moment to clarify the importance of the meeting. "I have worked for a number of months to bring these very influential men together. Discretion is of the utmost importance."

She nodded. "I understand. I've worked in your legal department for the past five years. Everything that passed over my desk was confidential. You can count on me."

He knew that. It was one of the reasons he'd agreed to this arrangement. Now, if he could just keep his mind from straying back to her luscious lips. His gaze zeroed in on them. They were painted up in a deep wine color. It was different from her usual earthy tones. But it was a good look on her.

He forced his mind back to business. "Did you reply to all of the outstanding emails?"

"I just finished them. The personal ones I've forwarded to your account as directed. I thought you might have some last-minute items you need completed before the meeting."

She was good. Really good. Normally that would be awesome, but when he was trying to keep her busy to avoid temptation, he wished she wasn't quite so competent.

"Have you returned all of the phone calls?"

She nodded. "I even called my mother."

"Your mother?"

"I just wanted to let her know that we arrived safely. She's actually off on her own holiday."

Was Holly attempting to make small talk? Boy, was he out of practice. He wasn't even sure how to respond. "That's good." He was better off sticking to business. "It sounds like you have everything under control. You can take the rest of the day off. We'll head out this evening as soon as all of our guests have arrived. Why don't you take a book and relax by the pool until then."

"I didn't bring a book. I didn't see a need since I planned to be working."

"But not from the time you woke up until you went to bed."

"You mean like you're doing?"

He glanced down at the papers littering his desk. "Guilty

as charged. But you don't want to end up like me. You're young and have so much to look forward to."

"You make it sound like you're old and your life is almost over."

"My life is Lockwood International. It's the reason I get out of bed in the morning."

"I'm sorry."

"Sorry? Sorry for what?"

"That you think that's all you have to live for."

"It's the way it has to be."

The pity reflected in her eyes had him recoiling. He didn't deserve pity or sympathy. She had no idea about his life—none whatsoever. Not even the press knew the entire truth.

Living and breathing everything about Lockwood International was his punishment. He'd lived while the rest of his family had perished. It was what his aunt had told him quite frequently when he rebelled about doing his schoolwork or having to stay in boarding schools. She told him he had no room to complain. He had lived while the others had died a painful death, and then she'd glare at him like it was all his fault. And for the most part, she was right.

Holly moved to the window. "Have you looked around this place? It's amazing. When's the last time you enjoyed it?"

"I don't have time for fun."

"Everyone needs to loosen up now and then. You don't want your guests showing up and finding that scowl on your face, do you?"

What scowl? He resisted the urge to run his hands over his face.

"I don't scowl." Her eyes widened at the grouchy tone of his voice. What was it about this woman that got under his skin? "I just need to stay on track and focus."

"Then I won't distract you any longer." She turned to the door.

She'd only tried to get him to relax, and yet he'd made her feel awkward. "Holly, wait." When she hesitated, he added, "I've been working so hard to pretend nothing happened between us that I've made matters worse. That was never my intention."

She turned. "Is it that hard to forget?"

"You know it is." His mind spiraled back to the kiss they'd shared on the plane. "But we can't go back there. It was a mistake the first time. And now that the fate of this project rests on how well you and I work together, we can't get distracted."

"I understand. I'll let you get back to work."

After Holly was gone, his concentration was severely lacking. He kept going over their conversation. Was his mood really that transparent? Usually business provided him solace from all that he'd done wrong in life and all that his life was lacking, but he couldn't find that escape anymore. He wondered if he'd done things differently, how his life would have turned out.

His chair scraped over the floor as he got to his feet. There was no point in staring blindly at the monitor. He wasn't going to get any more work done—at least not now. Maybe Holly was right. He should take a break. A run along the beach would be nice.

After changing his clothes, Finn stepped onto the patio. The splash of water drew his attention. He came to a complete halt as he watched Holly swim the length of the pool. He'd had no idea that she had taken him up on his suggestion that she go for a swim. He quietly watched, impressed with the ease of her strokes as she crossed the pool.

If he was smart, he'd head back inside before she noticed him. But his feet wouldn't cooperate. Sometimes being smart was overrated.

When she reached the edge of the pool, she stopped and

straightened. That was when he noticed her barely there turquoise bikini. The breath caught in his throat.

"Oh, hi." Droplets of water shimmered on her body as she smiled up at him. "Did you change your mind about unwinding?"

He struggled to keep his gaze on her face instead of admiring the way her swimsuit accented her curves. He made a point now of meeting her gaze. "I was going to take a run on the beach."

"In this heat?" When he shrugged, she added, "You'd be better off waiting until later when it cools down."

She was right, but he couldn't bring himself to admit it. "I'll be fine."

"Why don't you come swimming instead? The water is perfect."

He moved to the edge of the pool and crouched down. He dipped his hand in the water. She was right. The water was not too cold and not too warm. "I don't want to bother you."

"You won't be. The pool is plenty big for the both of us."

He had his doubts about the pool being big enough for him to keep his hands to himself. And with Holly in that swimsuit, he'd be so tempted to forget that they'd come to the island to work.

Finn raked his fingers through his hair. "I don't know. I really should be working."

"Your problem is that you think about work too much."

And then without warning, she swiped her arm along the top of the water, sending a small wave in his direction. By the time he figured out what she was up to, he was doused in water.

"Hey!" He stood upright and swiped the water from his face. "What was that all about?"

Her eyes twinkled with mischievousness. "Now you don't have an excuse not to join me."

Why was he letting his worries get the best of him and

missing out on this rare opportunity to have some fun? After all, it was just a swim.

"Okay. You win." He stripped off his T-shirt and tossed it on one of the lounge chairs.

He dove into the pool, enjoying the feel of the cool water against his heated body. He swam the length of the pool before returning to Holly. She was still smiling as she floated in the water.

"Not too bad for an old man—"

"Old man. I'll show you who's old. Let's race."

She eyed him up but didn't say a word.

"What's the matter?" he asked. "Afraid of the challenge."

"No. I'm just wondering if an old man like you can keep up with me."

"Seriously? You have to race me now."

She flashed him a teasing grin. "First one back gets their wish."

Without waiting for him, she took off. He smiled and shook his head. And then he set off in her wake. His muscles knew the motions by heart. He'd swam this pool countless times over the years, but this time was different. This time he wasn't alone.

He pushed himself harder. He reached the end of the pool and turned. He wanted to win. Not because he wanted to be the best. And not because he couldn't be a good loser. No. He wanted to win because the winner could name their wish.

And his wish—

His hand struck the end of the pool. His head bobbed above the water. A second later Holly joined him.

"About time you got here," he teased.

She sent him a cheesy grin before sending another splash of water in his direction. He backed away, avoiding most of the spray.

Holly was about to swim away when he said, "Not so fast. I won."

"And?"

"And I get my wish." He moved closer to her.

She didn't back away. It was as though she knew what he wanted. Was he that obvious?

Her voice grew softer. "And what did you have in mind?"

His gaze dipped to her lips. It seemed like forever since he last felt her kiss. There was something about her that got into his veins and made him crave her with every fiber of his being.

His gaze rose and met hers. His heart hammered against his ribs. Was she as turned on as he was? There was only one way to find out.

He reached out to her. Her skin was covered with goose bumps. He knew how to warm her up. His fingers slid over her narrow waist.

He'd never wanted anyone as much as Holly. And she was the last person he should desire. She was a serious kind of girl—the kind who didn't get around.

She was the type of woman you married.

The thought struck him like a lightning rod. As though she'd also had a moment of clarity, they both pulled back. Talk about an awkward moment.

"I...ah, should get back to work." Holly headed for the pool steps.

It was best that he didn't follow her, not right now. "I'll be in shortly. I think I'll swim a few more laps."

Finn groaned before setting off beneath the cool water, hoping to work Holly out of his system. He was beginning to wonder if that was even possible. He kicked harder and faster.

The one thing he knew was that he wasn't falling for Holly. No way. He didn't have room in his life for that major complication.

CHAPTER FIVE

ONE POUNDING HEART pressed to the other. Heated gazes locked. Lips a breath apart.

Holly gave herself a mental jerk. Not even a night's sleep had lessened the intensity of that moment in the pool with Finn. Oh, how she'd wanted to feel his touch again.

But then she'd spotted the passion in his eyes. One kiss wouldn't have been enough—for either of them. The acknowledgment of just how deep this attraction ran had startled her. She'd pulled back at the same time as Finn.

Now aboard Finn's luxury yacht, the *Rose Marie*, Holly took a seat off to the side of the room as the meeting commenced. With a handful of notable and influential businessmen in attendance, she couldn't let herself dwell on the almost-kiss. As each man took a seat at the long teakwood table, she quietly observed. Her job was to step in only when needed. Other than that, she was to remain virtually invisible on the sidelines.

So this is the hush-hush, wink-wink meeting.

A small smile pulled at Holly's lips as she glanced around the room. Finn sat at the head of the table in a white polo shirt and khaki shorts. A very different appearance from what she was accustomed to seeing on those rare times when she caught a glimpse of him at the office.

On either side of the table sat four men. Mr. Wallace, Mr. Santos, Mr. McMurray and Mr. Caruso. All influential men in their own rights—from toys to office supplies, electronics and snack foods. No wonder there were bodyguards littering the upper deck.

"Welcome." Finn began the meeting. "I've invited you all here in hopes that we will be able to rescue Project Santa."

He'd given her the information about this holiday project just before the meeting. He made it perfectly clear that it was not to be leaked to anyone for any reason. What took place on this boat was to remain top secret for now.

Talk about surprised.

Holly stared at Finn as though seeing him for the first time. He was a man known for his shrewd business dealings, not his philanthropy. And here she thought this meeting was about conquering the world—about a major corporate take-over. She couldn't have been more wrong.

Finn and his cohorts were planning a way to bring Christmas to many underprivileged children. If it worked, it would be the beginning of an ongoing project aimed at putting food and educational materials in the hands of children.

Holly was truly in awe of Finn. He was such a contra-diction at times. He worked long, hard hours, but he didn't expect his employees to do the same. He didn't celebrate Christmas, yet he planned Project Santa. At the office, he was all about profits and yet here he was planning to donate a portion of those profits to people in need.

For a man who hated Christmas, he certainly was doing a fine job of filling the boots of Santa this year. And she was more than willing to help him pull off this Christmas miracle. Although it was odd to have all of this talk about Christmas and presents surrounded by sunshine and the blue waters of the Caribbean.

Holly redirected her attention to the meeting, taking notes on her laptop and pulling up information as needed. She was tasked with running interference when tempers soared. Each of these men were billionaires and used to getting their own way, so compromise was not something they en-tertained often.

Some wanted to switch the Project Santa packaging to gift bags to cut costs. Others wanted to make the content more meaningful—something that wouldn't just entertain but help the recipient.

"Gentlemen." Finn's face was creased with stress lines. "This was all decided long ago. It's too late to change our plans. The gift boxes are strategically packed according to the location of each child."

Mr. McMurray leaned forward. "And how do we know these packages will get to the children?"

"Yeah, I've heard that a lot of these outreach programs are fronts for scams." Mr. Caruso, a gray-haired man, crossed his arms. "What if they steal them?"

"I hear your concerns. That's why some of my best Lockwood employees will escort each shipment to their destination. They are each tasked with making sure the packages get to their intended targets."

There was a murmur of voices. Holly noticed that Finn wasn't happy with the distractions, but he patiently let the men voice their concerns before they moved on to the reason for this meeting.

"Gentlemen, we need to address the problem we have with the lack of transportation now that Fred has suddenly pulled out."

Thanks to her research, Holly knew Fred Silver owned a delivery company that spanned the globe. As she listened to the men, she learned a federal raid on a number of Fred's distribution centers put his whole company in peril. It seemed Fred didn't have enough controls in place and the cartel got a foothold in his distribution routes. What a mess.

"Without Fred, I don't see how it's possible to complete Project Santa." Mr. Wallace shook his bald head in defeat.

"I agree." Mr. McMurray leaned back in his chair. "It's already December. It's too late to fix this."

The other men nodded in agreement.

Mr. Caruso stared at Finn. "But we still have all of the

books, toys and whatnot already allocated to this project. What do we do with it all?"

The men started talking at once. Voices were raised as each tried to talk over the other. Holly found it amusing that these men, who were well-respected in their own worlds, had a tough time playing nice with their peers. Each thought they had the right answer. And none wanted to stop and consider the other's perspective.

"Gentlemen!" Finn leaned forward, resting his elbows on the table. A hush fell over the room. "I think we need some coffee."

Finn glanced at Holly, prompting her into motion. She moved to grab the coffeepot with one hand and in the other she picked up a tray of pastries. As she headed for the table, each man settled back in their chair as though gathering their thoughts.

Holly pasted on her best and brightest smile. "Mr. Wallace, can I get you some coffee?"

The deep-set frown melted from the man's face and in its place was the beginning of a smile. "Why, yes, coffee sounds good."

She turned the coffee cup upright on the saucer and started to fill it. "I think what you all have come together to do is amazing. Project Santa will give hope to so many children." And then she had an idea. "And it will be such great publicity for your companies."

"Publicity." Mr. Wallace shook his head. "There's to be no publicity. Is that what Finn told you?"

"No, he didn't. I just presumed—obviously incorrectly." She was utterly confused. She'd missed something along the way. "Why then are all of you working so hard on this project when you each have global companies to tend to?"

They leaned back in their chairs as though contemplating her question. That was exactly what she was hoping would happen—that they'd remember why they were here and not give up. In the meantime, she served coffee for everyone.

"Finn should have told you." Mr. Santos reached for the creamer in the center of the table. "We each have so much that we wanted to do something to help those who have had a rough start in life. And with this being the season of giving, Finn came up with this idea. If we can make it work, it might be the beginning of something bigger."

"That sounds fantastic." Holly smiled, hoping to project her enthusiasm. "Too bad you can't make it work—you know, now that Mr. Silver isn't able to participate. I'm sure it's too big of a problem for you men to work around at this late date. Those poor children."

She turned to Finn, whose eyes widened. Oh, no. Had she gone too far? She'd merely wanted to remind these powerful men that they'd overcome greater obstacles in order to make their respective companies household names. If they really put their heads together and pulled in their resources, she was certain they could overcome this issue.

"She's right." Finn's voice commanded everyone's attention. "We can't stop now."

Tensions quickly rose as each powerful man became vocal about their approach to overcome these last hurdles and make the project a go. But this time they were pausing to hear each other out. And at times, building on each other's ideas.

Finn mouthed, "Thank you."

It wasn't exactly the use of her mind that she'd prefer, but the more she heard about this project, the more she believed in it—the more she believed in Finn. He was nothing like his ruthless businessman persona that was portrayed by the press. Why didn't he show the world this gentle, caring side of himself?

After spending hours to resolve the transportation problem with Project Santa, they were still no closer than they had been that morning.

Finn had just showered and changed into slacks and a dress shirt before meeting up with his associates for a card game. This trip wasn't all business. He'd learned long ago that keeping his allies happy was just as important as presenting them with a profitable deal.

He'd just stepped out of his cabin and glanced up to find Holly coming toward him. Her hair was wet and combed back. She looked refreshed and very tempting. His gaze dipped, finding she was wearing a white bikini. She must have been unwinding in the hot tub. He swallowed hard. *Look away. Concentrate on her face.*

Finn met her amused gaze. "Thank you."

"For what?" She adjusted a white towel around her slender waist.

His mouth grew dry. "For your help at the meeting. You were a big help getting everyone to work together."

"I'm glad I could help."

And then realizing they were talking in the hallway where anyone might overhear, he opened his cabin door. "But the distribution is more than we can overcome at this late date."

Holly didn't move. "Actually, I have some thoughts about your problem with the distribution. I don't think it's insurmountable."

He worried that she was a bit too confident. This was a national endeavor—coast to coast. But he had to admit he was intrigued. "Why don't you step in here a moment?"

Her hesitant gaze moved from him to the interior of his stateroom and then back to him. "I really shouldn't. I'm still wet."

"I promise I won't keep you for long. In fact, I'm due at a card game in a couple of minutes."

She noticeably relaxed. Without another word, she passed by him and entered the room. His heart thumped as he contemplated reaching out and pulling her close. What was it about her that had such a hold over him?

She turned as he pushed the door closed. She averted her gaze as her hands wrung together. Was she aware of the energy arching between them? Could she feel his draw to her? Was she as uncertain as he was about what to do about it?

"I don't think I told you, but your boat is amazing." She looked everywhere but at him. "I had no idea they were so elaborate."

"I'm glad you like your accommodations. I take it you enjoy sailing more than you do flying?"

"Definitely. I don't have to worry about falling out of the sky and—"

"No, you don't," he said, not wanting her to finish that graphic image. "If there's anything you want but can't find, just let me know."

"You know if you keep this up, you'll ruin your image."

"My image?"

At last, her gaze met his. "The one of you being a heartless corporate raider."

He pressed a hand to his chest. "I'm wounded. Do you really believe those nasty rumors?"

"Not anymore. I've seen the part you hide from the outside world." Her voice took on a sultry tone as her gaze dipped to his mouth. "Why do you do that?"

He swallowed hard, losing track of the conversation. "Do what?"

"Hide behind your villainous persona when in reality you're not like that at all."

His gaze shifted to her rosy lips. "How am I?"

"You're tough and hard on the outside, but inside..." She stepped closer, pressing a hand to his chest. "In there where it matters, you have a big heart."

"No one ever said that before."

Her hand remained on his chest as though branding him as hers and hers alone. "They just don't know you like I do."

His heart pounded against his ribs. "And do you like what you've gotten to know?"

"Most definitely."

His hand covered hers. "You do know if you don't leave right now that I'm not responsible for what happens next."

"But what about your guests?"

"They're involved in a card game."

"Oh, yes, the card game. You don't want to miss it."

By now she had to be able to feel the rapid beating of his heart. "I don't think they'll miss me."

"Are you sure?"

He nodded, not caring if they did. There was nowhere else he wanted to be at this moment. "Are you sure about this? You and me?"

"I'm sure that I want you to kiss me."

"Holly, I'm serious."

"I am, too. You do still want me, don't you?"

He groaned. "You know that I do."

His hands wrapped around her shapely hips and pulled her to him. In the process her towel came undone, pooling at her feet. He continued to stare into her eyes, watching to see if she'd change her mind, but he only found raw desire reflected in them.

She lifted up on her tiptoes and he didn't waste a moment claiming her lips. He was beginning to think he'd never tire of kissing her. The thought should worry him, but right now he had other things on his mind—things that were drowning out any common sense.

As their kiss deepened, so did his desires. Once was definitely not enough with Holly. Her beauty started on the inside and worked its way out. If he were to ever entertain the idea of getting serious with someone, it would be her.

Her fingers slid up his neck and combed through his hair. Her curves leaned into him, causing a moan to form in the back of his throat. Perhaps they could be friends with benefits. There wouldn't be any harm in that, would there?

He clearly recalled when things ended between them that Holly had said she didn't want anything serious. In fact, she was the first one to say there couldn't be anything more between them. For a moment he'd been floored and then relieved.

Now as her lips moved passionately over his, he wondered what he'd been thinking by letting her walk away. They had so much to offer each other with no strings attached.

But first he had to be sure Holly was still on board with the idea. He just couldn't have her expecting some sort of commitment from him because in the end, he'd wind up letting her down.

He grudgingly pulled back. Cupping her face in his hands, he gazed deep into her eyes. "Holly, are you sure about this?"

She nodded.

"Even though it'll never lead to anything serious?"

Again she nodded. "I told you I don't do serious."

A smile tugged at his lips. How could someone be as perfect as her? The thought got shoved to the back of his mind as she reached up and pulled his head down to meet her lips. This was going to be a night neither of them would forget—

Knock-knock.

"Hey, Finn, you coming?" Mr. Caruso's jovial voice came through the door. "Everyone's anxious to get the game started."

Holly and Finn jumped apart as though they were teenagers having been caught making out beneath the bleachers. She looked at the door and then him. Her lips lifted into a smile before she started to laugh. Finn frowned at her. She pressed a hand to her lips, stifling the stream of giggles.

"I'll be right with you." Finn ran a hand over his mouth,

making sure there were no lingering signs of lip gloss. And then he finger-combed his hair.

Holly gestured that she would wait in the bathroom. He expelled a sigh of relief. He really didn't want to have to explain what she was doing in his room scantily dressed in that tempting bikini.

With Holly out of sight and his clothes straightened, he opened the door. "Sorry I'm running late. I had something come up at the last minute. You know how it is."

The man clapped him on the shoulder. "You work too hard. Come on. The guys are waiting."

"I don't think so. I really need to finish this—"

"Work can wait, your guests can't." Mr. Caruso reached out, grabbed his arm and pulled him into the hallway. "After all, you're the host."

Finn glanced back in his suite longingly, knowing the exquisite night he'd be missing. Playing cards had never looked so dull and tedious before.

"You coming?"

With a sigh, Finn pulled the door shut. "Sure. The work can wait till later."

"Try the morning. I have a feeling this game is going to last most of the night. Should we invite your assistant?"

"I passed her in the hallway earlier. Holly—um, Ms. Abrams called it a night already."

"That's too bad. I like her."

He liked her, too—perhaps far more than was wise. Or perhaps he was blowing everything out of proportion since it'd been a while since he'd been dating. In fact, he hadn't dated anyone since his evening with Holly. No other woman had even tempted him after her. He wasn't sure what to make of that.

CHAPTER SIX

THE NEXT MORNING Holly awoke late. But she didn't feel too guilty. It was work that had her burning the midnight oil—not Finn.

She ran her fingers over her lips, recalling Finn's kiss before he'd left her for the card game. If there hadn't been a knock at his door, she knew where things would have led. Part of her knew it was for the best, but another part ached for the missed opportunity.

What was wrong with her? Why couldn't she be immune to his charms? It was like once his lips touched hers any logic disengaged and her impulses took over. She wondered if he had this effect over all women or just her.

She knew this thing between them couldn't go anywhere. Her experience with men should be proof enough. First, her father walked out on her and her mother. And then while she was earning her paralegal degree, she'd met Josh. He was good-looking and charming. Deciding all men couldn't be like her father, she let herself fall for him.

Holly felt ill as the memories washed over her. Everything between her and Josh had been great for a while. In fact, it was the happiest she'd ever been. And then she'd learned Josh had a gambling problem that led to him stealing from her—the person he was supposed to love. She'd arranged to get him help and he'd sworn he would complete the twelve-step program.

She'd wanted to believe him, but after what her father had done to her mother, Holly had to be sure. And that was when she'd caught Josh in a web of lies with another woman. Holly's stomach soured at the memory.

The depth of his betrayal had cut her deep. After Josh,

she'd sworn off relationships. Her independence gave her a much-needed sense of security. And with her full attention focused on her work, she didn't have time to be lonely. Guys just weren't worth the heartache. And she'd stuck by her pledge until now. Finn had her questioning everything—

Knock-knock-knock.

She had a feeling there'd only be one person who'd come calling at her door this early in the morning. Still, she asked, "Who is it?"

"It's me." The voice was very distinct. "Finn."

"Hang on." She scrambled out of bed and rushed to grab her robe. It was then that she noticed her stomach didn't feel right. It was way more than being upset about the unpleasant memories. She took a calming breath, willing the queasiness away.

She moved to the door and pulled it open. Finn stood there freshly showered and shaved, looking like he was ready to tackle the world. "Good morning."

His gaze narrowed in on her. "Everything okay?"

She ran a hand over her hair. "Sorry. I slept in." Her stomach lurched. She pressed a hand to her midsection, willing it to stop. "I'll, ah, take a quick shower and be right with you."

"You know, you don't look so good."

Right then her stomach totally revolted. She dashed to the bathroom. Thankfully her cabin wasn't that big. She was quite certain she wouldn't have made it another step. She dropped to her knees, sick as a dog. What in the world? She hadn't even eaten that morning.

Once her stomach calmed, she heard the sink turn on. Finn? He was here? He'd witnessed her at her worst. She would have groaned, but she feared doing anything that might upset her stomach again.

"Here. Take this." He handed her a cold cloth.

"You shouldn't be here."

"And leave you alone when you obviously don't feel well?"

No matter what she said, he wasn't leaving. And at that moment she didn't have the energy to argue. Once she'd cleaned up, she walked back to the bedroom. Her stomach wasn't totally right, but it did feel somewhat better.

"I'm sorry about that." Her gaze didn't fully meet his. "You...you were quite the gentleman. Thank you."

"Do you know what's bothering you? Is it something you ate?"

"I think it's seasickness."

"I'm sure it doesn't help that we hit some rough water this morning. Are you sure that's all it is?"

She nodded, certain it had to be the constant roll of the boat.

"You should lie down."

"I don't have time."

"Sure you do." He guided her back to the king-size bed. "Stay here. I'll be right back."

She did as he asked, hoping she'd soon feel like herself. He disappeared out the door like a man on a mission. As she lay there, her mind strayed to her plan for Project Santa. Perhaps she should run it by Finn first. She didn't want to do anything to embarrass either of them in front of those powerful men.

A few minutes later Finn came rushing back into the room. "How are you feeling now?"

"Better." It wasn't a lie.

"I grabbed some ginger ale and toast. Hopefully you'll be able to keep that down. And I grabbed some medicine for the motion sickness."

"Thank you." She sat up in bed and accepted the glass of soda. She tentatively took a sip, not sure what to expect when it hit her stomach. Thankfully, it remained calm.

"I also talked with the captain and he's set course for what he hopes is smoother water."

Finn was changing his trip just for her? She didn't know what to think, except that Finn was a lot more Santa-like than Grinchy.

She took another drink of the soda. So far, so good. Anxious to get on with her day, she got to her feet. She glanced over to find Finn staring at her. "What?"

"The look on your face. Something is bothering you. Is it your stomach again?"

She shook her head. "I told you I'm feeling better."

He sighed. "You're sure? You're not just telling me this to get rid of me?"

"I'm certain. I'll just get showered and be up to the meeting soon."

"I could use your help, but I don't want you pushing yourself." His gaze searched her face and then he moved to the door. "I should be going."

"Finn?"

"Yes."

"There is something I wanted to talk to you about."

His brow arched. "Is it about your health?"

"No. It's nothing like that. It's just an idea I wanted to run past you."

He glanced at his Rolex. "I'd be happy to hear you out, but not right now. I'm late." He opened the door. "I'll see you on deck." He rushed out the door.

"But—"

The door closed. Her words had been cut off. A frown pulled at her lips. She knew how to help him with Project Santa if he'd just slow down and listen to her. She refused to give up now. There had to be a way to get his attention.

Had he made a mistake?

Finn sat uncomfortably at the end of the table, knowing

if they didn't come up with a reasonable resolution to their transportation problem today that they would have to cut their losses and scrap the idea of Project Santa. The thought deeply troubled him.

He glanced at his watch for the third time in ten minutes. Where was Holly? Had she been struck with another bout of sickness?

"Listen, I know we need a solution regarding transportation, but all of my rigs are booked from now until Christmas, delivering our toys to stores." Mr. Wallace tapped his pen on the blank legal pad. "Besides, this wasn't my part of the arrangement. It's not my fault Fred wasn't on top of his business dealings and got in bed with the cartel."

Mr. Caruso sighed. "I couldn't possibly reroute all of my snack food shipments. It'd be a logistic disaster. And it would only cover the east coast. What about the children west of the Mississippi?"

All eyes turned to Mr. Santos. The guy shook his head. "I'm in the same boat. My network is on the east coast. And I have no transportation."

That left one man who hadn't spoken up, Mr. McMurray. He cleared his throat, visibly uncomfortable being in the hot seat. "And what makes you all think I can pull this off when none of you can?"

Immediately everyone spoke at once, defending why they couldn't take over the shipping part of the plan. Finn sat back quietly wondering why he ever thought they'd be able to pull off such a big project. It dashed his hopes for future projects of this scale.

At that moment Holly walked into the room. A hush fell over the men and Finn knew why. She looked like a knockout. She wore an aqua, sleeveless sundress. Her golden-brown hair had been piled on top of her head while corkscrew curls framed her face. She wore a little makeup, but definitely on the conservative side. If he hadn't known that she was feeling under the weather earlier, he wouldn't have been able to guess it by looking at her.

"Good morning, gentlemen. I'm sorry to be late. But I promise I was hard at work."

The tension around the table evaporated, replaced with smiles and warm greetings. Finn shook his head in disbelief. Who'd have thought a bunch of workaholics could be so easily swayed by a pretty face and long, toned legs?

"Don't let me interrupt your discussion." Holly moved to the chair she'd sat in the day before.

Mr. Wallace grunted. "You didn't interrupt much. Everyone was just making excuses about why they couldn't take on the shipping portion of Project Santa. We could use a fresh perspective. Do you have any thoughts on the matter?"

"Actually, I do. First, I want to say I'm very impressed with the endeavor you all are undertaking." She made a point of making eye contact with each man. "And if you would indulge me, I might have a suggestion about the transportation problem."

"Holly." The room grew silent. Finn had to give her a chance to gracefully bow out. "Perhaps I didn't make clear the enormity of this project. The gifts will need to be delivered from coast to coast in every town or city where our companies have a presence."

She nodded as her steady gaze met his. "I understood." She leveled her shoulders. "From what I understand, you have a master list of names and locations for the gifts. You also have all of the items sorted and boxed. All you're lacking is a delivery system."

Finn noticed a couple of the men had started to fidget with their cell phones. They didn't have faith in Holly's ability to overcome such a large obstacle. He had to admit he didn't know what she could do that they hadn't already considered.

"That would be correct." Finn really wanted to know where she was headed. He didn't like surprises. "We have a sorting facility in St. Louis. From there the packages need to be distributed to numerous cities."

"And if I understand correctly, you were planning to do this by way of long-haul trucks."

"Yes, until Fred's company was seized by the government. There's no way he'll be able to unravel that ugly mess in time to help us. So do you have a lead on some other trucking firm?"

She shook her head. "My idea is a little different. I started to think about all of the modes of transport. And then I started to think about who I knew in the transportation industry. And I realized my neighbor in New York is a pilot."

Finn cleared his throat. "So you're suggesting we have your friend fly all of the packages around the country."

She frowned at him. "Of course not. That wouldn't be possible considering there are thousands of packages."

"Then I'm not following what you're telling us."

"My friend is a pilot, but he's just one of many. When he's not flying commercially, he takes part in a national flying club." She glanced around the table and when no one said anything, she explained further. "This flying club has hundreds of members around the country. If we were to enlist their help, we could get the packages to their destinations."

"I don't know." Finn had to think this over. The men started chatting amongst themselves. Finn glanced up to find Holly with a determined look on her face. When she opened her mouth to elaborate, no one noticed.

Finn cleared his throat and then said loudly, "Gentlemen, shall we let Ms. Abrams finish her presentation?"

When silence fell over the room, Holly continued. "I've already put feelers out to see if there would be an interest in helping such a worthy cause, and I have close to a hundred pilots willing to fly the packages."

Finn rubbed his chin. "You trust these people? And they're going to do it out of the goodness of their hearts?"

"Yes, I trust them. And aren't you all doing this project out of the goodness of your hearts?"

One by one the men's heads nodded except Finn's. He didn't have faith in her plan. There were just too many moving parts. But he would give her credit for thinking outside the box. He was lucky to have her on staff at Lockwood.

Not about to discuss the pros and cons of her plan in front of her, Finn said, "Thank you for your input. We greatly appreciate your efforts. We'll need a little bit to discuss it. In the meantime, you could—"

"But don't you want to hear the rest of my plan?" Holly sent a pleading stare his way.

How could he say no when she turned those big brown eyes his way? He felt his resolve melting.

"Let her finish," Wallace chimed in.

The other men agreed.

Finn nodded at her to proceed.

"Getting the presents from the distribution center to the airstrip will take more transportation."

He was almost afraid to ask. "And what did you have in mind?"

"We'll go public and ask for volunteers."

"More volunteers?" He shook his head. "I don't think so."

"Listen, I know you were hoping to operate under the radar. And I know none of you are in this for the publicity, but if you would reconsider, this project might be bigger and better than before."

He wanted to put a stop to this, but he knew what it was like to be a child with no Christmas presents. Although his lack of presents had nothing to do with his parents' financial standing, it still hurt. He didn't want that to happen to other children, not if he could make a difference.

But he refused to put out a public plea asking for help. He didn't do it for the Mistletoe Ball, which meant so much to him—a continuation of his mother's work and a way to support the foundation seeking a cure to the horrible disease that stole his brother's life. Besides, he was the very last person in the country whom people would want to help. After all of the companies that he'd bought up and spun off into separate entities, causing job consolidation and ultimately downsizing, he was certain people would go out of their way to make sure he failed. He couldn't let that happen with Project Santa.

Finn met her gaze. "I'm not going to make this a publicity campaign."

"But at least hear me out."

He didn't want to. His gut told him she was about to give them a unique but tempting solution to their problem—but it would come at a steep price.

"Go ahead." Wallace spoke up. "Tell us how you would recruit these people?"

"We could start a media page on MyFace." She paused and looked around the table. "Do you know about the social networking service?"

They all nodded.

"Good. Well, it's hugely popular. With a page set up on it specifically for Project Santa, we can post updates and anything else. It even allows for spreadsheets and files. So there can be an official sign-up sheet. Or if you are worried about privacy, I could set up an online form that dumps into a private spreadsheet. In fact, last night when I couldn't sleep I started work on the graphics for the media page."

Caruso smiled at her. "You're a real go-getter. I can see why Finn scooped you up. You must make his life so easy at the office."

"Actually, he and I, well, we don't normally work together."

"Really?" Caruso turned to Finn. "What's wrong with you? How could you let this bright young lady get away from you?"

Finn kept a stony expression, not wanting any of them to get a hint that there was far more to this relationship than either of them was letting on. "I already had a fully capable assistant by the time Holly was hired. She normally works in the legal department, but with my assistant eloping, Holly agreed to fill in."

"And she's done an excellent job with her research." Caruso turned a smile to Holly.

"Yes, she has," Mr. McMurray agreed. "It isn't exactly the most straightforward option, but it definitely deserves further investigation."

Finn was proud that she'd taken the initiative, but he was not expecting the next words out of his mouth. "And we need to give her presentation some serious consideration."

"Agreed." The word echoed around the table.

Holly's hesitant smile broadened into a full-fledged smile that lit up her eyes. "Thank you all for listening to me." Her cloaked gaze met Finn's. "I have work to do. I'll be in my cabin should you need me."

CHAPTER SEVEN

WHAT HAD SHE been thinking?

Holly paced in her cabin, going over the meeting in her mind—more specifically the deepening frown on Finn's face as she'd presented her idea to distribute the gifts. Why had she even bothered? It wasn't like it was part of her job duties—far from it. But there was something about Project Santa that drew her in. She'd wanted to help.

And now she'd made a mess of things. Having Finn upset with her would not help her get the personal recommendation she needed to land the new job and get her the big pay increase she needed to secure her mother's early retirement.

She should have kept the ideas to herself. When would she ever learn? When it came to Finn, she found herself acting first and thinking later. Just like that kiss in his cabin. If they hadn't been interrupted, she knew there would have been no stopping them. Her logic and sanity had gotten lost in the steamy heat of the moment.

Going forward, she would be the perfect employee and that included keeping her hands to herself. She glanced down, realizing she'd been wringing her hands together. She groaned.

She knew Finn was going to shoot down her proposal. His disapproval had been written all over his face. She didn't understand his reaction. It wasn't like he had a better suggestion. No matter what Finn said, she still believed in her grass-roots approach.

Knock-knock.

For a moment she considered ignoring it. She wasn't in any state of mind to deal with Finn. She didn't think it was possible to paste on a smile right now and act like the perfect, obedient assistant. And that would be detrimental to her ultimate goal—leaving Lockwood—leaving Finn.

Knock-knock.

"Holly, I know you're in there. We need to talk." Finn's tone was cool and restrained.

She hesitated. He was obviously not happy with her. And on this yacht, even though it was quite spacious, she wouldn't be able to avoid him for long. So she might as well get it over with.

She took a calming breath, choking down her frustration. On wooden legs, she moved toward the door. Her stomach felt as though a rock had settled in the bottom of it. *You can do this.*

She swung the door open. "Can I do something for you?"

"Yes. I need an explanation of what happened at the meeting." He strode past her and stopped in the middle of the room.

Was it that he didn't like her idea? Or was he upset that it had been her idea and not his? She'd heard rumors that he was a bit of a control freak.

She swallowed hard. "I presented an idea I thought would save Project Santa. What else is there to explain?"

"When did you have time to come up with this idea?"

"Last night when you were playing cards."

His gaze narrowed in on her. "You should have brought it to my attention before making the presentation." His voice rumbled as he spoke. "We should have gone over it together. I'm not accustomed to having employees take the lead on one of my projects without consulting me."

Seriously? This was the thanks she got for going above and beyond her job duties—not to mention sacrificing her sleep—all in order to help him. Maybe it was her lack of sleep or her growing hunger, but she wasn't going to stand by quietly while he railed against her efforts to help.

She straightened her shoulders and lifted her chin. "I'll

have you know that I tried to tell you about my idea this morning, but you didn't have time to listen. And something tells me that isn't what has you riled up. So what is it?"

His heated gaze met hers. "I knew this was going to be a mistake—"

"What? My plan?"

"No. Your idea has some merit. I meant us trying to work together."

"Well, don't blame me. It wasn't my idea."

He sighed. "True enough."

"Wait. Did you say my plan has merit?"

"I did, but I don't think it's feasible."

Her body stiffened as her back teeth ground together. Really? That was what he was going with? Feasible?

She pressed her lips together, holding back her frustration. After all, he was the boss—even if he was being a jerk at the moment.

"I know you're not happy about this decision, but it's a lot to ask of so many pilots, and what happens if they back out at the last minute? It would be a disaster." He glanced down at his deck shoes. "I hope you'll understand. This is just the way it has to be."

"I don't understand." The cork came off her patience and out spewed her frustration and outrage. "I have given you a cost-effective, not to mention a timely solution, to your problem and yet you find every reason it won't work. If you didn't want to go through with Project Santa, why did you start it in the first place?"

"That's not what I said." He pressed his lips into a firm line as his hand came to rest on his trim waist. When she refused to glance away—to back down, he straightened his shoulders as though ready to do battle in the boardroom. "Okay. Your idea could work, but how do you plan on getting the message out to the people about Project Santa and the MyFace page?"

"We'll need a spokesperson."

"Where will you get that?"

She stared pointedly at him. "I'm looking at him."

"Me?"

"Yes, you."

"No way."

"Why not? All you have to do is a few promo spots to secure the public's assistance. What's the problem?"

His heated gaze met hers. "Why are you pushing this?"

She implored him with her eyes to truly hear her. "Do you realize the number of children you could help with your generous gifts?" When he refused to engage, she continued. "It would give them hope for the future. It might influence the path they follow in life." And then for good measure she added, "And without your cooperation, they'll never have that chance."

"That's not fair. You can't heap all of that guilt on me."

"Who else should I blame?"

A muscle flexed in his jaw. "You know, I didn't come here to fight with you."

"Then why are you here?"

A tense moment passed before he spoke again. "I wanted to tell you how impressed everyone was with your presentation."

"Everyone but you." The words slipped past her lips before she could stop them.

"Holly, that's not true." He raked his fingers through his hair, scattering it. "You don't know how hard this is for me."

"Then why don't you tell me?"

Conflict reflected in his eyes as though he was warring with himself. "I don't want to talk about it."

"Maybe you should. Sometimes getting it all out there helps." She walked over to the couch and had a seat. She patted the cushion next to her. "It might not seem like it at this particular time, but I am a good listener."

His gaze moved from her to the couch. She didn't think

he would do it—trust her with his deeply held secret. But if it stood in the way of his helping with the publicity for Project Santa, then they needed to sort it out.

When he returned his eyes to hers, it was as though she was looking at a haunted person. She hadn't even heard his story yet and still her heart swelled with sympathy for him. Whatever it was, it was big.

"Christmas wasn't always good at our house." His voice held a broken tone to it. "I mean it was when I was little, but not later." He expelled a deep breath.

"I'm sorry for pushing you. I shouldn't have done it—"

"Don't apologize. I understand why you want Project Santa to succeed. And I want the same thing."

"Then trust me. A little publicity is all we need to gain the public's assistance."

"But it has to be without me. Trust me. I'm not the right person to be the face of a charitable event."

"I disagree."

"That's because you don't know me." Pain reflected in his eyes. "Appearances can be deceiving. I'm not the man everyone thinks I am. I'm a fraud."

"A fraud?" She instinctively moved away. "If you aren't Finn Lockwood, who are you?"

"Relax. I'm Finn Lockwood. I'm just not supposed to be the CEO of Lockwood International. I got the job by default."

She was confused. "Who is supposed to be the CEO?"

"My brother."

"Oh." She still didn't understand. "He didn't want the job?"

"He wanted it but he died."

"I'm sorry." She slipped her hand in his. "Sometimes when I have an idea, I don't back off when I should."

For a while, they just sat there in silence. Hand in hand, Holly once again rested her head on Finn's shoulder as though it was natural for them to be snuggled together. Her heart ached for all he'd endured. She felt awful that she'd pushed him to the point where he felt he had to pull the scabs off those old scars.

"You didn't do anything wrong." Finn pulled away and got to his feet. "I should be going. I just wanted you to understand why I can't be the spokesman for Project Santa."

She rolled his words around in her mind, creating a whole new set of questions. She worried her bottom lip. After everything that had been said, she realized that it was best to keep her questions to herself. Enough had been said for one evening.

Finn placed a finger beneath her chin and lifted until they were eye to eye. "What is it?"

She glanced away. "It's nothing."

"Oh, no, you don't get off that easy. What are you thinking?"

She shook her head, refusing to say anything to upset him further. She was certain if she thought about it a bit longer, she'd be able to connect the dots. It was just that right now it was all a bit fuzzy. "It's not important."

"I'm not leaving here until you talk to me. Whatever it is, I promise not to get upset with you. Because that's what you're worried about, isn't it?"

She took a deep breath, trying to figure out how to word this without aggravating him further. "I'm sure it's my fault for not understanding. If I just think it over some more, it'll probably make perfect sense."

He moved his hand from her face and took her hands in his. "Holly, you're rambling. Just spit it out."

She glanced down at their clasped hands. "It's just that I don't understand why the way you became CEO would keep you from getting personally involved with the publicity for Project Santa."

He frowned. See, she knew she should have kept her questions to herself. Clearly she hadn't been listening to him as closely as she'd thought. She prepared herself to feel silly for missing something obvious.

"I don't deserve to take credit for the project. I don't deserve people thinking I'm some sort of great guy."

Really? That was what he thought? "Of course you do. This project was your brainchild. You're the one who brought all of those businessmen together to orchestrate such a generous act. There aren't many people in this world who could have done something like this."

"I'm not a good guy. I've done things—things I'm not proud of."

"We all have. You're being too hard on yourself."

He shook his head. "I wish that was the case. Besides, I'm not even supposed to be doing any of this. This company was supposed to be handed down to Derek, not me. I'm the spare heir. Anything I do is because of my brother's death. I don't deserve any pats on the back or praise."

What in the world had happened to him? Was this some sort of survivor's guilt? That had to be it. She had no idea what it must be like to step into not one but two pairs of shoes—his father's and his brother's.

"I disagree with you."

Finn's brows drew together. "You don't get it. If it weren't for my brother dying, I wouldn't be here."

"Where would you be?"

He shrugged. "I'm not sure. After my brother died, I gave up those dreams and embraced my inevitable role as the leader of Lockwood."

"Did you want to be a policeman or a soldier?" When he shook his head, she asked, "What did you dream of doing with your life?"

"I thought about going into medicine."

"You wanted to be a doctor?"

"I wanted something behind the scenes. I was thinking about medical research. My mother was always going on about how much money her charity work raised to find cures for diseases, but it was never enough. I excelled in math and science—I thought I could make a difference."

"But don't you see? You are making a difference. You gave up your dreams in order to take over the family business, but you've made a point of funding and planning charitable causes. You are a hero, no matter what you tell yourself."

His mouth opened and then he wordlessly closed it. She could tell he was stuck for words. Was it so hard for him to imagine himself as a good guy?

She squeezed his hand. "This is your chance to live up to your dreams."

"How do you get that?"

"You can make a difference to all of those children. You can give them the Christmas you missed out on. Maybe you'll give them a chance to dream of their future. Or at the very least, give them a reason to smile."

His eyes gleamed as though he liked the idea, but then he shook his head. "I'm not hero material." And then his eyes lit up. "But you are. You could be the face of Project Santa."

"Me?" She shook her head. "No one knows me. I won't garner the attention that Finn Lockwood will." Feeling as though she was finally getting through to him, she said, "Please, Finn, trust me. This will all work out. I know you aren't comfortable with the arrangement, but do it for the kids. Be their hero."

There was hesitation written all over his face. "There's no other way?"

"None that I can think of."

The silence stretched on as though Finn was truly rolling around the idea. The longer it took, the more optimistic she became.

His gaze met hers. "Okay. Let's do this."

"Really?" She couldn't quite believe her ears. "You mean it?"

He nodded his head. "As long as the promo is minimized."

"It will be. Trust me."

He didn't look so confident, but in time he'd see that her plan would work. And then a bunch of children wouldn't feel forgotten on Christmas morning. Knowing she'd had a small part in giving them some holiday cheer would make this the best Christmas ever.

"What are you smiling about?"

She was smiling? Yes, she supposed she was. Right now she felt on top of the world. Now that she'd proven her worth to Finn, she thought of asking him for that recommendation letter, but then she decided not to ruin the moment.

"I'm just happy to be part of this meaningful project."

"So where do we begin?" Finn sent her an expectant look.

In that moment all of her excitement and anticipation knotted up with nerves. She'd talked a good game but now it was time to put it all into action. Her stomach churned. She willed it to settle—not that it had any intention of listening to her.

When she didn't say a word, Finn spoke up. "Where do we start?"

The *we* in his question struck her. They were now a team. Not allowing herself to dwell on this new bond, she asked, "What about your guests? Shouldn't you be with them?"

"McMurray said he wasn't feeling so good and went to lie down. The other guys are taking in some sun and playing cards. So I'm all yours."

She eyed him up, surprised by his roll-up-his-sleeves-and-dive-in attitude. "The first place we start is on MyFace and work on recruiting additional pilots. Do you have a My-Face account?"

"No. I'll get my laptop." He got to his feet and headed for the door. He paused in the doorway and turned back to her. "On second thought, why don't you bring your laptop and work in my suite? It's a lot bigger."

Holly paused. The last time she'd been in his room, work had been the very last thing on either of their minds. The memory of him pulling her close, of his lips moving hungrily over hers, sent her heart pounding. She vividly remembered how he'd awakened her long-neglected body. Their arms had been entangled. Their breath had intermingled. And any rational thoughts had fled the room.

"I know what you're thinking."

Heat flared in her cheeks. *Are my thoughts that transparent?*

"But don't worry, it won't happen again. You have my word."

Maybe I can trust you, but it's me that I'm worried about.

CHAPTER EIGHT

SHE AMAZED HIM.

Finn awoke the next morning thinking of Holly. They'd worked together until late the night before. She had truly impressed him—which wasn't an easy feat. To top it off, she was efficient and organized. He knew she was good at her job, but he had no idea just how talented she was until last night.

They'd taken a long break for dinner with his associates. They updated them on all they'd accomplished and what Holly hoped to achieve over the next few days. The men promised to do their part to ensure the success of Project Santa, including putting out a call for volunteers to their employees and their families.

And to Finn's shock the two men who weren't active on social media were open to having Holly assist them with setting up a personal MyFace account. Everyone wanted to do their part to promote the project so that it was a success.

Finn slipped out of bed and quietly padded to the shower. With Project Santa underway, he had to concentrate on today's business agenda. He had a business venture that he wanted to entice these men to invest in. And thanks to Holly, everyone appeared to be in fine spirits. He hoped to capitalize on it.

Today he'd switched from his dress shorts and polos to slacks and a dress shirt. He couldn't help it. When he wanted to take charge of a business meeting, he wanted to look the part, too. He supposed that was something his father had taught him. Though his father had spiraled out of control after his brother's death, before that he was a pretty good guy, just a bit driven. He supposed his father was no more a workaholic than himself.

Finn straightened the collar of his light blue shirt with vertical white stripes sans the tie. Then he turned up the cuffs. After placing his Rolex on his wrist, he was ready to get down to business. Now he just needed Holly to take some notes.

He headed down the passageway to her cabin and knocked. There was no answer.

"Holly, are you in there?"

Knock-knock.

"Holly?"

That was strange. When they'd parted for the evening, they'd agreed to get together first thing in the morning to go over today's agenda. And then he recalled her picking her way through her dinner. Maybe he should be sure she was okay.

He tried the doorknob. It wasn't locked. He opened it a crack. "Holly, I'm coming in."

No response.

He hesitantly opened the door, not sure what he expected to find. He breathed easier when he found her bed empty. Before he could react, the bathroom door swung open and she came rushing out.

Dressed in a short pink nightie, she was a bit hunched over. Her arm was clutched over her stomach.

"Holly?"

She jumped. Her head swung around to face him. The color leached from her face. He wasn't sure if the lack of coloring was the result of his startling her or if it was because she didn't feel well.

"What are you doing here?"

"Sorry. I didn't mean to startle you. I…uh, well, we were supposed to meet up this morning. And when you didn't answer the door, I got worried. I came in to make sure you're all right."

Holly glanced down at herself as though realizing her lack of clothing. She moved to the bed and slid under the sheets. "I'm fine."

"You don't look fine."

"Well, thanks. You sure know how to make a girl feel better." She frowned at him.

"That's not what I meant. I...uh, just meant you don't look like yourself. What can I get for you?"

"Nothing."

"Are you sure? Maybe some eggs?" Was it possible that her pale face just turned a ghastly shade of green? She vehemently shook her head. Okay. Definitely no eggs. "How about toast?"

Again she shook her head. "No food. Not now."

"Are you sick?"

"No." Her answer came too quickly.

"Something is wrong or you wouldn't be curled up in bed."

"It's just the sway of the yacht. I'm not used to it."

He planted his hands on his waist. He supposed that was a reasonable explanation. "You aren't the only one with a bout of motion sickness. McMurray still isn't well. I guess my sailing expedition wasn't such a good idea."

"It was a great idea. And I'll be up on deck shortly."

"Take the morning off and rest—"

"No. I'm already feeling better. Just give me a bit to get ready."

"Why must you always be so stubborn?"

She sent him a scowl. "I'm not stubborn. It isn't like you know me that well."

"Since we started working together, I've learned a lot about you."

"Like what?"

He sighed but then decided to be truthful with her. "I know that you're honest. You're a hard worker. And you go above and beyond what is asked of you in order to do a good job."

A smile bloomed on her still-pale face. "Anything else?"

"I know you can be passionate—about causes you believe in. And sometimes you push too hard if you think it will help someone else."

She eyed him up. "You really believe all of that nice stuff about me? You're not saying it because you feel sorry for me, are you?"

Was she hunting for more compliments? He searched her eyes and found a gleam of uncertainty. He had to wonder, if only to himself, how someone so talented and sure of herself when it came to business could be so insecure behind closed doors.

"Yes, I meant everything I said. You're very talented."

Holly worried her bottom lip. When his gaze met hers, she glanced away. What did she have on her mind? Something told him whatever it was he wasn't going to like it. But they might as well get it over with.

"What else do you have on your mind?"

She blinked as though considering her options. Then she sat up straight, letting the sheet pool around her waist. He inwardly groaned as her nightie was not exactly conservative, and that was not something he needed to be contemplating at this moment.

Stay focused on the conversation! Don't let your eyes dip. Focus on her face.

Holly lifted her chin. "I would like to know if you'd write me a personal recommendation."

"Recommendation? For what?"

She visibly swallowed. The muscles in her slender neck worked in unison. "I have an inside source who says a prime opportunity is about to open up and I'd like to apply for the position."

"No problem. Just tell me what department it is and I'll make it happen. But I thought you liked working in the legal department."

"I did—I mean I do. But you don't understand. This job isn't within Lockwood."

He had to admit that he hadn't seen that one coming. And for a man that prided himself on being able to plan ahead, this was a bit much to swallow. "But I don't understand. You like your job, so this has to be about us."

Her slender shoulders rose and fell. "It's too complicated for me to stay on at Lockwood."

"You mean the kiss the other evening, don't you?"

Her gaze didn't quite meet his. "It would just be easier if I were to work elsewhere."

"When would you be taking this new position?"

"At the beginning of the year. So you don't have to worry about Project Santa. It will be completed before I leave and I'll be out of Lockwood before you return to New York."

"Sounds awfully convenient." His voice took on a disgruntled tone.

He didn't like the thought of Holly going to such lengths to keep her path from crossing his. Up until this trip, they'd done so well avoiding each other at the office. He had to admit a few times he'd hoped to bump into her in a hallway or the elevator, but that had never happened.

Holly was smart for wanting to get away from him. When his ex-fiancée hadn't been able to deal with his moods and distance, she'd left. He'd never blamed her. It was what he'd deserved. He should be relieved that Holly wanted to move on, but he couldn't work up the emotion.

He told himself that he didn't want to see her go because she was a good worker. She was smart and a go-getter. She wasn't afraid to think outside the box. His company needed more innovative people like her.

Holly smoothed the cream-colored sheet as though sorting her thoughts. "Listen, I know this comes as a surprise, but I really do think it would be for the best. It isn't like either one of us wants a serious relationship. You have your company to focus on."

"And what do you have?" He knew there was more to this request than she was saying, perhaps something even beyond what was going on between the two of them. Because if her reasons extended beyond the attraction between them, then he could fix it and she would stay, he hoped.

"I have my work, and this new position will help me to grow and to take on greater responsibility."

"And you can't do that at Lockwood?"

She shrugged, letting him know that she'd already dismissed that option.

Without Holly to liven things up, he would return to a downright boring existence. Before he handed over the golden ticket to another position, he needed more time to think this over. Surely there had to be a way to persuade her into staying.

"You've caught me off guard. Can I have some time to think over your request?"

"Of course. But don't take too long. Once word gets out about the opening, the candidates will flood the office with résumés."

He could see she'd given this a lot of thought and her mind was made up. "Just tell me one thing and be honest. Is this because you're trying to get away from me?"

Her gaze met his. "Maybe. Partly. But it's an amazing opportunity and I don't want to miss out on it."

"Would you be willing to tell me what the position is?"

"That would be telling you two things and you said you'd only ask one thing."

"And so I did." He sighed. "This isn't over."

"I didn't think that it was."

"I'll go get you some ginger ale and crackers."

"You don't have to do that. You have a business meeting to attend."

"Not before I see that you're cared for."

And with that he made a hasty exit from the cabin, still digesting the news. It left an uneasy feeling in his gut. And this was why he never got involved with employees of Lockwood. It made things sticky and awkward, not to mention he couldn't afford to lose such talent.

CHAPTER NINE

IT WAS SO good to be back on solid ground.

The next morning Holly stood on the balcony of Finn's beach house that was more like a mansion. He'd just escorted his last guest to the helipad. Their sailing trip had been cut short due to the rough waters. She thought for sure Finn would be upset, but he took it all in stride.

She shouldn't be standing here. There was work to be done on Project Santa—work that could be done from anywhere in the world, including New York.

The sound of footsteps caused her to turn around. Finn stopped at the edge of the deck. He didn't smile and the look in his eyes was unreadable.

"Did everyone get off okay?"

"They did."

The silence between them dragged on. Finn obviously had something on his mind. Maybe this was her chance to broach the subject of her leaving.

She turned to him.

"I was thinking I should get to work. You know, there's no reason I can't complete Project Santa in New York. I can make my travel arrangements and be out of your way shortly."

"You're not in my way." His voice dropped to a serious tone. "Have I somehow made you feel unwelcome?"

"Well, no, but I just thought that, ah, well, there's no point in me staying on the island. That is, unless you still need my assistance."

"You're right." His voice was calm and even. "Any work from here on out can be done via phone or the internet."

His sudden agreement stung. She knew she should be relieved, but she was conflicted. His eagerness to see her gone almost felt as though she was being dismissed—as though she hadn't quite measured up as his PA. Was that what he was thinking? Or had he merely grown tired of her like the other men in her life had done?

"I'll pack my bags and leave tomorrow."

She moved swiftly from the large deck and into the cool interior of the house. The sooner she got off this island, the better. She'd forget about Finn and how every time she was around him she wanted to follow up their kiss with another and another.

A new job was just what she needed. It'd give her the time and space to get over this silly crush she had on Finn. Because that was all it was, a crush. Nothing more.

So much for Holly's departure and having his life return to normal.

She was sick again.

Finn paced back and forth in his study.

He didn't care what Holly said, it obviously wasn't seasickness any longer. Her illness could be anything, including something serious. He hadn't gotten a bit of work done all morning. At least nothing worthwhile. And now that lunch was over and Holly hadn't shown up, he wasn't sure what to do. He'd never been in a position of worrying about someone else.

When his brother had been sick, it had been his parents who'd done most of the worrying and the caretaking. And then there had been his great-aunt who'd taken him in after his parents' deaths, but she was made of hearty stock or so she'd liked to tell him. She'd barely been sick a day while he'd known her. Even on the few times she'd gotten the sniffles, she carried on, doing what needed to be done until her final breath.

But he couldn't ignore how poorly Holly looked. And

her appetite at best was iffy. Then a thought came to him. He'd take a tray of food to her room. There had to be something she could eat.

When he entered the kitchen, Maria, his cook/housekeeper, glanced up from where she was pulling spices to prepare the evening dinner. "Can I get you something?"

Finn shook his head. "Don't let me bother you. I'm just going to put together a tray to take to Miss Abrams."

"I can do it for you."

"I've got it." There was a firm tone to his voice, more so than he'd intended. He just needed to do this on his own. "Sorry. I'm just a little worried."

Maria nodded as in understanding before turning back to her work.

Finn raided the fridge, settling on sandwich makings. It was what he ate late at night. And then he thought of something that Holly might enjoy. It was something his aunt swore by. Tea. "Maria, do we have some tea around here?"

The older woman smiled and nodded as though at last happy to be able to do something to help.

Between the two of them, they put together an extensive tray of food plus spearmint tea. And just to be on the safe side, he added a glass of ginger ale and crackers. As an afterthought, he snagged one of the pink rosebuds from the bouquet on the dining room table, slipped it into a bud vase and added it to the full tray. Hopefully this would cheer Holly up.

He strode down the hallway, up the steps and down another hallway until he stopped in front of her door. He tapped his knuckles on the door.

"Holly, it's me."

Within seconds, she pulled open the door. Her hair was mussed up and there was a sleepy look on her face. Her gaze lowered to the tray. "What's all of this?"

"It's for you. I noticed you missed lunch. I thought this might tide you over until dinner."

"Till dinner? I think that amount of food could last me for the next couple of days."

He glanced down at the sandwich. "I wasn't sure what meat and cheese you prefer so I added a little of everything. I figured you could just take off what you don't like."

"And the chips, fruit, vegetables and dip. Is there anything you forgot?"

He glanced over the tray and then a thought came to him. "I forgot to add some soup. Would you like some?"

"I think I'll get by with what you brought me."

A smile lifted her lips, easing the tired, stressed lines on her face. His gaze moved past her and trailed around the room, surprised to find that her laptop was closed. And then he spied the bed with the wrinkled comforter and the indent on the pillow. She'd been lying down.

"I'll put it over here." He moved toward the desk in the corner of her room. When she didn't follow him, he turned back to her. There were shadows under her eyes and her face was void of color. "Holly—"

She ran out of the room. She sent the bathroom door slamming shut.

That was it. He was done waiting for this bug or whatever was ailing her to pass. He pulled his cell phone from his pocket and requested that the chopper transport them to the big island where there would be medical help.

He didn't care how much she protested, this simply couldn't go on. There was something seriously wrong here. And he was worried—really worried.

"Finn, don't forget your promise."

"I won't." He stared straight ahead as he searched for a parking spot on the big island.

Before they flew here, Holly had extracted a promise from him. If she agreed to this totally unnecessary doctor's appointment, he would help her catch the next flight home.

She was certain whatever was plaguing her was no more than a flu bug. No big deal. She had no idea why Finn was so concerned.

Being an hour early for her appointment, Holly took advantage of the opportunity to meander through the colorful shops and the intriguing stands along the street. And in the end, it was a productive visit as she bought a few gifts.

When it was time to head to the clinic, Holly pleaded that it wasn't necessary. She was feeling better, but Finn insisted, reminding her that they had an agreement. And so they did. It also meant that she was almost homeward bound...just as soon as this appointment was concluded. She'd even packed her bag and brought it with her.

In the doctor's office Holly completed the paperwork and then they took her vital statistics. An older doctor examined her. He did a lot of hemming and hawing, but he gave her no insight into what those sounds meant. When she pointedly asked him what was wrong with her, he told her that he'd need to order a couple of tests.

Tests? That doesn't sound good.

She was feeling better. That had to be a good sign. But why was the doctor being so closemouthed? Although she recalled when her mother had suffered a stroke, trying to get information out of doctors was nearly impossible until they were ready to speak to you.

So she waited, but not alone. With her exam over, she invited Finn back to the room so he could hear with his own ears that she was fine. She was certain the doctor was only being cautious.

In the bright light, she noticed that Finn didn't look quite like himself. "Are you feeling all right?"

His gaze met hers. "I'm fine. It's you we should worry about."

She studied him a bit more. His face was pale and his eyes were dull. There was definitely something wrong with him.

"Oh, no, have I made you sick, too?"

He waved away her worry. "I'm like my great-aunt. I don't get sick."

"I don't believe you."

Finn's jaw tensed and a muscle in his cheek twitched, but he didn't argue with her. Okay, so maybe she was pushing it a bit. Doctor's offices made her uptight.

"I'm sorry," she said. "I didn't mean anything by that. I guess I don't do well with doctors."

The lines on Finn's handsome face smoothed out. "Why? What happened?"

She shrugged. "You don't want to hear about it."

"Sure, I do. That is, if you'll tell me."

Oh, well, what else did they have to do while waiting for the test results? There weren't even any glossy magazines in the small room. So while she sat on the exam table, Finn took a seat on the only chair in the room.

"It was a couple of days after you and I, you know, after—"

"The night we spent together?"

She nodded. "Yes, that. Well, I got a call from my mother's work. They were taking my mother to the hospital." She paused, recalling that frantic phone call when life as she knew it had come to a sudden standstill. "I'd never been so scared. I didn't know what was going on. I just knew an ambulance had been called for my mother. That's never a good sign."

"I'm sorry. I didn't know. I… I would have done something."

She glanced at him. "There was nothing for you to do. Remember, we agreed to stay clear of each other."

"Even so, I would have been there for you, if you'd have called me."

Holly shook her head. "I was fine. But thanks."

"I'm sure you had the rest of your family and friends to keep you company."

Holly shrugged. "I was fine."

He arched a brow. "When you said that the first time, I didn't believe you. And I don't believe it this time, either."

"Okay. I wasn't fine. I was scared to death. Is that what you want to hear?"

"No, it isn't what I want to hear. But I'm glad you're finally being honest with me."

Her gaze met his. "Why? It isn't like there's anything between us. At least, not anymore."

"Is that the truth? Or are you trying to convince yourself that you don't feel anything for me?"

She inwardly groaned. Why did everything have to be so complicated where Finn was concerned? Why couldn't things be simple, like her life had been before she'd walked into his office all those weeks ago?

CHAPTER TEN

Now, why had he gone and asked her if she had feelings for him?

Finn leaned his head back and sighed. It wasn't like he wanted to pick up where they'd left off. It didn't matter that they had chemistry and lots of it. In time, he'd forget about her sweet kisses and gentle caresses. He had to—she was better off without him.

He'd tried having a real relationship once. Talk about a mess. He wasn't going to repeat that mistake. Not that Holly was anything like Meryl. Not at all.

"Holly—"

The exam room door swung open. The doctor strode in and closed the door behind him. He lowered his reading glasses to the bridge of his nose. His dark head bent over a piece of paper. When he glanced up, his gaze immediately landed on Finn.

"Oh, hello." The doctor's puzzled gaze moved to Holly.

"It's okay. You can talk in front of him."

The doctor hesitated.

Holly sent the doctor a reassuring smile. "Finn's the one who insisted on bringing me here, and I just want to show him that he was overreacting."

"If you're sure."

She smiled and nodded.

"Okay then. I have the results back. It's what I initially suspected. You have morning sickness."

"Morning sickness? You mean I'm pregnant?" Holly vocalized Finn's stunned thoughts.

The doctor's bushy brows drew together. "I thought you knew."

Holly turned to Finn, the color in her face leaching away,

but no words crossed her lips. That was okay because for once, Finn couldn't think of anything to say, at least nothing that would make much sense.

A baby. We're having a baby.

Disbelief. Surprise. Excitement. Anger. It all balled together and washed over Finn.

Holly stared at him as though expecting him to say something, anything. But he didn't dare. Not yet. Not until he had his emotions under control. One wrong word and he wouldn't be able to rebound from it. And to be honest, he was stuck on six little—life-changing—words.

I'm going to be a father. I'm going to be a father.

Holly turned her attention back to the doctor. "You're sure? About the baby, that is."

The doctor's gaze moved to Finn and then back to her. The question was in his eyes, but he didn't vocalize it.

"Yes, he's the father."

Finn realized this was another of those moments where he should speak, but his mind drew a blank. It was though there was this pink-and-blue neon sign flashing in his mind that said *baby*.

"I'm one hundred percent certain you're pregnant." The doctor's forehead scrunched up. "I take it you have your doubts."

"Well, I, um—" she glanced at Finn before turning back to the doctor "—had my period since we were together. Granted it was light."

"Recently?"

"The week before last."

"Was there any cramping associated with it?"

She shook her head. "None that I recall."

"A little spotting is not uncommon. Have you had any spotting since then?"

"No. I'm just really tired. Are…are you sure everything is okay with the baby?"

"I'll be honest, you're still in your first trimester, which means the risk of miscarriage is higher. But I didn't tell you that to worry you. I just want you to realize that taking care of yourself is of the utmost importance."

"The baby." Her heart was racing so fast. "It's okay, right?"

"At this point, yes. I've arranged for a sonogram." He moved to the counter to retrieve a stack of literature. "You might like to read over these. They're about prenatal care and what to expect over the next several months. I'll be back."

Finn paced. Neither spoke as they each tried to grasp the news. Seconds turned to minutes. At last, Finn sank into the chair, feeling emotionally wiped out. His gaze moved to Holly but she appeared engrossed in a baby magazine the doctor had given her.

Where was the doctor? Had he forgotten them?

As though Finn's thoughts had summoned the man, the door swung open. A nurse walked in. Her eyes widened at the sight of Finn.

The nurse handed Holly a pink gown. "The straps go in the front." Then the nurse turned to him. "You might want to wait outside."

"I think you're right." That was it. Finn was out of there. He had no idea what was involved with a sonogram, but he'd give Holly her privacy.

When he reached the waiting room, he was tempted to keep going. In here he felt as though he couldn't quite catch his breath. Outside, in the fresh air, he would be able to breathe again. But he didn't want to move that far from Holly. What if she needed him?

And so he remained in the waiting room. He picked up a baby magazine, glanced at the cover and put it back down. He picked up another magazine, but it was for women. He put it down, too.

The door he'd just exited opened. A different nurse poked her head out. "Mr. Lockwood."

He approached her, not having a clue what she wanted. "I'm Mr. Lockwood."

"If you would come with me, sir." She led him back to Holly's exam room.

When he stood in the doorway, he found Holly lying on the exam table with a large sheet draped over her legs. He did not want to be here. He shouldn't be here.

Holly held her hand out to him. "Come see our baby."

He did want to see the baby. It would make it real for him. He moved to Holly's side, all the while keeping his gaze straight ahead, focused on the monitor. He slipped his hand in hers, finding her fingers cold. He assumed it was nerves. He sandwiched her hand between both of his, hoping to warm her up a little.

In no time at all, there was a fuzzy image on the monitor. Finn watched intently, trying to make out his child. And then it was there. It didn't look much like a baby at this point, but the doctor pointed out the head and spine.

"Wait a second, I need to check one more thing."

The doctor made an adjustment. Holly's fingers tightened their hold on Finn. Her worried gaze met his. Was there something wrong with their child?

Finn fervently hoped not. He just didn't think he could go through all his parents had endured with his brother. It was an experience he'd never forget.

"Okay." The doctor's voice rose. "Here we go. Just as I suspected."

Finn couldn't be left in the dark. He had to know what they were facing. "What's the matter?"

The doctor smiled up at him. "Nothing at all. You are having twins."

"Twins!" Holly said it at the same time as Finn.

"Yes, see here." The doctor showed them both babies.

It was the most amazing thing Finn had ever witnessed in his life. Twins. Who'd have thought? His vision started to blur, causing him to blink repeatedly. He was going to be a father—twice over.

He glanced down at Holly. A tear streamed down her cheek. His gut clenched. Was that a sign of joy or unhappiness? It was hard for him to tell. And then she turned and smiled at him. He released the pent-up breath in his lungs.

Holly squeezed his hand. "Did you see that? Those are our babies."

"I saw."

The doctor cleared his throat. "Well, you'll want to see your OB/GYN as soon as possible. But in the meantime, you need some rest and lots of fluids."

"Rest?"

"Yes and fluids. You have to be careful not to become dehydrated with the morning sickness."

"Okay. Whatever you say. I still can't believe I missed all of the signs."

"You aren't the first. Some women are in labor before they realize they are pregnant. These things happen."

Finn followed the doctor into the hallway while Holly got dressed. When they reentered the room, Holly looked different. Was it possible there was a bit of a glow about her? Or was he imagining things?

The doctor went over some suggestions on how to minimize her morning sickness and gave her a bottle of prenatal vitamins to get her started. "If you have any problems while you're in the islands, feel free to come back. I'm always here."

"I was planning to fly to New York today or tomorrow. Would that be all right?"

"I'd like to see you rested and hydrated before you travel. Get your morning sickness under control first."

Finn could feel everyone's attention turning his way, but he continued to study the random pattern of the floor tiles. He had nothing to contribute to this conversation, not at this point. This sudden turn of events was something he'd never envisioned.

The door opened and closed.

"Finn, are you okay?"

He glanced up, finding that he was alone with Holly. "Okay? No."

Her lips formed an O. "Can I say or do anything?"

He shook his head. He should be the one reassuring her, letting her know this was all going to be all right, but he couldn't lie to her. He had no idea how any of this was going to be all right. He was the last person in the world who should be a father. In fact, up until this point, he'd intended to leave all of his estate to designated charities.

But now, wow, everything had just changed. He raked his fingers through his hair. He had to rethink everything.

Pull it together. She's expecting me to say something.

He lifted his head and met her worried gaze that shimmered with unshed tears. That was the last thing he'd expected. Holly was always so strong and sure of what she wanted. Her tears socked him in the gut, jarring him back to reality. She was just as scared as he was, if not more so.

Oh, boy, were his children in big trouble here. Neither Holly nor himself was prepared to be a parent. They had so much to learn and so little time.

Finn stood. "Let's go back to the island."

Her worried gaze met his. "But what about New York?"

"You heard the doctor. You need to rest first." He held his hand out to her.

She hesitated but then grasped his hand.

He didn't know what the future held, but for now they were in it together. For better. Or for worse.

CHAPTER ELEVEN

WHAT WERE THEY supposed to do now?

A few days after returning from their trip to the big island, Holly was starting to feel better. The suggestions the doctor had given her for morning sickness were helping. And she'd been monitoring her fluid intake.

She was still trying to come to terms with the fact that she was pregnant. There was no question in her mind about keeping the babies, but that was the only thing she knew for sure.

Maria and Emilio had been called away from the island. This meant Holly and Finn had the entire island to themselves. In another time, that might have been exciting, even romantic, but right now, they had serious matters on their minds.

She paced back and forth in the study. Where would she live? How would she manage a job, helping out her mother and being a mom all on her own? And where did this leave her and Finn?

The questions continued to whirl around in her mind. She would figure it out—she had to—because she wasn't going to fall back on Finn. She'd counted on two men in her life and they'd both failed her. She knew better this time around. She could only count on herself.

Deciding she wasn't going to get any more work done, she headed for the kitchen. She needed something to do with her hands and she had an urge for something sweet.

As she searched the cabinets, looking for something to appease her craving, her thoughts turned to Finn. He'd barely spoken to her since they left the doctor's office. The occasional nod or grunt was about as much as she got out of him.

She couldn't blame him. It was a lot to adjust to. Her mind was still spinning. Her hand ran over her abdomen.

A baby. No, two babies. Inside her. Wow!

"How are you feeling?" Finn asked.

Four whole words strung together. She would take that as a positive sign. "Better."

"And the babies?"

"Are perfectly fine." She bent over to retrieve a cookie sheet from the cabinet.

"I can get that for you." Finn rushed around the counter with his hands outstretched.

"I can manage." She glared at him until he retreated to the other side of the counter.

She placed the cookie sheet on the counter before turning on the oven. "Did you need something?"

"You're planning to bake? Now?"

"Sure. Why not? I have a craving."

"Isn't it a little early for those?"

She sighed. Why did he have to pick now of all times to get chatty? She just wanted to eat some sugary goodness in peace. "Not that kind of craving."

"Then what kind?"

What was up with him? He'd never been so curious about her dietary habits before. Or maybe he was just attempting to be friendly and she was being supersensitive. She choked down her agitation, planning to give him the benefit of the doubt.

"These are cravings that I get when I'm stressed out." She pulled open the door on the stainless-steel fridge and withdrew a roll of premade cookie dough. "Do you want some cookies?"

"If you're stressed about Project Santa—?"

"It's not that!"

His eyes widened. "Oh. I see."

This was another opening for him to discuss the big pink

or perhaps blue elephant in the room. And yet, he said nothing. Her gaze met his and he glanced away. Was this his way of telling her that he wasn't interested in being a father?

She placed the package of cookie dough on the counter before moving to the oven to adjust the temperature. Next, she needed a cutting board. There had to be one around here somewhere. The kitchen was equipped with absolutely everything. At last, she spotted a small pineapple-shaped board propped against the stone backsplash.

With the cutting board and a knife in hand, she moved back to the counter. "I'll have some reindeer cookies ready in no time. I thought about some hot chocolate with the little marshmallows, but it's a little warm around here for that."

"Thanks. But I'll pass on the cookies. I have some emails I need to get to. By the way, do you have a copy of the Cutter contract?"

"I do. It's in my room. Just let me finish putting these cookies on the tray." She put a dozen on the tray and slipped it in the oven. "Okay. There." She turned back to him. "Stay here and I'll be right back."

She rushed to her spacious guest room that overlooked the ocean. It was a spectacular view. She was tempted to take a dip in the sea or at the very least walk along the beach, letting her feet get wet. Maybe she'd do it later, after she was done working for the day.

Turning away from the window, her gaze strayed over the colorful packages she'd brought back from the big island. She'd splurged a bit, buying a little something for everyone, including her half-sisters, Suzie and Kristi.

Holly worried her bottom lip. She always tried so hard to find something that would impress them and each year, she'd failed. Thankfully she'd bought the gifts before her doctor's appointment because afterward she hadn't been in a holly-jolly spirit. The bikinis, sunglasses, flip-flops and a cover-up with the name of the island were placed in yellow tissue-paper-lined shopping bags. The girls would be all set for summer. About the same time she was giving birth.

With a sigh, Holly continued her hunt for the contract. On top of the dresser, she found the file folder. She pulled it out from beneath a stack of papers and an expandable folder when the back of her hand struck the lamp. Before she could stop it, the lamp toppled over.

Holly gasped as it landed on the floor and shattered, sending shards of glass all over the room. As she knelt down to clean up the mess, she muttered to herself. It was then that she heard rapid footsteps in the hallway.

"What happened?" Finn's voice carried a note of concern. "Are you okay?"

"I am. But the same can't be said for the lamp."

"I'm not worried about it." His concerned gaze met hers.

"I'll have this cleaned up in no time. Your contract is on the edge of the dresser."

When he stepped forward, she thought it was to retrieve the contract. However, the next thing she knew, he knelt down beside her.

"What are you doing?" she asked, not quite believing her eyes.

"Helping you."

"I don't need your help—"

"Well, you better get used to it because I plan to help with these babies."

It wasn't a question. It was an emphatic statement.

Her stomach churned. She was losing her control—her independence. She was about to lose her sense of security because her life would no longer be her own—Finn and the babies would now be a part of it—forever.

Holly sucked in a deep breath, hoping it'd slow the rapid pounding of her heart.

"Did you cut yourself on the broken glass?" Finn glanced down at her hands.

"I'm fine." She got to her feet, needing some distance from him. And then she smelled something. She sniffed again. "Oh, no! The cookies."

She rushed to the kitchen and swung the oven door open. The Christmas cookies were all brown and burnt. With Finn hovering about, she'd forgotten to turn on the timer. She groaned aloud, not caring if he heard her or not.

She turned to the garbage and dumped the cookies in it. Her gaze blurred. The memory of Finn's words and the knowledge that life would never be the same made her feel off-kilter and scared. What were they supposed to do now?

CHAPTER TWELVE

HE HAD TO do something, but what?

The next evening, Finn did his best to concentrate on the details of a potential acquisition for Lockwood. Try as he might, his thoughts kept straying back to Holly and the babies. This was the time when his family would be invaluable. A deep sadness came over him, realizing that his children would never know his parents or his brother, Derek. In that moment he knew that it would be his responsibility to tell his children about their past—about their grandparents and uncle. Finn didn't take the notion lightly.

He glanced across the study to where Holly was sitting on the couch, working on her laptop. She'd been feeling better, which was a relief. Whatever the doctor had told her to do was helping. Now they could focus on the future.

His gaze moved to the windows behind her. The day was gray and glum just like his mood. He knew what needed to be done. They needed to get married.

He'd wrestled with the thought for days now. And it was the only solution that made sense. Although, he wasn't ready to get down on one knee and lay his heart on the line. Just the thought of loving someone else and losing them made his blood run cold. No, it was best their marriage was based on something more reliable—common goals.

The welfare of their children would be the tie that bound them. Finn's chest tightened when he realized that he knew less than nothing about babies. He would need help and lots of it. That was where Holly came in. He needed her guidance if he wanted to be the perfect parent—or as close to it as possible. Without her, he wouldn't even know where to start.

He assured himself that it would all work out. After all,

Holly was the mother to the Lockwood heirs. Their fates had been sealed as soon as she became pregnant. They would have to marry. And he would do his utmost to keep his family safe.

Holly leaned back. "I'm almost finished with the last details for Project Santa. I've reviewed the list of volunteers, state by state and city by city. I've been trying to determine whether there are enough volunteers to transport the gifts from the airports to the designated outreach centers."

Finn welcomed the distraction. "And what have you determined?"

"I think we need a few more drivers. I've already posted a request on MyFace. I'll wait and see what the response is before I take further steps."

"Good. It sounds like you have everything under control."

The fact that they worked well together was another thing they could build on. It would give their marriage a firm foundation. Because he just couldn't open his heart—he couldn't take that risk again.

A gust of wind made a shutter on the house rattle, jarring Finn from his thoughts. It was really picking up out there. So much for the sunshine in paradise. It looked like they'd soon be in for some rain.

"Finn, we need to talk." The banging continued, causing Holly to glance around. "What was that pounding sound?"

"I think it's a shutter that needs tightening."

Holly closed her laptop and set it aside. She got to her feet and moved to the window as though to inspect the problem. "Do you have a screwdriver and a ladder?"

"Yes, but why?"

"I'll go fix it."

"You?"

She frowned at him. "Yes, me. If you haven't noticed, I'm not one to sit around helplessly and wait for some guy to come take care of me."

"But you're pregnant and have doctor's orders to rest. You shouldn't be climbing on ladders. I'll take care of it later."

She sighed loudly. "I've been following his orders and I'm feeling much better. But if you insist, I'll leave the house repairs to you. Besides, there's something else we need to discuss."

"Is there another problem with Project Santa?"

"No. It's not that." She averted her gaze. "Remember how I asked you for a letter of recommendation?"

Why would she bring that up now? Surely she wasn't still considering it. Everything had changed what with the babies and all. "I remember."

Her gaze lifted to meet his. "Have you made a decision?"

"I didn't think it was still an issue."

"Why not?"

"Because you won't be leaving Lockwood, unless of course you want to stay home with the babies, which I'd totally understand. They are certainly going to be a handful and then some."

"Why do you think I won't leave to take that new job?"

Finn sent her a very puzzled look. "Because you're carrying the Lockwood heirs. And soon we'll be married—"

"Married?" Holly took a step back.

What was Finn talking about? They weren't getting married. Not now. Not ever.

"Of course. It's the next logical step—"

"No." She shook her head as her heart raced and her hands grew clammy. "It isn't logical and it certainly isn't my next step. You never even asked me, not that I want you to or anything."

"I thought it was implied."

"Implied? Maybe in your mind, but certainly not in mine. I'm not marrying you. I'm not going to marry anyone."

"Of course you are." His voice rumbled with irritation.

"This isn't the Stone Age. A woman can be pregnant without a husband. There are plenty of loving, single mothers in this world. Take a look around your office building. You'll find quite a few. But you won't find me there after the first of the year."

Had she really just said that? Oh, my. She'd gotten a little ahead of herself. What if he turned his back and walked away without giving her the recommendation? And she didn't have the job. It was still iffy at best. And without her position at Lockwood to fall back on, how would she support herself much less the babies and her mother?

"You're really serious about leaving, aren't you?"

She nodded, afraid to open her mouth again and make the situation worse.

"Do you really dislike me that much?"

"No! Not at all." In fact, it was quite the opposite.

She worried the inside of her lower lip as she glanced toward the window. The wind had picked up, whipping the fronds of the palm trees to and fro. She did not want to answer this question. Not at all.

"Holly?" Finn got to his feet and came to stand in front of her. "Why are you doing this? Why are you trying to drive us apart?"

"You…you're making this sound personal and it isn't." Heat rushed up her neck and made her face feel as though she'd been lying in the sun all day with no sunscreen.

"It is personal. It couldn't be more personal."

"No, it isn't. It's not like you and I, like we're involved."

"I don't know your definition of involved, but I don't think it gets much more involved than you carrying my babies."

"Finn, we both agreed after that night together that we wouldn't have anything to do with each other. We mutually decided that going our separate ways was for the best—for both of us."

"That was before."

"The pregnancy is a complication. I'll admit that. But we can work out an arrangement with the babies. We don't have to live out of each other's back pockets."

"I don't want to live in your back pocket. I want to provide a home for my children and their mother—"

"I don't need you to take care of me or the babies. I can manage on my own."

"But the point is you don't have to. I'm here to help. We can help each other."

She shook her head. "A marriage of convenience won't work."

"Sure it will, if we want it to."

Holly crossed her arms. "Why are you so certain you're right? It's not like we're in love. This thing between us will never last."

"And maybe you're wrong. Maybe the fact that we aren't in love is the reason that it will work. There won't be any unreasonable expectations. No emotional roller coaster."

"And that sounds good to you?"

He shrugged. "Do you have a better suggestion?"

"Yes. I think some space will be best for everyone."

"I don't agree. What would be best is if we became a family—a family that shares the same home as our children."

"And what happens—" She stopped herself just in time. She was going to utter, *What happens when you get bored*? Would he trade her in for a younger model? But she wasn't going there. It didn't matter because what Finn was proposing wasn't possible.

His gaze probed her. "Finish that statement."

"It's nothing."

"It was definitely something. And I want to know what it is." He moved closer to her.

His nearness sent her heart racing. It was hard to keep

her mind on the conversation. No man had a right to be so sexy. If only real life was like the movies and came with happily-ever-afters.

"Holly?"

"I honestly can't remember what I was going to say. But it's time I go back to New York."

Finn's eyes momentarily widened in surprise "What about the project?"

"The event is ready to go."

"You just said you had a problem with transportation."

"That...that's minor. I can deal with it from anywhere."

His gaze narrowed. "You're serious, aren't you?"

She settled her hands on her hips. "I am. You don't need me here. You can email me or phone, but you no longer need my presence here."

"Is there anything I can say to change your mind?"

There were so many things she wanted him to say. But she feared they were both too damaged—too cynical about life to be able to create a happily-ever-after.

And instead of trying and failing—of taking what they have and making it contentious, she'd rather part as friends. It'd be best for everyone, including the babies.

But finding herself a bit emotional, she didn't trust her voice. Instead, she averted her gaze and shook her head.

Finn sighed. "Fine. I'll call for the chopper."

"Really?" He was just going to let her walk out the door? It seemed too easy.

"It's what you want, isn't it?" He retrieved the phone.

"Yes, it is." She turned away and walked to the French doors. They were usually standing open, letting in the fresh air and sunshine, but not today. She stared off into the distant gray sky. Dark clouds scudded across it as rain began to fall.

She couldn't believe he was just going to let her walk away. A man who liked to control everything in his life surely couldn't live with just handing over his children with no strings attached.

In the background, she could hear the murmur of Finn's voice. He'd lowered it, but not before she caught the rumble in it. He wasn't happy—not at all. Well, that made two of them. But they'd have to make the best of the situation.

Her hand moved to her abdomen. It wouldn't be long now before she really started to show. She didn't even want to guess how big she'd get carrying not one but two babies. She had no doubt her figure would never be quite the same. But it would be worth it.

To be honest, she'd never thought of having children before. After her family had been ripped apart, she told herself she wasn't getting married or having children. She'd assured herself that life would be so much simpler when she only had herself to worry about.

Now she had two little ones counting on her to make all of the right decisions.

She turned, finding Finn with his back to her as he leaned against the desk. He certainly was different from Josh. Where Josh was a real charmer, Finn only gave a compliment when he truly meant it. Where Josh ran at the first sign of trouble, Finn was willing to stand by her. So why couldn't she give him a chance to prove that he truly was an exception?

He certainly was the most handsome man she'd laid her eyes on. Her gaze lingered on his golden hair that always seemed to be a bit scattered and made her long to run her fingers through it. And then there were his broad shoulders—shoulders that looked as though they could carry the weight of the world on them. She wondered how heavy a load he carried around.

Something told her he'd seen far too much in his young life. And she didn't want to add to his burden. That was never her intention. With time, she hoped he'd understand that she never meant to hurt him by turning down his suggestion of marriage.

Finn hung up the phone and turned to her. "We can't leave."

Surely she hadn't heard him correctly. "What do you mean we can't leave?"

"There's a storm moving in and with these high winds it's too dangerous to take up the chopper." His gaze met hers. "I'm sorry. I know how much you wanted off the island."

"So what are you saying? That we're stranded here?"

"Yes." He didn't look any happier about it than she did.

"What are we going to do?"

"You're going to wait here." He turned toward the door. "With Emilio and Maria away, I've got a lot of work to do before the storm. I won't get it all done tonight, but I can at least start."

"Wait for me. I want to help."

She rushed after him. There was no way she was planning to stand around and have him do all of the work. She knew her way around a toolbox and power tools. She could pull her own weight.

Hopefully this storm would pass by the island, leaving them unscathed. And then she'd be on her way home. She wasn't sure how much longer she could keep her common sense while around Finn.

Her gaze trailed down over Finn from his muscled arms to his trim waist and his firm backside. The blood heated in her veins. Enjoying each other's company didn't mean they had to make a formal commitment, right?

Wait. No. No. She couldn't let her desires override her logic. She jerked her gaze away from Finn. It had to be the pregnancy hormones that had her thinking these truly outlandish thoughts.

She was immune to Finn—about as immune as a bee to a field of wildflowers. She was in big trouble.

CHAPTER THIRTEEN

WHY WAS SHE fighting him?

The next day, Finn sighed as he stared blindly out the glass doors. No matter what he said to Holly, there was no reasoning with her. She was determined to have these babies on her own.

He knew that she wouldn't keep him from seeing them, but he also knew that visitation every other weekend was not enough. He would be a stranger to his own children—his only family. His hands clenched. That couldn't happen.

He'd never thought he'd be a part of a family again. And though he had worries about how well he'd measure up as a husband and father, he'd couldn't walk away. Why couldn't Holly understand that?

He didn't know how or when, but somehow he'd convince her that they were better parents together than apart. If only he knew how to get his point across to her—

The lights flickered, halting his thoughts. The power went completely out, shrouding the house in long shadows. After a night and day of rain, it had stopped, but the winds were starting to pick up again. And then the lights came back on.

Finn didn't like the looks of things outside—not one little bit. Normally there weren't big weather events at this time of the year, but every once in a while a late-season storm would make its way across the Atlantic. This just happened to be one of those times.

Finn rinsed a dinner plate and placed it in the dishwasher. Yes, to Holly's amazement, he did know his way around the kitchen. He was a man who preferred his privacy and he didn't have a regular household staff in New York, just a maid who came in a couple of times a week.

But here on the island, it was different. Maria and Emilio had a small house off in the distance. They lived here year-round. Maria looked after the house while Emilio took care of the grounds. They were as close to family as Finn had—until now.

He ran the dishcloth over the granite countertop before placing it next to the sink. Everything was clean and in its place. He wondered what Holly was up to. She'd been particularly quiet throughout dinner. He made his way to the study.

Though she wouldn't admit it, he could tell the storm had her on edge. He was concerned, too. The tide was much higher than normal and the wind was wicked. But this house had been built to withstand some of the harshest weather. They'd be safe here.

Now if only he could comfort Holly, but she resisted any attempt he made to get closer. He wondered what had happened for her to hide behind a defensive wall. It had to be something pretty bad. If only he could get her to open up to him.

He was in the hallway outside the study when the lights flickered and went out. This time they didn't come back on. He needed to check on Holly before he ventured outside to fire up the emergency generator.

He stepped into the study that was now long with shadows. He squinted, looking for her. "Holly, where are you?"

She stood up from behind one of the couches. "Over here."

"What in the world are you doing?"

"Looking for candles in this cabinet."

"There are no candles in here. I have some in the kitchen."

She followed him to the supply of candles. There were also flashlights and lanterns in the pantry. It was fully stocked in case of an emergency.

"Do you think we'll really need all of this?" She fingered

the packages of beef jerky and various other prepackaged foods.

"I hope not. The last I checked the weather radio, the storm was supposed to go south of us."

"And I think it's calming down outside. That has to be a good sign, doesn't it?"

When he glanced over at the hopefulness in her eyes, he didn't want to disappoint her. He wanted to be able to reassure her that everything would be fine, but something told him she'd already been lied to enough in her life. So he decided to change the subject.

He picked up a lantern. "I think this might be easier than the candles."

"Really?"

Was that a pout on her face? She wanted the candlelight? Was it possible there was a romantic side to her hidden somewhere beneath her practicality and cynicism?

Deciding it wouldn't hurt to indulge her, he retrieved some large candle jars. "Is this what you had in mind?"

She nodded. "But we won't need them, will we?"

Finn glanced outside. It was much darker than it normally would be at this time of the day. "Come on. I have a safe place for us to wait out the storm."

She didn't question him but rather she quietly followed him to the center of the house. He opened the door to a small room with reinforced walls and no windows.

"What is this?"

"A safe room. I know it's not very big, but trust me, it'll do the job. I had it specifically put in the house for this very reason." With a flashlight in hand, he started lighting the candles. "There. That's all of them." A loud bang echoed through the house. "Now, I'll go work on the generator."

Holly reached out, grasping his arm. "Please don't go outside."

"But I need to—"

"Stay safe. We've got everything we need right here."

"Holly, don't worry. This isn't my first storm."

"But it's mine. Promise me you won't go outside."

He stared into her big brown eyes and saw the fear reflected in them. It tore at his heart. He pulled her close until her cheek rested against his shoulder.

"Everything will be fine."

She pulled back in order to gaze into his eyes. "Promise me you won't go outside."

He couldn't deny her this. "Yes, I promise."

This time she squeezed him tight as though in relief.

Seconds later, Finn pulled away. "I think we'll need some more candles and I want to do one more walk through the house to make sure it's secure. I'll be back."

"I can come with you."

"No. Stay here and get comfortable. I'll be right back. I promise." He started for the door.

"Finn?"

He paused, hearing the fear in her voice. "Do you need something else?"

"Um, no. Just be careful."

"I will." Was it possible that through all of her defensiveness and need to assert her independence that she cared for him? The thought warmed a spot in his chest. But he didn't have time to dwell on this revelation. The winds were starting to howl.

He hurried back to the kitchen where he'd purposely forgotten the weather radio. He wanted to listen to it without Holly around. He didn't know much about pregnant women, but he knew enough to know stress would not be good for her.

The radio crackled. He adjusted it so he could make out most of the words. The eye of the storm had shifted. It was headed closer to them. And the winds were intensifying to hurricane strength. Finn's hands clenched tightly.

This was all his fault. He should have paid more attention to the weather instead of getting distracted with the babies and his plans for the future. Now, instead of worrying about what he'd be like as a father, he had to hope he'd get that chance. He knew how bad the tropical storms could get. He'd ridden one out in this very house a few years back. It was an experience he'd been hoping not to repeat.

With a sigh, he turned off the radio. He made the rounds. The house was as secure as he could make it. With the radio, satellite phone and a crate of candles and more water, he headed back to Holly.

"How is everything?" Her voice held a distinct thread of worry.

He closed the door and turned around to find a cozy setting awaiting him. There were blankets heaped on the floor and pillows lining the wall. With the soft glow of the candles, it swept him back in time—back to when his big brother was still alive. They were forever building blanket forts to their mother's frustration.

The memory of his mother and brother saddened him. Finn tried his best not to dwell on their absence from his life, but every now and then there would be a moment when a memory would drive home the fact that he was now all alone in this world.

"Finn, what is it?" Holly got to her feet and moved to him.

It wasn't until she pressed a hand to his arm that he was jarred from his thoughts. "Um, nothing. Everything is secure. It's started to rain."

"The storm's not going to miss us, is it?"

"I'm afraid not. But we'll be fine."

"With the door closed, it's amazing how quiet it is in here. I could almost pretend there isn't a big storm brewing outside."

He didn't want to keep talking about the weather. He didn't want her asking more questions, because the last thing he wanted to do was scare her with the word *hurricane*. After all, it wasn't even one yet, but there was a strong potential.

"I see you made the room comfortable."

She glanced around. "I hope you like it."

"I do." There was one thing about this arrangement—she couldn't get away from him. He had a feeling by the time the sun rose, things between them would be drastically different.

This was not working.

Holly wiggled around, trying to get comfortable. It wasn't the cushions so much as hearing the creaking of the house and wondering what was going on outside. Finn hadn't wanted to tell her so she hadn't pushed, but her best guess was that they were going to experience a hurricane. The thought sent a chill racing down her spine.

"Is something wrong?"

"Um, nothing."

She glanced across the short space to find Finn's handsome face illuminated in the candlelight. Why exactly had she insisted on the candles? Was she hoping there would be a bit of romance? Of course not. The soft light was comforting, was all.

His head lifted and his gaze met hers. "Do you need more cushions? Or a blanket?"

"Really, I'm fine." There was another loud creak of the house. "I... I'm just wondering what's going on outside. Should we go check?"

"No." His answer was fast and short. "I mean there could be broken glass and it's dark out there. We'll deal with it in the morning."

She swallowed hard. "You really think the windows have been blown out?"

"The shutters will protect them. Hopefully the house is holding its own."

"Maybe you should turn on the radio." Whatever the

weather people said couldn't be worse than what her imagination had conjured up.

"You know what I'd really like to do?" He didn't wait for her to respond. "How about we get to know each other better?"

"And how do you propose we do that?"

"How about a game of twenty questions? You can ask me anything you want and I have to be absolutely honest. In return, I get to ask you twenty questions and you have to be honest."

She wasn't so sure honesty right now would be such a good idea, especially if he asked if she cared about him. "I... I don't know."

"Oh, come on. Surely you have questions."

She did. She had lots of them, but she wasn't so sure she wanted to answer his in return. She didn't open up with many people. She told herself it was because she was introverted, but sometimes she wondered if it was more than that.

On this particular night everything felt surreal. Perhaps she could act outside her norm. "Okay, as long as I go first."

"Go for it. But remember you only get twenty questions so make them good ones."

CHAPTER FOURTEEN

HOLLY DIDN'T HAVE to think hard to come up with her first question. "Why did you look like you'd seen a ghost when you stepped in here?"

There was a pause as though Finn was figuring out how to answer her question. Was he thinking up a vague answer or would he really open up and give her a glimpse of the man beneath the business suits and intimidating reputation?

He glanced off into the shadows. "When I walked in here I was reminded of a time—long ago. My brother and I used to build blanket forts when we were kids. Especially in the winter when it was too cold or wet to go outside. My mother wasn't fond of them because we'd strip our beds."

Holly smiled, liking that he had a normal childhood with happy memories. She wondered why he kept them hidden. In all the time she'd been around him, she could count on one hand the number of times he spoke of his family. But she didn't say a word because she didn't want to interrupt him—she found herself wanting to learn everything she could about him.

"I remember there was this one Christmas where we'd built our biggest fort. But it was dark in there and my brother wanted to teach me to play cards. My mother would have been horrified that her proper young men were playing cards—it made it all the more fun. We tried a flashlight but it didn't have enough light. So my brother got an idea of where to get some lights."

Holly could tell by the gleam in Finn's eyes that mischief had been afoot. He and his brother must have been a handful. Would her twins be just as ornery? Her hand moved to her stomach. She had a feeling they would be and that she'd love every minute of it. She might even join them in their fort.

"While my parents were out at the Mistletoe Ball and the sitter was watching a movie in the family room, we took a string of white lights off the Christmas tree."

Holly gasped. "You didn't."

Finn nodded. "My brother assured me it was just one strand. There were plenty of other lights on the tree. After all, it was a big tree. So we strung the lights back and forth inside our fort. It gave it a nice glow, enough so that we could see the cards. There was just one problem."

"You got caught?"

He shook his head. "Not at first. The problem was my brother for all of his boasting had no clue how to play cards. So we ended up playing Go Fish."

Holly couldn't help but laugh, imagining those two little boys. "I bet you kept your parents on their toes."

"I suppose we did—for a while anyway." The smile slipped from his face and she wanted to put it back there. He was so handsome when he smiled.

"So what happened with the lights?"

"Well, when my parents got home, my mother called us down to the living room. It seems my father tried to fix the lights that were out on the lower part of the tree, but he soon found they were missing. My mother wanted to know if we knew anything about it. I looked at my brother and he looked at me. Then we both shrugged. We tried to assure her the tree looked good, but she wasn't buying any of it. My mother didn't have to look very long to find the lights. As I recall, we were grounded for a week. My father had the task of putting the lights back on the tree with all of the ornaments and ribbon still on it. He was not happy at all."

"I wouldn't think he would be."

"Okay. So now it's my turn. Let's see. Where did you grow up?"

She gave him a funny look. "Seriously, that's what you want to know?"

He shrugged. "Sure. Why not?"

"I grew up in Queens. A long way from your Upper East Side home."

"Not that far."

"Maybe not by train but it is by lifestyle." When Finn glanced away, she realized how that sounded. She just wasn't good at thinking about her family and the way things used to be so she always searched for a diversion.

"It's my turn." She thought for a moment and then asked, "Okay, what's your favorite color?"

He sent her a look of disbelief. "Are you serious?"

"Sure. Why wouldn't I be?"

"It's just that I thought these were questions to get to know each other. I don't know how my favorite color has much to do with anything."

"I'll tell you once you spit it out."

He sighed. "Green. Hunter green. Now why was that so important to you?"

"Are you sure it isn't money green?" He rolled his eyes and smiled at her before she continued. "It's important to me because I need a color to paint the babies' bedroom."

"Oh. I hadn't thought of that. Then I get to ask you what your favorite color is."

"Purple. A deep purple."

"Sounds like our children are going to have interesting bedrooms with purple and green walls."

Holly paused and thought about it for a minute. "I think we can make it work."

"Are you serious?"

"Very. Think about green foliage with purple skies. A palm tree with a monkey or two or three. And perhaps a bunch of bananas here and there for a splash of yellow."

His eyes widened. "How did you do that?"

"Do what?"

"Come up with that mural off the top of your head?"

She shrugged. "I don't know. It just sounded fun and like something our children might enjoy."

"I think you're right. I'll have the painters get started on it right away."

"Whoa! Slow down. I don't even know where we'll be living by the time these babies are born." When the smile slipped from his face, she knew it was time for a new question. "Why do you always leave New York at Christmastime? No, scratch that. I know that answer. I guess my real question is why do you hate Christmas?"

He frowned. "So now you're going for the really hard questions, huh? No, what's your middle name? Or what's your favorite food?"

She shrugged. "I just can't imagine hating Christmas. It's the season of hope."

There was a faraway look in his eyes. "My mother, she used to love it, too. She would deck out our house the day after Thanksgiving. It was a tradition. And it wasn't just her. The whole family took part, pulling the boxes of decorations out of the attic while Christmas carols played in the background. After we hung the outside lights, my mother would whip up hot chocolate with those little marshmallows."

"So you don't like it anymore because it reminds you of her?"

Finn frowned. "You don't get to ask another question yet. Besides, I wasn't finished with my answer."

"Oh. Sorry."

"Now that my family isn't around, I don't see any point in celebrating. I'll never get any of those moments back. When I'm here, I don't have to be surrounded by those memories or be reminded of what I lost."

There was more to that story, but she had to figure out the right question to get him to open up more. But how deep would he let her dig into his life? She had no idea. But if she didn't try to break through some of the protective layers that he had surrounding him, how in the world would they ever coparent? How would she ever be able to answer her children's questions about their father?

She didn't want to just ignore her kids' inquiries like her mother had done with her. Initially when her father had left, she'd been so confused. She thought it was something she'd done or not done. She didn't understand because to her naive thinking, things had been good. Then one day he packed his bags and walked out the door. Her mother refused to fill in the missing pieces. It was really hard for a ten-year-old to understand how her family had splintered apart overnight.

Finn cleared his throat. "Okay, next question. Do your parents still live in Queens?"

"Yes, however right now my mother's visiting my aunt in Florida. And my father moved to Brooklyn."

Finn's brow arched. "So they're divorced?"

"You already had your question, now it's my turn." Finn frowned but signaled with his hand for her to proceed, so she continued. "What happened to your brother?"

Finn's hands flexed. "He died."

She knew there had to be so much more to it. But she didn't push. If Finn was going to let down his guard, it had to be his choice, and pushing him would only keep him on the defensive.

And so she quietly waited. Either he expanded on his answer or he asked her another question. She would make peace with whatever he decided.

"My brother was the star of the family. He got top marks in school. He was on every sports team. And he shadowed my father on the weekends at the office. He was like my father in so many ways."

"And what about you?"

"I was a couple of years younger. I wasn't the Lockwood heir and so my father didn't have much time for me. I got the occasional clap on the back for my top marks, but then my father would turn his attention to my brother. For the most part, it didn't bother me. It was easier being forgotten than being expected to be perfect. My brother didn't have it easy. The pressure my father put on him to excel at everything was enormous."

Holly didn't care what Finn said, to be forgotten by a parent or easily dismissed hurt deeply. She knew all about it when her father left them to start his own family with his mistress, now wife number two.

But this wasn't her story, it was Finn's. And she knew it didn't have a happy ending, but she didn't know the details. Perhaps if she'd dug deeper on the internet, she might have learned how Finn's family splintered apart, but she'd rather hear it all from him.

"Everything was fine until my brother's grades started to fall and he began making mistakes on the football field. My father was irate. He blamed it on my brother being a teenager and being distracted by girls. My brother didn't even have a girlfriend at that point. He was too shy around them."

Holly tried to decide if that was true of Finn, as well. Somehow she had a hard time imagining this larger-than-life man being shy. Perhaps he could be purposely distant, but she couldn't imagine him being nervous around a woman.

"My brother, he started to tire easily. It progressed to the point where my mother took him to the doctor. It all snowballed from there. Tests and treatments became the sole focus of the whole house. Christmas that year was forgotten."

"How about you?" He didn't say it, but she got the feeling with so much on the line that Finn got lost in the shuffle.

He frowned at her, but it was the pain in his eyes that dug at her. "I didn't have any right to feel forgotten. My brother was fighting for his life."

She lowered her voice. "But it had to be tough for you with everyone running around looking after your brother. No one would blame you for feeling forgotten."

"I would blame me. I was selfish." His voice was gravelly with emotion. "And I had no right—no right to want presents on Christmas—no right to grow angry with my parents for not having time for me."

Her heart ached for him. "Of course you would want Christmas with all of its trimmings. Your life was spinning out of control and you wanted to cling to what you knew—what would make your life feel normal again."

"Aren't you listening? My brother was dying and I was sitting around feeling sorry for myself because I couldn't have some stupid toys under the Christmas tree. What kind of a person does that make me?"

"A real flesh-and-blood person who isn't perfect. But here's a news flash for you. None of us are—perfect that is. We just have to make the best of what we've been given."

He shook his head, blinking repeatedly. "I'm worse than most. I'm selfish and thoughtless. *Uncaring* is the word my mother threw at me." He swiped at his eyes. "And she was right. My brother deserved a better sibling than I'd turned out to be."

Holly placed her hand atop his before lacing their fingers together. A tingling sensation rushed from their clasped hands, up her arm and settled in her chest. It gave her the strength she needed to keep going—to keep trying to help this man who was in such pain.

"Did you ever think that you were just a kid in a truly horrific situation? Your big brother—the person you looked up to—your best friend—was sick, dying and there was nothing you could do for him. That's a lot to deal with as an adult, but as a child you must have felt utterly helpless. Not knowing what to do with the onslaught of emotions, you pushed them aside. Your brother's situation was totally out of your control. Instead you focused on trying to take control of your life."

Finn's wounded gaze searched hers. "You're just saying that to make me feel better."

"I'm saying it because it's what I believe." She freed her hand from his in order to gently caress his jaw. "Finn, you're a good man with a big heart—"

"I'm not. I'm selfish."

"Is that what your mother told you?"

"No." His head lowered. There was a slight pause as though he was lost in his own memories. "It's what my father told me."

"He was wrong." She placed a fingertip beneath Finn's chin and lifted until they were eye to eye. "He was very wrong. You have the biggest, most generous heart of anyone I know."

"Obviously you don't know me very well." His voice was barely more than a whisper.

"Look at how much you do for others. The Santa Project is a prime example. And you're a generous boss with an amazing benefits package for your employees—"

"That isn't what I meant. My father…he told me that I should have been the one in the hospital bed, not my brother." Holly gasped. Finn kept talking as though oblivious to her shocked reaction. "He was right. My brother was the golden boy. He was everything my parents could want. Derek and I were quite different."

Tears slipped down her cheeks. It was horrific that his father would spew such mean and hurtful things, but the fact that Finn believed them and still did to this day tore her up inside. How in the world did she make him see what a difference he continued to make in others' lives?

And then a thought occurred to her. She pulled his hand over to her slightly rounded abdomen. "This is the reason you're still here. You have a future. You have two little ones coming into this world that you can lavish with love and let them know how important each of them are to you. You can make sure they know that you don't have a favorite because they are equally important in your heart."

"What...what if I end up like my father and hurt our children?"

"You won't. The fact you're so worried about it proves my point."

His gaze searched hers. "Do you really believe that? You think I can be a good father?"

"I do." Her voice held a note of conviction. "Just follow your heart. It's a good, strong heart. It won't lead you astray."

"No one ever said anything like this to me. I... I just hope I don't let you down."

"You won't. I have faith in you."

His gaze dipped to her lips. She could read his thoughts and she wanted him too. Not waiting for him, she leaned forward, pressing her lips to his.

At first, he didn't move. Was he that surprised by her action? Didn't he know how much she wanted him? Needed him?

As his lips slowly moved beneath hers, she'd never felt so close to anyone in her life. It was though his words had touched her heart. He'd opened up and let her in. That was a beginning.

Her hands wound around his neck. He tasted sweet like the fresh batch of Christmas cookies that she'd left on a plate in the kitchen. She was definitely going to have to make more of those.

As their kiss deepened, her fingers combed through his hair. A moan rose in the back of her throat. She'd never been kissed so thoroughly. Her whole body tingled clear down to her toes.

Right now though, she didn't want anything but his arms around her as they sank down into the nest of blankets and pillows. While the storm raged outside, desire raged inside her.

CHAPTER FIFTEEN

IT COULD BE BETTER.

But it could have been so much worse.

The next morning, Finn returned to the safe room after a preliminary survey of the storm damage. He glanced down at the cocoon of blankets and pillows to find Holly awake and getting to her feet. With her hair slightly mussed up and her lips still rosy from a night of kissing, she'd never looked more beautiful.

She blushed. "What are you looking at?" She ran a hand over her hair. "I must be a mess."

"No. Actually you look amazing."

"You're just saying that because you want something from me."

He hadn't said it for any reason other than he meant it. However, now that she'd planted the idea into his head, perhaps now was as good a time as any to tell her what he had on his mind. He'd stared into the dark long after she'd fallen asleep the night before. He'd thought long and hard about where they went from here.

But now as she smiled up at him, his attention strayed to her soft, plump lips. "You're right, there is something I want." He reached out and pulled her close. "This."

Without giving her a chance to react, he leaned in and pressed his lips to hers. Her kisses were sweet as nectar and he knew he'd never ever tire of them. He pulled her closer, deepening the kiss. He needed to make sure that last night hadn't just been a figment of his imagination.

And now he had his proof. The chemistry between them was most definitely real. It was all the more reason to follow through with his plan—his duty.

When at last he let her go, she smiled up at him. "What was that about?"

"Just making sure you aren't a dream."

"I'm most definitely real and so was that storm last night. So, um, how bad is the damage?" She turned and started to collect the blankets.

"There's a lot of debris on the beach. It'll take a while until this place looks like it once did, but other than a few minor things, the house held its own."

"That's wonderful. How long until we have power?"

"I'm hoping not long. I plan to work on that first." They were getting off topic.

"Before I let you go, I do believe we got distracted last night before I could ask my next question."

"Hmm... I don't recall this." She sent him a teasing smile.

"Convenient memory is more like it."

"Okay. What's your question?"

Now that it was time to put his marriage plan in action, he had doubts—lots of them. What if she wanted more than he could offer? What if she wanted a traditional marriage with promises of love?

"Finn? What is it?"

"Will you marry me?"

Surprise reflected in her eyes. "We already had this conversation. It won't work."

"Just hear me out. It won't be a traditional marriage, but that doesn't mean we can't make it work. After all, we're friends—or I'd like to think we are." She nodded in agreement and he continued. "And we know we're good together in other areas."

Pink tinged her cheeks. "So this would be like a business arrangement?"

"Not exactly. It'll be what we make of it. So what do you say?"

She returned to folding a blanket. "We don't have to be

married to be a family. I still believe we'll all be happier if you have your life and I have my own."

A frown pulled at his lips. This wasn't the way it had played out in his imagination. In his mind, she'd jumped at the offer. If she was waiting for something more—something heartfelt—she'd be waiting a very long time.

There had to be a way to turn this around. The stakes were much too high for him to fold his hand and walk away. He needed to be close to his children—

"Stop." Her voice interrupted the flow of his thoughts.

"Stop what?"

"Wondering how you can get me to say yes. You can't. I told you before that I didn't want to get married. That hasn't changed."

But the part she'd forgotten was that he was a man used to getting his way. When he set his sights on something, nothing stood in his way. He would overcome her hesitation about them becoming a full-fledged family, no matter what it took.

He wanted to be a full-time father to his kids and do all the things his father had been too busy to do with him. He would make time for both of his children. He wouldn't demean one while building up the other. Or at least he would try his darnedest to be a fair and loving parent.

And that was where Holly came into the plan. She would be there to watch over things—to keep the peace and harmony in the family. He knew already that she wouldn't hesitate to call him out on the carpet if he started to mess up where the kids were concerned.

He needed that reassurance—Holly's guidance. There was no way that he was going to let her go. But could he give her his heart?

Everyone he'd ever loved or thought that he'd loved, he'd lost. He couldn't go through that again. He couldn't have Holly walk out on him. It was best that they go into this marriage as friends with benefits as well as parents to their twins. Emotions were overrated.

The storm had made a real mess of things.

And Holly found herself thankful for the distraction. She moved around the living room where one of the floor-to-ceiling window panes had been broken when a shutter had been torn off its hinge. There was a mess of shattered glass everywhere.

So while Finn worked on restoring the power to the house, she worked on making the living room inhabitable again. But as the winds whipped through the room, she knew that as soon as Finn was free, she needed his help to put plywood over the window. But for now she was happy for the solitude.

If she didn't know better, she'd swear she dreamed up that marriage proposal. Finn Lockwood proposed to little old her. She smiled. He had no idea how tempted she was to accept his proposal. She'd always envied her friends getting married...until a few years down the road when some of them were going through a nasty divorce.

No, she couldn't—she wouldn't set herself up to get hurt. And now it wasn't just her but her kids that would be hurt when the marriage fell apart. She was right in turning him down. She just had to stick to her resolve. Everyone would be better off because of it.

So then why didn't she feel good about her decision? Why did she feel as though she'd turned down the best offer in her entire life?

It wasn't like she was madly in love with him. Was she?

Oh, no. It was true.

She loved Finn Lockwood.

When exactly had that happened?

She wasn't quite sure.

Though the knowledge frightened her, she couldn't deny it. What did she do now?

"Holly?"

She jumped. Her other hand, holding some of the broken glass, automatically clenched. Pain sliced through her fingers and she gasped. She released her grip, letting the glass fall back to the hardwood floor.

Finn rushed to her side. "I'm sorry. I didn't mean to startle you." He gently took her hand in his to examine it. "You've cut yourself. Let's get you out of here."

"I... I'll be fine."

"We'll see about that." He led her to the bathroom and stuck her hand under the faucet. "What were you doing in there?"

"Cleaning up. What did you think?"

"You should have waited. I would have done it. Or I would have flown in a cleaning crew. But I never expected you to do it, not in your condition."

"My condition? You make it sound like I've got some sort of disease instead of being pregnant with two beautiful babies."

"That wasn't my intent."

She knew that. She was just being touchy because... because he'd gotten past all of her defenses. He'd gotten her to fall in love with him and she'd never felt more vulnerable.

"What had you so distracted when I walked in?" Finn's gaze met hers as he dabbed a soapy washcloth to her fingers and palm.

"It was nothing." Nothing that she was ready to share. Once she did, he'd reason away her hesitation to get further involved with him.

"It had to be something if it had you so distracted that you didn't even hear me enter the room. Were you reconsidering my proposal?"

He couldn't keep proposing to her. It was dangerous. One of these days he might catch her in a weak moment and she might say yes. It might have a happy beginning but it was the ending that worried her.

She knew how to put an end to it. She caught and held his gaze. Her heart *thump-thumped* as she swallowed hard, working up the courage to get the words out. "Do you love me?"

His mouth opened, but just as quickly he pressed his lips together. He didn't love her. Her heart pinched. In that moment she realized that she'd wanted him to say yes. She wanted him to say that he was absolutely crazy in love with her. Inwardly, she groaned. What was happening to her? She was the skeptic—the person who didn't believe in happily-ever-afters.

"We don't have to love each other to make a good marriage." He reached out to her, gripping her elbows and pulling her to him. "This will work. Trust me."

She wanted to say that she couldn't marry someone who didn't love her, but she didn't trust herself mentioning the L-word. "I do trust you. But we're better off as friends."

He sighed. "What I need is a wife and a mother for my children."

"You know what they say, two out of three isn't bad."

His brows scrunched together as though not following her comment.

She gazed into his eyes, trying to ignore the pain she saw reflected there. "We're friends or at least I'd like to think we are." He nodded in agreement and she continued. "And I'm the mother of your children. That's two things. But I just can't be your wife. I won't agree to something that in the end will hurt everyone. You've already experienced more than enough pain in your life. I won't add to it. Someday you'll find the right woman."

"What if I'm looking at her?"

She glanced away. "Now that the storm's over, I think I should get back to New York."

Finn dabbed antibiotic cream on her nicks and cuts before adding a couple of bandages. Without another word, he started cleaning up the mess in the bathroom. Fine. If he wanted to act this way, so could she.

She walked away, but inside her heart felt as though it'd been broken in two. Why did life have to be so difficult? Her vision blurred with unshed tears, but she blinked them away.

If only she could be like other people and believe in the impossible, then she could jump into his arms—she could be content with the present and not worry about the future.

CHAPTER SIXTEEN

TWO BUSY DAYS had now passed since the tropical storm. Finn had done everything in his power to put the house back to normal. The physical labor had been exactly what he needed to work out his frustrations.

Toward the end of the day, Emilio phoned to say that the storm was between them and he couldn't get a flight out of Florida yet. Finn told him not to worry, he had everything under control and that Emilio should enjoy his new grandchild.

"Do you want some more to eat?" Holly's voice drew him from his thoughts.

Finn glanced down at his empty dinner plate. She'd made spaghetti and meatballs. He'd had some jar sauce and frozen meatballs on hand. He didn't always want someone to cook for him—sometimes he liked the solitude. So he made sure to keep simple things on hand that he could make for himself.

"Thanks. It was good but I'm full."

"There's a lot of leftovers. I guess I'm not so good with portions. I'll put them in the fridge in case you get hungry later. I know how hard you worked today. I'm sorry I wasn't any help."

"You have those babies to care for now. Besides, you cooked. That was a huge help."

She sent him a look that said she didn't believe him, but she wasn't going to argue. "I'll just clean this up."

He got to his feet. "Let me help."

She shook her head. "You rest. I've got this."

"But I want to help. And I'd like to make a pot of coffee. Do you want some?"

"I can't have any now that I'm pregnant."

"That's right. I forgot. But don't worry. I plan to do lots of reading. I'll catch on to all of this pregnancy stuff. Well, come on. The kitchen isn't going to clean itself."

When he entered the kitchen, he smiled. For a woman who was utterly organized in the office, he never expected her skills in the kitchen to be so, um, chaotic.

Normally such a mess would have put him on edge, but this one had the opposite effect on him. He found himself relaxing a bit knowing she was human with flaws and all. Maybe she wouldn't expect him to be the perfect dad. Maybe she would be understanding about his shortcomings.

Holly insisted on cleaning off the dishes while he placed them in the dishwasher. In the background, the coffeemaker hissed and sputtered. They worked in silence. Together they had everything cleaned up in no time.

"There. That's it." Holly closed the fridge with the leftovers safely inside.

After filling a coffee mug, he turned to Holly. "Come with me. I think we need to talk some more."

She crossed her arms. "If this is about your marriage proposal, there's nothing left to say except when can I catch a flight back to New York?"

He'd already anticipated this and had a solution. "Talk with me while I drink my coffee and then I'll go check on the helipad."

"Do you think it's damaged?"

Luckily the helicopter had been on the big island for routine maintenance when the storm struck. It was unharmed. However, with so many other things that had snagged his immediate concern, he hadn't checked on the helipad. Anything could have happened during that storm, but his gut was telling him that if the house was in pretty good condition then the helipad wouldn't be so bad off.

"Don't worry. The storm wasn't nearly as bad as it could have been."

The worry lines marring Holly's face eased a bit. With a cup of coffee in one hand and a glass of water in the other for her, he followed Holly to his office. Luckily the windows had held in here.

"Why don't we sit on the couch?"

While she took a seat, he dimmed the lights and turned on some sexy jazz music. Cozy and relaxing. He liked it this way. And then he sat down next to Holly.

Her gaze narrowed in on him. "What are you up to?"

He held up his palms. "Nothing. I swear. This is how I like to unwind in the evenings."

The look in her eyes said that she didn't believe him.

"Listen, I'll sit on this end of the couch and you can stay at the other end. Will that work?"

She nodded. "I don't know why you'd have to unwind on a beautiful island like this—well, it's normally beautiful. Will you be able to get it back to normal?"

She was avoiding talking about them and their future. It was as though she was hoping he'd forget what he wanted to talk to her about. That was never going to happen.

Still needing time to figure out exactly how to handle this very sensitive situation, he'd come up with a way to give them both some time. "I have a proposition for you—"

"If this is about getting married—"

"Just hear me out." When she remained silent, he turned on the couch so that he could look at her. "Can I be honest with you?"

"Of course. I'd hope you wouldn't even have to ask the question. I'd like to think that you're always honest—but I know that isn't true for most people." Her voice trailed off as she glanced down at her clenched hands.

She'd been betrayed? Anger pumped through his veins. Was it some guy that she'd loved? How could anyone lie to her and hurt her so deeply? The thought was inconceivable until he realized how he'd unintentionally hurt those that were closest to him. And he realized that if he wasn't careful and kept her at a safe distance that he would most likely hurt her, too. The fire and rage went out of him.

Still, he had to know what had cost Holly her ability to trust in others. "What happened?"

Her gaze lifted to meet his. "What makes you think something happened?"

"I think it's obvious. I shared my past with you. It's your turn. What's your story?"

She sighed. "It's boring and will probably sound silly to you because it's nothing as horrific as what you went through with your brother."

"I'll be the judge of that. But if it hurt you, I highly doubt that it's silly. Far from it."

Her eyes widened. "You're really interested, aren't you?"

"Of course I am. Everything about you interests me."

Her cheeks grew rosy as she glanced away. "My early childhood was happy and for all I knew, normal. My father worked—a lot. But my mother was there. We did all sorts of things together from baking to shopping to going to the park. I didn't have any complaints. Well, I did want a little brother or sister, but my mother always had an excuse of why it was best with just the three of us. I never did figure out if she truly wanted another baby and couldn't get pregnant or if she knew in her gut that her marriage was in trouble and didn't want to put another child in the middle of it."

"Or maybe she was just very happy with the child she already had." He hoped that was the right thing to say. He wasn't experienced with comforting words.

"Anyway when I was ten, my father stopped coming home. At first, my mother brushed off my questions, telling me that he was on an extended business trip. But at night, when she thought I was sleeping, I could hear her crying in

her room. I knew something was seriously wrong. I started
to wonder if my father had died. So I asked her and that's
when she broke down and told me that he left us to start a
new family. Then he appeared one day and, with barely a
word, he packed his things and left."

"I'm so sorry." Finn moved closer to Holly. Not knowing what words to say at this point, he reached out, taking
her hand into his own.

"My mother, she didn't cope well with my father being
gone. She slipped into depression to the point where I got
myself up and dressed in the morning for school. I cooked
and cleaned up what I could. I even read to my mother, like
she used to do with me when I was little. I needed her to get
better, because I needed her since I didn't have anyone else."

"That must have been so hard for you. Your father...was
he around at all?"

Holly shook her head. "I didn't know it then, but later I
learned my stepmother was already pregnant with Suzie. My
father had moved on without even waiting for the divorce. He
had a new family and he'd forgotten about us...about me."

Finn's body tensed. He knew what it was like to be forgotten by a parent. But at least his parents had a really good
excuse, at first it was because his brother was sick and then
they'd been lost in their own grief. But Holly's father, he
didn't have that excuse. Finn disliked the man intensely and
he hadn't even met him.

"When the divorce was finalized, my father got visitation. Every other weekend, I went to stay with him and his
new family. Every time my parents came face-to-face it was
like a world war had erupted. My mother would grouch to
me about my father and in turn, my father would bad-mouth
my mother. It was awful." She visibly shuddered. "No child
should ever be a pawn between their parents."

"I agree." Finn hoped that was the right thing to say. Just
for good measure, he squeezed Holly's hand, hoping she'd

know that he really did care even if he didn't have all of the right words.

"I don't want any of that for our children. I don't want them to be pawns between us."

"They won't. I swear it. No matter what happens between us, we'll put the kids first. We both learned that lesson first-hand. But will you do something for me?"

"What's that?"

His heart pounded in his chest. He didn't know what he'd do if she turned him down. "Would you give us a chance?"

Her fine brows gathered. "What sort of chance?"

That was the catch. He wasn't quite sure what he was asking of her—or of himself. Returning to New York with the holiday season in full swing twisted his insides into a knot. The reminders of what he'd lost would be everywhere. But it was where Holly and the babies would be.

He stared deep into her eyes. His heart pounded. And yet within her gaze, he found the strength he needed to make this offer—a chance to build the family his children deserved.

He swallowed hard. "I'd like to see where this thing between us leads. Give me until the New Year—you know, with us working closely together. That will give Clara time for an extended honeymoon and to settle into married life. And we'll have time to let down our guards and really get to know each other."

"I thought that's what we've been doing."

"But as fast as you let down one wall, I feel like you're building another one."

She worried her bottom lip. "Perhaps you're right. It's been a very long time since I've been able to count on someone. It might take me a bit of time to get it right." She eyed him up. "But I have something I need you to do in return."

"Name it."

"Be honest with me. Even if you don't think that I'll like it, just tell me. I couldn't stand to be blindsided like my mother. And there was a guy I got serious with while I was getting my degree. Long story short, he lied to me about his gambling addiction and then he stole from me to cover his debts."

"Wow. You haven't had it easy."

She shrugged. "Let's just say I have my reasons to be cautious."

"I promise I won't lie to you." She meant too much to him to hurt her. "Now, I need to go check on the helipad."

"What about the recommendation?" When he sent her a puzzled look, she added, "You know, for that other job?"

"You still want to leave? Even though we agreed to see where this leads us?"

"What if it leads nowhere? It'll be best if you don't have to see me every day."

His back teeth ground together. Just the thought of her no longer being in his life tied his insides up in a knot. For so long, he'd sentenced himself to a solitary life. And now he couldn't imagine his life without Holly in it.

"Let's not worry about the future. We can take this one day at a time." It was about all he could manage at this point.

"It's a deal." And then she did something he hadn't expected. She held her hand out to him to shake on it.

It was as though she was making this arrangement something much more distant and methodical than what he had in mind. He slipped his hand into hers. As her fingertips grazed over his palm, the most delicious sensations pulsed up his arm, reminding him that they'd passed the business associates part of their relationship a long time ago.

He needed to give Holly something else to think about. Without giving himself the time to think of all the reasons that his next actions were a bad idea, he tightened his fingers around her hand and pulled her to him.

Her eyes widened as he lowered his head and caught her

lips with his own—her sweet, sweet lips. He didn't care how many times he kissed her, it wouldn't be enough.

And then not wanting to give her a reason to hide behind another defensive wall, he pulled away. Her eyes had darkened. Was that confusion? No. What he was seeing reflected in her eyes was desire. A smile tugged at his lips. His work was done here.

He got to his feet. "I'll go check on the helipad."

With a flashlight in hand, he made his way along the path to the helipad. He had no idea what to expect when he got there. If it was clear, there was no reason Holly couldn't leave in the morning. The thought gutted him.

He'd just reached the head of the path when the rays of his flashlight skimmed over the helipad. As though fate was on his side, there were a couple of downed trees, making the landing zone inaccessible. But luckily it didn't appear they'd done any permanent damage—at least nothing to make the helipad inoperable.

It was much too dark now, but in the morning he'd have to get the chain saw out here. He imagined it'd be at least a couple of days to get this stuff cleared. It was time that he could use to sort things out with Holly.

CHAPTER SEVENTEEN

A PAIN TORE through Holly's side.

The plates holding cold-cut sandwiches clattered onto the table. Holly pressed a hand to her waistline, willing the throbbing to subside. She rubbed the area, surprised by how much she was actually showing. But with twins on board, she figured that was to be expected. Thankfully when they'd visited the big island, she'd picked up some new, roomy clothes. They were all she wore now.

The discomfort ebbed away. Everything would be okay. It had to be. She was in the house alone. Finn had gone to the helipad first thing that morning to clear the debris. He didn't say exactly how bad it was, but she had a feeling he had a lot of work ahead of him if it was anything like the beach area.

She'd offered to help, but he'd stubbornly refused. So she set about cleaning the patio and washing it down so that it was usable again. All in all, they'd fared really well.

In a minute or so the discomfort passed. Realizing she might have overreacted, she shrugged it off and moved to the deck. She loved that Finn had installed a large bell. It could be rung in the case of an emergency or to call people for lunch, as she was about to do.

She wrapped her fingers around the weathered rope and pulled. The bell rang out.

Clang-clang. Clang-clang.

"Lunch!" She didn't know if he'd hear her, but hopefully he'd heard the bell.

She turned back to go inside the house to finish setting the table for lunch. She smiled, wondering if this was what it felt like to be a part of a couple. She knew they weren't a real couple, but they were working together. And she was happy—truly happy for the first time in a long while. She glanced around the island. Wouldn't it be nice to stay here until the babies were born?

A dreamy sigh escaped her lips. If only that could happen, but the realistic part of her knew it wasn't a possibility. Soon enough this fantasy would be over and she'd be back in New York, settling into a new job and trying to figure out how to juggle a job and newborns.

One day at a time. I have months until these little ones make their grand entrance.

At last, having the table set, she heard footsteps outside. Finn had heard her. Her heart beat a little faster, knowing she'd get to spend some time with him. Sure it was lunch, but he'd been gone all morning. She'd started to miss him.

Quit being ridiculous. You're acting like a teenager with a huge crush.

No. It's even worse. I'm a grown woman who is falling more in love with my babies' daddy with each passing day.

"I heard the bell. Is it time to eat?" He hustled through the doorway in his stocking feet. "I'm starved."

She glanced up to find Finn standing there in nothing but his jeans and socks. She had no idea what had happened to his shirt, but she heartily approved of his attire. Her gaze zeroed in on the tanned muscles of his shoulders and then slid down to his well-defined pecs and six-pack abs. Wow! She swallowed hard. Who knew hard work could look so good on a man?

His eyes twinkled when he smiled. "Is something wrong?"

Wrong? Absolutely nothing. Nothing at all.

"Um…no. I… I made up some sandwiches." Her face felt as though it was on fire. "The food, it's on the table. If you want to clean up a bit, we can eat." Realizing that she hadn't put out any refreshments, she asked, "What would you like to drink?"

"Water is good. Ice cold."

It did sound particularly good at the moment. "You got it."

She rushed around, getting a couple of big glasses and filling them with ice. Right about now she just wanted to climb in the freezer to cool off. It wasn't like he was the first guy she'd seen with his shirt off. Why in the world was she overreacting?

Get a grip, Holly.

She placed the glasses on the table and then decided something was missing. But what? She glanced around the kitchen, looking for something to dress up the table and then she spotted the colorful blooms she'd picked that morning. They were in a small vase on the counter. Their orange, yellow and pink petals would add a nice splash to the white tablecloth.

A pain shot through her left side again. Immediately her hand pressed to her side as she gripped the back of a chair with her other hand.

"What's the matter?" Finn's concerned voice filled the room, followed by his rapid footsteps.

She didn't want to worry him. "It's nothing."

"It's something. Tell me."

"It's the second time I've had a pain in my side."

"Pain?" His arm wrapped around her as he helped her sit down. "Is it the babies?"

"I... I don't know." She looked up at him, hoping to see reassurance in his eyes. Instead his worry reflected back at her. "It's gone now."

"You're sure?"

She nodded. "Let's eat."

"I think you need to see a doctor. The sooner, the better." He pulled out his cell phone. "In fact, I'm going to call the doctor now."

"What? But you can't. Honest, it's gone."

"I'll feel better once I hear it from someone who has experience in these matters."

A short time later, after Finn had gotten through to the doctor who'd examined her on the big island, Finn had relinquished the phone to Holly. She'd answered the doctor's questions and then breathed a sigh of relief.

When she returned the phone to Finn, his brow was knit into a worried line. She was touched that he cared so much. It just made her care about him all the more.

"Well, what did he say?"

"That without any other symptoms it sounds like growing pains. But it was hard for him to diagnose me over the phone. The only reason he did was because I told him we were stranded on the island due to the storm."

The stiff line of Finn's shoulders eased. "He doesn't think it's anything urgent?"

She shrugged. "He said I needed to make an appointment and see my OB/GYN as soon as possible just to be sure."

"Then that's what we'll do. We'll be out of here by this evening."

"What? But we can't. What about the trees and stuff at the helipad?"

"I just got the motivation I need to clear it. So you call your doctor and see if they can squeeze you in for tomorrow, and I'll call my pilot and have him fuel up the jet. We'll leave tonight."

"But you don't have to go. I know you don't want to be in New York for the holidays."

"That was before."

"Before what?"

"You know."

Her gaze narrowed in on him. "No, I don't know. Tell me."

"Before you and me...before the babies. We agreed we

were going to give this thing a go and this is me doing my part. You haven't changed your mind, have you?"

He cared enough to spend the holidays with her in the city. Her heart leaped for joy. Okay, so she shouldn't get too excited. She knew in the long run the odds were against them, but Christmas was the season of hope.

Things were looking up.

Finn stared out the back of the limo as they inched their way through the snarled Manhattan traffic. He could at last breathe a lot easier now. The babies and their mother were healthy. It was indeed growing pains. The doctor told them to expect more along the way.

Signs of Christmas were everywhere from the decorated storefronts to the large ornaments hung from the lampposts. As he stared out the window, he saw Santa ringing a bell next to his red kettle. It made Finn wish that he was back on the island. And then, without a word, Holly slipped her hand in his. Then again, this wasn't so bad.

She leaned over and softly said, "Relax. You might even find you like the holiday."

"Maybe you're right." He had his doubts, but he didn't want to give her any reason to back out of their arrangement. He only had until the first of the year to convince her that they were better off together than apart.

"We turned the wrong way. This is the opposite direction of my apartment." Obvious concern laced Holly's words. "Hey!" She waved, trying to gain the driver's attention. "We need to turn around."

"No, we don't," Finn said calmly. "It's okay, Ron. I've got this."

"You've got what?" She frowned at him.

"I've instructed Ron to drive us back to my penthouse—"

"What? No. I need to go home."

"Not yet. You heard the doctor. You have a high-risk pregnancy and your blood pressure is elevated—"

"Only slightly."

"She said not to overdo it. And from what you've told me, your apartment is a fifth-floor walk-up with no elevator."

"It… It's not that much. I'm used to it."

He wasn't going to change his mind about this arrangement. It was what was best for her and the babies. "And then there's the fact that your mother is out of town. There's no one around if you have any complications."

"I won't have any." Her hand moved to rest protectively over her slightly rounded midsection. "Nothing is going to happen."

"I sincerely hope you're right, but is it worth the risk? If you're wrong—"

"I won't be. But…your idea might not be so bad. As long as you understand that it's only temporary. Until my next appointment."

Which was at the beginning of the new year—not far off. "We'll see what the doctor says then. Now will you relax?"

"As long as you understand that this arrangement doesn't change anything between us—I'm still not accepting your proposal."

He wanted to tell her that she was wrong, but he couldn't. Maybe he was asking too much of her—of himself. He couldn't promise her forever.

An ache started deep in his chest.

What if he made her unhappy?

Maybe he was being selfish instead of doing what was best for Holly.

CHAPTER EIGHTEEN

IT DIDN'T FEEL like Christmas.

Holly strolled into the living room of Finn's penthouse. There was absolutely nothing that resembled Christmas anywhere. She knew he avoided the holiday because of the bad memories it held for him, but she wondered if it would be possible to create some new holiday memories.

She'd been here for two days and, so far, Finn had bent over backward to make her at home. He'd set her up in his study to monitor the final stages of Project Santa. And so far they'd only encountered minor glitches. It was nothing that couldn't be overcome with a bit of ingenuity.

That morning when she'd offered to go into the office, Finn had waved her off, telling her to stay here. Meanwhile, he'd gone to the office to pick up some papers. He'd said he'd be back in a couple of hours, but that was before lunch. And now it was after quitting time and he still wasn't back.

Perhaps this was the best opportunity for her to take care of something that had been weighing on her mind. She retraced her steps to the study where she'd left her phone. She had Finn's number on it because he refused to leave until he had entered it in her phone with orders for her to call if she needed anything at all.

Certain in her plan, she selected his number and listened to the phone ring. Once. That's all it rang before Finn answered. "Holly, what's the matter?"

"Does something have to be the matter?"

"No. I just… Oh, never mind, what did you need?"

"I wanted you to know that I'm going out. There's something I need to take care of."

"I'm almost home. Can I pick something up for you?"

"It's more like I have to drop off something."

"Tonight?" His voice sounded off.

"Yes, tonight."

"I just heard the weather report and they're calling for snow. A lot of it."

Holly glanced toward the window. "It's not snowing yet. I won't be gone long. I'll most likely be home before it starts."

"Holly, put it off—"

"No. I need to do this." She'd been thinking about it all day. Once the visit with her family was over, she could relax. It'd definitely help lower her blood pressure.

Finn expelled a heavy sigh. "If you aren't going to change your mind, at least let me drive you."

He had no idea what this trip entailed. To say her family dynamics were complicated was an understatement. It was best Finn stay home. "Thanks. But I'm sure you have other things to do—"

"Nothing as important as you."

The breath caught in her throat. Had he really just said that? Was she truly important to him? And then she realized he probably meant because she was carrying his babies. Because she'd asked him straight up if he loved her and he hadn't been able to say the words.

"Holly? Are you still there?"

"Um, yes."

"Good. I'm just pulling into the garage now. I'll be up in a minute. Just be ready to go."

She disconnected the call and moved to her spacious bedroom to retrieve the Christmas packages and her coat. Her stomach churned. Once this was done, she could relax. In and out quickly.

She'd just carried the packages to the foyer when Finn let himself in the door. She glanced up at him. "You know I can take a cab."

"I told you if you're going out tonight, I'm going with you."

"You don't even know where I'm going."

"Good point. What's our destination?"

"My father's house. I want to give my sisters the Christmas presents I bought while we were in the Caribbean."

He scooped up the packages before opening the door for her. "So we've progressed to the point where I get to meet the family." Finn sent her a teasing smile. "I don't know. Do you think I'll pass the father inspection?"

She stopped at the elevator and pressed the button before turning back to him. "I don't think you have a thing to worry about."

His smile broadened. "That's nice to know."

"Don't get any ideas. In fact, you can wait in the car. I won't be long."

"Are you sure you want to take the presents now? I mean Christmas isn't until the weekend after next."

"I don't spend Christmas with them. I usually spend it with my mother. But after talking with my mother and aunt, I decided to give them something extra special for Christmas—a cruise." It would definitely put a dent in her savings, but it was worth it. This was her mother's dream vacation.

"That was very generous of you."

Holly's voice lowered. "They deserve it."

"And what about you?" When she sent him a puzzled look, he added, "You deserve a special Christmas, too. What would you like Santa to bring you?"

"I... I don't know. I hadn't thought about it."

The elevator door slid open. Finn waited until Holly stepped inside before he followed. "You know without your mother around, perhaps you could spend the time with your father."

She shook her head. "I don't think that would be a good idea."

Finn had no idea about her family. Thankfully she'd thought to tell him to stay in the car. She didn't want to make an awkward situation even more so.

Something was amiss, but what?

Was she really that uncomfortable with him meeting her family? Or was it something else? Finn glanced over at Holly just before he pulled out from a stop sign. The wipers swished back and forth, knocking off the gently falling snow.

The sky was dark now and all Finn wanted to do was turn around. He wasn't worried about himself. He never let the weather stop him from being wherever he was needed. But it was different now that he had Holly next to him and those precious babies. He worried about the roads becoming slick.

"We're almost there." Holly's voice drew him from his thoughts.

It was the first thing she'd said in blocks. In fact, she hadn't volunteered any details about her family. Why was that?

As he proceeded through the next intersection, Holly pointed to a modest two-story white house with a well-kept yard that was now coated with snow. "There it is."

He pulled over to the curb and turned off his wipers. "You've been awfully quiet. Is everything all right?"

"Sure. Why wouldn't it be?"

"You haven't said a word the whole way here unless it was to give me directions."

"Oh. Sorry. I must be tired."

"Sounds like a good reason to head back to the penthouse and deal with this another day."

"No." She released the seat belt. "We're here now. And I want to get this over with."

"Okay. It's up to you."

When he released his seat belt and opened the door, she asked, "What are you doing?"

"Getting the packages from the trunk."

She really didn't want him to meet her family. Why was she so worried? He didn't think he made that bad of a first impression. In fact, when he tried he could be pretty charming. And if they were going to be a family, which they were because of the babies, he needed to meet her father. He was certain he could make a good impression and alleviate Holly's worries.

With the packages in hand, he closed the trunk and started up the walk. Every step was muffled by the thin layer of snow.

"Where do you think you're going?" Holly remained next to the car.

He turned back and noticed the way the big flakes coated the top of her head like a halo. "I presume we're taking the presents to the door and not leaving them in the front yard."

"There's no *we* about it."

"Listen, Holly, you've got to trust me. This will all work out."

"You're right. It will. You're going to wait in the car." Her tone brooked no room for a rebuttal.

Just then there was a noise behind him. "Who's there?" called out a male voice. "Holly, is that you?"

She glared at Finn before her face morphed into a smile. "Yes, Dad. It's me."

"Well, are you coming in?"

Obediently she started up the walk. When she got to Finn's side, she leaned closer and whispered, "Just let me do the talking."

Boy, she was really worried about having him around her family. "Trust me."

He wasn't sure if she'd heard his softly spoken words as

she continued up the walk. He followed behind her, wondering what to expect.

They stopped on the stoop. Her father was still blocking the doorway. The man's hair was dark with silver in the temples. He wore dark jeans and a sweatshirt with the Jets logo across the front. Finn made a mental note of it. If all else failed, maybe he could engage the man in football talk—even though he was more of a hockey fan.

"Who's at the door?" a female voice called out.

"It's Holly and some guy."

"Well, invite them in." And then a slender woman with long, bleached-blond hair appeared next to Holly's father. The woman elbowed her husband aside. "Don't mind him. Come in out of the cold."

Once they were all standing just inside the door, Finn could feel the stress coming off Holly in waves. What was up with that? Was she embarrassed of him? That would be a first. Most women liked to show him off to their friends. As for meeting a date's family, he avoided that at all costs. But Holly was different.

"Here, let me take your coats." Holly's stepmother didn't smile as she held out her hand. She kept giving Finn a look as though she should know him but couldn't quite place his face.

"That's okay." Holly didn't make any move to get comfortable. "We can't stay. I... I brought some gifts for the girls."

"Suzie! Kristi! Holly's here with gifts."

"I hope they like them. I saw them while I was out of town and thought of them."

"I'm sure they will." But there was no conviction in the woman's voice. "You can afford to go on vacation?"

Holly's face paled. "It was a business trip."

"Oh."

Her father retreated into the living room, which was off

to the right of the doorway. A staircase stood in front of them with a hallway trailing along the left side of it. And to the far left was a formal dining room. The house wasn't big, but it held a look of perfection—as though everything was in its place. There was nothing warm and welcoming about the house.

Finn wanted to say something to break up the awkward silence, but he wasn't sure what to say. Was it always this strained? If so, he understood why Holly wouldn't want to spend much time here.

"Who's your friend?" Her stepmother's gaze settled fully on him.

"Oh. This is Finn. He's my—"

"Boyfriend. It's nice to meet you." He held out his hand to the woman.

"I'm Helen." She flashed him a big, toothy smile as she accepted his handshake. "I feel like I should know you. Have we met before?"

"No."

"Are you sure?" She still held on to his hand.

He gently extracted his hand while returning her smile. "I'm certain of it. I wouldn't have forgotten meeting someone as lovely as you."

Her painted cheeks puffed up. "Well, I'm glad we've had a chance to meet. Isn't that right, Fred?" And then at last noticing that her husband had settled in the living room with a newspaper, she raised her voice. "Fred, you're ignoring our guests."

The man glanced over the top of his reading glasses. "You seem to be doing fine on your own."

"Don't I always?" the woman muttered under her breath. "Lately that man is hardly home. All he does is work." She moved to the bottom of the steps and craned her chin upward. "Suzie! Kristi! Get down here now!"

Doors slammed almost simultaneously. There was a rush

of footsteps as they crossed the landing and then stomped down the stairs.

"What do you want? I'm busy doing my nails." A teenage girl with hair similar to her mother's frowned.

"And I'm on the phone." The other teenager had dark hair with pink highlights.

"I know you're both busy, but I thought you'd want to know that your sister is here."

Both girls glanced toward the door. But they were staring—at him.

Both girls' eyes grew round. "Hey, you're Finn Lockwood." They continued down the steps and approached him. "What are you doing here?"

His stomach churned as they both batted their eyes at him and flashed him smiles.

"He's your sister's boyfriend."

Surprise lit up both sets of eyes. "You're dating her?"

He nodded. "I am. Your sister is amazing."

"I brought you some gifts." Holly stepped next to Finn. "I found them when I was in the Caribbean and I thought you would like them."

Each girl accepted a brightly wrapped package.

"What do you say?" prompted their mother.

"Thank you," they muttered to Holly.

"I'm Suzie," said the blonde.

"And I'm Kristi."

Helen stepped between her daughters. "Why don't you come in the living room and we can talk?"

"We really can't stay." Holly glanced at him with uncertainty in her eyes.

He smiled at her. "Holly's right. We have other obligations tonight, but she was anxious for me to meet you all."

"How did she bag you?" Suzie's brows drew together. "You're a billionaire and she's nothing."

Ouch! Finn's gaze went to the stepmother, but Helen

glanced away as though she hadn't heard a word. That was impossible because Suzie's voice was loud and quite clear.

His gaze settled back on Suzie. "Holly is amazing. She is quite talented. And she spearheaded the Project Santa initiative."

"The what?"

"It's nothing," Holly intervened. "We really should go."

Finn took Holly's hand in his. "We have a couple of minutes and they haven't opened their gifts yet."

Both girls glanced down as though they'd forgotten about the Christmas presents. They each pulled off the ribbons first and then tore through the wrapping paper. They lifted the lids and rooted through the bikinis and cover up as well as sunglasses and a small purse.

Kristi glanced up. "Does this mean you got us tickets to the Caribbean? My friends are going to be so jealous. I'll have to go to the tanning salon first. Otherwise I'll look like a snowman in a bikini."

Suzie's face lit up. "This will be great. I can't wait to get out of school."

"Oh, girls, we'll have to make sure you have everything you need. I'll need to go to the tanning salon, too."

"You?" The girls both turned to their mother.

"This is our gift, not yours," Suzie said bluntly. "You aren't invited."

"But—"

"Um, there is no trip," Holly said.

"No trip?" All heads turned to Holly. "You mean all you got us was some bikinis that we can't even use because if you hadn't noticed, it's snowing outside—"

"Suzie, that's enough. I'm sure your sister has something else in mind." Her stepmother sent her an expectant look.

Wow! This family was unbelievable. If Finn had his choice between having no family and this family, he'd be much happier on his own. He glanced around to find out why Holly's father hadn't interceded on his daughter's be-half, but the man couldn't be bothered to stop reading his paper long enough.

Finn inwardly seethed. As much as he'd like to let loose on these people and tell them exactly what he thought of them and their lack of manners, he had to think of Holly. For whatever reason, they meant enough to her to buy them gifts and come here to put up with their rudeness. Therefore, he had to respect her feelings because it certainly appeared that no one else would.

"There is one other thing." Finn looked at Holly, willing her to trust him with his eyes as he gave her hand a couple of quick squeezes. "Do you want me to tell them?"

"Um…uh, sure."

"You know how Holly is, never wanting to brag. But she used her connections and secured tickets to the Mistletoe Ball for the whole family."

For once, all three females were left speechless. Good. That was what he wanted.

"You did that? But how?" Her stepmother's eyes reflected her utter surprise. "Those tickets cost a fortune and I heard they sold out back in October."

Holly's face drained of color. "Well, the truth is—"

"She has an inside source that she promised not to re-veal to anyone," Finn said. "They'll be waiting for the four of you at the door of the museum."

The girls squealed with delight as Helen yelled in to her husband to tell him about the tickets to the ball. If a man could look utterly unimpressed, it was Holly's father. And through it all, Finn noticed that not one person thanked Holly. It was though they felt entitled to the tickets. A groan of frustration grew down deep in his throat. A glance at Holly's pale face had him swallowing down his outrage and disgust.

He made a point of checking his Rolex. "And now, we really must be going."

As they let themselves out the front door, the girls were talking over top of each other about dresses, shoes, haircuts and manicures. And he had never been so happy to leave anywhere in his entire life. Once outside, Finn felt as though he could breathe. He was no longer being smothered with fake pleasantries and outright nastiness.

CHAPTER NINETEEN

BIG FLUFFY SNOWFLAKES fell around them, adding a gentle softness to the world and smoothing out the rough edges. Finn continued to hold Holly's hand, enjoying the connection. When they reached the car, he used his free hand to open the door.

She paused.

"Holly?"

When she looked up at him, tears shimmered in her eyes. The words lodged in his throat. There was nothing in this world that he could say to lessen the pain for her.

Instead of speaking, he leaned forward and pressed his lips to hers. With the car door ajar between them, he couldn't pull her close like he wanted. Instead he had to be content with this simple but heartfelt gesture.

With great regret he pulled back. "You better get in. The snow is picking up."

She nodded and then did as he said.

Once they were on the now snow-covered road, Finn guided the car slowly along the streets. He should have been more insistent about putting off this visit, not that Holly would have listened to him. When she set her mind on something, there was no stopping her. Although after meeting her family, he could understand why she'd want to get that visit out of the way.

As the snow fell, covering up the markings on the street, his body tensed. This must have been how it'd been the night his parents died. The thought sent a chill through his body.

"Are you cold?" Holly asked.

"What?"

"I just saw you shiver. I'll turn up the fan. Hopefully the heat will kick in soon." After she adjusted the temperature controls, she leaned back in her seat. "What were you thinking by offering up those tickets to the ball? I don't have any connections."

"But I do. So don't worry." He didn't want to carry on a conversation now.

"You...you shouldn't have done it. It's too much."

"Sure, I should have." Not taking his eyes off the road, he reached out to her. His hand landed on her thigh and he squeezed. "I wanted to do it for you. I know how much your family means to you."

"They shouldn't, though. I know they don't treat me...like family. I just wish—oh, I don't know what I wish."

"It's done now so stop worrying." He returned his hand to the steering wheel.

"That's easy for you to say. You're not related to them."

"But they are related to you and the babies. Therefore, they are now part of my life." He could feel her eyeing him up. Had that been too strong? He didn't think so. Even if he never won over her heart, they would all still be one mixed-up sort of family.

"You do know what this means, don't you?"

His fingers tightened on the steering wheel, not liking the sound of her voice. "What?"

"That you and I must go to the ball now. And it's a well-known fact that you make a point of never attending the ball."

"For you, I'll make an exception." The snow came down heavier, making his every muscle tense. "Don't worry. It'll all work out."

"I'll pay you back."

Just then the tires started to slide. His heart lurched. *No! No! No!*

Holly reached out, placing a hand on his thigh. Her fingers tightened, but she didn't say a word.

When the tires caught on the asphalt, Finn expelled a pent-up breath. This was his fault. He promised to take care of his family and protect them like he hadn't been able to do with his parents and brother. And already he was failing.

Finn swallowed hard. "If you want to pay me back, the next time I tell you that we should stay in because of the weather, just listen to me."

She didn't say anything for a moment. And then ever so softly, she said, "I'm sorry. I didn't think it'd get this bad."

His fingers tightened on the steering wheel as he lowered his speed even more, wishing that they were closer to his building.

Just a little farther. Everything will be all right. It has to be.

His gut twisted into a knot. It was going to take him a long time to unwind after this. The snow kept falling, making visibility minimal at best. The wipers cleared the windshield in time for more snow to cover it.

His thoughts turned back to Holly. The truth was that no matter how much he'd fought it in the beginning, he'd fallen for Holly, hook, line and sinker. He couldn't bear to lose her or the babies. From now on, when they went out, he'd plan ahead. He'd be cautious. He'd do anything it took to keep them safe.

From here on out, they were a team. He had Holly's back. And he already knew that she had his—the success of Project Santa was evidence of it. Now he just had to concentrate on the roadway and make sure they didn't end up skidding into a ditch or worse.

What an utter disaster.

Back at the penthouse, Holly didn't know what to say to Finn. He'd been so quiet in the car. He must be upset that she let him walk into such a strained situation and then for him to feel obligated to come up with those tickets to the ball. They cost a small fortune. She didn't know how she'd ever repay him.

Now she was having second thoughts about telling Finn that they had to go to the ball. She didn't know how she'd explain it to her family, but she'd come up with a reason for their absence. Besides, it wasn't like she even had a dress, and the ball was just days away.

When she stepped into the living room, she found Finn had on the Rangers and Penguins hockey game. That was good. After the cleanup on the island, the work at the office and then meeting her family, he deserved some downtime.

She sat down on the couch near him. "I hope you don't mind that I ordered pizza for dinner."

"That's fine." His voice was soft as though he was lost in thought.

"Tomorrow I'll work on getting some food in the fridge."

He didn't say anything.

She glanced up at the large-screen television. She had to be honest, she didn't know anything about hockey or for that matter any other sport, but she might need to if these babies were anything like their father.

"Who's winning?"

He didn't say anything.

What was wrong with him? Was he mad at her? She hoped not. Maybe he was just absorbed by the game. "Who's winning?"

"What?"

"The score. What is it?"

"I don't know."

He didn't know? Wasn't he watching the game? But as she glanced at him, she noticed he was staring out the window at the snowy night. Okay, something was wrong and she couldn't just let it fester. If he had changed his mind about her staying here, she wanted to know up front. She realized she came with a lot of baggage and if he wanted out, she couldn't blame him.

She placed a hand on his arm. "Finn, talk to me."

He glanced at her. "What do you want to talk about?"

"Whatever's bothering you?"

"Nothing's bothering me." He glanced away.

"You might have been able to tell me that a while back, but now that I know you, I don't believe you. Something has been bothering you since we left my father's. It's my family, isn't it?"

"What? No. Of course not."

"Listen, I know those tickets are going to cost a fortune. I will pay you back."

"No, you won't. They are my gift. And so is your dress and whatever else you need for the ball."

"But I couldn't accept all of that. It… It's too much."

"The ball was my idea, not yours, so no arguments. Tomorrow we'll go to this boutique I know of that should have something for you to wear. If not, we'll keep looking."

"I don't know what to say."

"Good. Don't say anything. I just want you to enjoy yourself."

"But how am I supposed to after tonight? I'm really sorry about my family. It's complicated with them. I was less than cordial to my stepmother when she married my father. I blamed her for breaking up my parents' marriage since he had an ongoing affair with her for a couple of years before he left my mother."

Finn's gaze met hers. "And your mother didn't know?"

Holly shrugged. "She says she didn't, but I don't know how she couldn't know. He was gone all the time. But maybe it was a case of *she didn't want to know so she didn't look.*"

"Sometimes we protect ourselves by only seeing as much as we can handle."

"Maybe you're right. But I think my mother's happy now. I just want to keep her that way, because she did her best to be there for me and now it's my turn to be there for her."

"And you will be. I see how you stick by those you love."

"You mean how I still go to my father's house even though I'll never be one of them?"

"I didn't mean that."

"It's okay. I realize this, but as much as they can grate on my nerves, I also know that for better or worse, they are my family. I just insist on taking them in small doses. And I'm so sorry I let you walk into that—I should have made it clearer to you—"

"It's okay, Holly. You didn't do anything wrong."

"But you didn't talk on the way home."

"That had nothing to do with your family and everything to do with me and my poor judgment. I'm forever putting those I care about at risk."

Wait. Where did that come from? "I don't understand. You didn't put me at risk."

"Yes, I did. And it can't happen again. We shouldn't have been out on the roads tonight. We could have…"

"Could have what? Talk to me."

He sighed. "Maybe if I tell you, you'll understand why I don't deserve to be happy."

"Of course you do." She took his hand and pressed it to her slightly rounded abdomen. "And these babies are proof of it."

"You might change your mind after I tell you this."

"I highly doubt it, but I'm listening."

"It had been a snowy February night a year after my brother died. I'd been invited to my best friend's birthday party, but I wasn't going. I was jealous of my friend because my Christmas had come and gone without lights and a tree. I'd been given a couple of gift cards, more as an afterthought."

Holly settled closer to him. She rested her head on his shoulder as she slipped her hand in his. She didn't know where he was going with this story, but wherever it led, she'd be there with him.

"My birthday had been in January—my thirteenth birthday—I was so excited to be a teenager. You know how kids are, always in a rush to grow up. But my parents hadn't done anything for it. There was no surprise party—no friends invited over—just a store-bought cake that didn't even have my name on it. I was given one birthday gift. There were apologies and promises to make it up to me."

Her heart ached for him. She moved her other hand over and rested it on his arm.

"When the phone rang to find out why I wasn't at my friend's party, my mother insisted I go and take a gift. Our parents were close friends, so when I again refused to go, my mother took back the one birthday gift that I'd received but refused to open. She insisted on delivering it to the party, but the snow was mounting outside and she was afraid to drive. My father reluctantly agreed to drive, but not before calling me a selfish brat and ordering me to my room."

Finn inhaled a ragged breath as he squeezed her hand. She couldn't imagine how much he'd lived through as a child. The death of his brother had spun the whole family out of control. No wonder he was such a hands-on leader. He knew the devastating consequences of losing control.

Finn's voice grew softer. "They only had a few blocks to drive, but the roads were icy. They had to cross a major roadway. My father had been going too fast. When he slowed down for the red light, he hit a patch of ice and slid into the intersection...into the path of two oncoming vehicles."

"Oh, Finn. Is that what happened tonight? You were reliving your parents' accident?"

He nodded. "Don't you see? If I had gone to that party, I would have been there before the snow. My parents would have never been out on the road. And tonight if I had paid attention to the forecast, I would have known about the storm rolling in."

"No matter how much you want to, you can't control the future. You had no idea then or now about what was going to happen. You can't hold yourself responsible."

"But you and those babies are my responsibility. If anything had happened to you, I wouldn't have known what to do with myself."

"You'd lean on your friends."

He shook his head. "I don't have friends. I have associates at best."

"Maybe if you let down your guard, you'd find out those people really do like you for you and not for what you can do for them." Her mind started to weave a plan to show Finn that he didn't need to be all alone in this world.

"I don't know. I've kept to myself so long. I wouldn't know how to change—how to let people in."

"I bet it's easier than you're thinking. Look how quickly we became friends."

"Is that what we are?" His gaze delved deep into her as though he could see straight through to the secrets lurking within her heart. "Are we just friends?"

Her heart *thump-thumped*. They were so much more than friends, but her voice failed her. Maybe words weren't necessary. In this moment actions would speak so much louder.

Need thrummed in her veins. She needed to let go of her insecurities. She needed to feel connected to him—to feel the love and happiness he brought to her life. She needed all of Finn with a force that almost scared her.

He filled in those cracks and crevices in her heart, making it whole. And not even her father's indifference tonight, her stepmother's coldness or her stepsisters' rudeness could touch her now. In this moment the only person that mattered was the man holding her close.

So while the snow fell outside, Holly melted into Finn's arms. She couldn't think of any other place she'd rather be and no one else she'd rather be with on this cold, blustery night.

CHAPTER TWENTY

THIS WAS IT.

Holly stared at her reflection in the mirror. The blue spar-kly gown clung to her figure—showing the beginning of her baby bump. She frowned. What had she been thinking? Perhaps she should have selected something loose that hid her figure. But Finn had insisted this dress was his favor-ite. She turned this way and that way in front of the mirror. And truth be told, she did like it—a lot.

She took a calming breath. She was nervous about her first public outing on the arm of New York's most eligible bachelor. A smile pulled at her lips as she thought of Finn. He'd been so kind and generous supplying her family with tickets to the ball, and now she had a surprise for him.

It'd taken a bit of secrecy and a lot of help, but she'd pulled together an evening that Finn would not soon forget. To put the plan into action, she'd needed to get rid of him for just a bit. Unable to come up with a better excuse, she'd pleaded that her prenatal vitamin prescription needed refilling. To her surprise he'd jumped at the opportunity to go to the store. She might have worried about his eagerness to leave if her mind wasn't already on the details of her surprise. She liked to think of it as Project Finn.

She smoothed a hand over her up-do hairstyle. It was se-cured by an army of hairpins. Nothing could move it now. She then swiped a wand of pink gloss over her lips. She felt like she was forgetting something, but she couldn't figure out what it might be.

The doorbell rang. It was time for the evening's festivi-ties to begin. She rushed to the door and flung it open to find Clara standing there on the arm of her new husband. They were each holding a large shopping bag.

"Hi." Holly's gaze moved to Clara's husband. "I'm Holly. It's so nice to meet you."

"I'm Steve." He shook her hand. "Clara had a lot to say about you and Finn—all good. I swear."

Holly couldn't blame Clara. From the outside, she and Finn appeared to be an overnight romance. No one knew that it started a few months ago.

Then remembering her manners, she moved aside. "Please come inside. I sent Finn out on an errand. Hopefully he won't be back for a little bit. Is everything going according to plan?"

Clara nodded. "It is. Are you sure about this?"

"Yes." Her response sounded more certain than she felt at the moment. "This is my Christmas present to Finn."

"I didn't know he did Christmas presents."

"He doesn't, but that's all going to change now."

"Isn't this place amazing?" Clara glanced all around. "I'm always in awe of it every time I stop by with some papers for him. And as expected, there's not a single Christmas decoration in sight." Clara sent Holly a hesitant look. "Do you really think this is going to work?"

"As long as you have the ornaments in those bags, we're only missing the tree."

"Don't worry. I called on my way over and the tree is on its way."

"Oh, good. Thank you so much. I couldn't have done this without you. But no worries. If it doesn't go the way I planned, you're safe. I'll take full responsibility."

Holly thought of mentioning the baby news. She was getting anxious to tell people, but she didn't know how Finn would feel about her telling his PA without him. So she remained quiet—for now.

After pointing out where she thought a Christmas tree

would look best, Holly asked, "Where's everyone else? I was hoping they'd be here before he gets back."

As if on cue, the doorbell rang again.

"That must be them. I'll get it." Clara rushed over and swung open the door. "I was starting to wonder what happened to you guys."

A string of people came through the door carrying a Christmas tree and packages. Some people Holly recognized from the office and others were new to her. They were all invited to Finn's penthouse before attending the Mistletoe Ball. In all, there was close to a dozen people in the penthouse. Clara made sure to introduce Holly to all of them. Everyone was smiling and talking as they set to work decking Finn's halls with strands of twinkle light, garland and mistletoe.

Holly couldn't help but wonder what Finn would make of this impromptu Christmas party.

As though Clara could read her mind, she leaned in close. "Don't worry. He'll like this. Thanks to you, he's a changed man."

Holly wasn't so sure, but she hoped Clara was right. Instead of worrying, she joined the others as they trimmed the tree.

How long does it take to fill a prescription?

Finn rocked back on his heels, tired of standing in one spot. He checked his watch for the tenth time in ten minutes. There was plenty of time before they had to leave for the ball. Not that he wanted to go, but once he'd invited Holly's family there was no backing out.

He made a point of never going to the ball. Publicly, he distanced himself as much as he could from the event. He liked to think of himself as the man behind the magic curtain. He never felt worthy to take any of the credit for the prestigious event. He carried so much guilt around with him—always feeling like a poor replacement for his family.

But Holly was changing his outlook on life. Maybe she had a point—maybe punishing himself wasn't helping anyone.

He strolled through the aisles of the pharmacy. When he got to the baby aisle, he stopped. He gazed at the shelves crowded with formula, toys and diapers. All of this was needed for a baby? Oh, boy! He had no idea what most of the gizmos even did.

Then the image of the twins filled his mind. His fingers traced over a pacifier. He finally acknowledged to himself that he had to let go of the ghosts that haunted him if he had any hopes of embracing the future. Because deep down he wanted Holly and those babies more than anything in the world.

In no time, he was headed back to the penthouse with two pacifiers tucked in his inner jacket pocket and roses in his hand. He knew what he needed to do now. He needed to tell Holly how much he loved her and their babies—how he couldn't live without them.

But when he swung open the penthouse door, he came to a complete standstill. There were people everywhere. In front of the window now stood a Christmas tree. It was like he'd stepped into Santa's hideaway at the North Pole.

Where had all of these people come from? He studied their faces. Most were his coworkers. The unfamiliar faces he assumed were significant others. But where was Holly?

He closed the door and stepped farther into the room. People turned and smiled. Men shook his hand and women told him what a lovely home he had. He welcomed them and gave the appropriate responses all the while wondering what in the world they were doing there.

And then a hand touched his shoulder. He turned, finding Clara standing there, smiling at him. If this was her idea, they were going to have a long talk—a very long talk.

"Oh, I know who those are for. Nice touch." Clara sent him a smile of approval.

"What?"

She pointed to his hand.

Glancing down at the bouquet of red roses he'd picked up on his way home, he decided to give them to Holly later—when it was just the two of them. He moved off to the side and laid them on a shelf.

Finding Clara still close at hand, he turned back to her. "Looks like I arrived in time for the party."

"What do you think? Holly went all out planning this get-together."

Holly? She did this? "But why? I don't understand."

Clara shrugged. "Holly didn't tell me what prompted this little party. Maybe she just thought it would be a nice gesture before the ball. All I know is that she asked me to pull together all of your close friends."

Close friends? He turned to his PA and arched a brow. "And now you take directions from Holly?"

"Seemed like the right thing to do. After all, I'm all for helping the course of true love."

He turned away, afraid Clara would read too much in his eyes. True love? Were his feelings that obvious?

"Just be good to her. She's a special person." And with that, Clara went to mingle with the others.

His close friends? He glanced around the room. Yes, he knew many of these people. They'd been the ones to help him when he'd been old enough to step into his father's role as CEO. He'd had lunch or dinner with all of them at one point or another. He'd even discussed sports and family with them. He'd never thought it was any more than them being polite and doing what was expected, but maybe he hadn't been willing to admit that those connections had meant so much more.

Finn recalled the other night when he'd been snuggled with Holly on the couch. They'd been discussing friends and he'd said he didn't have any. Was this Holly's way of showing him that he wasn't alone in this world? That if he let down his guard, this could be his?

"Finn, there you are." Holly rushed up to him. "I have some explaining to do."

"I think I understand."

Her beautiful eyes widened. "You do?"

He nodded before he leaned down. With his mouth near hers, he whispered, "Thank you."

And then with all of his—their—friends around, he kissed her. And it wasn't just a peck. No, this was a passionate kiss and he didn't care who witnessed it. He was in love.

CHAPTER TWENTY-ONE

HOLLY COULDN'T STOP SMILING.

A 1950s big-band tune echoed through the enormous lobby of the Metropolitan Museum. It was Holly's first visit and she was awed by the amazing architecture, not to mention the famous faces in attendance, from professional athletes to movie stars. It was a Who's Who of New York.

It also didn't hurt that she was in the arms of the most handsome man. Holly lifted her chin in order to look up at Finn. This evening was the beginning of big things to come—she was certain of it.

Finn's gaze caught hers. "Are you having fun?"

"The time of my life. But you shouldn't be spending all of your time with me. There are a lot of people who want to speak with you, including the paparazzi out in front of the museum."

"The reporters always have questions."

"Did you even listen to any of them?"

"No. I don't want anyone or anything to ruin this evening."

"You don't understand. It's good news. In fact, it's great news. Project Santa was such a success that it garnered national attention. The website is getting hit after hit and tons of heartfelt thank-yous from project coordinators, outreach workers and parents. There have even been phone calls from other companies wanting to participate next year. Just think of all the children and families that could be helped."

Finn smiled. "And it's all thanks to you."

"Me?" She shook her head. "It was your idea."

"But it was your ingenuity that saved the project. You took a project that started as a corporate endeavor and put it in the hands of the employees and the community. To me, that's the true meaning of Christmas—people helping people."

His words touched her deeply. "Thank you. I really connected with the project and the people behind the scenes."

"And that's why I think you should take it over permanently. Just let me know what you need."

Holly stopped dancing. "Seriously?"

"I've never been more serious."

This was the most fulfilling job she'd ever had. She didn't have to think it over. She knew this was her calling. Not caring that they were in the middle of the dance floor, she lifted on her toes and kissed him.

When they made it to the edge of the dance floor, Finn was drawn away from her by a group of men needing his opinion on something. Holly smiled, enjoying watching Finn animated and outgoing.

Out of excuses, Holly made her way to her family. It was time she said hello. She made small talk with her stepmother and sisters, but her father was nowhere to be seen. As usual, they quickly ran out of things to say to each other and Holly made her departure.

On the other side of the dance floor, Holly spotted her father dancing too close with a young lady. He was chatting her up while the young woman smiled broadly. Then her father leaned closer, whispering in the woman's ear. The woman blushed.

The whole scene sickened Holly—reminding her of all the reasons she'd sworn off men. They just couldn't be trusted and it apparently didn't get better with age.

Her stepmother was in for a painful reality check when she found out that she'd been traded in for a younger model just like her father had done to Holly's mother. The thought didn't make Holly happy. It made her very sad because she knew all too well the pain her half-sisters were about to experience.

Deciding she wasn't in any frame of mind to make friendly chitchat, she veered toward a quiet corner. She needed to gather herself. And then a beautiful woman stepped in her path. Holly didn't recognize her, but apparently the woman knew her.

"Hi, Holly. I've been meaning to get a moment to speak with you." The polished woman in a red sparkly dress held out a manicured hand.

"Hi." Holly shook her hand, all the while experiencing a strange sensation that she should know this woman.

Her confusion must have registered on her face because the woman said, "I'm sorry. I should have introduced myself. I'm Meryl."

Surely she couldn't be Finn's ex, could she? But there was no way Holly was going to ask that question. If she was wrong, it would be humiliating. And if she was right, well, awkwardness would ensue.

"If you're wondering, yes, I am that Meryl. But don't worry, Finn and I were over ages ago. I saw you earlier, dancing with him. I've never seen him look so happy. I'm guessing you're the one to do that for him. He's a very lucky man."

At last, the shock subsided and Holly found her voice. "It's really nice to meet you. Finn has nothing but good things to say about you."

Meryl's eyes lit up. "That's good to know. I think he's pretty great, too."

Really? Finn had given her the impression that hard feelings lingered. Her gaze scanned the crowd for the man they had in common, but she didn't see him anywhere.

"Ah, I see I caught you by surprise." The woman's voice was gentle and friendly. "You thought there would be lots of hard feelings, but there aren't. I assure you. Finn is a very generous and kind man. He just doesn't give himself enough credit."

"I agree with you."

Holly wanted desperately to dislike this woman, but she couldn't. Meryl seemed so genuine—so down to earth. There was a kindness that reflected in her eyes. Why exactly had Finn let her get away?

"And the fact that you were able to get him to attend his very own ball is a big credit to you."

"His ball?"

The woman's eyes widened in surprise. "I'm sorry. I said too much."

"No, you didn't." Holly needed to know what was going on. "Why did you call this Finn's ball? As far as I know, he's never even attended before this year."

"I thought he would have told you, especially since he just told me that he intends to marry you."

"He told you that?"

The woman nodded as her brows scrunched together. "Anyway, I do the leg work for the ball, but he's the drive behind it. It's not made public but the ball is done in memory of Finn's mother and brother. He says that he remains in the background underwriting all of the associated expenses because he's made a number of unpopular business deals as far as the press is concerned, but I think it's something else."

The thought that this woman had insights into Finn that Holly lacked bothered her. "What do you think his reasons are?"

"I think the ball reminds him of his family and for whatever reason, he carries a truckload of guilt that he survived and they didn't."

And that was where Holly was able to fill in the missing pieces, but she kept what Finn had told her about his past to herself. She knew all about his survivor's guilt. And now she realized how much it'd cost him to come here tonight.

But what other secrets was he keeping from me? Tears stung the backs of her eyes. *Stupid hormones.* "There appears to be a lot I have to learn about Finn."

"I'm not surprised he didn't mention it. Finn doesn't open up easily."

Just to those that are closest to him. Holly finished Meryl's statement. After all of their talk about being open and honest with each other, he let her come here not knowing the facts. He'd lied to her by omission. Now she wondered what else he was keeping from her.

"I... I should be going." Holly was anxious to be alone with her thoughts.

"Well, there I go putting my foot in my mouth. Sorry about that. Sometimes when I'm nervous I talk too much."

"It's okay. I've really enjoyed talking with you."

Meryl's eyes lit up as a smile returned to her face. "I'm really glad we met. I think we might just end up friends, of course if you're willing."

"I'd like that."

But as they parted company, Holly didn't think their friendship would ever have a chance to flourish. She doubted they'd ever run into each other again.

She turned to come face-to-face with her father. He was the very last person she wanted to speak to that evening. "Excuse me."

Her father stepped in front of her. "Not so fast. I did a little research into that boyfriend of yours. And I think I should get to know him better."

Not a chance. Her father caused enough destruction wherever he went. She wasn't going to give him a chance to hurt Finn.

Holly pointed a finger at her father. "You stay away from him."

Her father's eyes widened with surprise. "But it's a father's place to make sure the guy is worthy of his daughter."

She clenched her hands. "And you would be an expert on character and integrity?"

"What's that supposed to mean?"

"I saw you—everybody saw you flirting with that young woman who's what? My age? How could you?"

"I didn't mean for it to happen."

"You never do."

Her father at least had the decency to grow red-faced. "You don't understand—"

"You're right. I don't. I have to go."

She rushed past her father. Suddenly the walls felt as though they were closing in on her and it was hard to breathe. She knew not to trust men. Her father had taught her that at an early age. And he'd reinforced that lesson tonight.

What made her think that Finn would be different? No, he wasn't a womanizer, but he was a man. And he only trusted her so far. Without complete trust, they had nothing.

Except the babies, which she'd never keep from him. But they didn't have to be together to coparent. Because she refused to end up like her mother and blindsided by a man.

The fairy tale was over.

It was time she got on with her life—without Finn.

She headed for the door, needing fresh air.

What in the world?

Finn had caught glimpses of Holly and Meryl with their heads together. His gut had churned. *Nothing good will come of that.*

He tried to get away from a couple of gentlemen, but they were his partners in an upcoming deal and he didn't want to offend them. But for every excuse he came up with to make his exit, they came up with a new aspect of their pending deal that needed further attention.

He should have forewarned Holly that Meryl would be here. But honestly, it slipped his mind. Between the news of the babies and then Holly's surprise holiday gathering at the penthouse, his thoughts were not his own these days.

He breathed easier when the women parted. But the next time he spotted Holly, she was having a conversation with her father and if the hand gestures and the distinct frown were anything to go by, it wasn't going well.

"Gentlemen, these are all great points. And I look forward to discussing them in great detail, but I promised my date I wouldn't work tonight."

The men admitted that they'd made similar promises to their wives. They agreed to meet again after the first of the year. With a shake of hands, they parted.

Finn turned around in time to witness Holly heading for the door. He took off after her, brushing off people with a smile and promising to catch up with them soon. It wasn't in him to be outright rude, but his sixth sense was telling him Holly's fast exit was not good—not good at all.

He rushed past the security guards posted at the entrance of the museum, past the impressive columns, and started down the flight of steps. Snow was starting to fall and Holly didn't have a coat. What was she thinking?

When he stepped on the sidewalk, his foot slipped on a patch of ice. He quickly caught his balance. He glanced to the left and then right. Which way had she gone?

And then he saw the shadow of a person. Was that her? He drew closer and realized the person was sitting on the sidewalk. His heart clenched. He took off at a sprint.

When he reached Holly's side, he knelt down. "Holly, are you all right?"

She looked up at him with a tear trailing down her cheek. "No. I'm not."

"Should I call an ambulance?"

"No." She sniffled. "I just need a hand up. I… I slipped on some ice."

"Are you sure it's okay if you stand? I mean, what about the babies?"

"Just give me your hand." He did as she asked.

Once she was on her feet, she ran her hands over her bare arms. He noticed the goose bumps, which prompted him to slip off his jacket and place it over her shoulders. "Thank you. But you need it."

"Keep it. I'm fine." He had so much adrenaline flooding through his system at that particular moment that he really didn't notice the cold.

"Do you want to go back inside?"

She lifted the skirt of her gown. "I don't think so. My heel broke."

He glanced down, finding her standing on one foot as the other heel had broken and slipped off her foot. Without a word, he retrieved the heel and handed to her. Then he scooped her up in his arms.

"Put me down! What are you doing?"

"Taking you home."

"Finn, stop. We need to talk."

"You're right. We do. But not out here in the cold."

CHAPTER TWENTY-TWO

So much for making a seamless exit.

Holly sat on the couch in Finn's penthouse feeling ridiculous for falling on the ice and breaking her shoe. The lights on the Christmas tree twinkled as though mocking her with their festiveness. She glanced away.

She'd trusted Finn and yet things about him and his past kept blindsiding her. How was she ever supposed to trust him? How was she supposed to believe he'd never hurt her?

Falling in love and trusting another human was like a free fall and trusting that your parachute would open. Holly wasn't sure she had the guts to free-fall. Her thoughts strayed back to her father. She inwardly shuddered, remembering him flirting with that young woman, and then he didn't even deny he was having an affair with her. Her mother had trusted him and then her stepmother. It was to their utter detriment.

Finn rushed back in the room with a damp cloth. "Here. Let me have your hand."

She held her injured hand out to him. He didn't say anything as he gently cleaned her scrapes and then applied some medicated cream before wrapping a bit of gauze around it.

"Did you hurt anything else?"

"Besides my pride? No."

"I wish you'd have talked to me before you took off. Anything could have happened to you—"

"If you hadn't noticed, I'm a grown woman. I can take care of myself."

He arched a brow at her outburst.

"Hey, anyone can slip on ice," he said calmly. "I just wish

you'd have talked to me. Why did you leave? Was it Meryl? Did she say something to upset you?"

"No. Actually she didn't. Not directly."

"What is that supposed to mean?"

"Why didn't you tell me she would be there? That you still interact with her?"

He shrugged and glanced away. "I don't know. I didn't think of it."

"Really? Is that the same reason you didn't tell me you're the mastermind behind the Mistletoe Ball? That without you, there wouldn't be a ball?"

"I guess I should have said something. I didn't think it was a big deal. I wasn't keeping it a secret from you, but I've been distracted. If you haven't noticed, we're having twins."

"What else haven't you told me?" Her fears and insecurities came rushing to the surface. "What else don't I know about you that's going to blindside me?"

His facial features hardened. "I'm sure there's lots you don't know about me, just like there's a lot I don't know about you." When she refused to back down, he added, "Do you want me to start with kindergarten or will a detailed report about my last five years do?"

She glared at him for being sarcastic. Then she realized she deserved it. She was overreacting. She'd let her family dig into her insecurities and her imagination had done the rest.

"You know what? Never mind." Finn got up from the couch. "If you don't trust me, this is never going to work. Just forget this—forget us. I was wrong to think it could work."

Her heart ached as she watched him walk out of the room. She didn't even know the person she'd become. It was like she was once again that insecure little girl who realized her father had lied to her—learning that her father had secretly exchanged his current family for a new one. And now her father was about to do it again.

But Finn hadn't done that. He hadn't done anything but be sweet and kind. Granted, he might not be totally forthcoming at times, but it wasn't because he was out to deceive her or hurt her. She couldn't punish him for the wrongs her father had done to her over the years.

If she was ever going to trust a man with her heart—it would be Finn. Because in truth she did love him. She'd fallen for him that first night when he'd invited her here to his penthouse. He'd been charming and entertaining.

Now, when it looked like she was going to have it all— the perfect guy, the amazing babies and a happily-ever-after—she was pulling away. In the light of day, the depth of her love for Finn scared her silly. Her instinct was to back away fast—just like she was doing now. And if she wasn't careful, she'd lose it all. If she hadn't already.

Still wearing Finn's jacket, she wrapped her arms around herself. She inhaled the lingering scent of his spicy cologne mingled with his unique male scent. Her eyes drifted closed.

There had to be a way to salvage things. Maybe she could plead a case of pregnancy hormones. Nah. She had to be honest with him about her fears and hope he'd be willing to work through them with her.

It was then she noticed something poking her. There was something in his inner jacket pocket. She reached inside and pulled out not one but two packages of pacifiers. One was pink and one was blue. Happy tears blurred her eyes as she realized just how invested Finn was in their expanding family. She had to talk to him—to apologize.

She swiped at her eyes and got to her feet, heading for the kitchen.

CHAPTER TWENTY-THREE

WHAT WAS HE DOING?

Finn chastised himself for losing his cool with Holly. Every time she questioned him, she poked at his insecurities about being a proper husband and father. He had so many doubts about doing a good job. He didn't even know what being a husband and father entailed. All he knew was that he wanted to do his best by his family.

And he wasn't a quitter. He fought for the things he believed in. Sometimes he fought too long for his own good. But this was his family—there was no retreating. He would somehow prove to Holly—and most of all to himself—that he could be there for her and the babies through the good and the bad.

Certain in what he needed to do, he turned on his heels and headed back to the living room, hoping Holly hadn't made a quick exit. If she had, it wouldn't deter him. He would find her. He would tell her that he loved her. Because that was what it all boiled down to. He was a man who was head over heels in love with the mother of his children.

When he entered the living room, he nearly collided with Holly. He put his hands on her shoulders to steady her. "Where are you going in such a rush?"

"To find you. There's something I need to say."

"There's something I need to say to you, too."

At the same time, they said, "I'm sorry."

Finn had to be sure he heard her correctly. "Really?"

She nodded before she lifted up on her tiptoes and with her hands on either side of his face, she pulled him down to her. The kiss wasn't light or hesitant. Instead her kiss was heated and demanding. Need thrummed in his veins. He never wanted to let her go.

It'd be oh, so easy to dispense with words. His hands wrapped around her waist, pulling her soft curves to his hard planes. A moan grew in the back of his throat and he didn't fight it. Holly had to know all of the crazy things she did to his body, to his mind, to his heart.

But he wanted—no, he needed to clear the air between them. Christmas was in the air and it was the time for setting aside the past and making a new start. That was exactly what he wanted to do with Holly.

It took every fiber of his being to pull away from her embrace. Her beautiful eyes blinked and stared at him in confusion. It'd be so easy to pull her close again and pick up where they'd left off.

No, Finn. Do the responsible thing. Make this right for both of you.

"Come sit down so we can talk." He led her to the couch.

"Talk? Now?"

"Trust me. It's important."

"As long as I go first," she said. "After all, I started this whole thing."

"Deal."

She inhaled a deep breath and then blew it out. She told him about running into her family and how her father's actions and her stepsisters' words had ripped the scabs off her insecurities. "I know that's not a good excuse, but it's the truth. I've spent most of my life swearing that I would never end up like my mother—that I'd never blindly trust a man."

"And then you ran into my ex and found out I'd left out some important details about my life."

Holly shrugged and glanced away. "I just let it all get to me." She lifted her chin until her gaze met his. "I know you're not my father. You are absolutely nothing like him. I trust you."

"You do?"

She nodded. "I can't promise that every once in a while my insecurities won't get the best of me, but I promise to work on them."

"I love you, Holly."

Her eyes grew shiny with unshed tears. "I love you, too."

He cleared his throat, hoping his voice wouldn't fail him before he got it all out. "I would never intentionally hurt you or our children. You and those babies mean everything to me. I'm really excited to be a father."

"I noticed." She reached in his jacket pocket and pulled out the pacifiers. "I found these. And they're so sweet. Our babies' first gifts."

"You like them?"

She nodded. "How could I have ever doubted you?"

"I promise you here and now that I'll work on being more forthcoming. I've spent so many years keeping things bottled up inside me that I might slip up now and then. Will you stick by me while I work on this partnership thing?"

She nodded. "As long as you'll stick by me while I learn to let go of the past."

"It's a deal." Then recalling the flowers, he jumped to his feet. "I have something for you." He moved to the bookcase and retrieved the flowers. "I got these for you when I went to the pharmacy earlier." He held them out to her.

She accepted the bouquet and sniffed them. "They're beautiful."

This was his chance to make this Christmas unforgettable. He took her hand in his and gazed up into her wide-open eyes. "Holly, the most important thing you need to know about me is that I love you. And I love those babies you're carrying. I want to be the best husband and father, if you'll let me. Will you marry me?"

A tear splashed onto her cheek. She moved his hand to

her slightly rounded abdomen. "We love you, too. And yes. Yes! Yes! I'll marry you."

His heart filled with love—the likes he'd never known. And it was all Holly's doing. She'd opened his eyes and his heart not only to the spirit of the season, but also to the possibilities of the future.

He leaned forward, pressing his lips to hers.

This was the best Christmas ever.

EPILOGUE

THERE—THAT SHOULD do it.

Finn stepped back from the twelve-foot Christmas tree that stood prominently in front of the bay windows of his new house—correction, *their* house…as in his and Holly's home. This was the very first Christmas tree that he'd decorated since he was a child. Surprisingly it didn't hurt nearly as much as he'd thought. The memories of his brother and parents were always there, lingering around the edges, but now he was busy making new memories with Holly and their twins, Derek, in honor of his brother, and Maggie, in honor of his mother.

"How's it going?" Holly ventured into the room carrying a twin in each arm.

"I just finished putting on the lights. And how about you? Is Project Santa a go?"

Holly's face lit up. "Yes. And this year will be even bigger than last year, which means we're able to help even more children."

"I knew you were the right person to put in charge."

Maggie let out a cry. Holly bounced her on her hip. "Sounds like someone is hungry."

"Did I hear someone cry out for food?" Holly's mother strolled into the room, making a beeline for Maggie.

Finn glanced over at his mother-in-law, Sandy, who now lived in a mother-in-law apartment on the other side of their pool. When Holly had suggested her mother move in, he had to admit that he'd been quite resistant to the idea. But when Holly really wanted something, he found himself unable to say no.

In the end, he and Sandy hit it off. The woman was a lot

more laid-back than he'd ever imagined. And she doted over her grandchildren, which won her a gold star. And with the help of a nanny and a housekeeper, they were one big, happy family—unless of course the twins were hungry or teething.

"I can do it, Mom," Holly insisted, hanging on to the baby.

"Nonsense. I wasn't doing anything important." Sandy glanced over at the tree. "And from the looks of things in here, your husband could use some help."

Holly smiled. "I think you're right." She handed over the fussing baby. "Thanks. I'll be in shortly."

"Don't hurry. I've got this." Sandy started toward the kitchen. "Isn't that right, Maggie? We're buddies."

Holly stepped up beside Finn. "Are you sure you bought enough lights to cover all of the tree?"

"Yes. I'll show you." He bent over and plugged them in.

His wife arched a brow at him as though she knew something that he didn't. This was never a good sign.

"You should have tested them before putting them on the tree."

"What?" He turned around to find the top and middle of the tree all lit up, but the bottom section was dark. But how could that be? "I swear I tested them before I strung them."

Holly moved up next to him and handed over Derek. "Maybe it's just payback."

He glanced at his wife, trying to figure out what payback she was referring to. And then he recalled that last Christmas he'd shared the story of how he and his brother had swiped a strand of lights from the Christmas tree in order to light up their blanket fort.

A smile pulled at Finn's lips at the memory. It was the first time he'd been able to look back on his past and smile. That was all thanks to Holly. Her gift to him last year was giving his life back to him. Instead of walking around a shell of a man, he was taking advantage of every breath he had on this earth.

"Perhaps you're right. Maybe Derek's playing tricks on me."

"Did you hear that?" Holly leaned forward and tickled their son's tummy, making him giggle and coo. "Are you playing tricks on your daddy?"

Finn knew she was adding a bit of levity to the moment to keep things from getting too serious. Finn liked the thought that his brother might be looking down over them and smiling. Right here and now the past and the present came together, making Finn feel complete.

"Would you do that?" Finn placed his finger in his son's hand. "Would you steal the lights from the Christmas tree to make a fort?"

"Don't give him ideas," Holly lightly scolded. "I have a feeling your son will get into enough trouble of his own without any help from you."

"I think you might be right."

"And if he has a little brother, we'll really have our hands full."

This was the first time Holly had ever mentioned having another baby. It was usually him going on about expanding their family because to his surprise and delight, he loved being a dad. He'd even considered quitting the day job to be a full-time parent until Holly put her foot down and told him that someone had to keep the family business going to hand down to their children. But he no longer worked from morning till late at night. He took vacations and weekends. He had other priorities now.

"I think it'd be great to have another baby. Just let me know when you want my assistance. I'm all yours."

"Oh, you've done plenty already."

"Hey, what's that supposed to mean?" Derek wiggled in his arms. "Oh, you mean the twins? What can I say? When I do something I go all out."

"Well, let's just hope this time around I'm not carrying

twins or you might just be staying home to take care of all of them while I run the office."

Surely he'd misunderstood her. She couldn't be—could she? "Are...are you pregnant?"

She turned to him and with tears of joy in her eyes, she nodded. "Merry Christmas."

Finn whooped with joy before leaning forward and planting a kiss on his wife's lips. He'd never been so happy in his life. In fact, he never knew it was possible to be this happy.

"You give the best Christmas presents ever, Mrs. Lockwood."

"Well, Mr. Lockwood, you inspire me." She smiled up at him. "I love you."

"I love you the mostest."

* * * * *

She felt his eyes on her.

He watched her every move as she came downstairs from putting the kids to bed.

"Thanks for babysitting," she said. "And for the pizza. I'm sure you have more exciting plans for your Friday night, but I appreciate that you stayed."

"I didn't have plans. And I enjoyed hanging out with you and the kids."

She sat across from him. "You're my daughter's new BFF, you know."

His eyes glinted. "We're more than BFFs. She asked me to marry her."

"Well, you gave her flowers and played Barbies with her. Of course she's head over heels in love with you."

"Is that all it takes?"

"For a three-year-old."

He leaned forward and settled his hands on her knees. Even through the denim she felt the heat of his touch—a heat that seared her whole body. "What about the three-year-old's mom?"

She eyed him warily. "Are you flirting with me?"

"If you have to ask, my skills must be rusty."

"It's more likely that mine are," she admitted, feeling out of her element here.

He lowered his head toward her. "Then maybe we should work on changing that."

* * *

Those Engaging Garrets
—The Carolina Cousins

BUILDING THE PERFECT DADDY

BY
BRENDA HARLEN

First Published in Great Britain 2016
By Mills & Boon, an imprint of HarperCollins*Publishers*
1 London Bridge Street, London, SE1 9GF

© 2016 Brenda Harlen

ISBN: 978-0-263-92025-3

23-1016

Our policy is to use papers that are natural, renewable and recyclable products and made from wood grown in sustainable forests. The logging and manufacturing processes conform to the legal environmental regulations of the country of origin.

Printed and bound in Spain
by CPI, Barcelona

Brenda Harlen is a former attorney who once had the privilege of appearing before the Supreme Court of Canada. The practice of law taught her a lot about the world and reinforced her determination to become a writer—because in fiction, she could promise a happy ending! Now she is an award-winning, national best-selling author of more than thirty titles for Mills & Boon. You can keep up-to-date with Brenda on Facebook and Twitter or through her website, www.brendaharlen.com.

This book is dedicated to my wonderful husband, who has proved, time and again over the years, he is capable of tackling the various home improvements our various homes have required (with thanks for finally putting up the new trim in the hallway!).

Chapter One

It was raining again.

The sound of the water drumming on the roof woke Lauryn up well before her seven-month-old son. She cracked an eyelid and squinted at the glowing numbers of her alarm clock—5:28 a.m.

Way too freakin' early.

She rolled over and pulled the covers up over her head, as if that might muffle the ominous sound of the rain. When she'd had a couple of leaky spots patched in the spring, the roofer had warned her that the whole thing needed to be redone. She'd nodded her understanding because she did understand. Unfortunately, she didn't have the money for that kind of major expense right now, and the sound of the water pounding down felt like Mother Nature beating on her head, chastising her for the foolish choices she'd made.

But she was no longer the idealistic twenty-seven-year-old who had been as much in love with the idea of being a bride as the man who had proposed to her. And she was still paying for that mistake—which was why she couldn't afford a new roof right now.

She looked up at the ceiling and sent up a silent prayer: *Please hold out for just one more year. Just long enough for me figure out my finances and my life.*

She didn't know who she was trying to bargain with—the roof or Mother Nature or God. At this point, she would willingly make a deal with anyone who had the power to change her fate.

Her parents—Tom and Susan Garrett—had given her and Rob the money to buy a house when they'd married. A proper house, like the simple Craftsman-style bungalow in Ridgemount that she'd thought would be perfect for a young couple starting out. But she'd let her charming new husband convince her that they could split the money between a less expensive fixer-upper and his start-up sporting-goods business, The Locker Room.

After six years, the house was still in need of major repairs, the business was failing and she was on her own with a preschooler and a baby. Was it any wonder that she only wanted to stay in bed all day with the covers over her head?

But she didn't have that option. She didn't get to follow her bliss, as Rob had claimed he was doing when he walked away from all of his responsibilities. She was stuck right where she was with the old roof, drafty windows, leaky plumbing and rotting porch.

Still, she tried to focus on the positive—her final divorce papers had come in the mail a few days earlier and she was grateful that it was done. She might have wished away her entire marriage, except then she wouldn't have Kylie and Zachary.

No matter what happened, she was determined not to let her mistakes impact their lives. She had to figure a way out of the precarious situation they were in, to give them a stable and loving home. Hopefully, the way out would be found within the business plan she'd prepared for her upcoming meeting at the bank, because taking more money from her family was definitely *not* an option.

She glanced at the clock again—5:57 a.m.

Knowing that Zachary would be up within the hour, she reluctantly pushed back the covers and slid out of bed. Avoiding the creakier floorboards, she tiptoed to his room to confirm that he was sleeping soundly in his crib. He was so big already. Almost eighteen pounds and twenty-eight inches long at his last checkup, he'd long since mastered rolling from his back to his stomach and over again and was now starting to use the rails of his crib to pull himself up.

She gently touched the ends of his baby-soft curls and felt her heart swell inside of her chest. She might hate her ex-husband for a lot of reasons, but she would always be grateful to him for the two precious children he'd given her.

Moving away from the crib, she headed to the master bath. Stripping away the tank top and boxer shorts she'd slept in, she showered quickly, determined to have herself put together and ready for the day before either of the kids woke up. But she hadn't even finished drying her hair when she heard the baby stirring. Zachary was inevitably up with the sun, but apparently he knew seven in the morning even when the sun wasn't shining.

She hurried downstairs to fix him a bottle of formula. He was eating some solid foods now and drinking from a sippy cup during the day, but a bottle continued to be part of his early morning and late-night routine, and Lauryn appreciated the quiet time snuggling with her baby. She returned to the bedroom with the bottle in hand and lifted him from his crib, changed his diaper and settled into the rocking chair by the window to feed him.

When Zachary was satisfied—at least for the moment— she headed across the hall to check on her daughter. Stepping into the little girl's bedroom was like stepping into the pages of a fairy tale. The interior walls were painted to look like they were made of stone blocks, with three arched "windows" providing spectacular views of the kingdom, including snowcapped mountains, a lush green forest and even a waterfall spilling into a crystal-clear lake. There was also an exquisite glass carriage drawn by a pair of white horses making its way down a long, winding road toward another castle with numerous turrets and towers. The castle was guarded by knights and dragons; there were wildflowers in the grass, fairies peeking out from the trees and butterflies, birds and hot air balloons in the sky.

She didn't know how many hours her sister had spent, first sketching and then painting the mural. Jordyn had created a complete fantasy world for her niece, and Kylie absolutely loved everything about it. It was only Lauryn who had recently started to worry that she wasn't doing her little girl any favors by encouraging her belief in fairy tales and happily-ever-afters.

Lauryn used to believe in those same things. And when Rob Schulte had proposed, she'd been certain that he was her Prince Charming. Even during the rocky periods in their marriage, she'd been confident that their love would guide them through the difficult terrain. And she'd remained optimistic right up until the day her prince had ridden off into the sunset with a yoga instructor, leaving her trapped in a crumbling castle surrounded by fire-breathing dragons in the form of unpaid creditors.

It had taken her a while, but she'd eventually come to accept that he'd never loved her the way she'd loved him. She could forgive him for walking out on their marriage—but not for walking away from their children. She was relieved, but not really surprised, that Rob hadn't shown any inclination to fight for custody. She had enough struggles trying to manage the business he'd left floundering and keep a leaky roof over all of their heads without battling on yet another front.

As she made her way down to the kitchen, Zachary let out a loud belch, then a relieved sigh.

She continued to rub his back as he settled. "Does that feel better now?"

The baby, of course, didn't answer.

Feeling dampness on her shoulder, she tore a paper towel off the roll and attempted to wipe off the spit-up that was now sliding down the front of her shirt. Obviously she would have to change, but Kylie would be up soon and she wanted to get her breakfast started.

She settled Zachary in his high chair with a handful of Cheerios on his tray to keep him occupied while she gathered the necessary ingredients to make French toast. Hopefully Kylie's favorite breakfast would make the little girl more amenable to spending the afternoon with her grandparents while Lauryn attended her meeting at the bank.

Susan and Tom Garrett absolutely doted on their grandchildren, and Kylie had always loved spending time with them, but since Rob had gone, the little girl had become unusually clingy and demanding. It was as if she was afraid to let her mother out of her sight in case she disappeared from her life, too.

Lauryn was turning the first slice of bread in the pan when she heard Kylie's footsteps on the stairs. A moment later, her daughter trudged into the kitchen, wearing her favorite princess nightgown made of a silky pink fabric with a ruffled hem, white silk underskirt and puffy sleeves—and a decidedly *un*-princess-like scowl on her face. Kylie had never been a morning person.

Climbing into her booster seat at the table, she reached for the cup of orange juice waiting for her. Lauryn cut up the fried bread and set the plate in front of her daughter, who picked up her fork and stabbed a piece of toast. Lauryn sat beside her and sipped her coffee.

Kylie finished about half of her breakfast, then pushed her plate aside. "Can we go to the park today?"

"Maybe later," Lauryn said.

"I wanna go now," her daughter insisted.

"It's raining now," she said. "And Mama has to take care of some paperwork this morning."

Kylie folded her arms over her chest in an all-too-familiar mutinous posture. "I wanna go to the park."

"Later," she promised, kissing the top of her daughter's

head before lifting Zachary out of his high chair. "Right now, we have to get the two of you washed up and dressed."

She'd just propped the baby on her hip when the doorbell rang. Kylie immediately raced down the hall.

With a weary sigh, Lauryn followed. If it had been up to her, she would have ignored the summons. She wasn't in the mood to deal with some kid selling chocolate bars or magazine subscriptions, especially when she could afford neither. And why anyone would be going door-to-door on a Wednesday morning in this weather was beyond her comprehension, but since Kylie had already climbed up on the sofa in the living room and was pushing the curtains apart to see who was at the door, she could hardly pretend that no one was home.

"There's lotsa peoples outside," Kylie told her.

Lots of people?

Lauryn knew she was frowning when she unlocked the door and pulled it open—a frown that deepened when she saw that her daughter hadn't been exaggerating. In addition to the mouthwateringly handsome and impressively muscled man on her porch wearing a hard hat and a tool belt—*Oh, please God, do* not *let this be some kind of stripper-gram, because I have no idea how I'd explain* that *to my daughter*—there was a man on the lawn with what looked like a video camera propped on his shoulder, a trio of people standing a little farther away under an umbrella and a van and two pickup trucks parked on the road in front of the house.

The hunk in the hard hat and the tool belt smiled, causing a fluttery sensation in her belly, along with a nagging suspicion that she'd seen him somewhere before.

"Are you Lauryn Schulte?" he asked.

"I am," she confirmed, her tone giving no hint of the unexpected and unwelcome awareness she was feeling. "But unless you're from the North Carolina State Lottery with one of those big checks for me, you can get yourself and your camera crew off my property."

Chapter Two

The experiences gained from three years in front of the camera had taught Ryder Wallace to keep a smile on his face under almost any circumstances. Circumstances certainly more challenging than a frazzled mother with a baby on her hip and what looked like baby vomit on the shoulder of the pale yellow T-shirt she wore over faded denim jeans.

Except that she then closed the door in his smiling face. *And locked it.*

He actually heard the click of the dead bolt sliding into place.

Not quite the reaction he'd anticipated.

"Cut!"

Owen Diercks jogged over to the rickety porch, where Ryder was still staring, slack jawed, at the closed door.

"What in the hell just happened?" the director demanded.

"I think we came at a bad time," Ryder said.

"I'm tired of standing around waiting for these women to primp for the camera," Owen grumbled. "Whoever decided to surprise the contest winners obviously didn't think that one through."

"I believe the surprise aspect was your idea," Ryder said, although the home owner's tone made him suspect that Lauryn Schulte's reasons for closing the door on his face were about more than an unwillingness to face the cameras without her lipstick on.

"Which is probably why no one ever listens to my ideas,"

the director acknowledged as lightning flashed in the distance. He glanced at the sky, a worried look on his face, then at his watch. "I don't particularly want to stand around in the rain for God only knows how long while our home owner does her hair and makeup."

"Do you want to wrap for today?" Ryder asked him.

"No, I want to stay on schedule," Owen grumbled as thunder rumbled and lightning flashed again. "But it doesn't look like that's going to happen today."

Ryder glanced back at Carl, who was using a garbage bag to keep his camera sheltered from the rain while he waited for further instructions.

"Pack it up," Owen called out to him.

Carl nodded and immediately moved toward the van with his equipment. The assistant to the director and the AV tech followed the cameraman.

"We need to get back on schedule," Owen said. "Which means that someone needs to remind Mrs. Schulte of the terms and conditions she agreed to when she submitted her application." He looked at Ryder. "Do you want me to do it?"

"I will," he offered. Because as great as Owen was in handling the numerous and various aspects of his job, he also had a tendency to piss people off. And after only a brief interaction with Lauryn Schulte, Ryder got the impression that she was already pissed off.

Owen nodded. "I expect to be back here first thing Monday morning with everyone ready to go."

"They will be," Ryder promised, with more conviction than he felt.

As the director made his way down the driveway to his own vehicle, Ryder considered his options. For him, walking away wasn't one of them.

He was accustomed to home owners opening their doors wide and inviting him and his *Ryder to the Rescue* crew to come inside—not just happy but grateful to see him. Because it was his job to fix other contractors' mistakes, to finish the projects that do-it-yourselfers gave up on doing. In sum, he gave people what they wanted and they were appreciative of his time and efforts. They hugged him and sent him thank-you cards. They were never dismissive or disinterested.

Clearly Lauryn Schulte didn't understand what was at stake here, so he knocked on her door again.

There was no response.

He knew she was home, and she knew that he knew she was home, and thinking about that began to piss *him* off.

He knocked once more, and once more she ignored him.

But the little girl pushed back the curtains at the front window and waved to him. Something about her looked vaguely familiar—or maybe she just looked like most little girls of a similar age, even if he didn't know what that age might be.

He lifted a hand and waved back.

She smiled and twin dimples creased her cheeks. She really was a cute kid. Through the glass, he heard her mother say something. Though he couldn't decipher the actual words, the message was clear enough when the child gave one last wave before the curtains fell back into place over the window.

He sat on the porch, mostly sheltered from the rain pounding down around him by the overhang, and waited.

As he did, he made a quick visual scan of the surrounding area. It was a decent neighborhood, showing some signs of age. Most of the houses were simple designs—primarily bungalows and two stories, between thirty and forty years old—but well kept, the lawns tidy, flower beds tended. There were no flowers in Mrs. Schulte's garden, only a few scraggly bushes and a plastic bucket and shovel likely intended for digging in beach sand rather than potting soil.

He heard a click behind him—the dead bolt releasing—then the sound of the door opening.

"Why are you sitting on my porch in the rain?" Lauryn asked wearily.

He stood up and turned. Though her sweetly curved mouth was unsmiling and her soft gray-green eyes were filled with suspicion, neither detracted from her beauty. But he'd known a lot of beautiful women, and he wasn't going to be distracted from his task by an unexpected tug of attraction.

"Because you didn't invite me to come inside," he responded.

"And I'm not going to," she said firmly.

"Let's start at the top again," he suggested, with a hopeful smile. "My name is Ryder Wallace—I'm the host of WNCC's home improvement show *Ryder to the Rescue*."

She was unimpressed. "That still doesn't explain what you're doing here."

"I'm here to discuss the details of the work you want done, and it would be really great if you'd let me come in out of the rain to talk about it."

Though she was still frowning, she finally stepped away from the door to allow him entry.

"Do you have any coffee?" he asked hopefully.

"I thought you wanted to talk."

He smiled again. "Talking over a cup of coffee in the kitchen is so much friendlier than standing in the foyer."

"You're right," she said, "but I'm not feeling particularly friendly."

The little girl, who had been hiding behind her mother, peeked out at him now. "You can have tea wif me," she offered.

Lauryn sighed. "Kylie, what did Mama tell you about strangers?"

But the little girl shook her head. "He gave me flowers."

Ryder looked at the mom for an explanation, but she seemed equally confused by her daughter's statement.

"At the weddin'," Kylie clarified.

"My sister's wedding," he guessed, because it was the only one he'd attended recently.

Lauryn's puzzlement gave way to speculation. "Are you telling me that Avery Wallace is your sister?"

He nodded, confirming his relationship to the obstetrician who had recently married Justin Garrett, another doctor at Charisma's Mercy Hospital.

"Okay," she finally—reluctantly—relented. "I guess I can offer you a cup of coffee."

"Were you at the wedding?" he asked, following mother and daughter through the hallway to the kitchen he recognized from the photos she'd submitted with her application.

She shook her head. "No. Zachary—" she glanced at the baby in the playpen, playing with colorful plastic rings "—was running a bit of a fever, so we stayed home. Kylie went with my parents. And when you caught the bride's bouquet—"

"Avery threw it at me," he felt compelled to point out in his defense. "It was an automatic reflex."

She shrugged, as if the details were unimportant, and set a filter into the basket of the coffeemaker on the counter—the only modern appliance visible in the whole room.

"And when you caught the bouquet," she said again, measuring grounds into the filter, "you gave the flowers to Kylie."

He looked at the little girl in the frilly nightgown and finally remembered. "You were wearing a dark blue dress?"

Kylie smiled and nodded.

"Then you must be related to Justin," he said to Lauryn.

"He's my cousin," she admitted. "Our fathers are brothers."

"Small world," he mused, wondering if the loose familial connection would help or hinder his case.

"Small town," she corrected, handing him the mug of coffee. "Cream or sugar?"

"Sugar, please."

She offered him the sugar bowl and a spoon so he could fix it the way he liked it.

As he did, he asked, "Why do I get the impression that you changed your mind about being on the show?"

"What are you talking about?"

He frowned at the genuine bafflement in her tone. "You applied for a Room Rescue from *Ryder to the Rescue*."

"My sister Tristyn is addicted to the show, but I don't think I've ever seen it," she told him. "I don't have time to watch a lot of television, and when I do, it's usually *Nick Jr.*"

He acknowledged that with a nod. "So was it your sister who told you about the Room Rescue contest?"

She shook her head. "I honestly don't know anything about a contest."

He pulled the application out of his pocket and passed it across the table as Kylie tugged on her mother's arm and whispered something close to her ear.

"Yes, you can go up to your room to play for a little while," she said, and her daughter skipped off.

Lauryn unfolded the page and immediately began skimming the document, her brows furrowing. She finished reading and set the page down. "Well, it's all true," she admitted. "Except that I didn't send this in."

He pointed to the signature box. "That's not you?"

"It's my name—and a pretty good replica of my signature, which leads me to believe that one or both of my sisters filled out the application."

He winced. "The application is a contract, so I'll pretend I didn't hear you say that, then my director won't want to get our legal department involved."

"Can't you just tell him that I changed my mind?" she suggested hopefully.

"I don't understand," he admitted. "Most people would be thrilled by the prospect of a brand-new kitchen."

She looked around the dull and outdated room. "Rob had plans for this space—new cabinets, granite counter, ceramic floor."

"We can certainly consult with your husband about the design," he offered, attempting to appease her.

She shook her head. "He's not here."

"When will he be back?"

"Well, he left nine months ago, so I don't expect him to return anytime soon."

"I'm sorry," he said automatically.

"Don't be," she said. "I'm not."

He took a moment to regroup and reconsider his strategy. "Then forget about his plans," he urged. "What do *you* want?"

Lauryn stood up to lift the now-fussing baby from his playpen. "I don't even know where to begin to answer that question."

Opening a cupboard, she took a cookie out of a box. The little guy reached for it eagerly and immediately began gnawing on it.

Kylie returned to the kitchen, walking past the table to the back door, where she shoved her feet into a pair of pink rain boots.

"I told you we could go to the park later," Lauryn reminded her daughter. "You're supposed to be playing in your room now."

The little girl nodded. "But it's wainin' in the castle."

Her mother frowned. "What do you mean 'it's raining in the castle'? The rain is outside, honey."

This time Kylie shook her head. "The wain's on my bed."

Lauryn pushed back her chair and, with the baby propped on her hip, raced down the narrow hallway and up the stairs.

Instinctively, Ryder followed.

She stood in the doorway of what was obviously her daughter's bedroom, staring at the water dripping from the ceiling onto the little girl's bed. And puddling beside her tall dresser. And in front of her closet.

Her bottom lip trembled as she fought to hold back the tears that now filled her eyes.

"Why's it wainin' inside, Mama?" Kylie asked.

"Because it wasn't a crappy enough day already," her mother muttered in weary response.

The little girl gasped. "You said a bad word."

"Yes, I did," she admitted.

"Where's your attic access?" Ryder asked her.

"My bedroom," she told him.

He followed her across the hall. She reached for the loop of white rope in the ceiling. Of course, even on tiptoe, her fingertips barely brushed the rope. He easily reached up to grasp the handle and pull down the stairs.

She looked up into the yawning darkness overhead. "I can't remember the last time I was up there," she admitted. "I don't even know if there's a light."

Even if there was, there was also water coming into the house and Ryder wasn't willing to take a chance on forty-year-old wiring. Instead, he pulled the flashlight from his tool belt, switched on the beam and began his ascent.

It was a fairly typical attic—with a wide-planked floor over the joists of the ceiling below so that he didn't have to worry about where he stepped. A tiny window at each end illuminated dust and cobwebs along with various boxes and some old furniture. He lifted the beam of light to the ceiling and noted the distinct wet patches that showed him where the rain was coming in.

He walked back to the access and called down to Lauryn. "Can you get me some old towels and buckets?"

"I only have one bucket," she told him.

"Wastebaskets or big pasta pots would work."

She nodded and disappeared to gather the required items while he continued his inspection of the attic ceiling.

"Why's it wainin' in the castle?"

The little voice, so unexpected and close behind him, made Ryder start.

"How did you get up here?" he demanded.

"I comed up the ladder," Kylie told him.

"I'm not sure your mom would want you climbing up ladders when she's not around."

"Why's it wainin' in the castle?" she asked again, a little impatiently this time.

"There's a hole in the roof," he explained, shining the light to show her where the water was coming in. "Actually, a few holes."

"You fix it?"

"Yeah, I can fix it," he said, and was rewarded with a smile that lit up the dim space and tugged at his heart.

"Kylie?" her mother shouted out from below, her voice panicky. "Kylie—where are you?"

"She's with me," Ryder called down, taking the little girl's hand to lead her back to the stairs.

Though Kylie had bravely made the climb up, the sudden death grip on his hand as they approached the opening warned him that she wasn't so keen about going down again.

"Do you want me to carry you?" he asked her.

Eyes wide, she nodded quickly.

Her arms immediately went around his neck when he scooped her up. And in that moment, that quickly, he fell for this brave and terrified little girl who so openly and willingly placed her trust in him.

Lauryn was reaching for her daughter even before he hit the last step, simultaneously hugging her tight and chastising her for disappearing. Ryder left her to that task while he picked up the items she'd gathered and returned to the attic.

It didn't take him long to direct the water from the various points of origin into the bucket and pots she'd supplied. Of course, that would only contain the rain, not stop it from coming in, but it was the best he could do for now.

When he came back downstairs, the baby had fallen asleep in his crib, Kylie was dressed and Lauryn was tying a ribbon in her daughter's hair. The puddles in the little girl's room had been mopped up, and plastic bowls put in place to capture any more water that leaked through.

Ryder took a moment to look around the room and appreciate the detailed painting on the walls that he'd barely noticed earlier. "Did you do this?"

Lauryn shook her head. "My sister did."

"It's incredible," he said.

"Jordyn is incredibly talented." She looked worriedly at the ceiling, where a dragon flew in the sky above the castle walls.

"It won't take much to touch up after the roof is fixed."

She nodded, though she didn't look reassured.

In fact, she looked as if she had the weight of the enormous dragon—and entire fairy-tale kingdom—resting on her narrow shoulders.

Damn, but he'd always been a sucker for a damsel in distress. And this damsel had a lot more distress than she seemed to be able to handle right now.

"In the interim, I could put tarps up on the roof to give you some extra protection," he offered.

But she squared her shoulders and turned to face him. "You've done enough already, thanks. And now, I really need you to go so that I can run my errands."

"Do you want me to recommend a good roofer?"

"No, thanks," she said. "I've got someone who came out once before."

"If your roof is still leaking, maybe you need somebody different," he suggested.

Her cheeks flushed. "He warned me that I would need to redo the whole roof."

"When was that?"

"April," she admitted.

"You were told, *five months ago*, that you needed a new roof, and you haven't done anything about it?" he asked incredulously.

She lifted her chin. "Not that I owe you any explanations, but I've been kind of busy trying to take care of my two kids and run the business that my husband walked away from."

"I wasn't implying that you should have climbed up onto the roof to strip and reapply shingles yourself, just that you should have scheduled the work to be done."

"And I would have," she said. "But in my experience, most people generally want to be paid for the work that they do."

And that was when he realized she hadn't been neglectful— she couldn't afford a new roof. Obviously, he didn't have any details about her financial situation, but he suspected that she'd just given him the leverage he needed to secure her cooperation for the show.

"That's usually the way those things work," he acknowledged. "But, sometimes, other arrangements can be made."

She narrowed her gaze. "I really think you should go now."

He held up his hands in mock surrender. "I wasn't suggesting anything inappropriate," he assured her. "It seems apparent that, as much as you'd like a new kitchen, there are other issues that require more immediate attention."

"Your observational skills must be why your name is in the title of the show," she remarked dryly.

"And I know you're reluctant to participate in the show—"

"I'm not reluctant," she denied. "I'm refusing."

"But why?"

"Because this isn't a television studio, it's my home," she told him. "Maybe there are some things that I'd like to change and other things that need to be changed—like the roof—but I have no desire to open up the doors and let your camera crews dissect my personal space for your television viewers."

"You'd get a brand-new kitchen," he reminded her.

She shook her head stubbornly. "I don't need a new kitchen that desperately."

"But you do need a new roof—and I can get you that, too. In fact, we can specify whatever home improvements you want in the contract."

For the first time, he saw a hint of interest in her gray-green eyes. "You can really get my roof fixed?"

"Yes, I can," he assured her.

"What will it cost me?"

"Not a dime. We have a generous budget, as well as numerous sponsors and endorsement deals that will cover everything. *If*," he said, clearly emphasizing the word, "you agree to appear on the show."

He could see her weighing the pros and cons in her mind. In the end, practicality triumphed.

"When can you start?"

Chapter Three

Ryder left shortly after that, promising to have the contract revised to reflect the terms of their verbal agreement.

Lauryn still had some concerns, but she pushed them aside and packed the kids into the van to take them to her parents' house before her appointment with Howard Greenbaum, the loans manager at the bank. Howard and her father were old friends and she'd known the man since she was a little girl. She also knew that Howard would never let that long-term friendship affect any decisions that had to be made on the job—a fact that he confirmed before she left the bank.

When Lauryn returned to her childhood home, Zachary was napping in his playpen and Kylie was playing with some of her mother's old dolls in front of the television in the living room—keeping Grandpa company while he watched his favorite afternoon game shows. Looking at her children now, everything seemed so normal, so right. But she was suddenly and painfully aware of how quickly their situation could change.

Still, she was lucky. She knew that no matter what else happened, her parents would never let her kids go hungry or sleep on a park bench. And while there was undoubtedly some comfort in that realization, she wanted to provide for her own family—even if she was becoming increasingly doubtful that she could.

"Is everything okay?" Susan Garrett asked when Lauryn made her way to the kitchen, where her mother was tidying up after baking cookies.

She could only shake her head.

"Do you want to talk about it?" her mother prompted.

She shook her head again, then let out a sigh.

"Actually I do," she admitted. "But if I talk about it, I'll fall apart, and I don't want Kylie to see me fall apart."

Susan pulled a glass from the cupboard, filled it with milk, then set the drink and a plate of chocolate-chip cookies on the table and instructed her daughter to sit.

So Lauryn did. And, unable to resist, she reached for a cookie and broke off a piece. The still-warm morsel flooded her mouth with the flavor of her childhood and made her yearn—almost desperately—for those simpler times when her mother could make all of her troubles go away. But she was the mother now; she had to handle her own troubles and make things right for her children.

"Are there problems at The Locker Room?" Susan asked, aware that Lauryn was trying to pull the sporting goods store back from the brink of financial disaster.

She managed a wry smile. "Aren't there always?"

"Then something else—something more—is weighing on your mind," her mother noted. "Have you heard from Rob?"

She shook her head. "Not a single word. And believe me, that's a relief not a disappointment."

"I can understand that," Susan acknowledged. "What I can't understand is how he could walk away from his children. Regardless of what happened between the two of you, he's their father."

"Apparently, that title doesn't mean the same thing to all men," Lauryn noted.

"Has Kylie asked about him lately?"

She shook her head. "Not in a while."

"Maybe that's for the best," her mother said.

"I'm sure she misses him," Lauryn said, then reconsidered. "Or maybe not. Even when he was around, he wasn't much of a hands-on dad."

"So if you're not worried about Rob," Susan prompted.

"I've just got a lot on my mind."

"If there's anything I can do to help, you know—"

"I do know," Lauryn interjected. "But you already do so much."

Her mother seemed genuinely surprised by that. "What do I do?"

"You look after Kylie and Zachary whenever I need you to."

"Honey, that's not a favor to you but a treat for me," Susan told her.

"I love you for saying that, but I know my kids—they're not always a treat."

"They are for their grandparents," her mother insisted.

Lauryn managed a smile. "They're so lucky to have both of you. *I'm* so lucky to have both of you."

Susan lifted a hand to brush her daughter's bangs away from her eyes. "Can you stay for dinner?"

Of course, they could. And no doubt, whatever her mother had planned for the evening meal would be better than the meat loaf Lauryn had thrown together that morning. But her parents had already been with the kids for four hours, fed them lunch and probably numerous snacks.

"Thanks, but I've got dinner ready to go in the oven at home."

"We're having roast pork with fingerling potatoes and green beans," Susan said in a final attempt at persuasion.

"Enjoy," Lauryn said, kissing her mother's cheek.

When the rain finally stopped early in the afternoon, Ryder loaded up the necessary supplies and headed back to the Schulte residence. It wouldn't take him long to tack down the tarps, and since Lauryn had said she had errands to run, he expected to complete the task and be gone before she returned.

He didn't quite make it. He was securing his ladder into the bed of his truck when she pulled an aging minivan into the driveway beside his truck.

The Garretts were one of the wealthiest and most well-known families in Charisma. Of course, Lauryn's last name was different, which was why he hadn't immediately made the connection, but as soon as Kylie had mentioned the flowers and the wedding, he'd started to put the pieces together into a more complete picture. But there were still big, gaping holes in the form of the ancient van, leaking roof and outdated kitchen. He finished the tying down while she got the kids out of the vehicle and decided that, sooner or later, he would fill those holes.

He noticed that she'd changed out of the yellow T-shirt and jeans into a slim-fitting navy skirt and jacket and tucked her feet into high-heeled sandals. He also noticed that she had some pretty nice curves beneath the buttoned-up suit.

He shook his head, as if that might dislodge the unwelcome thought from his brain. She was his client—and if he expected to be able to work with her, he had no business ogling her. Not to mention that she really wasn't his type. He preferred uncomplicated women and simple relationships—a single mother, no matter how beautiful and desirable, didn't fit that criteria.

"What are you doing here, Mr. Wallace?" she asked.

"Ryder," he reminded her.

"What are you doing here, *Ryder*?"

He smiled at the pique in her tone. "I took advantage of the break in the weather to put some tarps up."

Her gaze shifted to the roof of the house. "You didn't have to do that," she protested.

"I wanted to make sure you wouldn't get any more rain in the castle," he said, winking at Kylie. "And give the wood a chance to dry out so that it will be ready when the roofers are."

"You're really going to get my roof fixed?"

"I said I would," he reminded her.

She nodded. "Rob used to say a lot of things, too," she admitted. "But he didn't follow through on many of them."

"Home renovations aren't as easy as a lot of people think," he said, even as he wondered what had gone wrong in her marriage and if she was still hung up on her ex-husband.

"Well, thanks for putting up the tarps." She started to move past him toward the house.

"Since we're going to be spending a lot of time together over the next few weeks, you might want to ease up on the hostility a little," he suggested.

"I'm not—" She blew out a breath and shook her head. "I'm sorry. It's been a really bad day and I'm taking it out on you, and after you went out of your way to help me out—which I do appreciate."

"You're welcome."

She started toward the door again, then hesitated. "Are you one of those people who drinks coffee all day?"

He smiled. "Is that a roundabout way of offering me a cup?"

She shrugged. "It seems the least I can do—if you're interested."

Yeah, he was interested, and apparently in more than just the hot beverage she was offering. The tug of attraction he felt for the home owner was more than a little disconcerting because, aside from the fact that single mothers weren't his type, Ryder had a very strict rule against mixing business with pleasure. If he was smart, he'd say, *Thanks, but no thanks*, climb into his truck and head home. Maybe he'd even return Holly's call and accept her offer of dinner—and dessert. His occasional friend-with-benefits was fun and single and, most importantly, she'd never asked for anything more than he was willing to give. Yes, he should definitely call Holly back.

"Coffee would be great," he said instead.

Lauryn led him into the house. After setting Zachary in his playpen, she started the coffee brewing.

"I wanna dwink, too," Kylie said, retrieving a juice box from the fridge.

"Okay," Lauryn agreed, unwrapping the straw and inserting it into the top of the box.

The little girl took a sip, then set it aside. "Cookie?"

This time her mother shook her head. "You already had cookies at Grandma's."

So Kylie turned her attention to Ryder. "Cookie?" she asked hopefully, adding a smile for good measure.

He chuckled. "Sorry—I don't have any cookies."

The little girl pouted.

"Your coloring book and crayons are still on the table in the living room," Lauryn told her daughter.

With an exaggerated sigh, Kylie turned toward the living room.

"You're going to have your hands full with that one," Ryder said to Lauryn.

"They're full enough already," she admitted, setting a mug of coffee and the sugar in front of him.

"How old is she?"

"Three and a half."

"And the little guy?" he asked, glancing at the playpen where the baby had managed to pull himself to his feet and was gnawing on the frame.

Lauryn's gaze followed his as she sat down across from him with her own mug. "Seven months and—as you can see—teething."

He frowned. "Didn't you say your husband left nine months ago?"

"I did," she confirmed.

"It must have been hard on you—having the baby without him," he noted.

She shrugged. "My sister Tristyn was there."

"The one who forged your signature on the application?"

"I thought we were going to pretend I didn't tell you that."

"We were," he acknowledged. "But then I thought that we might be able to use your sisters in the introductory segment—put them in front of the cameras and let them explain why they wanted this renovation for you."

"They'd probably love that," she said. "But Tristyn's job requires her to travel a lot, so it would depend on when you planned to film the segment."

"Monday," he told her.

"Monday—as in five days from now?"

"Is that a problem?"

"No," she admitted. "I mean—I'm still not entirely comfortable with this, but I guess Monday is as good a day as any to begin."

"Do you think your sisters can be here?" he asked.

She shrugged again. "It shouldn't be a problem. Besides, they owe me—even if they don't know it yet."

"Hopefully, by the time we're done, you'll be thanking rather than blaming them," he told her.

"Hopefully," she agreed, then sighed when she saw Kylie slip back into the room and open a cupboard beside the fridge. "No more cookies."

"But I'm hungwy."

Lauryn stood up and moved to the stove, twisting a knob to turn it on. "Dinner won't be too long," she promised.

She took a yogurt tube out of the fridge and snipped off the top.

"Is Mister Wyder gonna have dinner wif us?" Kylie asked, taking the tube from her.

"Oh. Um." She felt her cheeks flush as she delicately tried to wiggle out of the awkward position her daughter had put her in. "I'm sure Ryder already has plans for dinner."

Kylie turned to him. "Do you?"

"Actually, I don't have plans," he told her.

"You have dinner wif us?" she asked again.

His gaze shifted from the little girl to her mother. "What are you cooking?"

"Meat loaf," she told him, taking the already prepared pan from the refrigerator and sliding it into the oven. "With a side of mac and cheese and salad."

She hadn't planned on adding macaroni and cheese to the meal, but she wasn't sure that the meat loaf and salad would stretch far enough to feed all of them if he decided to stay.

"Sounds good," he decided.

She eyed him skeptically. "Really?"

He smiled, and she felt an unexpected warmth spread through her veins. "Well, it sounds a lot better than the pizza I probably would have ordered at home."

"I like pizza," Kylie told him.

"So do I," he admitted. "But it gets kind of monotonous when you eat it four or five times a week."

"What's mon-tin-us?"

"Monotonous," he said again, enunciating clearly. "And it means boring."

Lauryn took a pot out of the cupboard and filled it with water, then set it on the stove to boil.

Although she would have been able to get two meals out of the meat loaf if she was only feeding herself and the kids, she was glad he was staying. She'd had a really crappy day and while she certainly wouldn't have sought out any company, she was grateful for the distraction. Because as long as Ryder was there, she didn't have to think about how spectacularly she'd screwed up her life or try to figure out how she was supposed to put all of the broken pieces back together again. As an added bonus, he was great with her kids—and, she admitted to herself, really nice to look at.

"Can I help with anything?" Ryder offered.

She shook her head. "The salad is in the fridge, the meat loaf is in the oven, and the mac and cheese will only take ten minutes after the water boils. But if you'll excuse me for a minute, I'm just going to run upstairs to change into something more forgiving of sticky fingers."

Ryder nodded.

She was gone less than three minutes, exchanging her dry-clean-only business attire for a comfortable pair of faded jeans and a peasant-style blouse. When she returned to the kitchen, he was refilling his mug of coffee from the pot.

She picked up her own abandoned cup and sat down across from him.

Ryder ran his fingers over the surface of the table. He had really great hands—a workman's hands—strong and capable. "I noticed you've got a lot of quality furniture inside this house with the leaky roof, falling-down porch and ugly kitchen."

"I took advantage of the employee discount at Garrett Furniture," she told him.

He lifted a brow. "Not the family discount?"

"I didn't think it would take you too long to figure it out after Kylie mentioned Justin and Avery's wedding."

"Did you want it to remain a secret?" he asked.

She sipped her coffee. "No. But I don't want the Garrett name used on the show."

"Why not?"

Because she was embarrassed enough about her financial situation, and the last thing she wanted was to cause embarrassment to her family. She knew it wasn't easy for her parents to overlook all of the work that needed to be done in her home. More than once, her father had offered to call a handyman friend to fix the leaky plumbing in the kitchen, to replace some questionable boards in the front porch, to secure the wobbly ceiling fan in the master bedroom. Every time, Lauryn had refused because her husband had promised to take care of the problems.

It was harder to turn away her cousins when they showed up at the door, as Andrew and Nathan had done a few times. It was thanks to them that she had a secure handrail leading to the laundry room in the basement and shelves in the nursery. And the new locks on the doors were courtesy of Daniel, who had installed them within hours of learning that Rob had walked out on his family. Not that she intended to admit any of that to the man seated across the table from her now.

"Can't you just respect my wishes on this?" she finally said.

He considered for a minute, then nodded. "Okay."

"Well, that was easy," she said both grateful and a little dubious.

"Did you expect me to be difficult?"

"You weren't nearly as agreeable when I asked you to get off my property this morning," she reminded him.

"I know you're not thrilled about being part of the show, but everything will go much more smoothly if you accept that we're on the same team," he told her.

"Are we?"

"Why do you doubt it?"

She shrugged. "A lot of so-called reality-TV shows are all about the conflict and drama."

"Maybe you should watch a few episodes of *Ryder to the Rescue* before you sign the contract," he advised.

"Maybe I will," she agreed.

"In the meantime—" he nodded toward the stove "—your water is boiling."

She hurried to open the window above the sink, to let the steamy air escape, because the range fan didn't work. Then she opened the box of macaroni and dumped the noodles into the pot.

Ryder found plates and cutlery and set the table. She started to tell him that she would do it, because she was accustomed to doing everything on her own, then she decided that it was nice—at least this once—to have some help. Besides, while she finished the preparations for dinner, she was able to watch him move around her kitchen— and she really liked watching him move.

After making the pasta sauce, she called Kylie for dinner, then dished up her food while the little girl was washing up. She cut up some meat for Zachary and added a spoonful of macaroni, then slid his plate into the freezer while she settled him into his high chair and buckled the belt around his middle. Kylie had already climbed into her booster seat and was shoveling spoonfuls of macaroni and cheese into her mouth.

"Ketchup, please."

Lauryn grabbed the bottle of ketchup from the fridge, shook it up and squirted a dollop onto her daughter's plate—close to but not touching the meat—then set the bottle on the table.

"Umm umm," Zachary was making his hungry noises and reaching toward his sister's plate.

"Yours is just cooling off," Lauryn promised, offering a sippy cup of milk to tide him over.

He immediately put the spout in his mouth, took a drink, then tossed the cup aside. "Umm umm," he demanded.

Holding back a sigh, she bent to retrieve it, but Ryder had already scooped it off the floor and set it on the table.

It was then she noticed that his fork was still beside his plate, his food untouched.

"Please don't wait for me," Lauryn told him. "Your dinner will get cold if you do."

"No colder than yours," he pointed out.

She opened the door of the freezer to check on Zachary's meal. "I'm used to it. Sometimes the kids are finished before I get a chance to start."

Satisfied with the temperature of the baby's food, she set the plate in front of him. Zachary, like his sister, did not stand on ceremony but immediately shoved a hand into the macaroni.

Lauryn uncurled his fingers and wrapped them around the handle of the spoon she'd given to him. He held on to the utensil, then used the other hand to pick up a piece of meat. Shaking her head, she sat down at her plate and wiped her fingers on a napkin.

Only when she was seated did Ryder pick up his own fork. Not even her husband had ever waited for her to sit down before digging into his own meal, but she pushed that memory aside.

She'd taken the first bite of her dinner when the sky suddenly grew dark and she heard the rumble of thunder in the distance. But it was distant—far, far away, she assured herself, stabbing her fork into a piece of meat just as the skies opened up and rain poured down.

She pushed the meat around until Ryder reached across the table and put his hand over hers. She jolted at the unexpected contact, her fork slipping from her fingers and clattering against the edge of her plate, but he didn't pull his hand away.

"The tarps will hold," he told her.

She nodded, grateful for his reassurance and a little unnerved that this man, whom she'd met only hours earlier, had so easily followed the direction of her thoughts. Even more unnerving was the way her skin had warmed and her pulse had leaped in response to his touch.

She slowly drew her hand away. "Did you want more meat loaf?"

"I wouldn't mind another slice."

She pushed away from the table and reached for his plate.

"I can get it," he told her.

"More milk, please," Kylie said, lifting up her empty cup.

"I can get that, too," Ryder said, when she started to rise again.

Settling back in her seat, Lauryn forced herself to take another bite of her dinner. She blamed the rain for her loss of appetite, because she was worried about potential new leaks.

But she was more worried about the sudden and unexpected tingles she'd felt all the way to her toes when Ryder touched her.

Chapter Four

Meat loaf and macaroni and cheese seemed to Ryder like a traditional family meal, but he couldn't be certain. He'd grown up in a family that was anything but traditional, with two parents who spent more time at their respective jobs than at home and happily abdicated responsibility for the upbringing of their children to the nanny.

He and Avery had been lucky there, because Hennie had been wonderful. Right up until Ryder was twelve and Avery fifteen, when George and Cristina—long divorced but still making such decisions together—had concluded that their children didn't need a caregiver anymore.

Spending time with Lauryn and her children was almost like entering a whole new world—and not one in which he felt entirely comfortable. He was accustomed to eating alone, and usually in front of the television. Except when his sister took pity on him and invited him over for a meal. He appreciated those invitations for a lot of reasons, not the least of which was that Avery was a fabulous cook. He also suspected that those invitations would be fewer and further between now that his sister had a husband and a baby.

By the time Zachary had finished all of his meat and noodles, his face and fingers were covered with cheese sauce. He even had bits of ground beef and macaroni in his hair.

"I think someone needs a bath," Lauryn said, when she took his empty plate away.

"Zach!" Kylie declared.

"Well, Zachary's going to get his first," her mother agreed.

"Why don't Kylie and I tidy up the kitchen while you clean up the little guy?" Ryder suggested.

"You don't have to do that," she protested.

"I don't mind," he told her, because it seemed only fair that he should do something to show his appreciation for the delicious meal. On the other hand, he couldn't deny there was a part of him that was itching to make his escape from this unfamiliar yet somehow temptingly cozy situation.

The whole dinner scene had been a little too domestic for him—and a lot outside his comfort zone. Being around the sexy single mom and her adorable kids was creating some unfamiliar and unwelcome feelings.

Attraction was a simple emotion, and he had no trouble recognizing and acknowledging his attraction to Lauryn. It was the other stuff that was getting all tangled up inside of him. Because aside from the fact that she turned him on, there were a lot of reasons that he simply liked her. She was smart and warm and kind, and it was readily obvious that she doted on her kids.

And that was the crux of the problem right there—she had children. Children were a complication and Ryder didn't want complications in his life. At least he never had before.

But since his sister had gotten married and had had her baby and he'd seen how those new bonds had enriched her life, he'd begun to wonder if there wasn't something to be said for familial connections.

He'd always admired Avery's intelligence and drive and ambition. But since she'd fallen in love with Justin Garrett, he saw something in her that he hadn't before: joy. It was almost as if there had been a piece missing from her life, but she'd never known it until she met him.

Ryder wasn't looking for anyone to complete him. He was perfectly content with his life. Yet, spending time with

Lauryn and Kylie and Zachary tonight, he found himself wondering if maybe he wasn't ready for something more.

Uncomfortable with those feelings, he pushed them aside to be considered at a later date—or preferably not at all.

"I think you should stop arguing with me," he said to Lauryn now, "and get Zachary in the bath before he falls asleep in his high chair."

She shifted her attention to the baby, whose chin was against his chest, his eyelids visibly drooping. "That's a good plan," she agreed, unhooking the tray and then lifting him out of his seat.

As soon as she picked him up, Zachary rubbed his face against her shoulder, leaving a smear of cheese sauce on her shirt. Lauryn either didn't notice or didn't care, and for some reason he found that incredibly appealing.

Most of the women he'd dated over the past few years had been preoccupied with their clothes and hair and makeup, and he found it tiresome to date a woman who rushed off to reapply her lipstick after a meal or was constantly fluffing her hair or adjusting her hemlines. Of course, he'd never dated someone with kids, and he suspected it was natural for a woman's priorities to change when she became a mother—his own being an obvious exception.

Kids were loud and messy and demanding, and he already knew that was true of both Kylie and Zachary. They were also innocent and trusting and adorable. And while he'd been immediately charmed by the little girl who was full of energy and curiosity, and undoubtedly intrigued by the little boy who seemed to see everything but say nothing, he decided that it would be smart to take a step back. Maybe even two.

Because Lauryn and Kylie and Zachary were a family, and he was a contented bachelor with no desire to change that status.

Wasn't he?

* * *

At eleven o'clock on Saturday, Lauryn met both of her sisters at the Morning Glory Café for brunch. After Lauryn had married Rob, she'd discovered that she didn't get to see Jordyn and Tristyn nearly as often as she used to, and that was how the monthly "Sisters' Saturday" tradition began.

"I had an interesting visitor Wednesday morning," Lauryn said, sprinkling pepper on the home fries that accompanied her scrambled eggs and sausage.

"Who?" Jordyn asked, drowning her pancakes in syrup.

"Can't you guess?"

Tristyn stabbed a piece of melon with her fork. "Is it someone that we know?"

"It turns out that there is a loose familial connection."

"Now you've piqued my curiosity," Jordyn admitted.

"Ryder Wallace."

Tristyn's fork slipped from her fingers. *"Ryder to the Rescue?"*

Lauryn nodded. "Apparently the home renovation expert is Justin's new wife's brother."

"I knew that," Tristyn admitted, picking up her utensil again.

"But why was he at your house?" Jordyn asked, her tone equal parts curious and cautious as she cut into a pancake.

"That's what I wondered—and then he told me that my application was selected as one of the grand prize winners in WNCC's Room Rescue contest."

"Oh, my God!" Tristyn practically squealed with delight. "That is *so* awesome."

"And surprising, considering that I never submitted an application," Lauryn pointed out. "In fact, I'd never even heard of the contest. So imagine my surprise when he showed me the application with my name and signature on it."

Her sisters exchanged a look.

"Actually, that's kind of a funny story," Jordyn began.

"I can't wait to hear it," Lauryn told her.

"Obviously you know it was us," Tristyn said, stirring her yogurt and granola. "And we're not going to apologize, because somebody had to do something."

"So why didn't you tell me?"

"Because we never expected that our—*your*—application would actually be chosen," Jordyn admitted.

"But it was," she pointed out. "And I felt like a complete idiot when Ryder Wallace showed up at my door and I had absolutely no idea why he was there."

"I can see how that might have been a little awkward," Jordyn conceded.

"It was more than a little awkward."

"Is he as hot in person as he is on TV?" Tristyn asked curiously.

She'd followed Ryder's advice and decided to watch a few episodes of his show. As a result, she could answer her sister's question sincerely. "Much hotter."

"Damn, I wish I'd been there."

Lauryn couldn't deny that there was an indescribable something about the man that any woman would find appealing. He was strong and sexy and incredibly charismatic, and after only a few hours in his company, she was halfway toward a serious infatuation. Of course, after being married to a man who didn't know how to hang a picture on the wall, it probably wasn't surprising that she'd be intrigued by a take-charge guy who owned his tools and knew how to use them. "You can be there Monday."

"What's Monday?" Jordyn asked, smiling her thanks to the waitress who refilled her mug with coffee.

"The whole crew is coming to the house on Monday and Ryder wants the two of you to explain, on camera, why you submitted the application for me," she told her sisters.

"Then he is going to remodel your kitchen?"

"And fix a few other things," she acknowledged.

"Why don't you sound more excited?" Tristyn asked. "You're finally going to get rid of those ugly cupboards and even uglier linoleum."

She swallowed a mouthful of eggs. "With the added bonus of a bunch of strangers traipsing through my house."

"They're not going to be there forever," Tristyn pointed out. "Just long enough to give you a fabulous kitchen makeover—which you've wanted since you bought that place."

"I know. But I thought…" She sighed. "I thought Rob and I would do it."

There was silence for a moment before Jordyn cautiously asked, "Do you…miss him?"

"No," she replied, a little ashamed to admit that it was true. But her ex-husband had stopped being a factor in her life long before he walked out on their marriage.

"Good."

Her eyes widened in response to the vehemence in her sister's tone.

"I'm sorry," Jordyn said. "But none of us ever thought he was good enough for you."

"I thought he was perfect—and I felt so lucky that he picked me."

"You *are* lucky," Tristyn said. "Because you got two wonderful kids out of the deal."

"And because you've got the two best sisters in the world," Jordyn chimed in.

Lauryn smiled. "You're right—on both counts."

"And you get to spend the afternoon at Serenity Spa with those sisters," Jordyn added.

She shook her head regretfully. "I'm sorry, I can't go today."

"What do you mean—you can't go?" Tristyn demanded.

"I don't have the time…or the money," she admitted.

"It's a Garrett sisters' tradition," Jordyn reminded her. "And we're not letting you skip out on it—*again*."

Lauryn looked away. "I appreciate what you're trying to do, but I had an appointment at the bank on Wednesday and discovered that my financial situation is even more dismal than I realized."

"How dismal?" Tristyn asked gently.

"The business is mortgaged to the hilt."

"But you knew that," Jordyn reminded her. "That's why you should sell it, or let the bank take it and all of the headaches that go with it."

"I was starting to see the benefits of that plan," Lauryn admitted. "Until I found out the business also has a secured line of credit."

Her sisters exchanged another look, this one confirming that they'd both guessed how it was secured.

Jordyn winced. "Oh, no."

"The house," Tristyn whispered.

Lauryn nodded and pushed her plate away, her appetite gone.

"But how is that possible?" Jordyn wondered. "Wouldn't Rob have needed you to sign any paperwork?"

"Signatures can be forged," Tristyn reminded her, looking guilty because they'd done exactly that for the Room Rescue.

"They can," Lauryn agreed. "But he didn't forge my signature."

"You didn't—you *wouldn't*—jeopardize your home," Jordyn asserted.

"You're right—I wouldn't. At least not knowingly. But I did sign the papers," she admitted. "Based on the date of the application, when Kylie was about three months old."

"And colicky," Tristyn remembered.

She nodded. "I remember Rob came home early one

day with flowers. That should have been a clue, because he never came home early. Or with flowers.

"He told me that the business was doing well, but there was some new vendor—I don't remember whether it was equipment or apparel—but they were offering him exclusive retail rights for the area if he could commit to carrying the entire line in his inventory. He said that he'd been to the bank to get a loan and, because he was married, they wanted my signature, too."

She looked away, embarrassed and ashamed that she'd been so foolish. "I just signed the papers where he told me to. I didn't even read them.

"And now—" she fought against the tears that burned behind her eyes "—if I let the bank foreclose on the business, they could take the house, too."

"Then we need to come up with a plan to save the business," Jordyn said.

"And since my brain functions much better when I'm relaxed, we'll brainstorm some ideas after the spa."

"I already told you, I can't—"

"You can't say no," Tristyn interjected. "Mom made all the arrangements—*and* paid for it."

Lauryn sighed. "She shouldn't have done that."

"She didn't just do it for you, but for all of us. Because she knows how much we all enjoy the monthly ritual."

Because it was true—and because she loved being with the women who weren't just her sisters but her best friends—Lauryn gave up her protest.

Sweet Serenity Boutique & Spa was located in a renovated three-story Colonial Revival home in Northbrook, offering different services on different levels. The three sisters were on the lower level now, continuing their conversation as they perused the selection of polishes for their pedicures.

"I had no idea things were as bad as they are at the store," Lauryn confided. "Rob didn't let me see the books. He said it was because he wanted to take care of the business, to prove that he could take care of us."

"And a piss-poor job he did of both," Jordyn said bluntly.

Lauryn could only nod. "But I loved him. Maybe I was naive but, for a long time, I really did love him."

"I know you did," Tristyn said sympathetically.

"And you'll fall in love again," Jordyn told her.

"Jesus, I hope not," Lauryn said.

Her recently—and happily—married sister frowned. "Why would you say something like that?"

"Because I have no desire to repeat past mistakes." She sipped from her glass of cucumber-and-lime-infused spring water.

"You wouldn't," Jordyn said confidently. "Your relationship with Rob was a learning experience."

"Most importantly, I learned that I don't need a man to complete my life."

"As if he ever did," Tristyn remarked dryly.

"I didn't think I'd fall in love again," Jordyn confided. "I didn't think I could. And then I met Marco."

Lauryn couldn't help but smile at that. Marco Palermo had fallen head over heels for Jordyn and immediately set his sights on winning her heart—not an easy task. Four years earlier, Jordyn had been only weeks away from her wedding when her fiancé was killed in a car crash. As a result, she'd put up all kinds of barriers around her heart, refusing to let any man get too close. Until Marco.

While he wasn't at all the type of guy that Lauryn would have expected to steal her sister's heart, he was absolutely perfect for her. And they were perfect together. Lauryn was thrilled for both of them, and just a little bit envious. Because when she was with Jordyn and Marco, she realized that she'd never shared that kind of soul-deep love and connection with her own husband. But even as she lamented that fact, she wasn't looking for the same thing now—she had more important concerns.

"I just want my kids to be safe and happy and know that I love them."

"They are and they do," Jordyn assured her. "And while that's a legitimate and even admirable goal, you can't live your life for your children."

"Why don't we table this discussion until you have kids of your own?" Lauryn's tone was a little harsher than she'd intended, but neither of her sisters really understood what she was going through. They couldn't know the joy that filled her heart every time she looked at her children—or how much pressure she felt always trying to do what was best for them.

Thankfully, Jordyn wasn't offended by her sharp retort. And the thought of a baby—Marco's baby—was enough to make her deep green eyes go all misty and dreamy.

Unfortunately, Tristyn wasn't so easily distracted. "But what do *you* want?" she asked Lauryn.

I want to not worry that my bank card is going to be declined at the gas station because I just bought diapers and formula.

Not that she would admit as much to her sisters. Telling them about the business was one thing; whining about her personal finances was something else entirely. Her mistakes were her own and she was determined to fix them on her own. Of course, now that the bank had rejected her proposal, her options had gone from limited to almost nonexistent, but she wasn't ready to give up yet.

"Well, I have been thinking about making some changes in my life," she finally confided. "Maybe dyeing my hair to test the old adage about blondes having more fun."

Her sisters exchanged a look, and she knew they were

both thinking of Roxi—the perky blonde yoga instructor that Lauryn's husband had run off with.

"Or red," she said, because the color didn't matter as much as the change it would symbolize.

Tristyn shook her head. "Do you remember when I went red—or tried to? It took my stylist three hours to undo what I'd done, and he made me promise that if I ever wanted a drastic change I would stick to the color on my toes."

Lauryn looked at the pale pink and white polishes she'd chosen for her standard French pedicure.

Tristyn handed her the bottle of sparkly purple that she'd selected. "Go wild," she advised. "But in a way that won't do any long-term damage."

Lauryn looked at the color—equal parts intrigued and wary—and decided it was time to step out of her comfort zone. At least a little.

Chapter Five

Ryder loved his job. Of course, he'd prefer doing it without cameras recording him every step of the way, but he'd long ago accepted that as a necessary trade-off for being able to do the work he wanted to do. *Ryder to the Rescue* was currently one of the top-rated programs at WNCC, with a viewership that continued to grow with each successive season, but Virginia Gennings, the producer, wanted to keep the show fresh and the Room Rescue contest was her latest brainstorm.

Ryder's only real objection had come when Owen had delegated the task of choosing the contest winners to him. Three winners out of more than nine hundred entries from as far away as Texas and Seattle, with requests that ranged from a modest bathroom rehab to the complete reconfiguration of a floor plan. Owen's criteria for selection: stories that would appeal to viewers. Which meant that Ryder's original plan—to put all of the entries in a box and draw three at random—fell by the wayside as he spent hours reading application after application, sorting them into three distinct groupings of Maybe, No and No Way in Hell.

The majority of applications that went into the third pile were those that included naked pictures and explicit offers to express appreciation for his work when the cameras were gone or, in one notable case, with the cameras still rolling. The requests for free renovations by home owners who could well afford to pay for the work they wanted done landed in the No file. And then there was the Maybe group, from which he selected the winners.

Lauryn Schulte's application had appealed to him for several reasons, including her reference to the husband who didn't have time to do the renovation. Because the existence of a husband meant it was much less likely that he'd have to fend off the attention of an overzealous fan—a sticky situation that was occurring more frequently, seemingly in direct correlation to the show's increasing popularity.

According to Virginia, Ryder was the whole package—smart, sexy, strong and charismatic—and the female viewership of *Ryder to the Rescue* was so high because women trusted him and wanted to invite him into their homes. But Ryder liked to keep his private life private. Okay, so maybe he did date a lot of women, but he didn't dish about any of them and he made it clear that if they dished, they were history. As a result, for the first few seasons that the show was on the air, he'd mostly managed to keep a low profile.

Until the previous spring when he'd agreed to help Carl, one of his cameramen, build a deck on the back of his house. It was a simple project—a few hours' work on a sunny Saturday afternoon—and he hadn't hesitated when Carl asked if he was available. But it was a sunny and *hot* Saturday afternoon, and it hadn't taken him long to decide to strip off his T-shirt, as the other guys had also done. But he was the only one whose name was in the title of the show, and one of Carl's wife's friends had snapped a photo of #shirtlessRyder #summerdays and tweeted it to all of her friends. Apparently, the damn photo had gone viral, resulting in an endless discussion on social media about his #yummymuscles. He'd been appalled when Carl sheepishly brought it to his attention; Virginia had been delighted.

Since then, he'd been heralded not just as America's Hottest Handyman but also the Sexiest Man on WNCC. As a result, he'd become the target of much female admiration and media attention. And when WNCC launched the Room Rescue contest and had let it be known that all applications would be personally reviewed by the show's host, it was an opportunity for women to throw their pictures and phone numbers at Ryder in the hopes that, even if he didn't bring his construction crew to their homes, he might call.

He didn't.

The first project chosen was a master suite reno for a young couple near Anderson, South Carolina. The second assignment took his crew to Montana to finish a basement apartment for the college freshman son of a forty-seven-year-old widow in Miles City. The final winning application was Lauryn's.

Kitchen and bathroom renovations tended to be popular because they directly added to the value of a home, providing a good return on investment when it came time to resell the property. As a result, he'd done a lot of kitchen upgrades and remodels on the show. And while he wasn't overjoyed at the thought of starting yet another one, he was happy to finally be back home and able to sleep in his own bed.

Of course, he now knew that one of the main factors that had weighed in favor of Lauryn's application was no longer valid—the husband who had never found the time to do the renovation work was gone from her life. On the other hand, her two children obviously kept her busy enough that he didn't anticipate she would be an impediment to the project. She'd also shown less than zero interest in his celebrity status or #yummymuscles, making it clear that the only reason he was being allowed access to her house was that she desperately needed the new roof he'd promised to provide.

So what was it about the single mother that made her so unforgettable? With her long, dark hair, creamy skin, gray-green eyes and perfectly sculpted mouth, she was undeniably beautiful, but he'd met a lot of beautiful women over the years without becoming fixated on any of them.

Or maybe his fascination was with the kids rather than their mother. Because when he looked at Kylie and Zachary, he couldn't help but think about his sister and himself and the scars that were a result of growing up in a broken home. But Kylie and Zachary had one clear advantage over Avery and Ryder: an amazing mother who, despite the weight of so many responsibilities on her slender shoulders, did everything she could to ensure her children felt loved and secure.

And they were great kids. Zachary was an adorable and affectionate child with big blue eyes that seemed to take everything in. Kylie was a dynamo with silky dark curls and the sweetest Cupid's-bow mouth that was always quick to smile. She was fearless enough to climb up an open staircase into a dark attic, smart enough to be uncertain about making the trip back down and trusting enough to let him carry her out again.

Her mother wasn't nearly as trusting—but maybe she had reasons to be wary, having been abandoned by her husband when she was pregnant with their second child. Not only that, he'd gotten the impression that she hadn't heard from the guy since. Ryder shook his head, wondering what kind of person walked out on his family. But why did he care? Why did he wish he could make things better for her? Especially when she'd given no indication that she wanted or needed anyone to take care of her.

Whatever the reasons, he was suddenly looking forward to this project a lot more than he'd expected.

After the spa, Lauryn and her sisters browsed a few of the local shops. Jordyn oohed and aahed over the jewelry display in Zahara's but didn't buy anything. She'd always loved fun and funky accessories, but since her marriage to

Marco, she rarely wore anything more than the rings he'd put on her finger.

"Look at this," Jordyn said, holding up a hanger with a purple satin demi-cup bra with matching bikini panties.

"Why do you need something like that? You're practically still on your honeymoon," Tristyn noted.

"I wasn't thinking for me, but for Lauryn."

She eyed the lingerie warily. "I don't think that's quite my style."

"The color matches your toenails," her sister pointed out.

"Which is proof that I've ventured far enough out of my comfort zone for today."

"I think Jordyn's right," Tristyn said. "You need to make a statement. Be bold. Be sexy."

"Who am I making a statement to?"

"Yourself," Jordyn said. "You're the only one who matters."

"I'm more of a white lace kind of girl," she told them.

"Because you like white lace or because Rob liked you in white lace?" Tristyn challenged.

Realizing that the answer to her sister's question was the latter, Lauryn impulsively grabbed the hanger from Jordyn's hand. "You're right—just because I've never worn purple satin doesn't mean that I shouldn't try it."

Tristyn handed her a red lace set. "Try this one, too."

After more shopping and dinner at Valentino's, Jordyn went home to her husband, but Tristyn convinced Lauryn—who wasn't in any hurry to go back to her empty house because the kids were spending the night with their grandparents—to go to Marg & Rita's for a drink. They arrived as another group was leaving and immediately snagged the just-vacated table by the bar.

Lauryn was sipping her second icy drink when Tristyn bobbled her own glass, nearly sloshing its contents over the rim.

"Ohmygod—he's here."

Lauryn glanced over her shoulder. "Who's here?"

Her sister sighed dreamily. "Hashtag yummy muscles."

She blinked. "Who?"

"We really need to get you on Twitter," Tristyn said, which didn't answer Lauryn's question at all. "Now he's at the bar."

She shifted her gaze, but there were so many people crowded around that area she still had no idea who was the focus of her sister's attention.

"Chatting with the fake blonde in the red dress," Tristyn told her.

She found the blonde in the red dress more easily and nodded in agreement with her sister's description. "Definitely fake."

Tristyn sighed. "Focus on the man."

Lauryn's gaze shifted again—and her heart actually skipped a beat when her gaze fell on Ryder Wallace.

"You *have* to introduce me. Please," her sister implored.

"You'll meet him on Monday," Lauryn reminded her.

Tristyn wiggled her eyebrows suggestively. "I want to meet him tonight and have breakfast with him in the morning."

She shook her head. "When are you going to realize that you spend so much time ogling other men because you don't want to admit that you have the hots for your boss?"

"Eww," Tristyn said. "My boss is our cousin."

"I was referring to the *other* half of Garrett-Slater Racing," she noted dryly.

"Josh Slater is *not* my boss," her sister said. "And I most assuredly do *not* have the hots for him."

Lauryn shrugged. "Go ahead—continue to live in denial."

Tristyn seemed happy enough to do that—and even happier still a minute later when she reached across the table to grab Lauryn's hand. "He's coming this way."

And only a few seconds later, he was standing beside their table.

Lauryn sighed, wondering how she'd gone so long without knowing who he was, and now it seemed that every time she turned around he was there. *"Ryder to the Rescue."*

She didn't know she'd spoken the words aloud until his lips curved.

"Actually, my last name is Wallace," he reminded her. "The 'to the Rescue' part is just for the show."

"I'm Tristyn," her sister said, offering her hand and a big smile. "And a huge fan of your show."

"It's a pleasure to meet you," he said, taking the proffered hand. "And this is my buddy, Dalton."

Lauryn hadn't even noticed the other man with Ryder, which proved she was as pathetic as her sister—only a little less obvious about it.

"Would it be all right if we joined you?" Ryder asked.

It would be rude to refuse when they were two people sitting at a table for four and there were no empty tables, but Lauryn was less interested in common courtesy than she was in self-preservation. The more time she spent in Ryder's company the more aware she was of him, and she definitely did not need to be crushing on the man who would be renovating her kitchen.

"Actually, you can have this table," she said. "We were just on our way out."

"No, we weren't," her sister immediately denied. "And yes, you can join us."

Ryder took the chair beside Lauryn; Dalton sat beside Tristyn. Although she suspected that her sister was a little disappointed by the seating arrangement, she didn't show it. She immediately started chatting with Ryder's friend—

who was, Lauryn finally noticed, almost as well-built and good-looking as America's Hottest Handyman.

"So what are you doing here?" she asked Ryder. "I would have thought Bar Down was more your style."

"And you'd be right," he confirmed. "But it was closed for a private party tonight."

She lifted her glass to her lips, frowning when she discovered it was empty. Before she could protest, Ryder had snagged the waitress to order another round of drinks for the table.

"We really should be going," Lauryn said, kicking her sister under the table. "It's getting late and—"

"And Kylie and Zachary are spending the night with their grandparents," Tristyn interjected.

Dalton seemed surprised by the revelation. "You have kids?"

Lauryn nodded. "Two of them."

"Husband?" he prompted.

"Not anymore."

"Hallelujah to that," Tristyn said, lifting her glass.

"My sister wasn't a fan," Lauryn noted dryly.

"What about you?" Tristyn asked Dalton. "Wife? Kids?"

He shook his head firmly. "Absolutely no entanglements."

"Good to know," Tristyn said, with a smile that conveyed a lot more than her words.

Which baffled Lauryn, because her sister had been all about Ryder until he actually came over to their table.

Ryder shifted a little closer to Lauryn to make room for the waitress who had returned with their drinks. As he did, his thigh brushed against hers, sending a jolt through her veins. Dalton took some bills out of his wallet as the waitress passed the drinks around. Lauryn immediately picked up her glass and took a long swallow of the icy liquid in a desperate attempt to cool her suddenly overheated body.

She pulled her phone out of her pocket, checked the screen.

"Expecting a call?" Ryder asked.

"Not really," she admitted. "But sometimes Kylie wakes up in the night looking for me. And this is Zachary's first sleepover because I was nursing him until a few weeks ago, when he started teething and it just got to be too painful to—" She broke off as heat flooded her cheeks. "And that was a little too much information."

Ryder just chuckled.

"I'm going to shut up now," she decided.

He touched her hand and she felt another jolt. "When I was four years old, my sister convinced me that I had a crack in my butt because the doctor dropped me when I was born."

She laughed at the outrageousness of the claim. "She did not."

"She did," he assured her solemnly. "And after that, every time I fell down, I was afraid parts of me would break off."

She shook her head, still smiling. "Why would you tell me something like that?"

"So that you wouldn't feel self-conscious about what you said. Now that you know something embarrassing about me, it levels the playing field."

"Do you always play fair?" she asked curiously.

His lips curved as he squeezed her hand gently before pulling his own away to pick up his beer. "Not always."

She wondered why it sounded more like a warning than an admission.

Chapter Six

After about an hour, Lauryn was forced to acknowledge that Ryder was more of a celebrity than she'd realized. During that time, several people—most of them female—had stopped by the table to say "hi" and tell him how much they enjoyed watching him on TV. Lauryn had assumed he would appreciate the attention, but she noticed that the ready smile on his lips wasn't reflected in his eyes. Apparently having legions of adoring fans could grow tiresome after a while.

Another frosty glass was set in front of her—was it her third? Fourth?—when she saw Dalton elbow his friend as the blonde in the red dress started toward their table. The woman looked a little unsteady and Ryder immediately murmured, "Excuse me," and rose to his feet to intercept her.

Lauryn sipped her drink as she watched him steer the woman toward the door and outside. He returned a few minutes later, giving a slight nod to his friend when he caught Dalton's eye.

"We've got to get an early start on a roofing job in the morning," Ryder said, winking at Lauryn, "so we're going to call it a night."

Dalton reluctantly pushed away from the table. "It was a pleasure meeting both of you."

Though his words encompassed both of them, Lauryn wasn't surprised that his gaze lingered on Tristyn. Her sister had that effect on a lot of men.

"Maybe we'll see you again," Tristyn said.

Dalton grinned. "I'm counting on it."

After Lauryn and Tristyn finished their drinks, they took a cab back to Lauryn's house. She lent her sister a pair of pajamas, and they crashed together in her bed like they'd done on many occasions in the past.

"If Jordyn was here, it would be just like old times," Tristyn noted.

"I don't remember my head spinning during those old times."

"It's the tequila," her sister told her.

"I don't drink tequila," Lauryn said. "Not since college."

"What do you think is in a margarita?"

She hadn't thought about it—she'd just enjoyed the sweet flavor of the pink lemonade margaritas. But thinking about it now elicited a regretful moan. "Tequila?"

"Yep."

Lauryn closed her eyes. "I guess I shouldn't drink margaritas, either."

She was almost drifting off to sleep before Tristyn spoke again. "Do you usually sleep in the middle now?"

"What?" She cracked open an eye to look at her sister.

"I assume you had a specific side of the bed when you shared it with Rob. I just wondered if you slept in the middle now that he's gone."

"We stopped sleeping together long before he walked out," she admitted. "He always claimed he fell asleep on the sofa, but I think that was just an excuse. In fact, I think the last time we had sex was when Zachary was conceived."

"You're kidding."

She shook her head, then grabbed the edge of the night table when the room spun around her. "He always blamed me for getting pregnant, as if it was something I'd done on my own."

Her sister was quiet for a minute, considering this information. "Did you ever suspect…that he was cheating on you?" she asked.

"After a few months without any physical connection, I started to wonder if maybe there was someone else," she admitted. "But I never asked, because I didn't want to know. Despite the obvious disconnect between us, I didn't want our marriage to be over."

"Have you had sex with anyone else since he left?"

"Of course not!"

"Why not?" Tristyn pressed.

"Because," she sputtered, so flustered by the question it took her a moment to come up with a more reasoned response. "I have two kids—I don't have the time or energy to even think about sex. And even if I had the time and the energy and a willing partner, I'm not exactly eager to bare a body that's not as tight or toned as it used to be."

"I saw you in that purple satin bra and undies—you look fabulous," Tristyn said loyally.

"And that's why you're my favorite sister tonight."

"I'm your favorite sister because I didn't make you come home alone to an empty house."

"I do appreciate that," Lauryn confirmed.

"Do you miss being married?" Tristyn asked curiously.

"No."

"Do you miss sex?"

Lauryn sighed. "I'm not even sure I remember what it is."

"We need to get you a Rabbit," her sister decided.

"Don't you think I have enough to keep me busy without adding a pet to the mix?"

Tristyn smirked. "I'm not referring to a furry bunny."

"What are you referring to?"

"A battery-operated adult toy."

She felt her cheeks burn. "I can't believe we're having this conversation."

"Sweetie, you've gone almost a year and a half without sex—that sure as heck can't be healthy."

"Things change when you have kids," Lauryn told her, a little defensively. "You don't have as much time for intimacy—or even the inclination."

"I don't believe it," Tristyn said. "If you're with the right guy, you find the time to be with him."

"Obviously, Rob wasn't the right guy," she said.

"Obviously," her sister agreed. "But he's been gone for almost nine months, and when I saw you with Ryder tonight, I got the distinct impression that he revs your engine."

Lauryn rolled her eyes. "You've been working in the racing industry for too long," she said, attempting to divert the conversation even as her thoughts drifted to Ryder and the completely unexpected—and unwelcome—tingles that danced over her skin whenever he was near.

"You're not denying it," Tristyn noted.

"I'm sure he revs the engine of every woman in America between the ages of seventeen and seventy."

"Undoubtedly," her sister agreed, then her tone became contemplative. "But while I've always found Ryder Wallace to be incredibly appealing, you're usually attracted to pretty boys."

"You think Rob was a pretty boy?"

"Just because I didn't like him doesn't mean I couldn't appreciate that he had a certain metrosexual appeal," Tristyn said. "Ryder Wallace is the complete opposite—a man's man. And the more I think about it, the more I think it might be interesting to stick around and watch the two of you together."

"We're not going to be together. He's going to renovate my kitchen and I'm going to keep the kids out of the way."

"That's disappointing."

"And anyway, he left the bar tonight with the blonde in the red dress."

"He walked out with her," Tristyn acknowledged. "But I don't think he went home with her."

"What makes you say that?"

"Because even as he was walking out the door, he was looking at you."

Lauryn squinted at her sister. "How many margaritas did you have?"

"He was looking at *you*," Tristyn said again. "And you were looking right back at him."

She sighed. "He is really nice to look at."

And with that thought and his image lingering in her mind, she finally drifted off to sleep.

Lauryn had never been much of a drinker. Even back in college, she rarely overindulged, and since becoming a mother, "rarely" became "never." She did enjoy the occasional glass of wine—sometimes even two, but the four cocktails she'd tossed back the night before were an unprecedented experience. And the banging inside her head the next morning confirmed it was an experience she could have lived without.

"What the hell?" Tristyn grumbled, her face buried in the pillow beside her.

Lauryn winced as her sister's words sliced through her skull like daggers. "Can you 'what the hell' a little more quietly, please?" she begged softly. "The pounding inside my head is punishment enough for last night."

"The pounding's not in your head," Tristyn told her. "I think it's on the roof."

Lauryn reluctantly pulled the covers off her face and pried open her eyelids to look at the ceiling, then frowned. "What the... Oh."

"Oh?" her sister prompted.

Throwing back the covers, she jumped out of bed, hurried down the stairs and out the front door. Heedless of the damp grass beneath her bare feet, she ventured into the middle of the lawn so that she could see the roof, holding up a hand to shield her eyes from the piercing glare of daylight.

The sun was behind him, outlining his impressive physique: incredibly broad shoulders stretching out a forest green T-shirt, strong arms tightly corded with muscle and lightly dusted with gold hair, long powerful legs hugged by faded denim.

Looking at him standing there, Lauryn's mouth actually went dry. Or maybe that was a residual effect of the tequila.

"Good morning." he called down, when he saw her looking up at him.

Her response was much less amiable. "What the hell are you doing on my roof, Ryder?"

Ryder knew he shouldn't stare, but the sight of Lauryn standing on the front lawn—her fists propped on hips clad in a pair of silky boxer shorts, her sexily tousled hair spilling over her shoulders and her green eyes blazing— rendered him unable to do anything else. The top of her head barely came up to his chin, but her shapely bare legs seemed endless and the skimpy little tank top she wore over the boxers hugged her feminine curves and made him wish he could do the same.

His crew chief, always attuned to any potential problems, put down his nail gun to join Ryder at the edge of the roof. Stan whistled under his breath. "Is that the home owner?"

"That's Mrs. Schulte," Ryder confirmed.

Stan was quiet for a minute, taking in the situation—or maybe just admiring the view.

"You won't have to worry about anyone showing up late for this job," his crew chief assured him. "The guys will be more than happy to work under her. Or over her. Or—" He wisely swallowed the rest of his words when Ryder slid him a glance, then cleared his throat. "No disrespect intended."

He nodded. "Help Dalton finish up here with the water shield. I'll go see what Mrs. Schulte wants."

As he climbed down the ladder propped up at the side of the house, Lauryn headed to meet him. She made quite a picture striding across the grass, and he let his gaze skim over her again. Though he knew she couldn't see his eyes through the dark lenses of his sunglasses, he forced his gaze up to her face when she halted in front of him. "Is there a problem?" he asked.

"That depends on whether or not you consider a bunch of men banging on your roof at seven thirty in the morning a problem."

"I'm guessing we woke you up."

She shoved a wayward strand of dark hair away from her face. "Good guess."

"I'm sorry," he said. "There was no answer when I knocked and no vehicle in the driveway, so I assumed you were out."

"At seven thirty in the morning?"

He shrugged. "Or didn't come home."

"What do you mean—my van isn't here?" She glanced over her shoulder and discovered that there were two trucks—one bearing the Renovations by Ryder logo and the other advertising Dalton's Roofing—taking up the length of driveway. "Oh, right. Tristyn and I cabbed it back last night."

He tilted his head to study her more closely. "I'm guessing that was a good idea. Head hurt this morning?"

"Only because I woke up to someone banging on my roof," she told him.

"The tequila had nothing to do with it?" he challenged.

"The effects of the tequila would have worn off after a couple more hours of sleep," she said, her cheeks flushing.

"Then I'll apologize for waking you, but the forecast was for clear skies and Dalton had the weekend free. I thought you would appreciate getting the roof done as soon as possible."

"I do, of course," she agreed. "I just didn't realize it would be this soon."

"We actually started yesterday," he told her. "Tearing off the old shingles and replacing the wet plywood. You didn't see the Dumpster at the side of the house?"

"No, I didn't," she admitted as her sister—fully clothed—crossed the lawn toward them.

"And when we left Marg & Rita's last night, I told you it was because we needed to get an early start today."

She vaguely remembered him saying something about a roofing job, but she hadn't realized he'd been referring to her roof. "Will you be finished today?" Lauryn asked.

He glanced up at the clear sky. "I can't imagine why not."

"Perhaps because the men who are supposed to be working are all focused on your conversation," Tristyn suggested.

He shifted his gaze to his buddies, who were staring down from the roof without any pretense of working. He shook his head, but he knew he really couldn't blame them. "I don't think they're as interested in any conversation as they are in your sister's underwear."

Lauryn gasped softly and immediately folded her arms over her chest. The action succeeded in covering up her puckered nipples but also pushed up her breasts, enhancing the cleavage displayed by the low neckline of her tank.

"This isn't my underwear," she denied hotly.

"Then what is it?" he asked.

"My pajamas."

"Semantics," her sister said, handing her a robe. "And irrelevant when the curve of your butt cheeks is visible for the workmen and all of your neighbors to see."

Lauryn shoved her arms into the sleeves of the garment and yanked the belt around her waist, glaring at Ryder the whole time. "This is *your* fault."

He lifted a brow. "How is it my fault?"

"You were making so much noise on the roof I didn't stop to think about what I was wearing."

"Or not wearing," her sister interjected.

Ryder fought against the smile that wanted to curve his lips in response to the words that perfectly echoed his own thoughts. Of course, Tristyn could afford to tease Lauryn because she was wearing actual clothes.

The color in Lauryn's cheeks deepened in response to the teasing. "You remember my sister, Tristyn?"

He nodded. "I apologize for the wake-up call."

"Please don't," she said, her eyes sparkling with humor. "I'm happy to tell everyone I know that I was awakened by America's Hottest Handyman."

He winced. "I'd rather you didn't."

"While you two conduct your meeting of the Ryder Wallace Fan Club, I'm going to go drown myself in the shower," Lauryn told them.

"There's coffee on in the kitchen," Tristyn said.

Lauryn nodded as she headed back toward the house.

"Coffee?" Ryder echoed hopefully.

"Come on in," she invited.

He followed her through the front door, down the short, wide hallway to the kitchen, where the scent of the fresh brew teased his nostrils.

Tristyn, obviously at home in her sister's kitchen, took down two mugs from the cupboard and filled them from the carafe. "Cream or sugar?" she asked him.

"Sugar, please."

She retrieved the bowl and a spoon and set them on the counter. She drank her own black—and watched him so intently he began to feel as if he was in *his* pajamas.

"Is something wrong?" he finally asked.

"Not at all," she assured him. "The dim lighting in the bar didn't really do you justice, and I was just appreciating the fact that you're even better looking in person than on TV."

"Thank you," he said cautiously.

"Don't worry—I'm not hitting on you. Not that I wouldn't be tempted, under other circumstances," she admitted. "But even a little foggy from the tequila last night, I could see the sparks between you and Lauryn. Which is why I was so puzzled when you left with the clingy blonde in the clingier red dress."

"I think the tequila had more of an effect than you realized," he told her, ignoring her comment about the blonde.

"Are you denying that there's a certain…chemistry… between you and my sister?"

"I think you're misinterpreting friction as attraction," he told her. "She's not at all looking forward to her home being invaded by me and my crew."

"I know," she admitted.

"But you didn't anticipate that when you forged her name on an application?"

"I suspected that she might have some objections," Tristyn acknowledged. "But when we sent in the application, we didn't really think it would be chosen. Not out of the hundreds you must have received."

"Actually, we got close to a thousand," he told her.

"And somehow, out of all of those, you selected Lauryn's application," she mused.

"You mean *your* application."

She chose to ignore the clarification. "It kind of makes me think that fate had a hand in your selection."

"Fate?" he echoed dubiously.

"I was a skeptic, too," she told him. "But the way the stars aligned for my other sister and her husband last year,

I'm starting to believe some things might be written in the heavens."

"And that excuses you signing your sister's name?"

"Sometimes the end does justify the means. And Lauryn deserves this. She *needs* this. After everything she's been through this past year…and years before."

He didn't ask. Though Ryder was undeniably curious about Lauryn's history, it wasn't really any of his business.

"So how did you get her to agree to it?" Tristyn asked him.

"I had a little help from Mother Nature," he admitted.

"The leaky roof?" she guessed.

He nodded. "The rain was coming into Kylie's bedroom."

"If it had been her own bedroom, she would have put out buckets and lived with it as long as she had to," Tristyn said. "If you've been given a tour of the house, you probably noticed that Kylie's and Zachary's rooms are the only ones that have been updated in forty years."

"I noticed," he confirmed.

"Rob made her so many promises…" Tristyn trailed off, shaking her head. "He agreed to everything she wanted when they were first married—and did absolutely nothing."

"You obviously weren't a fan."

"No," she admitted. "I tried to like him, because Lauryn loved him, but I couldn't get beyond reluctant tolerance."

"He couldn't have been that bad if your sister stayed with him for so long," Ryder surmised.

"Lauryn doesn't like to fail at anything. Once she spoke her vows, she was determined to do everything in her power to make the marriage work. But a relationship takes two people, and Rob wasn't half as committed as she was."

Maybe he should have felt guilty that he was talking to Lauryn's sister about her, but he wasn't interrogating her—they were just having a conversation. And he suspected that Tristyn wouldn't tell him anything she didn't want him to know.

Especially not with Lauryn's footsteps coming down the stairs.

"Feel better?" Tristyn asked when her sister entered the kitchen.

"Much." Lauryn poured herself a mug of coffee, added a splash of milk and took a long sip.

"You found your clothes," Ryder noted. "I'm disappointed."

She narrowed her gaze. "Aren't you supposed to be working on the roof?"

"Everything's under control," he assured her.

"Where's the camera crew?" Tristyn asked. "There doesn't seem to be anyone filming what you're doing today."

"Lucky for your sister," he teased.

Now that the shower had washed away the tequila-induced cobwebs, Lauryn could admit that her decision to storm outside and confront Ryder had been both impulsive and regrettable. Unfortunately, there was no way to undo what she had done, so she attempted to appeal to his sense of decency instead. "Can we *please* just forget about this morning?"

"I don't think so," he said. "But I can stop talking about your underwear, if it makes you uncomfortable."

"I was wearing *pajamas*," she said through gritted teeth.

"The camera crew?" Tristyn prompted again, in an obvious attempt to redirect the conversation.

"They don't usually work weekends and they don't work at all without a signed contract." He slid an envelope across the table. "The terms have been revised, per our previous discussion. Now we just need your signature."

"If you don't have a contract, why are you here?" Tristyn asked.

"Because I wanted to get the roof done before it rained again. Thankfully, it's in pretty good shape." He turned his attention back to Lauryn. "Dalton said the biggest problem was some patchwork that was done around the chimney without replacing the flashing—that's why the water was getting into your attic and then Kylie's bedroom from there.

"And speaking of the attic," he continued, "do you mind if I take another look up there to ensure everything's drying out?"

"Of course not," she said. Then Lauryn thought about the fact that the attic access was in her bedroom—and the new lingerie her sisters had bought for her was on top of her dresser. "But why don't you have another cup of coffee first?"

"Why?" he asked, obviously having picked up on something in her tone.

"Because...I can't remember if I made my bed," she improvised, setting down her mug and heading back to the stairs.

"I've seen unmade beds before," he assured her.

"Just give me a minute," she said, hurrying up to her bedroom. She swept the lingerie off the dresser and into the top drawer. And then, because her bed was unmade, she took a minute to pull up the sheets and comforter.

Ryder stepped into the room just as she was tying back the curtains. Sunlight spilled through the window, illuminating a scrap of red fabric on the floor in front of the dresser.

He bent down and picked it up.

She suspected that her face burned a brighter shade of crimson than the thong dangling from Ryder's finger.

"As much as I liked your pajamas," he said, "I like your underwear even more."

Chapter Seven

Lauryn snatched the lacy fabric out of his hand and stuffed it into the drawer. "You wanted to look in the attic," she reminded him.

"I did," he agreed, intrigued by the color in her cheeks. "But now I'm much more interested in the goodies you have in that dresser."

"Could you *please* focus on the reason you're here?"

"I can multitask," he assured her, reaching up to lower the staircase. "As for the reason I'm here...did you ever consider that this room could use a makeover?"

"Never," she told him.

"That was sarcasm, right?"

"No, I think the blue-and-green-plaid wallpaper really works with the chocolate comforter and pink accents."

"That was definitely sarcasm," he noted.

She looked around the room, shrugged. "I was going to tear it down," she admitted. "Whoever owned the house before we bought it obviously loved bold-patterned wallpaper, because it was *everywhere*. But after the hassle of scraping ugly roosters off Kylie's walls, I decided I could live with this plaid a little while longer."

"There were roosters in Kylie's room?"

"And flocked velvet flowers on a black background in what is now Zachary's room," she told him.

"I guess there's no accounting for taste," he acknowledged.

"And while I obviously want to get rid of this plaid at some point in time, it's not something I'm anxious to tackle with two kids underfoot. And, truthfully, I've become so accustomed to it that I don't even see it anymore." She shrugged. "And since nobody else usually sees it, I don't worry about it."

He figured he'd have to be blind not to see the wallpaper, but he chose to focus on the first part of her statement, instead. "The kids aren't here now, and I'd be happy to help you strip." He grinned. "The wallpaper, I mean."

"While I appreciate the offer," she said, in a tone that sounded less than appreciative, "I don't have time today. I have to be at The Locker Room before noon."

"Zumba class?" he guessed, because she didn't look like the type to pump iron.

"What?"

"Is that what you do at the gym?" He'd dated a Zumba instructor a few months previously and now had a keen appreciation for the benefits of aerobic dance on the female body.

She smiled as she shook her head. "I'm not going to work out but to work. The Locker Room is my business."

"I thought you worked at Garrett Furniture."

"Not since my ex left me his failing sporting goods store in exchange for all of the money in our joint bank accounts."

"Your husband really was a prince, wasn't he?"

"There was a time when I thought he was," she admitted. "And that was my mistake."

While her tone was matter-of-fact, her eyes were filled with so much sadness he was immediately contrite. "I'm sorry."

"You were on your way up to the attic," she reminded him again, a clear indication that their conversation was at an end.

He nodded and started up the stairs, but while he was inspecting the space, his mind was only half on the task. Or maybe only a third. Because another part of him was wanting to soothe her obvious heartache, and another part was wanting to see her in the lacy red thong that he'd found on the floor of her bedroom.

Until she'd stormed outside in her pajamas earlier that morning, he hadn't given a single thought to her underwear. And why would he? He was a contractor, she was his client and he'd never before crossed that line. Even when a client had made it clear that she'd be interested in playing with his tools, he'd never been tempted. Until now.

But he could—and would—resist the temptation. Because a divorcée with two small children had *complication* written all over her, and he preferred simple relationships. And red lace. Yeah, he really liked red lace. And soft curves and fragrant skin and—

Damn, her sister was right. There was some definite chemistry there. And while he was both attracted and intrigued, he knew that the best thing he could do was keep his distance from the sexy single mom. Because she was all about family, and he didn't have the first clue what it meant to be part of one.

He pushed her out of his mind and returned his attention to the ceiling. He was able to confirm that everything was drying out nicely and there were no other problem areas. There were some boxes piled in one corner, many of them marked "Christmas decorations" and several others indicating Kylie's first birthday, Kylie's baby clothes, Kylie's art and crafts. There were no less than half a dozen boxes for a child who wasn't even four years old. Obviously, Lauryn was a doting and sentimental mother—or a hopeless pack rat. His own mother had been neither—she'd never even put her children's artwork on the refrigerator, and when their nanny had done so, she'd complained about the clutter.

He shook off the memories and the melancholy, gathered the pots that he'd set out a few days earlier to collect the leaking water and headed back downstairs.

He could hear Lauryn talking before he entered the kitchen. Since it sounded like a one-sided conversation, he guessed that she was on the phone. He hesitated in the hallway, not wanting to interrupt but not wanting to eavesdrop, either.

"You're a sweetie, Jackson." Those brief words alleviated his reluctance to listen in on her conversation. "I don't know a lot of lawyers who would take time out of their Sunday mornings to help out a nonpaying client."

Of course, Ryder couldn't hear what Jackson said after that, but his response made Lauryn chuckle—and made Ryder wonder about her relationship with the lawyer.

"True," she agreed. "Give my love to Kelly and the kids."

Ryder waited until she'd set down the phone before he stepped into the kitchen. "Jackson?" he queried.

"My cousin," she explained. "He's an attorney in upstate New York."

He was inexplicably relieved by her explanation and glanced at the papers spread out on the table, with notes penciled in the margins. "Do you have questions about the contract?"

"Not now," she said. "But I learned the hard way not to sign anything unless and until I understand every word."

The slight edge to her tone suggested there was a story there—no doubt involving the ex-husband in some way—but he reminded himself that he would be doing them both a favor by keeping their relationship strictly business. No confidences or confessions required.

"And you're still not thrilled about doing the show," he guessed.

"No, but I won't renege on our agreement," she promised.

"Look on the bright side," he suggested.

"There's a bright side?" she asked, sounding skeptical.

"You can finally say goodbye to this ugly brown linoleum."

Lauryn managed a tight smile as she picked up her pen

and turned to the final page, scrawling her name on the signature line without further hesitation.

Because he was right. She'd hated that floor for more than six years—although much like the plaid wallpaper in her bedroom, she'd become so accustomed to the cracked vinyl that she barely noticed it anymore. And even if Kylie had taken her first steps on that linoleum, the memories wouldn't be torn away along with the flooring. And maybe Zachary would take his first steps in the new kitchen.

Still, as she added her signature to the second copy of the contract, she couldn't help feeling that she'd sold out. Not that she really had a choice. Whether or not the producers of *Ryder to the Rescue* would really take legal action against Tristyn and Jordyn for falsifying the application, she wasn't willing to take the chance of causing any negative publicity for her family. And with the financial difficulties of The Locker Room hanging over her head, she knew there wasn't going to be any extra money for home improvements anytime soon, not to mention the new roof that was—thank you, Ryder Wallace—already being installed.

"Where'd your sister go?" he asked her now.

"My cousin Daniel picked her up to take her to Charlotte for the race today." She slid the signed papers back into the envelope and handed it to Ryder. "So it all starts tomorrow?"

He nodded. "We'll be here by eight—I hope that's not too early."

"That's fine." She checked her purse for the essentials—wallet, keys, cell phone. "Are we done here now? Because I need to call a cab so that I can pick up my van."

"I can give you a ride."

"Oh." While she appreciated his willingness to help her out, she knew that she should decline his offer. To another woman, the butterflies that fluttered in her tummy whenever he was near might indicate anticipation, but to

Lauryn they were a warning sign—and one that she intended to heed. Which meant that she needed to set very clear boundaries for a strictly professional relationship with Ryder Wallace. "Thanks, but I don't want to take you away from your work."

"It's not a problem," he insisted. "And it will give us a chance to talk about your ideas for the kitchen."

Which sounded perfectly reasonable and definitely within the boundaries of their working relationship. And it would save her the cost of cab fare. "That would be great—thanks."

After Ryder dropped Lauryn off at her van and watched her drive away, he made a quick detour to the grocery store, then stopped by the condo where his sister now lived with her husband and new baby.

"This is a nice surprise," Avery said, opening the door to let him in. "But definitely a surprise."

"I wanted to see how my beautiful niece is doing."

"What about your beautiful sister?"

He grinned and kissed her cheek. "Her, too, of course. In fact, I brought her a present," he said, handing Avery the tub of ice cream he'd picked up.

She eyed the gift in her hand warily. "Why did you bring me ice cream?"

He frowned at her unexpected response. "It's cookies 'n' cream—isn't that your favorite?"

"It is," she confirmed with a sigh. "But I just had a baby three weeks ago and I've still got fourteen pounds to lose."

He reached for the container that she was eyeing with equal parts longing and suspicion. "Fine—I'll take it home with me."

She hugged the tub to her chest and slapped at his hand. "No, you won't. You can't come in here waving ice cream around and then take it away."

"Can I trade it for a cup of coffee?" he asked.

"That sounds reasonable," she decided.

He followed her to the kitchen, marveling over how much her life had changed this year. As much as Avery loved babies, she'd had deep-seated doubts about her ability to be a good mother—an understandable consequence of their dysfunctional upbringing.

But from the minute she learned of her pregnancy, she'd done everything possible to be the best mother that she could be. Ryder was happy for his sister because she was happy, but that didn't mean he wanted the same thing for himself. He liked being single and couldn't imagine that he'd ever want to complicate his life with marriage and kids.

"There she is," he said softly, moving toward the kitchen island where his niece was sleeping, securely buckled into some kind of baby seat. "Is it possible that she gets cuter every time I see her?"

"Of course. And I say that with absolutely no bias whatsoever," Avery told him.

He shifted his attention to her. "I had some reservations when you first told me about your pregnancy—and especially when you told me the father was a doctor," he admitted. "But looking at you now…I honestly don't think I've ever seen you look happier or more content."

"I never thought I could be this happy," she admitted, sliding a mug of coffee across the table to him. "I lucked out with Justin—he's a wonderful husband and father. And Vanessa, fingers crossed, is a very good baby."

"Of course, she is. She's perfect."

Avery rolled her eyes. "So tell me what's happening with you."

"We're finally ready to start the last Room Rescue."

"You say that as if there was a delay."

"It turns out the home owner wasn't thrilled by the idea of camera crews on her property," he confided, lifting the mug to his lips to sip the coffee she'd already sweetened for him.

"She didn't think about that before she filled out the application?" his sister asked, sounding surprised.

"Well, that's another story," he said, then realized she might be able to fill in some of the missing details. "How well do you know Justin's cousin, Lauryn?"

"Not well," she said. "And not because of Justin. I delivered her baby."

"Zachary."

Her brows lifted at his use of the baby's name. "How do you—oh," she realized. "Lauryn is the third winner of your contest?"

He nodded.

"It's starting to make sense now," she said. "From the little that Justin has said, she's an intensely private person—not the type to compete for a spot on a television program."

"You're right," he confirmed, and told her about Lauryn's sisters submitting the application on her behalf.

"How did you end up picking her application, anyway?"

"I thought she was married," he admitted. "In addition to the mention of a husband, there was a notable absence of nude photos and explicit propositions."

She chuckled at that. "If you'd chosen an application with nude photos, you'd be facing a lot less resistance right now."

"I'd rather deal with resistance than sexual harassment." A slight movement caught the corner of his eye and he turned to see Vanessa lifting her arms up, her little hands clenched into fists, her tiny rosebud mouth opening in a yawn. "Hey, look who's waking up. And smiling at me."

"It's gas," Avery said, rolling her eyes.

"It is *not*," he denied. "She knows her favorite uncle when she's looking at him."

"Justin has two brothers who might want to challenge that title."

"But they're not here right now and I am," he said, unfastening the plastic buckle around the baby's belly and lifting her from her seat.

"She's going to be hungry," Avery said. "Every three hours like clockwork."

"Well, she's not fussing right now," he noted, tucking her into the crook of his arm. "But maybe she should eat—she still doesn't weight half as much as my tool belt."

"She's gained over a pound since we brought her home from the hospital."

"That hardly makes her a heavyweight."

"Dr. Kertz is pleased with her progress," she assured him.

"What does he think of that flower growing out of her head?" he asked, studying the fabric daisy with apparent concern.

"It's a headband," she said. "She doesn't have a lot of hair yet, and I want people to know that she's a girl."

He looked around the condo. "What people? And isn't the pink outfit enough of a clue?"

She shrugged. "Justin came home with all of these little accessories for her—headbands and frilly socks—and I know he likes to see her wearing them."

"Speaking of your husband, this is the first time I've been here and not found him hovering over both of you."

"He's at the hospital today."

"Are you itching to get back?" he wondered.

"I thought I would be," she admitted. "But I'm going to take some time, then Justin and I want to coordinate our schedules so that one of us is with Vanessa as much as possible."

"Not planning on hiring a nanny?"

"Not ruling it out," she acknowledged. "But if we did, it would only be for a few hours a day—I have no intention of paying someone else to raise my child."

"You're already a better mother than ours ever was," Ryder told her.

"Daddyhood looks like it would fit you pretty well, too," she noted.

He immediately shook his head and shoved the baby at his sister. "No way. I'm not ready to be domesticated."

But then he remembered the way Kylie had looked at him, with absolute trust in her big blue eyes. And the way he'd felt, like he was a superhero, when she'd wrapped her arms around him. And he considered that being a daddy—under the right circumstances and in the distant future—might not be so bad.

"Since you mentioned our mother," Avery began, settling the baby against her shoulder.

"Just a slip of the tongue," he assured her.

"Well, she's coming to town next weekend to meet her granddaughter."

"Really?"

"I was as surprised as you are," she admitted. "And I'm not entirely convinced that her plans won't change between now and then, but if they don't…could you pick her up at the airport?"

"Can't she take a cab?"

"Come on, Ryder—she's our mother."

"I'm still not entirely convinced," he said. "When I visited her lab in Atlanta, I got a much warmer feeling from one of the test tubes."

"Ha-ha." But he could tell his sister wasn't amused.

He sighed. "When does her flight get in?"

"I'll text the details to you as soon as they're confirmed," she told him. "Thank you."

"You know I can't say 'no' to you, but if you're expecting a happy family reunion next weekend, you're going to be disappointed."

"I was thinking birthday party rather than reunion," she admitted.

"No way," he said firmly.

"But I always make dinner for you on your birthday."

"That was before you had a husband and a baby to take care of."

"As surprising as it may seem, neither getting married nor giving birth stripped me of my ability to cook."

"I'm sure that's true," he said. "But, as it turns out, I already have plans for dinner on my birthday."

Her eyes narrowed. "Why don't I believe you?"

"Apparently you're cynical and untrusting—you should work on that."

His sister was undeterred. "Who are these plans with?"

"You know I don't kiss and tell."

"Well, don't be kissing my husband's cousin," she said.

He frowned, uncomfortable with his sister's uncanny ability to read his thoughts and feelings. "Where did *that* come from?"

"I've known you forever," she reminded him. "So I know that what you don't say is often more telling than what you do."

"Well, you're way off base this time," he told her.

"I hope I am," she said. "But you've never walked away from anything that needed to be fixed."

"Houses," he clarified. "I fix houses."

"And while you're renovating Lauryn's kitchen, you'll likely be spending a fair amount of time with her."

"I've lost count of the number of kitchen renos I've done," he told her. "There's no cause for concern on this one."

"Those Garretts have a way of sneaking into your heart when you least expect it," she warned.

"You don't have to worry—single moms aren't my type," he assured her.

"And doctors weren't mine," she said pointedly.

Chapter Eight

Lauryn was on her way back downstairs after tucking Kylie into bed Sunday night when she saw headlights turn into the driveway. As the vehicle drew closer to the house, she recognized it as Jordyn's hatchback.

She didn't know why her sister had stopped by, but she was grateful for any distraction from thoughts of the upcoming renovation that had plagued her throughout the day. She only hoped it was the inevitable mess and presence of the construction crews that worried her, rather than the man who was the center of the show.

"You're eleven hours early," she said, meeting her sister at the door.

"I didn't forget about the taping tomorrow," Jordyn assured her. "But I wanted to get this to you tonight."

"What's this?" she asked, taking the proffered folder.

"A business proposal." Jordyn kicked off her shoes and headed down the hall.

As her sister helped herself to a can of soda from the fridge, Lauryn settled at the table and opened the cover of the folder. She quickly scanned the contents and was already shaking her head before she got to the bottom of the first page. "I can't let you invest in the business."

"Why not?"

"Because it's too risky. The Locker Room hasn't been in the black for the past three years."

"Because it's been poorly inventoried, overstaffed and

mismanaged," her sister pointed out, pouring the soda into a glass.

"All of that's true," she agreed. "And there's no guarantee that I can turn it around."

"You're a Garrett," Jordyn reminded her, conveniently ignoring the fact that Lauryn's surname had been Schulte for more than six years. And while Lauryn had been tempted to take back "Garrett" when her husband walked out, she'd decided to keep "Schulte" for the sake of her kids.

"And with two more Garretts on board—and countless others waiting in the wings to offer advice and expertise you may not want or need—I don't see any other possible scenario," Jordyn continued.

Lauryn couldn't help but smile at that, but still she hesitated to take what her sisters were offering. She'd made mistakes in her life and she was paying for them—she didn't want her sisters to pay, too. The amount of money that Rob had dumped into the store—and lost—was staggering to her, and she didn't know if it was even possible to get out of the mountain of debt he'd left behind. "I appreciate what you're trying to do, but—"

"No buts," Jordyn said, sitting across from her. "Tristyn and I are both committed to this."

"When did you come up with this plan? I only told you about the situation at breakfast yesterday."

"She stopped by the house on her way to Charlotte this morning. Interestingly enough, we were both already thinking along the same lines."

"Did you talk to Marco about this?" she asked, aware that her sister's husband had a lot invested in his own business ventures.

"Of course, I did. And he fully supports what we're doing."

"Because he hasn't seen the books," Lauryn said, only half joking.

"Because he knows that I wouldn't be doing this if I didn't have complete faith in you," her sister clarified.

Still, Lauryn hesitated.

"Stop being stubborn," Jordyn told her. "You don't have to do everything on your own."

"I know. I just don't want to count on other people to clean up my messes."

"This wasn't your mess."

"Wasn't it?" Lauryn challenged.

"Your only mistake was marrying a man who didn't deserve you," her sister insisted.

Lauryn pulled the glass across the table and picked it up for a sip. "And I'm in the financial mess I'm in now because I married him."

"Now you're being stupid as well as stubborn," Jordyn said. "And if you don't take the deal that we're offering, we'll tell Dad."

She choked on the soda. "Are we in grade school? If I don't do what you want, you're going to run and tell Daddy?"

"Yep." Jordyn was unapologetic as she took her drink back. "And you know what he'll do—he'll buy the building, even the whole block, if necessary."

Lauryn didn't doubt that it was true. It was one of the reasons she hadn't shared any of the details of the situation with her parents.

"The bank wouldn't give me any money." She felt compelled to point that out to her sister. "Doesn't that tell you something about the state of the business?"

"It only tells me that I need to switch banks—and you probably should, too."

Lauryn thumbed through the clearly drafted agreement again. Jordyn took a pen out of her pocket and set it down on top of the papers.

"I'm not signing anything without talking to my lawyer," she said, attempting to stall her sister.

"Your lawyer drafted the agreement," Jordyn told her.

"He did?"

"Do you think we'd trust anyone but Jackson with this?"

Of course not. And there wasn't anyone Lauryn trusted more than her sisters. This time when Jordyn nudged the pen toward her, Lauryn picked it up and signed her name.

Lauryn was expecting Ryder and his crew when they showed up at eight o'clock the next morning, but that didn't mean she was any more comfortable about the whole scenario. She hovered in the background as the camera operators and AV techs walked through the hall and the kitchen, figuring out where to set up lights and microphones and stationary cameras. By nine, they were ready to begin.

"This is our home owner, Lauryn Schulte, who lives in this 1972 traditional Foursquare with her children."

The show's director, Owen Diercks, had wanted the kids on camera. "Our viewers love kids," he told Lauryn. But Kylie, although already a fan of Ryder, was less certain about all of the other people who had invaded her home, and Lauryn wasn't prepared to force her outside of her comfort zone. As a result, after seeing her daughter safely onto the school bus, she'd opted for Zachary to remain off screen, too, under the watchful eyes of Jordyn and Tristyn.

"How long have you lived here, Lauryn?" Ryder asked her.

"A little more than six years now."

"And how long have you been planning to renovate?"

"A little more than six years," she admitted. "When we bought the house, the plan was to update the kitchen as soon as possible."

"Obviously, that plan changed."

"My husband had his own business, so he didn't have the time to do the renovations we wanted to do.

"In the beginning, I was employed full-time outside of

the home, too. Then, after our daughter was born, I continued to work part-time in retail as well as take care of her."

"And now you have two children?" Ryder prompted.

She nodded. "Kylie's three and a half and Zachary is seven months."

"So when you heard about the Room Rescue contest, did you decide that would be the perfect opportunity to get a new kitchen?"

"Well, that's not quite how it happened," she admitted. "In fact, I didn't even know about the contest—it was my sisters who filled out the application on my behalf."

"How did you feel when you found out what they'd done?" he prompted.

"I was embarrassed that they had believed it was necessary to bring in outside help to complete the renovation—and because they were right. I've hated this kitchen for more than six years. I certainly didn't want to go on TV and show it off to your viewers."

"Well, let's bring in your sisters now so that they can tell their side of the story."

After Tristyn and Jordyn were introduced, they explained their decision to fill out an application on Lauryn's behalf—and expressed their excitement that the application had actually been chosen by Ryder for inclusion in the program.

"At this point, I would usually introduce you to Monica Snyder, our design expert," Ryder said, speaking to the viewers as much as to Lauryn. "It's her job to meet with the home owners, to determine what changes they consider essential and what other features they would like to add to the room under renovation, then decide how to make it happen within the allotted budget.

"But Monica spent the weekend mountain biking at Warrior Creek, where she took an unfortunate spill and broke her leg."

"Oh, my goodness," Lauryn said, her concern immediate and genuine. "Is she going to be okay?"

Ryder nodded. "She's going to be fine, but she's also going to be in the hospital for a few days and laid up for several weeks after that."

"So who's going to design my kitchen?" Lauryn asked, feeling slightly panicked.

"You are," he told her. Then he dropped an enormous binder on the table in front of her. "With a little assistance from what Monica refers to as her planning bible."

"I think I'm going to need a lot of assistance."

"Haven't you been thinking about this kitchen renovation since you bought the house?"

She nodded. "I must have redesigned this room a dozen times in my mind over the years, but I never made any final decisions. Probably because I wasn't sure this renovation was ever going to happen."

"It's going to happen now," Ryder assured her.

And, surrounded by the cameras and his crew, she was finally starting to believe it.

The morning taping kept Lauryn tied up longer than she'd expected, and it was after noon before she was able to make her escape. Then she had to meet Kylie's bus, load both of the kids into the van and head over to her parents' house so that Susan could watch them while Lauryn relieved Bree, one of only two part-time employees at The Locker Room.

Thankfully, she didn't have to worry about feeding Kylie and Zachary. She'd called her mother before she left home to let her know they were going to be hungry, and Susan had lunch ready when they arrived—including a sandwich for Lauryn to take with her. *Thank goodness for my family*, she thought to herself as she kissed Kylie and Zachary, then gave her mom a quick hug. She honestly didn't know how she would've have made it through the past nine months without them.

Mondays tended to be quiet at the store. Not that The Locker Room did a brisk business any day of the week, but on Mondays, in particular, the hours seemed to drag. With few customers to tend to, Lauryn spent her time tidying up displays and re-shelving misplaced merchandise. When the bell over the door rang, she turned toward the front of the store with a ready smile on her face.

The smile froze when she recognized the man who walked through the door.

"Ryder."

"Hello, Lauryn."

"Is there something I can help you find?" she asked, pretending he was just another customer.

"Actually, I was looking for you," he said. But he took a minute to glance around the store. "You've recently done some work in here."

"A few cosmetic touches to refresh the store's image."

"I like the color."

"Jordyn has a good eye for that kind of thing."

"An important quality in an artist, I would think."

She seemed surprised that he'd remembered the detail that she'd dropped into a casual conversation several days earlier, but Ryder had always believed that good customer service started with paying attention to his clients and listening to what they wanted—which was why he was here.

"We need to decide on a cabinet style and color as soon as possible. My supplier is expecting a big order for a new development in the north end, and we want to get yours in ahead of that or the original four- to six-week time frame could end up being ten to twelve."

"Then I guess I'd better decide on my cabinets."

"Based on what seemed to catch your eye when you were looking through Monica's book, I've narrowed it down to three choices," he told her, setting three photos on the counter.

"This is a shaker style, obviously in white. This is a mission style in cherry, and this is an inset design in dark walnut," he told her, pointing to each picture in turn. "Of course, there are numerous other colors available in each of the styles—including birch and maple, which are both very popular."

Her gaze shifted from one picture to the next and back again. "I like the crisp, clean look of this one," she said, indicating the shaker style.

"It's a classic," he assured her.

"But I'm not sure about the white—more specifically, how it will hold up against sticky fingers."

"Peanut butter and jelly won't magically disappear, but they will wipe off easily."

"On the other hand, this dark walnut has real impact."

He smiled. "You're all over the map, aren't you?"

"I've been waiting a long time for this and I can't imagine that I'll ever want to redo the kitchen again, so I want to be sure that, whatever I choose, I'll be just as happy with it five or ten years from now as I am today."

"That makes sense," he agreed. "So why don't you hold on to the photos for now, but try to make a decision by Wednesday."

She nodded as she gathered up the photos and tucked them beneath the counter. "I'll let you know when I've decided, but it won't be before tomorrow. I'm working here until the store closes at eight tonight."

He scowled at that. "And then you've got to go home and pack up your kitchen?"

"Don't worry. Everything will be cleared out by the time your crew arrives in the morning," she assured him.

"I'm not as concerned about the cupboards as I am about you—that's a long day."

"I'm used to long days," she said.

The next words were out of his mouth before he considered what he was offering—or wondered why. "I could bring over some boxes later and help with the packing up."

"Thanks, but I can manage."

"I'm sure you can," he agreed. "But I don't understand why would you refuse the offer of free labor?"

"Because I learned the hard way that nothing in life is ever really free."

"Cynical, aren't you?"

"Realistic," she countered.

"You can call it what you want," he told her, "but you'll see me around nine."

She sighed. "Why are you doing this?"

He wasn't entirely sure of the answer to that question himself. Since she'd first opened the door to him on a rainy morning, he'd had more questions than answers. But for now, he only shrugged. "Maybe I feel guilty that I pushed you into agreeing to do the show without fully appreciating the impact it would have on your life."

"I am getting a new kitchen out of it," she reminded him.

He nodded. "And tonight, I'll help you clear out the old one."

Lauryn had found a few empty boxes in the storage room at The Locker Room, so she threw those into the back of the van when she finally left the store after closing up. Then she detoured to her parents' house again to pick up Kylie and Zachary, who had been fed and bathed and were all ready for bed. Still, she had barely finished tucking them in when she heard a soft knock at the back door.

Ryder had brought more boxes with him, and while she was still skeptical of the reasons behind his offer, she couldn't deny that he did provide the labor he'd promised. He started on the top cabinets while she concentrated her efforts on the bottom. And he meticulously itemized the contents of each box on the outside, then carried them into the dining room where he stacked them against an empty wall.

"What's all of this stuff?"

Lauryn looked up. "What stuff?"

He handed her an old shoe box. She lifted the lid to peek inside. "Oh. I'd almost forgotten about these."

"What are they?"

"Cookie cutters."

"That's a lot of cookie cutters."

She sifted through the metal shapes, her lips curving a little. "I used to bake a lot of cookies."

"Why?"

She shrugged and put the lid back on the box. "It was fun. My sisters and I used to bake and decorate cookies with our mom, and it was a tradition I'd always imagined sharing with my own kids. Of course, that was before I realized that simply taking care of the kids would take so much time."

"You don't bake anymore?"

"Rarely." She dropped the shoe box inside the larger box he was filling. "And when I do, they're not the kind that I decorate with icing and colored sugars. I should probably get rid of that stuff, but I keep thinking—or at least hoping—that I'll get back to it someday."

"Then you will," he said, opening another shoe box filled with icing bags, tips and various other utensils that he assumed were also for her cookie decorating. He packed it up and Lauryn returned to boxing up the everyday dishes.

"Did your mom bake cookies for you?" she asked.

"No."

The blunt, dismissive tone surprised her even more than the response. "Never?"

"She was always far too busy to concern herself with any kind of domestic or maternal duties."

"Busy doing what?" she wondered.

"Back then, I'm not sure—probably medical research of some kind. Now Dr. Cristina Tobin is a research supervisor at the Centers for Disease Control in Atlanta."

"Then maybe it's a good thing that she wasn't baking cookies for you when she came home from the lab," Lauryn said, making him smile.

"I'm sure that was her primary concern," he noted dryly.

"So your sister followed your mother's footsteps into medicine," she said, intrigued by this unexpected insight into his family. "Did your father work in construction?"

"No, he's a doctor, too. A cardiac surgeon at Emory."

"Wow," she said, clearly impressed. "But you had no interest in medicine?"

"Less than zero," he told her.

"A rebellion against your parents?"

He considered her question for a minute. "I don't think so. As soon as I got my first LEGO set, I always liked to build things, then knock them down and build them up again even better. Becoming a contractor seemed a natural progression from that."

"I'd say there are a lot of home owners who are extremely happy that you chose home renovations over medicine."

"Would you be one of them?"

"Maybe you should ask me that question after my new kitchen has been unveiled," she suggested.

"I will," he told her.

Although the baby monitor was up in Zachary's room, Kylie's scream came through loud and clear, followed by gulping sobs that twisted Lauryn's heart.

"Mama! Mama! Where are you, Mama?"

Lauryn raced up the stairs, anxious not only to alleviate

Kylie's growing panic but to quiet her before she managed to wake up her brother, too.

When she entered the room, she found her daughter sitting up in bed, her eyes wide and her cheeks streaked with tears.

"I'm here," Lauryn told her, lowering herself onto the edge of the mattress.

Kylie threw herself at Lauryn, sobbing against her chest. "I had a bad dweam, Mama."

She stroked a hand over her daughter's silky hair, gently untangling the twisted strands. "I know, honey. But the dream's over now and Mama's here."

"You stay wif me?"

"For a minute," she agreed.

Kylie scooted over to make room and patted the empty space on her pillow.

Lauryn hesitated, not wanting to be away from her kitchen assignment for too long but knowing her daughter would settle more easily if she stayed with her awhile. So she lay down beside her. "Close your eyes and go back to sleep, honey."

"You close your eyes," Kylie said.

So Lauryn did…for just a minute. Because comforting her children always comforted her, too. And maybe taking an extra minute away from the not just sexy but sweet Ryder Wallace would help her restore her equilibrium. Maybe.

Chapter Nine

Through the baby monitor on the counter, Ryder could hear the soft murmur of voices, though he couldn't hear the actual words. Kylie's outburst had given him quite a jolt, and before he even realized what was happening, Lauryn was racing up the stairs to her daughter.

He was surprised by the urge to follow her, to see for himself that everything was okay with the little girl. But it really wasn't any of his concern. Whatever monsters existed in Kylie's nightmares, he had no doubt that Lauryn would handle them. After only a short acquaintance with her, Ryder didn't doubt that she could handle anything.

Though she might look all soft and fragile, he knew that there was a steely strength beneath her silky skin. She was as much a warrior as a nurturer, and he was in danger of becoming infatuated with both parts of her.

He focused his attention on his task, pausing only to reply to a couple of text messages that came through on his cell phone. One from Arielle—a veterinarian assistant he'd dated for a few weeks in the summer—and two from Samantha—a high school gym teacher he'd gone out with exactly once. He replied to both that he was busy with work and unavailable for the foreseeable future, without a hint of regret that it was true.

Even before *Ryder to the Rescue* had made him a pseudo-celebrity, he'd attracted a fair amount of attention from women, and he couldn't deny that he'd enjoyed his popularity. His sister had occasionally accused him of enjoying it too much. But he was always honest about what he wanted and he always treated the women he dated with respect. Recently, though, he'd found himself starting to grow weary of the whole dating scene and wondering if he wasn't ready for something more.

He immediately shook his head, appalled that such a thought would even cross his mind. Of course, he wasn't weary of the dating scene. Short-term relationships were the hallmark of his life; commitments and entanglements were to be avoided at all costs. Then his thoughts drifted to the mother who was upstairs now, soothing her frightened child, and he acknowledged that there might be circumstances in which the benefits exceeded the costs.

Ryder pushed the tempting thought aside. He was nearly finished in the kitchen when Lauryn made her way back downstairs.

"I'm so sorry," she said. "I just snuggled with Kylie for a few minutes, to make sure she was settled, and I guess I fell asleep, too."

"That's okay," he told her. "I managed to carry on without you."

She looked at the stacked and labeled boxes, then at the empty cupboards. "I feel like the shoemaker who wakes up to discover the elves have done all of his work."

"You still have to figure out where you want everything in the dining room," he told her. "But that can wait until the morning."

"Thank you."

"Is Kylie okay?" he asked, sincerely concerned about the terror he'd heard in the little girl's voice.

Lauryn nodded. "She's sleeping soundly now."

"Does she often have bad dreams?"

"Not so much recently—thank God," she told him. "But for a while, she was waking up almost every night, and occasionally several times in one night."

"Any idea what triggers that?"

"You mean other than her father suddenly disappearing from her life?"

He winced. "I guess that would do it."

She nodded. "The pediatrician has assured me that it's a fairly normal response to what she's been through and that she'll eventually outgrow them."

"Was she okay last Saturday night—at her sleepover?"

"She was," Lauryn confirmed. "Which is a big step. She used to love staying at my parents' house, but sleepovers have been few and far between over the past nine months."

He could understand that Kylie would want to stick close to the one parent she had left, and he wondered again about the kind of man who could walk away from not only his wife but his beautiful daughter and unborn son. His own parents had hardly been role models, but they'd accepted the responsibilities of parenthood—or at least those they couldn't abdicate to the nanny.

"It's hard to see the changes in her," Lauryn admitted softly. "She was always an outgoing and affectionate child who never shied away from strangers."

"She certainly didn't shy away from me," he noted. "Even on day one, after you'd closed the door in my face, she invited me to have tea with her."

Lauryn smiled a little at the memory. "Well, you did give her flowers. A girl never forgets the first boy who gives her flowers."

He didn't know if that was true, but he liked to think the little girl would remember him when he was gone. And as soon as the kitchen was done, he would be gone, so it would be crazy to even think about starting something with Lauryn. But he couldn't deny that he was tempted.

"Everything changed after Rob left," she said, picking up the thread of their previous conversation. "She started to panic anytime I was out of her sight. I was in the hospital for two nights when Zachary was born, and she was almost inconsolable during that time."

"Who stayed with her then?"

"She stayed with my parents." Lauryn went to the fridge—relocated to the dining room—and retrieved a bottle of chardonnay, then looked around as if trying to remember what she'd done with the wineglasses. Since he'd packed them away, he found the box easily.

"You're not having one?" she asked, when he handed her a glass.

"Are you offering to share?"

"Sure."

So he retrieved a second glass and poured wine for himself while Lauryn sipped hers.

"My parents have been so great through this whole thing," she told him. "Actually, my whole family's been great, but my parents have gone above and beyond."

Although he had no personal experience with that kind of support, he knew that family were supposed to be the people to turn to in a time of crisis. He couldn't imagine ever relying on either of his parents, but he knew his sister would be there for him—as he would for her.

"My mom understood Kylie's apprehension, but she also believed that her granddaughter needed to stop clinging to me twenty-four/seven. When Zachary was about six months old, she planned a special day for Kylie. She and my dad took her to the zoo in Asheville, then to Buster Bear's and finally back to their house for the night."

"Any three-year-old's fantasy," he remarked with a smile.

She sipped her wine, then nodded. "And Kylie had a fabulous time—until she found out that she was sleeping over. Then she had a complete meltdown. She cried and screamed, but my mother remained firm. She told Kylie that she could call me to say good-night, but only if she stopped crying."

"Sounds like tough love."

"A little tougher than I was prepared for," Lauryn admitted. "I understood what she was doing, that she wanted Kylie to learn to trust that I would be there in the morning, but it was so hard for me to hear my little girl fighting against tears." She smiled wryly. "I don't think any of us slept that night, but the panic attacks finally started to fade. In fact, this is the first one she's had in several weeks."

"But when they happen, they upset you as much as they upset her," he guessed.

"When you're a parent, there's nothing worse than a child who is hurting—especially when you can't do anything about it."

Maybe a parent like Lauryn, but he already knew that she was one of a kind. He touched her hand, and her quick intake of breath confirmed that she wasn't oblivious to the chemistry between them, either.

"But you are doing something," he told her, as she carefully drew her hand away from his. "You're showing her that she can depend on you to be there for her."

She lifted her glass to her lips again, swallowed the final sip. "I'm not sure that's much consolation to a little girl who's missing her daddy."

He tipped the bottle, emptying the last of the wine into her glass. "Do you miss him, too?"

Ryder wasn't sure what compelled him to ask the question, except that he wanted to know. When she'd first told him that her husband was gone, she'd said that she wasn't sorry. But she'd been on the defensive that day, and he wondered if she'd held back her true feelings.

"I got used to Rob not being here a long time before he ever left," she told him. "When he packed up and moved out, it was almost a relief, because I could finally stop pretending that everything was normal. And then, of course, I felt guilty for being relieved, because of Kylie and Zachary."

"Divorce is hardly uncommon today," he pointed out to her.

"It is in my family," she retorted. "My parents have been married thirty-nine years, and both of my father's brothers have been married to their wives for more than forty. And all of my cousins who are married—and most of them are—have figured out how to make it work.

"Well, Matt was divorced from his first wife," she acknowledged. "But that wasn't his fault."

"There doesn't have to be fault," Ryder told her. "Sometimes things just don't work out."

"Are you speaking from personal experience?" she challenged.

He nodded. "I was around Kylie's age when my parents split up."

The confession succeeded in banking some of the fire in her eyes, and when she spoke again, her tone was more curious than confrontational. "Do you remember much from that time?"

"It's hard to separate what I actually remember from what I've been told, but it wasn't particularly traumatic. We were living in Brookhaven at the time, so my mom chose to move out, to get a place closer to the Northeast Georgia Medical Center, where she was working."

Her forehead crinkled. "Your mother left—and left you and your sister behind?"

He smiled at the outrage in her voice. "We were well taken care of," he assured her.

"By your father?"

"By the nanny," he clarified. "And when my mom was settled again, she and my dad shared custody, which meant that we moved back and forth every two weeks."

"How was that?" she asked curiously.

He shrugged. "It was the status quo, as far as I knew, and Hennie moved back and forth with us."

"That's one good thing about Rob moving to California," she said. "At least there wasn't any fighting over custody."

"I have a feeling he wouldn't have stood a chance."

She managed a smile at that, and the sweet curve of her lips seemed to arrow straight to his heart—which was Ryder's cue to make his escape, before he became even more mired in his unbidden awareness of Lauryn.

He finished his wine and set the empty glass on the table. She automatically rose to her feet as he did. "Thank you—for all of your help tonight."

"You're welcome."

"I guess I'll see you in the morning," she said, following him to the door.

"You will," he confirmed, but he hesitated with his hand on the knob.

When he looked at her again, he saw in her expression a combination of awareness and wariness. The former tempted him to move closer; the latter propelled him to walk away.

He did so, already counting the hours.

Friday afternoon, Lauryn enlisted Jordyn to babysit Kylie and Zachary while she went into Raleigh to meet with Adam Carr, a former assistant manager of The Locker Room. The college student had worked for Rob for four years before taking a job at a bigger store in the bigger city. At least, that was her ex-husband's explanation for his employee's departure. When she'd crossed paths with Adam a few weeks earlier, she'd discovered that the truth was a little bit different.

Adam had left The Locker Room because he had a lot of ideas to generate more business for the store and he was frustrated by Rob's refusal to hear them. Lauryn was desperate for ideas and eager to listen, and after their conversation, she'd immediately offered him a management position.

All the way home, she anticipated sharing the details with her sister. But when she pulled into her driveway, Jordyn's car wasn't there.

Lauryn hurried into the house, halting abruptly in the entrance of the living room where Kylie was kneeling on the floor, a coloring book and crayons on the coffee table in front of her, and Zachary was asleep in his playpen, his favorite blanket clutched in one hand, the thumb of the other in his mouth.

She pressed a hand to her racing heart and released an unsteady breath. Her children were here. They were fine.

And sitting on the sofa, watching over them, was Ryder.

"Where's Jordyn?" she asked, when she managed to catch her breath again.

"She got a call from the author she works with—something about an emergency last-minute revision—and said she had to go."

Lauryn was incredulous. "And she just left?"

"Only after she asked me to hang around until you got home," he explained.

"I'm so sorry," Lauryn said. "She never should have imposed on you that way."

"It's okay," he assured her. "Your sister had somewhere to be. I didn't."

But Lauryn had deliberately stayed away until she was sure he'd be gone, because after the time they'd spent together Monday night, she'd worried that she'd shared too much. Revealed too much. And the insights he'd given her into his own family had changed her perspective on him. He wasn't just America's Hottest Handyman to her now—he was a real person, with real-life experiences and scars. And it was that man she was drawn to more and more every time she was near him.

"Well, thank you for staying, but I'm sure you want to get home now, and I need to get supper on."

"Wyder said we can have pizza," Kylie chimed in.

Lauryn shook her head. "Not tonight, honey. I've got spaghetti sauce in the freezer—"

"Pizza," her daughter insisted.

She sighed. "Kylie, please don't do this now."

"But Wyder—"

"Should have checked with your mom first," he said to the little girl. Then he addressed Lauryn, his tone apologetic. "But it's already ordered."

She sighed, a little frustrated at the unexpected changes to their usual routine. "You definitely should have checked with me first."

"I know, but we were hungry and I didn't know when you would be home."

Which she knew wasn't unreasonable from his perspective, but the whole situation had caught her off guard. She'd come home expecting to find her sister with her kids—not the man who'd rescued Kylie's mural from ruin and fixed her roof and stirred feelings inside of her that she didn't want to have stirred.

But maybe it wasn't surprising that she was attracted to him. In the space of a week, he'd done more to help around the house than her ex-husband had done in a year—maybe even six years. And now he was hanging out with her children, and looking not just at ease but as if he belonged.

"In fact," Ryder said, in response to the peal of the doorbell, "that's probably our dinner now."

Holding back another sigh, she reached for her purse, wondering if the delivery person would take her credit card to pay for the pizza—and silently crossing her fingers that it wasn't maxed out because she'd relied on it to cover other essentials, such as groceries and gas for her car.

"I've got it," he said, moving past her with cash in hand.

She should insist on paying for the meal. But the truth was, she didn't even have twenty dollars in her wallet and she'd rather not run up her credit card. Which meant that she had to accept his offer—and that he would be staying to eat with them.

"It looks like you ordered more than just pizza," she said when he returned with the food.

"I got some wings and Caesar salad, too," he told her. "Because Kylie said it was her favorite and I figured you'd want her to have some kind of vegetable."

Which was true, but not something she would have expected him to consider. "I also want her to go wash up," she said, looking pointedly at her daughter.

Kylie, eager for pizza, obediently scampered off.

"Do you want this in the dining room?" Ryder asked.

"Yes, please." She headed to the bookcase that was serving as a makeshift cabinet while her kitchen was under construction. "I'll get plates."

"There should be paper plates and plastic cutlery in the bag," he told her.

"You really did think of everything," she noted.

"I know it can't be easy carting your dishes downstairs to the laundry tub."

"It's not easy, but it works. And it's only for a few more weeks, right?" she asked, her tone hopeful.

She was managing well enough with her refrigerator, microwave and toaster oven set up in the dining room, but after only four days, she was already missing a real kitchen—and excited about the unveiling of the completed job.

Ryder's crew had completed the demolition work in the first two days, filling a Dumpster in the backyard with her old cabinets and the ugly brown linoleum—even pieces of drywall and chunks of wood that suggested bigger changes than she'd anticipated. But since she'd approved the basic layout, picked out her cabinets, countertops, backsplash, floor tile and lighting fixtures, she'd been banned from the area.

In fact, the director was so determined to ensure that she not get a glimpse of the work until they'd finished, he'd closed off the doorways from the kitchen to the hallway and dining room and covered the inside of the kitchen windows with dark paper.

"All clean," Kylie announced, holding up her dripping hands for her mother to see.

"Yes, but you missed the drying that usually comes after washing."

Her daughter wiped her hands down the front of her pink overalls, then held them up again.

Lauryn shook her head as Ryder bit back a smile. "Take a seat."

While Kylie climbed into her booster seat, Lauryn got the milk out of the fridge and poured a cup for her.

Kylie ate one slice of pizza—but not the crust. She also had a helping of Caesar salad. Of course, Zachary woke up as soon as Lauryn took the first bite out of her own pizza, so she got up to change his diaper, then settled him in his high chair at the table. While she warmed up some leftover roast beef, mashed potatoes and corn, she let him chew on Kylie's abandoned crust, keeping a close eye on him to ensure he didn't manage to tear off any pieces.

When she returned to the table, Ryder was putting more salad on Kylie's plate.

"An' that one," Kylie said, pointing to a crouton.

Ryder scooped it out with the tongs and set it on top of the salad already on her plate.

"An' that one." She pointed to another, which he dutifully scooped out for her.

"An' that one."

"And that's all," Lauryn said firmly when Ryder had added the last crouton to her plate.

Kylie picked up her fork.

"How's your pizza?" Ryder asked Lauryn.

"It's really good."

He gestured to her plate. "So why aren't you eating it?"

"Sorry, I guess my mind was wandering." But she picked up her slice and took another bite.

"Anything you want to talk about?"

She shook her head as she continued to chew.

"I'm all done, Mama," Kylie said.

Lauryn glanced at her daughter's plate. "You didn't eat any of the salad you said you wanted."

"I ate the cwoutons."

"Did you drink your milk?"

Kylie nodded.

"Okay, you can go wash up again—and dry this time," she reminded her daughter, who was already climbing down from the table.

"'Kay."

"You really should let me pay you for dinner," she said to Ryder.

"I would have ordered all of this even if I wasn't sharing it," he told her.

"Even the salad?"

"Maybe not the salad," he acknowledged. "But if it makes you feel better, you can consider this payback for the meat loaf you shared with me last week."

It might have made her feel better, except that he'd only been at her house on meat loaf night because he'd spent the afternoon putting up tarps on her roof. But before she could say anything else, Kylie wheeled a pink case into the room.

"You play Barbie wif me, Wyder?"

"Sure," Ryder agreed easily.

Kylie beamed at him and opened the case, spilling dolls and clothes and accessories onto the floor. "I fowgot

Darcy," she said, and raced up to her bedroom to retrieve her favorite doll.

"She named all of her Barbies after the girls in her preschool class," Lauryn explained. "Darcy is currently her best friend."

"Well, it never made any sense to me that they'd all be named Barbie," Ryder said.

"You've given this matter some thought, have you?" she asked, amused by his matter-of-fact statement.

"I had an older sister growing up," he reminded her. "I spent a lot of time playing with Barbies."

She couldn't picture the strong, broad-shouldered man sitting across from her playing with skinny plastic dolls. "You did?"

He nodded. "I had to if I wanted Avery to catch for me while I practiced pitching for Little League."

Kylie came skipping back into the room with Darcy.

"You play, too, Mama?"

"No, thanks. I'll let you and Ryder play while I give Zachary his bath."

After her little guy was bathed, diapered and dressed in a one-piece sleeper, she went downstairs to fix his bottle. By the time she had it ready, he was rubbing his fists against his eyes.

"Clean up your toys, Kylie—it's your turn in the tub next."

"Perfect timing," Ryder said. "Darcy and Ken were just getting ready to go to bed."

Lauryn's brows lifted.

"I mean—each to their own beds," he hastened to clarify. "In their separate houses."

"But they're gettin' mawied tomowow," Kylie said. "Then they can live in the same house."

"Tomorrow? That doesn't give you a lot of time to plan the big event," Lauryn told her. "And you definitely need to pack up all of her clothes and shoes before you can have a wedding."

The little girl immediately began shoving everything back into her pink case. "I can't find the weddin' dwess, Mama."

"I'm sure it's around here somewhere."

"She can't get mawied wifout a weddin' dwess."

"We'll find it tomorrow," Lauryn promised.

Zachary squirmed, reaching for his bottle, and Ryder held out his arms, offering. Lauryn hesitated.

"You can hardly feed him and bathe Kylie at the same time," he pointed out.

"Not very easily," she agreed. And not without Kylie splashing around so much that Zachary would likely need to be changed again, so she passed the bottle and the baby to him.

Zachary had other men in his life: his grandfather and Jordyn's husband—Uncle Marco—and numerous other honorary uncles who were actually her cousins, so maybe it wasn't surprising that he'd immediately taken to Ryder. But still it unsettled Lauryn to see her baby nestled so contentedly in his strong arms.

"Do you mind if I turn on the television so we can watch the baseball game?"

"Go ahead," she said. "Baseball usually helps him fall asleep."

Ryder gasped. "Say it ain't so."

"If I did, I'd be lying."

He looked down at the baby, who was looking at him with wide blue eyes. "Well, you're young yet," he decided. "Your opinion will change when you're strong enough to hold a bat."

"I don't think that's going to happen anytime soon," she told him. "He's only just started holding his bottle."

Chapter Ten

Lauryn wasn't surprised to find that Zachary was asleep by the time she'd tucked Kylie into bed, read her a quick story and returned downstairs. She *was* surprised to find that Ryder had fallen asleep, too, with the baby securely tucked against his chest.

Rob had never sat and cuddled with his daughter like that. He'd held her, usually when Lauryn had thrust the baby into his arms and didn't give him a choice, but he'd always claimed he felt awkward and afraid of hurting her. She didn't know anyone who was stronger than Ryder or who had such an appealing softer side. The combination was incredibly enticing. The fact that he'd actually sat on the floor playing Barbies with her little girl made him almost irresistible.

The attraction she could deal with. As she'd told her sister, there likely wasn't a woman between seventeen and seventy who didn't find him attractive. But the more time she spent with him, the more she found herself drawn to his kindness and generosity and thinking of him not as a TV star but simply a man. A man who made her remember that she wasn't just a mother but a woman, too.

But Lauryn was determined to resist his magnetism. Her life was already complicated enough without adding a new man to the mix. Not that she had any reason to believe that was even an option. Aside from some lighthearted banter and the occasional flirtatious smile, he'd given her no indication that the attraction she felt might be shared.

Ryder's eyes opened when she lifted the baby's weight off his chest.

"Obviously, the game wasn't stimulating enough to keep even you awake," she said lightly.

"The Braves are winning," he told her.

"What's the score?"

"Five-three, top of the sixth."

"Six-three, bottom of the seventh," she informed him. "One on and one out."

"You know baseball?" Ryder sounded surprised.

"I dated a varsity third baseman in high school."

"Did he get to third base with you?" he asked, with a teasing smile.

She just shook her head, not willing to discuss her romantic past with a man who made her wish she had a romantic present. "I'm going to take Zachary up to his crib now."

The baby was in such a deep sleep he didn't stir when she settled him in his bed and covered him with a light blanket. She lightly stroked a finger over his cheek and sent up a silent prayer of thanks for her good fortune. In his short life, he'd given her very little cause for concern— and endless joy.

She checked on Kylie again before she headed downstairs, happy to see that she was sound asleep, too, her favorite stuffed dog tucked under her arm.

"Thank you for babysitting," she said to Ryder when she returned to the living room. "And for the pizza."

"It was my pleasure."

She smiled at the automatic response. "I'm sure you had more exciting plans for your Friday night, but I appreciate that you stayed."

"Actually, I didn't have any plans at all," he told her, sounding a little surprised by the fact himself. "And I quite enjoyed hanging out with you and the kids."

"I have to confess, as much as I love Kylie and Zachary, it's nice to have some adult company every once in a while."

"And it was nice for me to be able to pretend to be a kid again for a little while," he said.

"I know that you're Kylie's new BFF," she confided. "Even I don't have the patience to play Barbies with her for as long as you did."

He grinned. "We're more than BFFs—she asked me to marry her."

"Well, you gave her flowers, stopped it from raining in her castle and played with her," Lauryn reminded him. "Of course, she's head over heels in love with you."

"Is that all it takes?" he wondered aloud.

"For a three-year-old," she confirmed.

He leaned forward and settled his hands on her knees. Even through the denim, she felt the heat of his touch—a heat that quickly spread through her whole body. "What about the three-year-old's mom?"

"Are you flirting with me?" she asked, not sure if she was more wary or hopeful.

One side of his mouth tipped up in a wry smile. "If you have to ask, obviously my skills are rusty."

"It's more likely that mine are," she admitted, feeling more than a little out of her element.

"Then maybe we should work on changing that," he suggested, as his hands skimmed her outer thighs.

It was a friendly caress, not overtly sexual in any way. But to a woman who hadn't been touched by a man in a very long time, the casual slide of his palms over the soft denim was both erotic and enticing.

"Why?" she asked, the question barely more than a whisper.

His gaze held hers as his lips curved again. "Because flirting is only one of the many fun things that men and women can do together."

"But why are you flirting with *me*?" she asked.

"Because you're a beautiful and intriguing woman."

And he was seducing her with nothing more than his eyes and his voice, and she wasn't ready to be seduced.

"I'm a mess," Lauryn told him, trying to ground herself back in reality again. "My life is a mess. Surely, in the past week, you've figured that out."

"Yeah, but you're a hot mess."

She managed a smile. "Flatterer."

He must have sensed the shift in her mood, because he lifted his hands away and reached for something on the sofa. "By the way—" he held up one of Kylie's Barbies "—I found this stuck between the cushions."

"That's the wedding dress she was looking for."

"But she's still missing the veil."

"You're quite the expert on Barbie's wardrobe," she teased, grateful for the change of topic and the lessening of the tension between them. "I'm starting to believe that you really did play with your sister's dolls when you were a kid."

"I wouldn't make something like that up," he assured her.

"Well, I think it's pretty cool that your parents let you play with Barbies and let Avery play baseball without trying to force gender stereotypes on you," she noted.

"A consequence of absenteeism rather than open-mindedness," he assured her. "My guess is that they both thought parenthood would be an interesting experiment—and then they lost interest in it."

This time she reached out to him, touching a tentative hand to his arm. "I'm sorry."

He shrugged. "It wasn't so bad," he said. "Because when you're a kid, you think all families are like your own."

"Not everyone is cut out to be a parent," she acknowledged, her ex-husband having proven that to her.

Then, because she regretted introducing the unhappy

topic, she shifted their conversation in another direction. "I've been watching your show."

His brows lifted. "Why?"

"I was curious."

"You were checking my references," he accused, but his tone was light, teasing.

"That might have been part of it, too," she acknowledged.

"And what did you think?"

"I think they really like the close-ups of you in tight T-shirts."

His gaze shifted away, as if he was embarrassed by her observation. "According to Virginia Gennings—the producer—we have a strong female demographic."

"I'm not surprised," she told him.

"And women are more likely to push their husbands to make changes around the house, while most men are content with the status quo and resistant to change."

"How did Virginia Gennings discover that you look good in a tool belt?"

"I built a solarium for a client in Winston-Salem. We were just finishing up the project when her sister came to town for a visit. Virginia was that sister."

"It was that easy?"

He grinned. "I guess that would depend on who you ask. Virginia would say it wasn't easy at all. She'd apparently pitched the idea to the studio and got the green light, but when she pitched it to me, I turned her down."

"Why?" she asked, genuinely interested in his reasons.

"First, I'm not a fan of reality TV shows in general. Second, I'm a contractor, not an actor. Third, I started my own business because I like being my own boss, so I wasn't keen to work for someone else again."

"What changed your mind?" Lauryn asked.

"She wouldn't take no for an answer," he admitted. "She

thought I was holding out for more money. She came back three times with more lucrative contracts before she realized that what I really wanted was some degree of control over my life.

"So I got the big paycheck, a one-year contract, the right to choose the projects and my crew, final approval of editing and the option to bail if I didn't like what they were doing with the show."

"And now the show's in its sixth season?"

He nodded. "Because we film two seasons a year. Your reno will air at the end of season seven."

She was excited about the renovation, but not so much to know that her friends and neighbors and hundreds of thousands of strangers would be able to watch it on TV.

"So tell me what you've been doing while we've been tearing apart your kitchen," Ryder suggested.

"Mostly trying to find someone else to manage The Locker Room," she admitted. "Soon to be 'Sports Destination—where your quest for the right equipment ends.' And, in smaller letters, 'A Garrett Family Business.'"

He considered the slogan for a minute, then nodded. "It's catchy."

"But not too cheesy?" she asked hopefully.

"Not too cheesy," he assured her. "But maybe you should consider 'where your quest for the *perfect* equipment ends'—it sets a higher standard."

"Oh, I like that. And Tristyn will be so irked that she didn't think of it."

He raised a brow.

"The new name and slogan were her ideas," she said, answering the unspoken question. "Of course, PR is her specialty. She said it was going to be enough of a challenge to bring customers into the store without having to fight against their preconceptions about The Locker Room."

"She's right," he agreed.

"I balked initially," she admitted. "It almost seemed like cheating, using my family's name, as if I was trying to capitalize on the goodwill that they've built up in this town over the past fifty years."

"Isn't it your name, too?"

"The one I was born with, anyway. And the one I shared with my sisters for a lot of years, which I guess makes it appropriate for our joint venture."

"You're lucky to have the support of your family."

She knew it was true. And she knew that Ryder hadn't been nearly as fortunate.

From what he'd told her about his sister, she could tell they were close. From what he'd revealed about his parents, she guessed they were not. And while she was undeniably curious, she was also determined to respect the boundaries of their professional relationship.

Even if those boundaries had already shifted more than a little bit.

After meeting with Adam early Saturday morning to hand off the keys to her new store manager and review the tasks that needed immediate attention, Lauryn happily left him in charge and headed over to her sister's house.

Lauryn took two minutes to set up Zachary's playpen and put the television on for Kylie before she joined her sister in the kitchen of the new home she shared with her husband.

"Coffee?" Jordyn offered. "I picked up some of that cinnamon one you like."

"Okay," she agreed. "But that's not getting you off the hook for last night."

Her sister dropped the pod into the brewer. "What did I do last night?"

"You were supposed to be watching Kylie and Zachary. Instead, you left them in the care of a virtual stranger."

"Ryder's not a stranger," Jordyn denied.

"He was until ten days ago," she pointed out.

"And in that short span of time, your children have come to adore him."

"They adore everyone."

Her sister nodded, conceding the point. "And when I couldn't figure out why Zachary wouldn't stop fussing, Ryder suggested that I give him a teething biscuit—which worked like a charm."

"My mistake," she said dryly. "Obviously, the man is a childcare expert."

"And even if he's not," Jordyn said, "Kylie and Zachary appear relatively unscathed."

She wrapped her hands around the mug her sister passed to her. "That's hardly the point."

"What *is* your point?"

"If you really had to leave, you should have called *me*."

"I was going to," Jordyn said. "But I knew you were in Raleigh, and then Ryder offered to hang around. By the way, how did things go with Adam?"

"Now you're trying to sidetrack me," Lauryn accused.

"No, I'm trying to find out if you persuaded the former assistant manager to come back."

"He's the manager now," she said. "I handed over the keys this morning."

"Well, that's a huge step in the right direction," her sister said.

"It will free up a lot of my time," Lauryn agreed. "I felt so guilty for dumping the kids on Mom every time I turned around. Which, incidentally, is why I asked *you* to take care of them yesterday."

"So…how did Ryder screw up?" Jordyn asked cautiously.

"What do you mean?" She lifted the mug to her lips.

"I assume you came in here all fired up because he'd done something wrong."

"No, he didn't do anything wrong," she admitted.

"Then why are you scowling?"

"Because…" She faltered, aware that her explanation wasn't going to sound rational or reasonable—and probably wasn't rational or reasonable. "Because he was so good with both of them."

"And that's a problem…why?" Jordyn prompted.

She sighed. "I know it shouldn't be, and you're probably going to tell me I'm being ridiculous—"

"You're being ridiculous," her sister confirmed.

"—but he scares me."

Jordyn's teasing immediately gave way to concern. "What do you mean? What did he do?"

"I don't mean that I'm afraid of him," she hastened to clarify, wary of the warrior gleam in her sister's eyes. "But I am afraid of the way he makes feel."

Jordyn relaxed again. "How does he make you feel?"

Lauryn didn't know if there was a simple answer to that question. For the past year and a half, as her efforts to save her crumbling marriage had ended with the acceptance of its demise, she'd gone through the motions. She'd focused on her daughter and preparations for the new baby, her emotions with respect to her husband mostly numb.

Ryder had awakened those long-dormant emotions, and she wasn't entirely sure that was a good thing.

"Unsettled," she finally responded.

"Hmm," Jordyn mused.

"What does *that* mean?" she asked warily.

"I'm getting the impression that he didn't rush off when you got home last night."

She shook her head. "He'd already ordered pizza for dinner, then he stayed to eat with us. Then he played with

Kylie while I got Zachary ready for bed, and he gave Zachary his bottle while Kylie had her bath."

"Wow," Jordyn said. "In one night, he acted more like a husband and father than your ex-husband ever did."

She nodded. "And it scares me to realize that there's a part of me that still wants that. And how crazy is it that I can actually envision this man—who I barely know—in that role?"

"I don't think it's crazy at all," her sister told her. "You deserve to be happy, Laur. And if he makes you happy, then you should go for it."

She shook her head. "My divorce was finalized three weeks ago. There's no way I should be thinking about—"

"Your divorce *is* final," Jordyn interjected. "It's okay for you to move on."

"I have moved on."

"Prove it."

"I have a new business partnership with my sisters and I'm having my kitchen renovated—isn't that proof enough?"

"No," Jordyn said bluntly. "You should do something to thank Ryder for babysitting last night."

"I said thank you. Several times, in fact."

The music emanating from the television in the other room warned that Kylie's favorite program had ended. As if on cue, her daughter skipped into the kitchen—and directly to the cupboard beside the stove.

"What are you doing?" Lauryn asked her.

"Gwyff wantsa tweat," she said, referring to Jordyn's tailless, one-eyed cat. The creature was notoriously antisocial but highly food-motivated, which made him willing to tolerate anyone who fed him. He tolerated Kylie extremely well.

"Gryff always wants treats," Jordyn noted.

"Can I give him tweats?" Kylie asked.

"One treat," her aunt instructed.

"'Kay," the little girl agreed, reaching into the box.

"Speaking of treats," Jordyn said, "I think the situation calls for cupcakes."

"Cupcakes?" Kylie echoed hopefully.

"What situation?" Lauryn asked warily.

"The Ryder situation."

Lauryn shook her head. "He's not a situation and I'm not baking cupcakes."

"I like cupcakes," Kylie chimed in. "Choc'ate cupcakes."

"I know, honey. And Gryff would really like his treat now," Lauryn said, urging her daughter back to the living room.

But, of course, the cat—even with half an ear missing— had heard the box of treats being opened and had come to find Kylie, who simply opened up her hand and let Gryff have his snack.

"See? Even Kylie's in favor of the plan," Jordyn said.

Still, Lauryn hesitated. "I don't want to send the wrong message."

"That you're grateful to him for looking after your kids?"

"And I don't have a kitchen," she pointed out.

"You could use this one."

"I suppose you have all the ingredients I'd need, too?" she challenged.

"Probably not," Jordyn admitted. "But I can pop out to the grocery store."

"I thought you were in a hurry to run errands."

"And the grocery store errand just moved to the top of the list. What do you need to make cupcakes?"

"Spwinkles," Kylie chimed in. "We needs lots an' lotsa spwinkles."

Even as Lauryn added the necessary ingredients to her sister's list, she wondered if the cupcakes were somehow going to say a lot more than a simple "thank you." And was that a message she was ready to send?

Chapter Eleven

Ryder's morning didn't start out too badly. After a meeting with the production team, he went for breakfast with Owen and Virginia. The waitress at the Morning Glory Café brought his breakfast platter with a candle in it, undoubtedly Virginia's idea. The show's producer never missed a detail.

As he was driving away from the restaurant, his phone rang. When he connected the call, he was greeted by his sister singing "Happy Birthday," loudly and off-key.

"I'm on my way to the airport," he said when Avery paused to take a breath. "Isn't that punishment enough without adding your singing to the mix?"

"Actually, that's the other reason I called," his sister said. "To tell you that your chauffeur services aren't required."

It was possible that Justin had changed his shift at the hospital and was available to meet his mother-in-law's flight, but Ryder suspected otherwise. "She's not coming, is she?"

"No," Avery admitted.

He shook his head. Just when he thought his mother couldn't disappoint him anymore, she proved otherwise. Her last-minute cancellation didn't bother him—meetings with his mother were inevitably awkward and strained—but he knew that Avery had been looking forward to her visit. More importantly, she'd been looking forward to Vanessa meeting her maternal grandmother.

"Did she say why?"

"The usual."

Which, of course, meant work. Nothing mattered more to Dr. Cristina Tobin—not even her children. Ryder used to admire her dedication—he'd certainly been told often enough that her research was important, that what she did saved lives. Now it just made him sad. Maybe she did save lives, but she did so at the cost of living her own.

"Are you okay?" he asked his sister now.

"Of course, I'm okay," she said, her tone just a little too bright. "It's not as if I didn't know this might happen."

"Just because you're not surprised doesn't mean you're not disappointed."

"You're right," she admitted. "And I was a little disappointed at first. Then I called Justin's mom and dad and invited them to come for dinner tonight because I'd already bought the groceries to make chicken piccata, and Ellen was absolutely thrilled by the invitation because they haven't seen their granddaughter in three whole days."

"Three whole days, huh?"

Avery chuckled. "Are you feeling guilty now that it's been seven days since you stopped by?"

"I'll see you soon," he promised.

"You could come tonight, too," she offered. "There's going to be plenty of food."

"I told you—I have plans for tonight."

"I remember that's what you said," she acknowledged. "I just wasn't sure you were sticking with that story now that our mother isn't going to be in town."

"I'm sticking with that story," he told her.

"Well, I hope you have a wonderful birthday, little brother."

"Thanks, big sis." He disconnected the call and turned his vehicle around.

He hadn't been completely honest when he told his sister he had plans, but he was optimistic. He knew any number of women who would happily make themselves available to celebrate his birthday, but he didn't want to celebrate with any of them. Instead he drove to the lumber yard, because he wasn't opposed to a little bit of manipulation to get what he wanted.

He was hammering the final replacement board into place in the front porch when Lauryn's van pulled into the driveway. He quickly moved his tools and debris away from the door so that she could get to it without tripping over anything.

Kylie walked beside her mother, balancing a covered plastic container in her hands. Lauryn was weighted down with a diaper bag and purse over her shoulder, the baby's car seat in one hand and three grocery bags in the other. He dumped his tool belt and went to meet her.

"Do you not understand the concept of a day off?" she asked in lieu of a greeting.

"I like to fix things," he told her.

"Then you've definitely come to the right place."

He grinned at that. "Can I give you a hand with something, since both of yours appear to be full?"

She jiggled the keys that were dangling from a finger. "If you could open the door, that would be great."

He did as she requested, then took Zachary's car seat from her, too.

"Thanks," she said. "I swear he's getting heavier every day."

"He's got a few pounds on my niece, that's for sure."

"He's also six months older than Vanessa," Lauryn pointed out. To Kylie, she said, "Go put those on the table in the dining room, please."

The little girl did as she was requested, then turned to Ryder. "We made cupcakes for you."

"For me?" he asked, surprised.

She nodded.

"As a thank-you for last night," Lauryn said, starting to put her groceries away.

"You already said thank you," he reminded her, unbuckling Zachary's restraints and lifting him out of his car seat. "And how did you make cupcakes without an oven?"

"Jordyn let us use hers."

She was still busy with her groceries, so he gently laid the sleeping baby down in his playpen. "What kind of cupcakes?"

"Choc'ate," Kylie chimed in.

"We made vanilla, too," Lauryn said. "Because we didn't know what you'd like."

"Chocolate are my favorite."

"Me, too," the little girl told him.

He smiled. "Did you help make them?"

She nodded. "I put on the icin' an' spwinkles."

"Sprinkles, too? You must have known it was my birthday."

Lauryn closed the fridge and turned to him. "It's your birthday—today?"

He nodded.

"Why didn't you tell me?"

He shrugged. "It didn't exactly come up in conversation."

"We needs birfday candles," Kylie told her mother.

"You're right," Lauryn agreed. "Let's see if I can remember where I put them."

She put on a pot of coffee first, and it only took her a minute after that to find the candles and matches—tucked away on the top shelf of the bookcase, far out of reach of her children. Then she selected one of the chocolate cupcakes—with lots of sprinkles on top—and set it on a plate before inserting a single blue-and-white-striped candle into the middle of it.

Kylie looked at the candle, then at Ryder. "I fink he needs more candles," her daughter whispered to Lauryn.

"I think you're right," she whispered back. "But the number of candles he needs probably wouldn't fit on a cupcake."

"How many candles are you, Wyder?"

He smiled at her phrasing of the question. "Twenty-eight," he told her.

"Thatsa lotta candles," Kylie said solemnly.

"Of course, it seems like a lot to her," Lauryn explained. "She just learned to count to ten—and sometimes she skips over nine."

But he could tell the number had surprised her, too, prompting him to ask, "Do you think it's a lot of candles?"

"It's fewer than were on my last birthday cake," she admitted, putting another cupcake on a plate for her daughter. "Did you wash up?" she asked Kylie.

As the little girl scrambled down from the table to do so, Lauryn reminded her, "And don't forget to dry."

"How many candles did you have?" he asked.

Lauryn shook her head. "Not telling."

"Thirty?" he guessed.

She ignored his question and focused on inspecting Kylie's hands when her daughter returned to the table. After Lauryn nodded her approval, Kylie climbed back into her chair and Lauryn struck a match, then set the flame to the wick of his candle.

"Now you hafta make a wish an' blow out the candle," Kylie told him.

"What should I wish for?" he asked her.

"What you want most," she told her, lifting her cupcake to her mouth.

"Hmm." He glanced up at Lauryn. "I might have to give that some thought."

"While you're thinking, wax is melting onto your cupcake," she warned.

He continued to hold her gaze as he let out a puff of air, extinguishing the flame.

"Whad'ya wish?" Kylie asked, her mouth full of cake and icing.

"I wished that you and Zach and your mom would have dinner with me tonight," he confided.

"You're not supposed to tell your wish," Lauryn told him, then admonished her daughter, "And you're not supposed to talk with food in your mouth."

Kylie, still chewing on her cupcake, said nothing.

"Why am I not supposed to tell my wish?" Ryder asked.

"Because then it won't come true," she warned.

He accepted the mug of coffee she set in front of him, stirred in a spoonful of sugar. "Are you really going to deny my birthday wish?"

"You don't have plans to spend your birthday with friends or family?"

"Avery wanted to cook dinner for me, but my mother was supposed to be in town and I didn't want to be part of a dysfunctional family reunion."

"Your mother was planning to come to town for your birthday and you weren't going to spend it with her?"

"Her plans had nothing to do with my birthday," he assured her. "If not for the fact that she always sends me a card and a check, I'd think she didn't even remember the date I was born."

"I'm getting the impression that you're not very close to your mother," she said lightly.

"We're as close as we both want to be."

She frowned at that. "There are times that it feels as if I can't move in this town without tripping over one of my relatives but, at the same time, it's comforting to know that they're never far away if I need them."

"Your family is obviously a little different from mine."

"Still, I'm sure your mother is proud of your success."

He shook his head. "She's never forgiven me for not going to medical school."

"Maybe you don't have an MD, but you do have your own television show," she pointed out.

"My mother doesn't watch television."

She sat down at the table with her own cup of coffee. "Has she seen the billboards proclaiming that you're America's Hottest Handyman?"

"I sincerely hope not," he told her.

"Has she ever actually seen the results of what you do?" she asked curiously.

"She's not impressed—any man can hammer a nail."

"If she met my ex-husband, she'd know that's not true," Lauryn remarked dryly.

Ryder managed a smile at that.

"All done, Mama," Kylie said. "Can I go wash up now?"

They both shifted their attention to the little girl, who had chocolate icing, crumbs and sprinkles smeared on her face and hands.

"No," Lauryn told her. "You sit right there—I'll get a washcloth."

"Are you gonna eat your cupcake?" Kylie asked him, eyeing Ryder's plate hopefully when her mother had left the room.

He might have offered it to her if he wasn't sure his generosity would result in a scolding from Lauryn. "Of course," he told her. "It's my birthday cupcake and extra-special because you made it for me. But there's one sprinkle—" he carefully picked a pink one off the icing "—that's just for you."

He dropped the candy into her outstretched palm and she immediately transferred it to her mouth—and more icing from her hand to her face in the process.

Ryder lifted the cupcake to his mouth to hide his smile. At that moment, Lauryn came back with a washcloth to wipe Kylie's face and hands, carefully scrubbing each and every digit on both hands and the spaces in between. "Now you may go play," she said to her daughter when she was done.

Kylie slid off her seat and scampered away.

"That was really sweet," Lauryn said to him. "Sharing your sprinkles with her."

He shrugged. "It wasn't a big deal."

"It was to Kylie," she told him. "And to me."

"It was one sprinkle," he said, uncomfortable with the way she was looking at him—as if there was something special about him because he'd had a two minute conversation with her kid.

Apparently sensing his unease, she shifted the topic of the conversation again. "You were telling me about your mother's visit," she reminded him.

"Just that her intended visit is why I told Avery that I already had plans for tonight."

"You lied to your sister to avoid seeing your mother who didn't end up coming to town, anyway?"

"It wasn't really a lie," he denied. "I did have plans—to stay far away from my mother. So...will you let me take you out for dinner tonight?"

"Actually, my cousin's wife and daughter are coming over tonight. Maura's taking a babysitting certification course and I'm going to take advantage of her services to complete the inventory I left unfinished at the store yesterday."

He studied her for a minute. "I can't figure out if you really have stock to count or if you're brushing me off."

"I really have stock to count," she said, with enough reluctance in her tone to convince him that it was true.

"And if you didn't?" he wondered.

"I still wouldn't go out for dinner with you," she admitted.

"Because you're not attracted to me?" he challenged.

"Because you should be having dinner with the blonde in the red dress."

He didn't expect that she would give a direct answer to his question—and he definitely hadn't expected the answer that she did give. "What blonde in the red dress?"

"The one you were with at Marg & Rita's last week."

"I wasn't *with* her," he denied.

"You left the bar with her."

Damn. He'd hoped no one had seen him slip out the door with Debby, but not for the reasons that Lauryn apparently suspected. "Only to give her a ride home."

"You don't owe me any explanations."

But he wanted to explain. "She's Brody's little sister, who had a little too much to drink in an attempt to forget that she'd recently broken up with her boyfriend. I took her home, saw her safely inside, then went back to my own place because I knew that I had a roofing job to oversee early the next morning."

"You might have told me about the roofing job when I saw you that night," she told him.

He smiled. "I sort of did," he reminded her. "But I'm glad you didn't pick up on my hints or I might have missed seeing you in your…pajamas."

Maura knocked at the door promptly at six o'clock. Though her stepmother, Rachel, was there to supervise, Rachel had asked Lauryn to pretend she wasn't and to give her instructions to the babysitter as if she was on her own. So Lauryn invited Maura inside and showed her the notes she'd left by the phone, with appropriate snack instructions, television guidelines, bedtimes and her cell phone number clearly enumerated.

"An' I gets stowies before bed," Kylie piped up.

"She gets *one* story before bed," Lauryn clarified.

Maura nodded. "What time do you think you'll be home?"

"The inventory shouldn't take more than a couple of hours."

"I need seven more hours for my certification," her niece reminded her.

She smiled at that. "I'm definitely not going to be out *that* long."

"Stay out as long or as short as you need," Rachel told her. "We can come back for more hours another time."

"You play Barbies?" Kylie asked her babysitter.

"I can play whatever you want," Maura told her.

The little girl beamed and skipped off to get her dolls.

"I guess that's everything," Lauryn said, picking up her purse and heading to the door.

"Not quite," Maura said, following her.

"What did I forget?"

The babysitter held out her arms to take the baby.

"Oh, right." Feeling foolish and oddly reluctant, she pressed a kiss to Zachary's forehead and passed him to Maura.

Rachel followed her out the door. "They'll be fine," she promised.

"I know they will," Lauryn agreed.

"I see Andrew finally remembered to come over and replace those weak boards," Rachel noted, looking at the new wood beneath her feet.

"Actually, that was Ryder," Lauryn told her.

"Oh, right—I heard that his crew is doing some work on the house." The other woman's eyes twinkled. "How's that going?"

"I wouldn't know, I'm not allowed to even peek in the kitchen."

"I'm not talking about the kitchen but the man."

"I guess you're a fan of *Ryder to the Rescue*, too?"

"I do like the look of a man in a tool belt," Rachel confirmed. "Why do you think I married your cousin?"

Lauryn sighed. "I wish I'd been half as smart and found a man who was handy around the house—or at least one who knew how to change a toilet paper roll."

"Well, you've got a Mr. Fix-It now."

"I don't have him," she denied.

"Then you're not trying hard enough," her cousin's wife said, followed by an exaggerated wink.

Lauryn shook her head, but she was smiling when she drove away, and feeling incredibly grateful for the support of her often outrageous but always loving family.

Because she was still thinking about Rachel and Maura when she pulled into a parking space in front of The Locker Room, she didn't pay much attention to the pickup that occupied another space. It wasn't until she got out of the van that she spotted the Renovations by Ryder logo on the side—and then saw the man himself leaning against the building near the door.

"I came to help you with inventory," he said, before she had a chance to ask.

"Why?"

"Because we can go for dinner when it's done."

She narrowed her gaze. "I never agreed to that plan."

"I know. And I never suggested the plan because I knew you would think of some reason to shoot it down," he admitted.

He was right, and it irked her that he was right, that he could read her so easily. And, of course, now that he was here, she would feel ridiculous sending him away so that she could complete the task on her own. Instead, she shrugged, "I can't say I understand why you want to spend your birthday counting golf balls, but I'm not going to refuse your help."

"I think you'll figure out the why—" he flashed a quick grin "—eventually."

She slid a key into the lock to release the dead bolt, then stepped inside to disarm the alarm and gestured for him to enter, locking the door again at his back when he'd done so.

"I've inventoried everything in the storeroom," she told him, heading toward the back of the store. "But I haven't had a chance to check what's on the floor. I just need to get the lists from the office."

He followed her lead. She found the documents in the folder where she'd left them, but they weren't exactly as she'd left them.

"Is something wrong?" Ryder asked.

"These are all complete." She noted the initials in the corner of each page. "Somehow Adam got this all done today."

"I think your new manager is bucking for a raise."

She managed a smile. "He knows he'll get one, as soon as I can afford to give it to him."

"Well, I'm glad that was quick, because I'm starving. All I've eaten since breakfast is a cupcake, and that's only thanks to you."

"I've got half a dozen more that I meant to send home with you," she told him.

"We can get them after," he told her, clearly not budging on the dinner idea.

But sharing a meal with him—just the two of them—would really mess with the boundaries she was anxious to maintain. "Look, Ryder," she said, trying to reason with him. "I'm flattered by the attention—as any woman would be—but you can't possibly be interested in me."

"Why can't I be?" he challenged.

She hadn't expected him to make her spell it out, but because she'd been thinking about him—and thinking about all of the reasons she shouldn't be thinking about him—

she had a ready answer. "Because you're Charisma's most famous handyman and heartthrob, and I've got one failed marriage, two kids and a few years on you."

"You're really hung up on the age thing, aren't you?" he mused.

She shook her head. "Out of everything I just said, that's the one fact you focused on?"

"It's the only fact I can't dispute, because you refuse to tell me how old you are," he pointed out. "Aside from that, I think I've figured out a way to prove my interest is real."

"How?" she asked warily.

"Like this," he said, and lowered his head to kiss her.

Chapter Twelve

Lauryn had seen the warning signs.

The way her heart beat just a little bit faster whenever Ryder was near. The way even an accidental touch made her skin tingle. The way his smile made her feel all warm and fluttery inside. But she'd ignored those signs, attributing them to the fact that he was just so darn sexy and it had been so long since she'd felt anything.

Still, she didn't expect that her body would shift from slow burn to full blaze within a second of the first brush of his lips against hers.

Then he lifted his hands to her face, his fingertips trailing gently along the line of her jaw, down her throat. The feather-light touch raised goose bumps on her skin and made everything inside her quiver. He slid a finger beneath her chin, tipping her head back just a little so that he could deepen the kiss.

He coaxed her lips apart, slowly and gently, as if they had all the time in the world and he'd be happy to spend every minute of it kissing her. Then his tongue slid between them to dance with hers—a slow, sensual seduction that made everything inside her tremble and yearn.

She'd never thought a kiss was a big deal. How could she have known when no one had ever kissed her the way that Ryder was kissing her now?

When he finally eased his mouth from hers, they were both breathless.

"Do you still think I'm not interested?" he asked her.

"I can't think at all when you kiss me," she admitted.

He smiled, apparently pleased with her response. "Good," he said, and lowered his head again.

She stepped back, quickly.

Thankfully, he didn't follow, because Lauryn wasn't sure she had the willpower to turn away from him a second time.

"What are you in the mood for?" he asked.

She blinked, uncomprehending. "What?"

His lips curved again in response to her obvious befuddlement. "For dinner," he clarified.

"Oh." She exhaled a slow, unsteady breath and tried to refocus her thoughts.

"Casa Mercado?" he suggested.

She glanced down at her jeans and T-shirt. "I don't think I'm appropriately dressed."

"Valentino's?" he offered as an alternative.

She shook her head. "Too much risk of running into my sister or her husband or someone else in his family who would report back to her."

"Report what?" he asked curiously.

"That I was having dinner with America's Hottest Handyman."

"An event not worthy of any tabloid headlines," he assured her.

"My sisters would disagree."

"Do you have a better suggestion for dinner?"

She considered for a minute, then nodded decisively. "Eli's."

Eli's was famous for juicy cooked-to-order burgers and thick, hand-dipped milk shakes. The atmosphere of the diner-style restaurant, on the other hand, was nothing spectacular. The booths were red vinyl, the tables white Formica, the walls decorated with retro movie posters and all of it was illuminated by bright fluorescent lights.

It certainly wasn't the type of place that Ryder would have chosen to take any woman on a date. On the other hand, he hoped the casual atmosphere would help Lauryn relax in a way he suspected she wouldn't in an establishment with linen tablecloths and a wine list.

She ordered a bacon cheeseburger with curly fries and a vanilla milk shake; he went for the double, also with fries and a chocolate shake.

"Mmm, this is good," she said, after taking the first bite of her burger.

"Anyone ever tell you that you're a cheap date?" he asked teasingly.

"This isn't a date," she said firmly.

He just smiled. "You say to-may-to—"

"I say, this isn't a date," she interjected.

"I invited you to dinner and you, after some bribing and cajoling, agreed. That sounds like a date to me."

Her lips twitched as she fought against a smile. "Are bribing and cajoling part of your usual dating routine?"

"No, I have to admit this is a first for me," he told her. "You're not the first woman to ever say no, but you're the first who's intrigued me enough to want to change the no to a yes." A fact that probably surprised him as much as it surprised her.

He'd been perfectly content with his life. He certainly hadn't been looking for any entanglements. And then Lauryn had opened her front door—with a sweetly smiling child by her side and a chubby-cheeked baby on her hip and all kinds of attitude in her gray-green eyes—and he'd been hooked.

He'd dated all kinds of women—blondes, brunettes and redheads, tall and short, slender and curvy. All that was required was a mutual attraction—and an understanding that there would be no strings, no regrets and definitely no heartache when it was over.

His feelings for Lauryn were different, and he hadn't yet figured out what he was going to do about them. He wasn't looking for love. Truth be told, he wasn't entirely sure he even believed in it. While he couldn't deny that his sister had found something special with her husband, he wasn't certain it would last for a lifetime. He hoped it would—for the sake of Avery and Justin and especially Vanessa—but he wouldn't put any bets on it. Being with Lauryn made him want to gamble on his own future.

"I have two kids," she reminded him.

"You have two wonderful kids," he agreed.

"And Kylie is just starting to get used to her father being gone."

"I'm not trying to take his place," Ryder said, wanting to be clear about that.

"I know that, but Kylie doesn't. She only knows that there's an empty place in her life, and suddenly you're there and you're letting her have pizza and playing Barbies and…"

"And you don't want her to get attached," he finished for her.

"I don't want her to get hurt. Again."

He nodded, because he understood that she had reasons to be cautious. He could even acknowledge that she was smart to want to put on the brakes; he just wasn't convinced that she would succeed. The kiss they'd shared proved the attraction between them was both mutual and intense, and he was looking forward to following wherever it might lead. "I can't change the fact that I'm going to be around a lot over the next couple of months—maybe longer."

She narrowed her gaze. "Why 'maybe longer'?"

"Virginia thinks our viewers might appreciate seeing the results of a more comprehensive project, and she wanted me to discuss the possibility with you."

She took another sip of her milk shake. "What would a more comprehensive project entail?"

"Letting us loose in other rooms of your house," he explained.

"I didn't even want you in my kitchen," she reminded him.

"But it hasn't been so bad, has it?"

"It's only been a week," she pointed out.

"You're right," he admitted. "But Owen doesn't like gaps in the schedule, so he'd probably agree to anything you want."

"Why is there a gap in your schedule?"

"We were originally supposed to head to Georgia to work on the restoration of an antebellum mansion in Watkinsville, but the purchasers have encountered a few snags in their attempts to finalize the paperwork." Having finished his own meal, he stole a fry from her plate. "So what do you think about letting us tackle some more jobs around your house?"

"I'm tempted," she admitted, nudging her plate toward him. "But I'm not sure how I feel about my kids living in a construction zone for an extended period of time."

"That's a valid consideration," he acknowledged. "On the other hand, we're talking about work that you're going to want to have done eventually, and if you have it done now, you won't have to look forward to the noise and debris in the future."

She sighed. "You sure do know how to tempt a girl."

He grinned. "Imagine what I could do if I was actually trying."

Lauryn didn't want to imagine.

She didn't dare let her mind travel too far down the path of any temptation connected to Ryder Wallace. Because more than an hour after they'd left the store—after the kiss—her blood was still humming in her veins.

If he makes you happy, you should go for it.

She didn't know if he made her happy, but there was no doubt he made her yearn. After almost a year and a half of hibernation, her hormones were suddenly wide-awake and clamoring for attention.

Ryder's attention.

Which was precisely why she should thank him for dinner and walk away. Instead, when they left the restaurant she asked, "Did you want to come back to my place to get those cupcakes?"

"Inviting me home after a first date?" he teased.

"It wasn't a date," she said again.

He just grinned.

"And I'm only inviting you to come over to pick up the cupcakes," she further clarified, as much for herself as for him. Besides, Maura and Rachel would be there to chaperone so she didn't have to worry about him trying to steal any more kisses—or her own desire to give them away.

"I'll be right behind you," he promised.

Except that her cousin's wife and daughter stayed only long enough to say hello before they hurried out the door, with Rachel giving her an encouraging wink as she waved goodbye.

Lauryn pulled one of her dining room chairs across the floor, then stood on the seat to reach the top of the hutch where she'd put the box to ensure it was out of reach of her daughter's sweet tooth and eager grasp.

Ryder was immediately behind her. She sucked in a breath as his hands grasped her hips. "What are you doing?"

"Making sure you don't fall."

"I'm not going to fall," she assured him. "I do this all of the time."

"Do you know how many household accidents occur every day because people think any piece of furniture is a ladder?" he asked her.

"No, I don't. How many?"

"I don't know the number offhand," he admitted. "But it's a lot."

"This is sturdy Garrett-made furniture," she told him. "And you can let go of me now."

His eyes, when they lifted to hers, were filled with heat and wicked promise. "Maybe I don't want to."

Her tongue flicked out to moisten her suddenly dry lips. "Do you want your cupcakes to end up on the floor?"

He lifted his hands away, then removed the box from her hands. Lauryn stepped down off the chair.

"Thanks for these," he said.

"Those were to thank you," she reminded him. "And thank you for dinner, too."

"It was my pleasure."

She walked him to the door. "Happy birthday, Ryder."

"Thanks to you and the kids, it was," he said.

And then he kissed her again.

And though she knew kissing him back was a very bad idea, he felt too good to want to stop. In fact, he tasted so good that she wanted to get closer, but there was a box between them. As if he could read her thoughts, he set the container on the table by the door, freeing his hands to touch her. And those strong hands proved to be every bit as talented as his mouth.

Watching him on television, she couldn't help but admire his confident skill as he swung a sledgehammer or taped drywall or nailed trim. Since getting to know him, she'd wondered how it might feel to have his hands stroking over her body, those callused palms sliding against the soft skin of her breasts, her belly, her thighs. It had been a long time since she'd had a man's hands on her—a long time since she'd wanted a man's hands on her. And when those strong and oh-so-clever hands slid beneath the hem of her T-shirt, his warm touch surpassed every one of her fantasies.

A soft, blissful sigh whispered between her lips. She didn't want him to stop—she didn't ever want him to stop kissing her and touching her. But somewhere in the back of her mind, where a few brain cells were still functioning, she accepted that while getting naked with Ryder might feel really good tonight, she needed to think about tomorrow.

She eased away from him. Breathlessly. Reluctantly. "We can't do this."

"I can't think of a single reason why not," he said.

"For starters, because you're renovating my kitchen."

"The cameras are gone," he pointed out. "There's only you and me here now."

"And my two children," she said, a reminder to herself as much as to Ryder.

"Who are sleeping upstairs."

Upstairs—where her big, empty bed was also located. A bed that would feel a lot less empty with Ryder in it. But as tempting as the idea was, she shook her head. "I don't know how to have an affair."

"Since neither of us is currently involved with anyone else, it wouldn't be an affair," he told her.

"What would it be?"

He smiled, a slow curving of his lips that made her toes curl. "A pleasure." His hands skimmed up her back, raising goose bumps on her flesh and warming the blood in her veins. "A very definite pleasure," he promised.

The way her body was reacting to his touch, she had no doubt that he could fulfill that promise. But she'd never been the type to jump in with both feet, and she had to think about Kylie and Zachary, because everything she did affected her children.

"Don't you think that giving in to this…attraction would complicate our business arrangement?"

"It's already complicated," he told her.

"And getting involved would complicate it even further."

"Maybe," he acknowledged. "Or maybe it would alleviate some of the tension between us."

And there was no doubt she was feeling...tense. But she had to be smart.

"I want you, Lauryn. I didn't want to want you," he admitted. "But I've given up denying that I do."

"Ryder—" He touched a finger to her lips, silencing her so that he could continue.

"I want to strip you naked and make love to you." His voice was as seductive as a caress, the words sliding over her skin like a lover's touch. "But we'll wait until you're sure that it's what you want, too."

"You might be waiting a long time," she warned.

His lips curved again in a smile that was slow and sexy and just a little bit smug. "I don't think so."

"Good night, Ryder," she said firmly.

"Good night, Lauryn." He brushed his lips over hers once more. "Sweet dreams."

After a rain delay in Martinsville necessitated postponing Sunday's scheduled race, Tristyn finally returned to Charisma on Tuesday. Lauryn was in the store when her sister came in, her arms full of bags of Halloween decorations. She tried to protest that they were a sporting goods store and no one cared if there weren't any pumpkins or ghosts on display, but Tristyn waved off her arguments and got busy transforming the front window mannequins into zombies—albeit zombies wearing high-end sporting apparel and top-of-the-line athletic shoes.

When Adam came in at noon—because Lauryn opened the store on Tuesdays, Wednesdays and Thursdays—she was finally able to escape from her position at the front register.

"I need to talk to you about something," she said to

Tristyn when she found her sister arranging fake cobwebs and creepy plastic spiders on a skateboard display.

Her sister set another spider in place, then turned to face her. "You didn't forget to cancel the order for those ski jackets, did you?"

"No, I canceled the order. This has nothing to do with the inventory. Well, maybe it does. Indirectly."

"You're flustered," Tristyn mused. "And you never get flustered."

"I kissed Ryder." She blurted the words out like a confession. "Or he kissed me. But then I kissed him back."

Her sister's lips curved. "I think I understand now why you're flustered. This is certainly an interesting—if not unexpected—development."

"No, it's *not* interesting," Lauryn denied. "It's…crazy and irresponsible and reckless and dangerous and crazy—"

"You said 'crazy' twice," Tristyn pointed out.

"Because it needs to be said twice. Maybe even three times or ten times. Because I never should have let it happen and it's all Jordyn's fault."

"How is it Jordyn's fault?" her sister wanted to know. "And why are you assigning blame? Unless he's a really lousy kisser, and if he is, I don't want to know—it will ruin all of my fantasies."

"Of course, he isn't a lousy kisser. He's at the complete opposite end of the spectrum of kissers. And it's Jordyn's fault because she told me to make the cupcakes."

"You made cupcakes for his birthday?" Tristyn queried.

Lauryn frowned at that. "How did you know it was his birthday?"

"There were about a thousand 'happy birthday' messages to him on Twitter."

"You follow him on Twitter?"

"Half a million people follow him on Twitter," her sister said matter-of-factly.

"Well, I'm not on Twitter and I didn't know it was his birthday," Lauryn said. "The cupcakes were supposed to be a thank-you because he stayed to watch the kids on Friday when Jordyn abandoned them."

Tristyn waved away her explanation as if it was inconsequential. "Tell me about the kiss."

Just the memory of the kiss had heat flooding through her body, warming her from the top of her head to the toes curling inside of her shoes. "I can't remember the last time I was kissed like that," she admitted. "If ever. It was... pretty much perfect."

Her sister sighed dreamily. "I suspected that about him. He has the aura of a man who knows what he's doing in all aspects of his life."

"He knows what he's doing," she confirmed.

"What happened after the kiss?" Tristyn asked.

"We went out for dinner. To Eli's."

Her sister was clearly unimpressed. "He kissed you senseless and then bought you a burger?"

"Eli's was my choice."

Tristyn sighed. "Sometimes I can't believe we're sisters."

"We had a good time," she said, just a little defensively.

"You had milk shakes under fluorescent lights when you deserve wine and candlelight."

"We had a good time," she repeated. Then she thought about the kiss again—the kiss she hadn't been able to stop thinking about—and mentally amended "good" to "great."

"I'm not disputing that you probably did," Tristyn told her. "I just think you should expect more. You deserve more."

"Maybe I should consider one of those Rabbits you were talking about."

Her sister shook her head. "A battery-operated device is no substitute for a flesh-and-blood man, especially not when that man is Ryder Wallace."

She didn't disagree, but there were still a lot of reasons to be wary. "He's six years younger than me."

"So?"

"So I'm looking ahead at forty and he's not even thirty."

"You're thirty-four," her sister noted. "Forty is a long way off."

"Maybe, but I still graduated from college before he'd finished high school."

"So?" Tristyn said again.

She sighed and finally confided her biggest concern. "I have to think about my children—especially Kylie."

"Of course, you have to think about the children," her sister agreed. "But you need to think about yourself, too. What do *you* want? Are you looking for a fling or a relationship?"

"I wasn't looking for anything," she denied. "Not until he kissed me."

"And now?" Tristyn prompted.

"Now—" She blew out a frustrated breath. "Now I can't seem to think about anything but how much I want him naked and in my bed."

"An admirable goal," her sister assured her.

"I thought you would be the voice of reason, that you would point out all of the reasons that even thinking about getting naked with him is a bad idea."

"No, you didn't," Tristyn said. "If you really wanted to be talked out of this, you'd be talking to Jordyn."

"Except that Jordyn advised me to 'go for it.'"

"Obviously falling in love again has changed her perspective on life. And maybe that should be a lesson to you."

Lauryn shook her head. "I can't afford to make any more mistakes in my life."

"Relationships are always a risk," Tristyn acknowledged. "If you don't put your heart on the line you can't lose. On the other hand, you can't win, either."

Chapter Thirteen

Ryder was pleased with the progress his crew was making on Lauryn's kitchen—and frustrated that he'd made absolutely zero progress with the woman herself. He thought they'd had a good time together on his birthday. They'd talked and laughed and shared a couple of sizzling kisses. But in the almost two weeks that had passed since then, he'd barely seen her—and he never had an opportunity to be alone with her.

He really wanted to be alone with her. He wanted to kiss her and touch her and—

And there she was. Once again on her way out the door when he was coming in. But this time, he changed direction, falling into step beside her as she headed out with Zachary in his stroller and Kylie by her side. The backpack on the little girl told him that she was on her way to meet the school bus, which picked her up at the bottom of the driveway every morning.

"What have you got stuffed into that pack today?" Ryder asked Kylie.

"My Halloween costume," she told him. "We're havin' a party at school an' I'm gonna be a pwincess."

"I bet you'll be the prettiest princess in the whole school," he told her.

"You wanna come to my party?" she asked.

"As much fun as I'm sure that would be, I think your mom would prefer if I stayed here and worked on her kitchen."

"Definitely," Lauryn agreed.

Kylie tipped her head back to look at her mother. "Are you comin' to my party?"

"Yes, I'll be there," she confirmed.

"You hafta bwing tweats," the little girl reminded her.

"Mrs. Shea knows that I'm bringing a fruit tray," Lauryn told her as the school bus pulled up.

"'Kay," Kylie said. She quickly hugged her mom, then Ryder, then she leaned in to kiss her brother's cheek before she tackled the big stairs leading onto the bus.

"There's one Garrett female who isn't stingy with her affection," Ryder noted as the bus doors closed, swallowing the little girl up inside.

"Schulte," her mother corrected automatically.

He shook his head. "That might be her name, but the blood in her veins is pure Garrett."

Lauryn's lips curved just a little, as if she was pleased by the thought, but all she said was, "Aren't you supposed to be working on my kitchen?"

"The work will get done," he promised. "And I want to know why you've been dodging me for the last couple of weeks."

"I haven't been dodging you," she denied, pivoting the stroller around and heading back up the driveway. "I've seen you almost every day."

"But you're careful never to be alone with me."

She lifted Zachary out of the stroller and put him in his car seat, while Ryder collapsed the stroller for her and set it in the back of the van. "There's no reason for me to be alone with you."

"I didn't mean to scare you off," he said, when he had her full attention again.

"You didn't." But she was looking at her car keys when she said it.

He tipped her chin up, forcing her to meet his gaze. "Prove it," he said. "Have dinner with me tonight."

"Tonight is Halloween," she reminded him.

"You don't eat on Halloween?"

Her lips curved. "Usually only chocolate bars and gummy bears."

"After trick-or-treating," he guessed.

She nodded.

"Can I come along?"

"Only if you don't expect me to share the candy."

"You can have all of it, but—" he winked at her "—I have dibs on your kisses."

I have dibs on your kisses.

His words continued to echo in the back of Lauryn's mind throughout the day—while she was at the store, while she was assembling the fruit tray in her mother's kitchen, even while she was at the Halloween party at Kylie's preschool. Because she knew he wasn't talking about candy kisses, and she would gladly trade away every last gummy bear to feel his lips on hers again.

But she wanted more than his kisses. She wanted *him*. And that was why she'd been dodging him. Not that staying away from him had stopped the wanting, so when he'd asked if he could join them for trick-or-treating, she didn't see any point in denying his request.

When the doorbell rang, Lauryn was struggling to get Zachary into the pumpkin costume his sister had worn a few years earlier. Of course, Kylie had been two months younger—and about five pounds lighter—on her first Halloween.

After instructing Kylie to look out the window to ensure it was Ryder at the door, Lauryn gave her daughter permission to let him in.

"Hi, Wyder!" Kylie greeted him.

He took in her costume and immediately offered a deep, courtly bow. "Good evening, Your Highness."

She giggled. "You like my costume?"

"Very much," he told her. "But…I think you're missing something."

Her hands immediately went to the top of her head to ensure that her sparkly crown was in place. "What's missin'?"

"A trick-or-treat bag. Something worthy of a princess." He held up the one he carried—made of white satin fabric and decorated with ribbons and sparkly beads with a lace drawstring.

Kylie gasped, her eyes wide. "Is that for me?"

Ryder nodded. "Thank you!" she said, and threw herself into his arms.

He caught her as best he could, considering that his hands were full, and hugged her back. "You're welcome."

She accepted the bag and peered inside. "Look, Mama—there's even candy inside."

"You just made her day," Lauryn said, when Kylie had skipped away. "That's quite an improvement over a reusable grocery bag."

"I brought something for you, too," he said, offering her a bottle of wine. "The clerk assured me that nothing goes better with gummy bears than a nice merlot."

"I find a cool, crisp chardonnay really brings out the flavor of the green ones."

He lifted a brow. "You separate out the colors as you eat them?"

"Doesn't everyone?"

He chuckled. "No." He moved toward the refrigerator with a grocery bag in hand. "I also brought a couple of steaks and baking potatoes that we can throw on the grill later."

Kyle returned with sparkly shoes now on her feet. "Can we go, Mama?" she asked. "Is it time?"

"I think somebody's getting anxious," Ryder told her.

"She's been asking the same question since we got home from the school party," Lauryn told him.

"Are you comin' twick-or-tweatin' wif us, Wyder?"

"Yes, I am," he said.

"But you're not dwessed up."

He feigned shock. "You don't recognize my costume?" She shook her head.

"I'm Ryder to the Rescue," he said with a dramatic flourish, making her giggle. "I save home owners from leaky pipes and crumbling plaster. And sometimes I even take princesses door-to-door on Halloween night."

Lauryn boosted Zachary onto her hip. "Let's go, princess and Ryder to the Rescue, before this pumpkin turns into a grumpy bear."

It was nice to have company on the outing. Lauryn particularly appreciated a second set of adult eyes watching over Kylie as there were always so many people milling about—many of them unrecognizable in their costumes—that she worried about losing sight of her daughter. At least she didn't have to be concerned about Zachary, who was content—at least this year—to ride along in his stroller.

"Did you make her costume?" Ryder asked when they were stopped at the end of a driveway watching Kylie make her way to the front door. "It looks like a real dress."

"It was Maura's flower girl dress when her dad married Rachel." She smiled at the memory. "Of course, she was eight at the time, so I had to take in the sides and chop several inches off the hem. But after that, I just sewed on a lot of sparkling beads and stuff to make it look more princess-y."

"You did a great job."

"Thanks, but I was actually hoping she'd want to be

something more traditional—like a black cat or a ghost," she admitted.

"What's wrong with her being a princess?" he asked.

Lauryn shrugged. "I'm just worried that I'm not doing her any favors by perpetuating her illusions about fairy tales and happy endings."

"She's three," he reminded her. "She should believe in happy endings."

"Maybe," she said dubiously.

"Just because your Prince Charming turned out to be a frog is no reason to undermine her beliefs," he chided gently.

"Is that what you think I'm doing?" she asked, frowning as she realized he might be right.

"I don't know—is it?"

She sighed. "Maybe."

"And maybe your Prince Charming wasn't really a prince but the big bad wolf in disguise," he suggested.

"Now you're mixing up your fairy tales," she told him.

"My point is that you should have faith that the real Prince Charming is somewhere in your future. Or maybe even—" he slung an arm across her shoulders "—in your present."

She tipped her head back to look at him. "I always thought Prince Charming would wear a crown."

"That's only in the storybooks—in real life, he sometimes wears a tool belt."

When they had headed out at six thirty, Kylie had skipped down the driveway with an empty trick-or-treat bag and a heart full of excitement and enthusiasm. It wasn't even seven thirty when Kylie opened her bag to show her mother the contents. "Look, Mama, it's almost fulled up."

"Already? That's great."

"You're only saying that because you want to go home,"

Ryder guessed, speaking in a low tone so that only Lauryn could hear.

"I would like to get Zachary into bed at his usual time," she acknowledged.

"I can stay out with Kylie if you want to take him home," Ryder offered.

"That's not necessary," she said, watching as Kylie made her way up the flagstone walk of the next house. "Her energy will fade before much longer."

"That's something I have yet to see," he noted.

Lauryn smiled. "You will tonight. She'll go full speed ahead right up to the moment that she crashes."

Which was exactly what she did a short while later. They were three blocks from home when Kylie suddenly seemed to droop at her mother's feet, her bag of candy falling to the sidewalk. "I tired, Mama. You ca-wy me?"

Lauryn had no objections to carrying her daughter from the living room to her bed when she fell asleep downstairs—or even from the van into the house—but three blocks was another matter.

"Why don't you stand on the back of Zachary's stroller?" she suggested as an alternative.

Kylie shook her head. "My feets hurt."

"This sounds like a job for Ryder to the Rescue," he interjected, swooping down and lifting her high in the air to settle her on his shoulders.

The little girl screeched with terrified glee and grabbed hold of his hair so that it stood up in little tufts where her fingers grasped it. The scream had given Lauryn's heart a jolt—her daughter's precarious position jolted it again. She opened her mouth to demand that Ryder put Kylie down, then she saw the breathless smile on Kylie's face and the words stuck in her throat.

Lauryn couldn't begin to count the number of times she'd been carried like that on her father's shoulders when she was a child. It had been the perfect vantage point to watch the Fourth of July parade on Main Street or to look at the newly hatched baby birds in a nest in their backyard, and it was her favorite way to be carried when her own legs had been too tired to walk any farther.

The memories flooded back to her as she watched Ryder with her daughter, and something deep inside of her opened up, like a flower blooming in response to the warmth of the sun.

And that was before Kylie rested her chin on top of Ryder's head and said, "This was the bestest Halloween ever."

Ryder had just poured the wine when Kylie came back downstairs after her bath. Her costume was gone, but she was wearing a princess nightgown with fuzzy slippers on her feet.

"She wanted to say good-night," Lauryn explained.

"Of course," he said. Then to Kylie, he said, "Good night, princess."

She smiled shyly. "Kiss?"

He kissed her puckered lips.

"Will you come twick-or-tweatin' wif me again next year?" she asked softly.

Over the years, he'd been invited to countless events by numerous women, but he was certain he'd never received a more beguiling invitation. He nodded without hesitation. "It's a date."

She smiled again. "Night night, Wyder."

Lauryn took her hand and led her daughter up to bed. When she came back a few minutes later, it was with a worried expression on her face.

"I wish you hadn't done that," she said to him.

"What did I do?"

"You told Kylie that you'd go trick-or-treating with her next year."

"I don't see the problem," he admitted.

She folded her arms across her chest. "She might only be three and a half, but she's already had enough experience with disappointment in her life."

"I have no intention of disappointing your daughter," he assured her.

"Next Halloween is a whole year away," she pointed out. "You probably don't even know where you'll be next October."

He nodded his head in acknowledgment of the fact. "That's true."

"And when you're not here, Kylie will be left wondering what she did wrong."

"Wherever I might be, I'm sure I can come back to take her trick-or-treating," he said reasonably. "And if I can't, I'll at least talk to her and let her know why."

"Assuming that, twelve months from now, you remember an offhand promise that you made to a little girl."

He unfolded her arms and linked their hands together. "I'll remember, Lauryn."

But the furrow in her brow remained.

"Are you really worried that I'm going to disappoint Kylie?" he wondered aloud. "Or are you worried that I'll disappoint you?"

Her eyes flashed with something that might have been anger—or guilt. "I don't worry about being disappointed anymore. I expect it."

"Is that why you're trying to piss me off?" he asked quietly. "So that I'll get mad and leave, and your disappointment will be justified?"

"I'm not trying to do any such thing," she denied, then she sighed wearily. "Or maybe I am. I don't know—this whole situation is outside my realm of experience."

He dropped a brief but firm kiss on her lips before he released her hands. "The only place I'm going right now is to fire up the grill to cook the steaks, because man—and woman—cannot live on gummy bears alone."

"We also have fun-sized chocolate bars and marshmallow ghosts," she reminded him.

"Those will be for dessert."

So they ate steaks and baked potatoes, washing both down with the excellent merlot he'd brought over. Sitting across from Ryder, Lauryn found herself replaying their earlier conversation and wondering why she was continuing to deny what she wanted. Did she expect him to disappoint her? Or was she more worried that she might disappoint him?

She'd only had one lover in the past eight years, and only one lover prior to that. And in each of those situations, she'd been in love with the man before she'd made love with him. She'd never had a fling.

She wasn't in love with Ryder, but she was definitely in lust. She wanted him with an intensity that bordered on desperation—and that was definitely something she hadn't experienced before. But she still didn't know if she had the courage to follow her sisters' advice and "go for it."

"I think Kylie was right," Lauryn said, setting her fork and knife on her empty plate. "This was a really good Halloween."

"Actually, she said it was the bestest," he reminded her.

"Well, at three and a half, she hasn't experienced many Halloweens." She nudged a bowl of candy toward him. "Gummy bear?"

He peered inside. "You ate all of the red ones."

"And left all of the green ones for you."

"I'm in the mood for something sweeter," he said, edging his chair closer to hers.

He captured her mouth slowly, but it was indeed a capture. She had no hope of evading—and no desire to even try. She savored his kiss—the warmth, the texture, the flavor. She'd never known a kiss could be so much and make her want so much more.

As his mouth moved over hers, patiently, seductively, her mind clouded and her body yearned. Yes, what she was feeling was definitely lust. And maybe just a little bit more.

"I'll load up these dishes and take them downstairs for you," he said when he ended the kiss.

It frustrated her that he could switch gears so effortlessly while her body continued to battle with her brain.

"Why do you do that?" she asked when he came back, the frustration in her voice mirroring that of her body.

"Do what?" he asked, a little warily.

"Get me all stirred up and then walk away."

"You said you needed some time," he reminded her, sliding his chair back into place at the table. "I'm trying to give it to you."

She should be grateful for that, but right now she was feeling too turned-on to appreciate his restraint. "I haven't had sex in a year and a half," she admitted. "That's probably enough time."

His fingers tightened on the chair. "Are you saying that if I were to make a move, you wouldn't object?"

She shook her head and moved closer to him, sliding her hands up his chest to link behind his head. "I'm tired of waiting for you to make a move."

And then *she* kissed *him*.

Ryder thought he was pretty good at reading her, but Lauryn definitely surprised him when she moved forward to press her lips to his. Her mouth was soft and cool and just a little bit uncertain—as if she wasn't quite sure how he would respond.

He responded by sliding his arms around her and drawing her closer. Her body swayed into his, her soft womanly curves pressing against him and causing all of the blood in his head to quickly migrate south. But he held his own desire in check, letting her set the tone and the pace of the kiss.

One hand slid off his shoulder to trail down his arm until her hand caught his. She linked their fingers together as she eased her lips from his, then turned and led him toward the stairs.

He followed her willingly. Happily. Eagerly.

She paused at the door of her bedroom. "I should—"

"Check on the kids," he guessed.

She nodded.

"I'll wait right here," he promised, because he understood that she was, first and foremost, a mother. And surprisingly, he didn't find that aspect of her life off-putting at all.

She didn't make him wait long, but he could tell by the uncertainty in her eyes when she returned that those few moments she was away had been sufficient to create doubts about the next step. He was confident that he could erase all of those doubts in thirty seconds if he put his hands on her, but it needed to be her decision, so he held his ground.

"They're both sleeping," she told him.

"They had a lot of excitement today."

"It was a great day," she said, "but I'm still not convinced it was the bestest Halloween ever."

He recognized a challenge when it was issued. "I bet I could convince you."

"I'm willing to let you give it your best shot," she said.

It was all the invitation he needed.

He lifted her off her feet and carried her across the threshold into her bedroom.

Chapter Fourteen

Lauryn's breath whooshed out of her lungs; her heart fluttered wildly inside her chest. She'd watched many movie heroes carry their lovers off into the sunset, but she'd never imagined that it would happen to her. The fact that the sun had set hours earlier didn't detract at all from the sheer romance of the moment when Ryder swept her into his arms.

A thin sliver of moonlight slanted into the room, guiding him toward the bed, where he set her back on her feet and kissed her again.

Nerves jumped in her belly, twisted into knots. Now that they were here, she expected a race toward the finish line. And that was okay—her body was more than ready for the intimate connection they both craved. But she was apprehensive, too. Eighteen months was a long time and she wanted this—wanted *him*—so much she was a little worried that the anticipation might supersede the main event.

Then his hands moved over her as he deepened the kiss, and she stopped worrying. He found the buttons at the front of her shirt, his fingers adeptly unfastening them. It was only when he parted the fabric and she felt a rush of cool air against her skin that she remembered she had a plan for this eventuality.

"Wait."

He paused with his hands at the button of her jeans. "What am I waiting for?"

"I need a minute to change into something…"

"More comfortable?" he guessed.

"More seductive," she admitted.

"*You* are seductive enough," he told her.

"I can do better," she promised.

"Naked would be better."

She pressed a brief kiss to his lips. "I just need one minute."

"One minute," he agreed.

She opened her top drawer and pulled out the black silk slip with lace inserts that she'd recently bought in anticipation of showing it to Ryder, even before she was sure that she would ever do so. She ducked into the bathroom and quickly stripped away her clothes, spritzed some of her favorite but rarely used fragrance on her skin, then slipped into the silk. The fabric was cool against her body, making her nipples tighten, and the hem flirted with the tops of her thighs. Drawing in a long, deep breath for courage, she opened the door.

Ryder had turned on the lamp beside the bed and was lounging on top of the covers, staring at his watch, when she stepped back into the bedroom. Though she didn't say anything, he immediately looked up, as if he somehow sensed her presence. Then he rose from the bed, his eyes skimming over her from her head to her toes with obvious appreciation. "Wow."

She smiled, the single word successfully untangling most of the knots in her belly. "I told you I'd only be a minute."

"You were actually behind that closed door for almost a minute and a half."

"You were keeping track?"

"It felt like the longest eighty-five seconds of my life— but you are definitely worth the wait." He took her hands to draw her closer and felt her fingers tremble. "Are you nervous?"

"A little," she admitted. "It's been a long time for me."

"There's nothing to be afraid of," he promised.

"Should we talk first?"

"If you wanted to talk, you should have said so before you came out of the bathroom wearing nothing but…that."

"I just wanted to reassure you that I have no expectations beyond tonight," she said.

"I might not be the forever-after type, but I don't do one-night stands anymore, either," he told her. "So why don't we agree to simply enjoy being together for so long as we do?"

"One day at a time?"

"Something like that," he agreed.

"That works for me," she said.

"Good. Are we done talking now?"

He didn't give her a chance to answer before he covered her lips in a slow, deep kiss that had all of her worries fading away like a bad dream. He had a way of kissing her that made her feel not just wanted but adored, not just desired but cherished.

She tugged his T-shirt out of his jeans so that her hands could explore beneath it. Her palms slid over the warm, taut skin of his stomach, slowly tracing each rippling contour. He took his hands off her only long enough to lift his shirt over his head and toss it aside, allowing her to continue her exploration of his glorious muscles unimpeded.

And his muscles were indeed glorious. As tantalizing as he'd appeared in all those close-ups on TV, the images didn't do justice to him. She pressed her mouth to the warm skin, just above his heart that was beating as rapidly as her own.

He took a minute to shed most of his clothes, with the exception of a pair of very sexy black boxer-style briefs, then he laid her down on top of the bed and straddled her thighs. His fingers caught the edge of her slip and began to slide it upward over her skin.

She grabbed his wrists. "What are you doing?"

"As fabulous as this looks on you, I want it off—I want to see *you*."

"No, you don't."

"Yes, I do," he insisted.

She shook her head. "Ryder, I've given birth to two children—"

"Two beautiful children," he agreed. "Why would you think that carrying them would somehow make you any less beautiful?"

How was it that he always seemed to know exactly what to say? It was unnerving…and incredibly appealing. But she'd lived with her own doubts and insecurities too long to give them up easily now. "I thought guys your age were only interested in perfect bodies."

"And I thought women your age were more comfortable in their own skin," he countered, his hands continuing to explore her body in a way that assured her even more than his words that he wasn't finding any flaws.

"Touché," she said. "But you still don't know how old I am."

"Thirty-three," he guessed.

She frowned. "Where did you come up with that number?"

"I figured you did four years of college to get your business degree, then another two for your master's. If you started college at eighteen, then you would have been twenty-four when you finished, and Tristyn mentioned that you worked at Garrett Furniture for four years after you graduated and before you got married, and you were married for five and a half years." He looked at her. "Am I close?"

"Actually, I turned thirty-four on my last birthday." She eyed him warily. "It doesn't bother you that I'm six years older than you?"

"No," he said. "I just wish it didn't bother you that I'm six years younger than you."

"I'm trying not to think about it."

"Let me help you not think," he suggested, lowering his head to kiss her again.

"Okay," she said. "But the slip is not coming off."

"If you really want to keep it on, I won't object…this time."

Despite his opposition to the silk covering her body, it didn't seem to get in his way or inhibit his exploration of her body—or her enjoyment. He brushed his thumbs over her nipples, already tightly beaded beneath the silk, the brief contact making her gasp as arrows of pleasure streaked toward her core. Then he lowered his head and suckled her through the fabric until she was panting and squirming and desperately wishing that his mouth was on her bare flesh.

Thankfully, he had no inhibitions about his own body. And why would he? He was hard and strong and so perfectly put together he might have been sculpted by a master. But he wasn't a monument of cold, hard marble—he was a man, warm and strong. And he was in her bed. All those yummy muscles were right there for her to explore with her hands and lips and body.

His hands slid beneath the fabric, his fingertips trailing along the sensitive skin on the inside of her thighs, gently urging them apart. When he parted the soft folds of skin at the apex of her thighs, he hummed his approval.

Not quite brave enough to slide her hand beneath the waistband of his boxers, she explored the size and shape of him through the fabric.

She bit down on her lip when his hands slid between her thighs again. Keeping his gaze focused on her face, he dallied beneath the hem of her slip. When his thumb grazed the aching nub at her center, the light touch set off a myriad of sensations that made her gasp with shock and pleasure.

"I think I found a sensitive spot," he teased, brushing his thumb over it again.

"Ryder…*please*."

He slid a finger deep inside of her and slowly withdrew it. She clenched her teeth together to prevent herself from making any sound as he repeated the action, with two fingers this time. Then his thumb found that ultrasensitive spot again and circled around it. Her breath caught in her lungs as everything inside her tensed and tightened...and... finally...shattered.

He captured her mouth with his, swallowing the cries she could no longer hold back and holding her close while the aftershocks continued to shudder through her body.

"Definitely a sensitive spot," he mused, smiling against her mouth.

"I told you it's been a really long time for me," she said, her tone accusing.

"So you did," he acknowledged. "And I wanted to make sure the experience was enjoyable for you."

"Do you have any doubts?"

He grinned as he discarded his boxers. "Not one. And we're not close to being done yet."

"Condom," she said, suddenly remembering the box she'd bought *just in case*. "In the night table drawer."

"I've already got that covered," he said. "Or I will in a second."

It took a little longer than that, but once he'd ensured her protection, he parted her thighs with his knees and, in one smooth, powerful stroke, buried himself inside of her. She closed her eyes and sighed her appreciation. He was so hard and so deep...and it felt so good.

Then he began to move, thrusting deep, deeper, and sending fresh waves of pleasure straight to her core. She wrapped her arms and legs around him, anchoring herself to him as wave after wave of sensation washed over her. She tried to hold on, but it was too much. So she gave herself over to the storm and let it carry her away, and finally Ryder let himself sink into the abyss with her.

* * *

It was a long time later before her breathing evened out. Minutes? Hours? Days? She didn't know; she didn't care. She felt too completely sated to worry about anything.

Several more minutes passed after that before Ryder eased himself off her and brushed her hair away from her face. "You were...wow."

She shook her head. "The wow was all your doing."

"Or maybe the wow was the two of us together," he suggested, wrapping his arm around her and pulling her against his body.

She smiled as she laid her head on his shoulder and her palm on his chest, beneath which she could feel the still-rapid beating of his heart. "I'm convinced," she told him. "This was definitely the bestest Halloween ever."

"For me, too."

He continued just to hold her for a long time, his hand stroking leisurely down her back. She felt comfortable and contented and was starting to drift off to sleep when reality jolted her awake again.

She lifted her head to look at him. "You can't stay."

"I know," he admitted.

"I wish you could, but—"

"You don't have to explain," he told her. "I understand."

He eased himself into a sitting position, then brought her mouth to his and kissed her, long and slow and deep.

When he finally pulled away and reached for his shirt, she glanced at the clock. "You know, it really isn't that late," she decided.

He paused, one arm in a sleeve. "There are still a lot of hours before sunrise," he agreed.

"So you can stay a little longer, if you want."

The shirt dropped back to the floor.

"I want," he said, and proceeded to show her how much.

* * *

When Lauryn arrived home the next day and saw Ryder's truck still in her driveway, her heart did a happy dance inside her chest. While the rational part of her brain warned that she was venturing into dangerous territory, she didn't care. All that mattered was that he was there.

And when she finally got the kids into the house and he smiled at her, the intensity of his gaze made her suspect that he'd been thinking about her as much as she'd been thinking about him throughout the day.

"I missed you," he told her.

The simple sincerity of the words filled her heart, but she kept her own tone casual and light when she said, "I would have hoped you'd be too busy finishing my kitchen to miss me."

"We finished at two," he told her. "The unveiling is to-morrow morning, if you can be here."

She would have to call Adam to open the store for her, but she didn't want to wait a minute longer than necessary to see her new kitchen. "I *will* be here," she promised.

"Good."

"What's in the microwave?" she asked, when she heard the appliance ding.

"Pasta sauce."

"You're making dinner again?"

"Last night I grilled," he said, as if that didn't count. "And this is just spaghetti."

But it wasn't "just" anything to Lauryn. Finding a hand-some man in her ad hoc kitchen, making dinner for her family, was a big deal to her. And it made her question again the wisdom of what she was doing.

Could she really have a physical relationship with him— and the greatest sex she'd ever imagined—and not expect it to develop into something more? After one night, it was already more. Because even more than she enjoyed being with him, she loved how comfortable and natural he was with Kylie and Zachary. Not surprisingly, her children were both becoming more attached to Ryder every day, and maybe that should have been the biggest warning sign—her signal to back off. But she knew it was already too late for that, and she was already more than halfway in love with him.

Her sisters had encouraged her to have a fling—and she hadn't been looking for anything more than that. But Ryder tempted her to want more. A lot more. And though it was undoubtedly foolish to be falling for another man only weeks after her divorce was finalized, she couldn't deny that she was.

He stirred the pasta, peeked into the living room to make sure the kids were otherwise occupied, then tugged Lauryn out of sight to put his arms around her. "I've been thinking about kissing you all day."

"I've been thinking about that, too—and all of the other fun things that go along with kissing," she admitted.

He slid his hands up her back and slowly down again. "Does that mean I might get an invitation to stay late tonight?"

"You can stay as late as you want," she promised.

Since Tristyn and Jordyn had been part of the introductory segment, Lauryn invited them back for the unveiling. Over the past five weeks, Kylie had become accustomed to the presence of Ryder's crew and the cameras, and so both children would be with her when she entered their new kitchen for the first time.

She'd watched countless episodes of *Ryder to the Rescue* since the project started and never failed to be impressed by the transformations effected by his crew. There was absolutely no reason to be nervous, but she couldn't deny that she was.

Ryder went through his usual introductory spiel before he turned to face Lauryn. "Are you ready for this?"

She nodded.

"Are you excited or apprehensive?" he asked.

"A little of both," she admitted.

"Then let's not keep you in suspense any longer," he said, gesturing for Stan to open the door.

"Oh." Her eyes went wide and almost immediately filled with tears. "Wow."

She stepped into the center of the room and slowly turned in a circle so that she could take in the view from all angles. "It doesn't even look like the same room."

Ryder smiled. "Wasn't that the idea?"

"It was," she agreed. "I just never expected anything like this."

"You picked the white shaker-style cabinets, the charcoal granite countertops, glass-and-polished-stone-mosaic backsplash and graphite ceramic floor tiles, even the stainless steel hardware," he reminded her.

There were also brand-new stainless steel appliances, including a countertop range, chimney-style range hood, double wall ovens, French door refrigerator and dishwasher.

"You've got the island you wanted, with lots of extra storage and pendant lights over the breakfast bar. The sink has been moved to the short wall, so you've got a lot more usable counter space. And instead of a single window looking into the backyard, you now have a whole wall of windows, which will let in tons of natural light and allow you to keep an eye on the kids when they're out there."

"Everything is...perfect."

"But there's one more little surprise," Ryder said, opening the double doors of a pantry-style cupboard with pullout drawers.

Lauryn stepped closer, already loving the drawers that would make all of the space so much more accessible. Then she saw that the drawer was already stocked with baking supplies—different kinds of flours and sugars and more. The next drawer held baking trays, measuring cups and utensils—and her cookie cutters, neatly organized in clear stackable containers so that she could see what was inside.

The whole kitchen was amazing, but this cupboard showed her more clearly than anything else that Ryder really knew her. And despite the public unveiling, she understood that this was his personal gift to her.

"When you were packing up your old kitchen, you mentioned that you wished you had time to do more of the baking you used to enjoy. Unfortunately, we couldn't put more hours into your days, but we wanted to ensure that everything was available for you whenever you might find the time."

Conscious of the cameras that were rolling, she blinked back the tears. "This is so much more than I ever expected," she said. "I don't think there's any way that I could ever thank you and your crew enough."

She heard a voice—she thought maybe it was Brody's—pipe up from the background. "You could start by baking us some cookies."

Lauryn laughed as she wiped an errant tear from her cheek. "I'll be baking this weekend," she promised.

While Ryder said a final few words for the benefit of his television viewers, she gestured for Tristyn and Jordyn to come in to check out the space.

After they'd opened all of the cupboards and drawers, her sisters flanked her by the island. "Does this mean we're forgiven?" Jordyn asked.

"You think I'm going to forget that you forged my signature on the application just because I have a fabulous new kitchen?"

"How about the fact that you have a fabulous new man?" Tristyn suggested.

"That's more likely," she acknowledged.

"So…things are good between you and the hunky handyman?" Jordyn prompted.

She was helpless to prevent the smile that curved her lips. "Things are very good."

Tristyn had started to say something else when her cell phone chimed. She pulled it out of her pocket, then cursed softly beneath her breath. "Shoot, I've gotta run—no sharing any details until Saturday."

"What's Saturday?"

"Spa day," Jordyn answered, because Tristyn had already gone.

"I can't make this Saturday," Lauryn told her.

"Why not?" her sister demanded.

"Because Mom and Dad are going to Emerald Isle for the Goodens anniversary party, which means I don't have a babysitter."

"Isn't there someone else you usually call if Mom's busy?" Jordyn asked.

"Yeah," she admitted. "You."

"Well, that won't work," Jordyn said glumly. Then she brightened. "What about Ryder?"

Lauryn shook her head. "I'm not going to ask Ryder."

"Why not? Kylie and Zachary love him."

"Because Saturday is one of his rare days off and I'm not going to ask him to give it up to babysit my kids."

"Then I'll ask him," Jordyn said.

"Ask who what?" Ryder asked, coming over to join their conversation.

"No, you won't," Lauryn said pointedly.

Jordyn sighed but kept her lips zipped.

Ryder's glance shifted from one to the other questioningly until Lauryn finally explained. "Tristyn scheduled a spa day for Saturday, but my parents are going to be out of town."

"If you need someone to look after Kylie and Zachary, I'd be happy to," he said.

Jordyn shot her a triumphant look.

"I'll be gone most of the afternoon," she told him.

"And we might want to go for dinner after the spa," Jordyn added.

"That's not a problem. But if you end up at Marg & Rita's—" he winked at Lauryn "—I'd suggest taking it easy on the tequila."

Chapter Fifteen

After the big reveal episode had finished taping, Ryder helped Lauryn move her dishes and cookware back into the kitchen. Of course, the unpacking took twice as long as the packing because Kylie was running around the kitchen with her arms outstretched, pretending to be an airplane circling the island. Of course, Zachary thought his sister's antics were the funniest thing ever, and as he watched her through the mesh screen of his playpen, his whole body shook with his giggles.

"I love to listen to his laugh," Lauryn said to Ryder. "And to know, after wondering and worrying for so long, that they're both settled and happy now."

He slid an arm across her shoulders and drew her close to his side. "It doesn't look like you have anything to worry about now."

"Today has been a very good day," she agreed. "Thanks to you and your crew."

"While your words are appreciated, the guys are going to expect cookies when they come back on Monday," he told her.

"Then I guess I'll have to bake some cookies this weekend."

And she did. She found her favorite sugar cookie recipe and she spent Friday afternoon measuring and mixing and rolling and cutting. Of course, Kylie wanted to help, too, so she gave her daughter a portion of the dough and let her do her own thing. By the time Ryder showed up with pizza for dinner, she had six-dozen cookies in the shapes of hammers, saws and tape measures cooling on racks—and flour on every horizontal surface.

After they ate, they cleaned up the kitchen together. It didn't seem to matter to Ryder that she and Kylie had made the mess—he never hesitated to pitch in and help. Which gave her an idea...

"I was thinking about something we might do tonight, after the kids are in bed," she told him, as she was loading their dinner plates into her sparkling new dishwasher.

He finished wiping down the island, then folded the cloth over the faucet. "What's that?"

"It's something you suggested a while back but that I've resisted until now," she said.

"You have my complete and undivided attention," he assured her.

"It could get messy and sweaty," she warned, her tone deliberately provocative.

"Tell me more," he urged.

She laughed softly. "You don't have any idea what I'm suggesting, do you?"

"No," he admitted. "But I'm keeping an open mind."

"I'm talking about stripping—"

"Yes," he said, the word a heartfelt plea. "Please."

"—wallpaper."

"Oh."

She folded her arms over her chest. "That's a disappointing response considering how many times you've mentioned that you hate the plaid in the bedroom."

"Have I said a single word about it recently?" he asked.

"No," she admitted.

"Because when I'm with you, I don't see the wallpaper," he told her. "I don't see anything but you."

Her heart did a slow roll inside her chest. "You're good at that."

He put his arms around her. "At what?"

"Saying just the right thing so that I completely forget what we were talking about and just want to jump your bones."

He grinned. "Go ahead and jump—I'll catch you."

Ryder was happy to spend the day with Kylie and Zachary on Saturday, but he missed Lauryn. Somehow, in less than a week, he'd become accustomed to spending most of his free time with her. Regardless of whether they were hanging out with the kids or cuddling on the sofa together to watch television or snuggling naked in her bed, he was happy just to be with her.

He'd never before experienced the simple comfort of being with a woman without any particular plan or agenda—he'd never thought he wanted it. Until Lauryn. And although he was missing her, she deserved this time with her sisters, and he was glad—for a lot of reasons—that she'd taken it today.

When the kids were finally settled into their beds later that night, he had a whole new appreciation for what she did every day. Being a single parent was definitely not a job for the fainthearted.

He was picking up Barbie clothes and Candy Land pieces when he heard her key in the lock.

"Hey, you," he said, meeting Lauryn at the door.

"Hi," she responded in a whisper that matched his. "Where are the kids?"

"Sleeping."

She glanced at the watch on her wrist. "I didn't realize it had gotten so late."

"It's not all that late—just past their bedtime."

"Did they settle down without any trouble?" she asked.

"Without any trouble," he confirmed. "Although I have to confess—I wavered on the one-bedtime-story rule."

"How many did you read?"

"Three," he admitted.

Lauryn shook her head, but she was smiling. "Pushover."

He didn't deny it. "Did you have a good day?"

"I did," she confirmed. "Maybe the most surprising part is that I didn't worry about Kylie and Zachary at all. I thought about them, of course, and about you. But the whole time I was gone, I didn't worry because I knew you were taking care of them."

"I'm glad," he said sincerely.

"So what did you do with your day?"

"We went to the park, played twenty-three games of Candy Land, watched some princess movie and made peanut butter cookies."

"*You* made cookies with the kids?"

"With Kylie," he said. "Zachary was napping."

"What did you have for dinner?"

"Peanut butter cookies."

She looked so appalled he couldn't help but chuckle. "I'm kidding. We had chicken fingers and French fries with carrot and celery sticks, then peanut butter cookies for dessert. There are some left in the kitchen, if you want to try them."

"Maybe later," she said, sliding her palms up his chest. "Right now, I want to take you upstairs to my bed."

Her touch had an immediate and predictable effect on his body, but he tried to focus on their conversation while he still had some blood in his head. "And right now I really want to be taken upstairs," he agreed. "But there's something I need to tell you first."

She brushed her lips against his. "I'm listening."

"You had an unexpected visitor today."

"I'm not interested in anyone but you right now," she promised, starting to unfasten the buttons on his shirt.

He really didn't want to distract her from what she was

doing, but he knew she needed to hear this. "Not even your ex-husband?"

"What?" Lauryn dropped her hands and took a step back, her playful mood gone. "Why would you bring him up now?"

"Because he was here," Ryder said.

She shook her head, refusing to believe it. "He's in California."

"No, he's not," he said. "He showed up at your front door today, around three o'clock, grumbling about his key not working and demanding to know where you were."

"Are you sure it was Rob?" she asked, clearly hoping that he'd made a mistake.

"How many other men are there who would claim to be your husband?"

"*Ex*-husband," she said, firmly emphasizing the "ex."

But he could tell the news was finally starting to sink in, because she moved into the living room and lowered herself onto the arm of the sofa.

She looked up at him, the earlier sparkle in her eyes replaced by wariness. "He was really here?"

He nodded.

"But...why?"

"I don't know," he told her. "He didn't share his reasons with me."

She folded her arms over her chest, an instinctive and protective gesture. "Did Kylie see him?"

He shook his head. "No. She was in the kitchen, up to her elbows in peanut butter cookie dough, and I didn't let him past the front door."

She breathed out a weary sigh. "Thank you for that. I don't know what it would do to Kylie to see her father now, just when she's finally gotten used to him being gone."

He was more concerned about what it would do to Lauryn to see her ex-husband again. Yes, they were divorced, but he suspected that a piece of paper hadn't magically erased the feelings she'd had for the man she'd married—and the father of her children. And while he wasn't generally insecure, he couldn't deny that their shared history made him a little uneasy.

"If he's come back to see them, I don't know that you're going to be able to keep him away," Ryder warned gently.

"He left without even saying goodbye to Kylie," she reminded him. "He left before Zachary was even born."

"He's still their father."

She nodded, unable to deny that basic truth. "Was he a jerk to you?"

"Not really," he said. "He referred to me as the babysitter, but I don't think he meant to be deliberately insulting."

"I'm sorry," she said.

"Why are *you* apologizing?"

"Because I don't know what else to say—what to think," she admitted. "When he signed the separation agreement, I assumed that was it, that we were done forever and I wouldn't ever have to see him again. I certainly never expected that he would just show up at the door, and when I asked you to stay with the kids today, I didn't anticipate that you'd have to deal with him."

"Maybe you should call your cousin, the lawyer," Ryder suggested.

"I had a local attorney, Shelly Watts, handle the divorce for me," she told him. "Not that there was much to handle, but she drafted the terms of our separation agreement, he signed it, and the judge granted the divorce."

"Then you should call her."

"Now?"

He glanced at the clock. "Probably not now. Assuming your attorney has a life outside of the law, she might not want to be interrupted at nine thirty on a Saturday night. But definitely in the morning—to let her know what's going on."

"How can I tell her what's going on when I don't have a clue? For all I know, he came back for the leather jacket he left in the back of his closet."

"Maybe," he acknowledged. "But he introduced himself as your husband, not your ex-husband."

"So?"

"So…" He hesitated, reluctant to even speak the thought aloud. But he knew that, as unpalatable as it was to him, she needed to consider the possibility—and so did he. "Maybe he came back because he wants *you* back."

She pushed herself up from the sofa and headed toward the stairs. Ryder followed her up to the landing, watching from the doorway of Kylie's room as she tiptoed across the floor to check on her daughter, pulling up her covers and bending to touch her lips to the little girl's cheek. Then she crossed the hall to Zachary's room and followed the same routine with him.

"I called Rob after Zachary was born," she told Ryder now, her voice barely more than a whisper. "No one knows about that—not even my sisters."

"I don't think they'd be surprised to hear that you reached out to your husband to let him know that you'd given birth to his child."

"Maybe not," she acknowledged. "But it was more than that. I asked him to come home—no, I practically *begged* him to come home, to give us another chance to be a family."

He looked at the beautiful, strong, stubborn woman in front of him and his heart sank as he realized there could only be one reason she would do something like that. "You were still in love with him."

And if she was then, maybe she was now.

But Lauryn shook her head. "I didn't still love him. I didn't even *like* him very much at that point. But I looked at my baby and I felt that I owed it to him to try to give him a real family."

"Do you think that's why he's back?" And if it was, would she be willing to give her ex-husband that second chance now?

She shook her head again. "Rob's never cared about anyone but Rob, and I don't care where he goes or what he does," she insisted, though the tears that shone in her eyes suggested otherwise. "But this is so unfair to the children. Zachary is such a happy baby, and Kylie hasn't had a panic attack in weeks. And now...just seeing him could turn her whole world upside down again."

"What about your world?" Ryder asked.

"My children are my world," she reminded him.

"And me?" he wondered. "What am I?"

She was quiet for a minute, as if considering her response. "You're my 'one day at a time,'" she finally said, referring back to the conversation they'd had the first night they were together.

And that was all he'd wanted to be then—or so he'd believed. But now... "What if I want to be more than that?"

She closed her eyes. "Please don't do this. Not now."

He wanted to press her for an answer, but she was right. This wasn't the time. She needed to focus on her children and what her ex-husband's return would mean to them. They would have plenty of time to figure out their own relationship later—he hoped.

"Okay," he relented. "Tell me what you want me to do."

She looked up at him, those beautiful gray-green eyes filled with desperation. "I want you to take me to bed and let me pretend that we never had this conversation," she said, lifting her sweater over her head and tossing it aside, revealing a silky purple demi-cup bra and lots of tantalizing skin. "Help me forget about everything but the way I feel when I'm with you."

It wasn't much, but if it was the only thing he could do for her, he would give it his very best effort.

Lauryn didn't know what time Ryder left, she only knew that when she woke up in the early hours of the morning, he was gone. Her bed always seemed so much bigger and emptier without him, but this morning—with the specter of her ex-husband's return in the forefront of her mind—she felt even more alone.

She'd lain awake for half the night wondering why Rob had come back to Charisma, to no avail. What she did know was that if he was determined to see her, he wouldn't wait too long to show up at her door again.

As soon as she was up and dressed, she called Jordyn and asked her if she could take the kids for a few hours. He was waiting on the front porch—sitting in her favorite chair with his feet propped up on the railing—when she returned.

She tucked her keys in her pocket, because she had no intention of unlocking the door and inviting him inside. "So the rumors are true," she said.

"You heard I was back," he guessed.

"Why are you here, Rob?"

"California was too far away from my wife and kids," he said, his tone as deliberately casual as his pose.

"*Ex*-wife," she said pointedly.

"You asked me to come back," he reminded her. "To give us another chance to be a family."

"That was eight months ago. I'd just given birth and still had a lot of drugs in my system," she said by way of explanation.

"Don't tell me it's too late," he said, the plea accompanied by his most charming smile.

That smile used to make her forgive him all manner of things, but it had no power over her anymore. "It's way past too late, so why don't you tell me what you really want?"

"I'm hurt that you don't trust I'm telling you the truth," he said, his tone as false as the claim.

"I learned the hard way not to trust anything that comes out of your mouth," she said bluntly.

He dropped his feet from the railing and stood up, moving closer to her. She had to tip her head back to meet his gaze, but she held her ground.

"We were married for five and a half years," he said, lowering his voice to a more intimate tone. "I don't believe that your feelings for me are gone."

"Our five-and-a-half-year marriage ended when you ran off with the twenty-two-year-old you were screwing in your office at The Locker Room."

He finally took a step back. "Speaking of The Locker Room," he said, pointedly ignoring the rest of her statement, "I went by the store and saw that you changed the name."

"I've made a lot of changes there, and in the rest of my life," she told him.

He nodded as he looked around. "New porch, new roof, new lover."

She narrowed her gaze on him. "Is there a point to this or are you just talking out loud?"

"I was hoping you would deny that you're sleeping with your babysitter."

"It's none of your business who I'm sleeping with," she said, pleased that her cool tone gave no hint of the fury churning inside.

"I just never expected that you'd do something so… tawdry."

She shrugged. "I couldn't find a hunky yoga instructor. And he's not the babysitter—he's Ryder Wallace."

He seemed surprised by this revelation. "The host of that home renovation show?"

"Yes," she admitted.

He shrugged. "Well, he's not your usual type, but I guess

you saw the benefits of having a man around who didn't mind banging up some drywall after he finished banging you."

She curled her fingers around the porch railing and managed to resist the urge to slap his smirking face. "You are every bit the ass that Tristyn always thought you were."

"You think I don't know that your family never approved of me? That no one ever thought I was good enough for you?" he asked bitterly. "They all stood around watching me, waiting for me to fail."

She shook her head. "I'm not going to claim that everyone was overjoyed when we told them we were getting married, but they would have done anything to support us because you were my husband. You were the only one who felt the need to compete with my family."

Rob slid his foot along one of the new boards in the porch. "Did Daddy write a check for all of the work you've had done around here? Or did you have money hidden away that you failed to disclose when we settled our finances?"

"There were no assets—only debts," she snapped back at him. "And most of those were your debts."

"For richer or poorer," he reminded her.

"So it was just the faithful part of the vows that you couldn't remember?" she challenged.

"Let's not throw stones," he admonished.

"I'd rather throw you off my property, anyway," she shot back.

"We bought this house together," he reminded her.

"With money from my parents."

"Money they gave to us in celebration of our marriage."

She shook her head. "Have you rewritten our entire history in your mind?"

"We had a lot of good times together," he said.

"The good times were a long time ago," she told him. "And memory lane is closed."

His tone grew cold. "I'm entitled to see my kids."

Which was what she'd both anticipated and feared. And while she wanted to refuse, she knew that she couldn't. It didn't matter that he'd been a horrible husband or a neglectful parent—he was still the father of her children. And when she'd talked to her attorney earlier that morning, Shelly had warned her that Kylie's abandonment issues were as inconsequential as the fact that Zachary didn't even know his father. Absent evidence of abuse, no judge would deny Rob access to his children.

"They're not here right now," she said, grateful that it was true.

"You can't stop me from seeing them," he warned her.

"I don't want to stop you from seeing them," she said, although that wasn't exactly true. "I just want to know the truth about why you're here and how long you're planning to stay before you turn their lives upside down."

"I'm here because I missed my family," he insisted.

"The daughter you barely spent any time with and the son you've never even seen because you took off before he was born?" she challenged.

He dropped his gaze. "I panicked," he told her. "I knew the business was in trouble. I was barely bringing home enough money to pay the bills and put food on the table, and soon we were going to have another baby and another mouth to feed. I just couldn't bear to fail you."

"And screwing the yoga instructor somehow fixed all of that?" she asked derisively.

"I made mistakes," he admitted. "But I have the right to be with my kids."

"I'm not going to oppose visitation," she told him. She would fight tooth and nail if he tried to go after custody, but she was going to try to play nice—for now. "If you really want to see your children, meet us at Oakridge Park at two o'clock."

Chapter Sixteen

When Lauryn headed to the park with the kids, she didn't tell Kylie that her daddy would be there. She'd learned a long time ago not to count on her ex-husband for anything, and she didn't want her daughter to experience the same disappointment of being let down by a man she should be able to count on.

After all, the first man any little girl falls in love with is her father, and she knew that Rob's abandonment of his daughter had left deep scars. Thankfully, Kylie's life was filled with men she could depend on: her grandfather, her uncles and now Ryder.

But she couldn't think about Ryder now. She couldn't let herself be distracted.

It was a short walk to the park but the wind was brisk, and Lauryn was glad she'd put a hat and mittens on Kylie and tucked a blanket around Zachary.

"Can I go on the swings, Mama?" Kylie asked, as soon as the playground was within her sight.

"Of course," Lauryn agreed. "But I think there's someone over by the slide who wants to see you."

Kylie immediately pivoted in that direction, a bright smile lighting her whole face. "Wyder?"

"No, honey—it's Daddy."

"Daddy?" Kylie echoed, sounding more confused than excited. "Daddy's in Califownia."

"He came from California for a visit," she explained, hoping he wouldn't stay much longer than that.

Kylie, so eager to skip ahead a moment ago, stuck close to her mother now.

Lauryn couldn't blame her daughter for being wary, and she hated that she'd felt compelled to make this visit happen. Just because Rob was here today wasn't any guarantee that he would be around tomorrow. In fact, she hoped he wouldn't be around tomorrow, but she was following her attorney's advice and cooperating—at least for now.

She bent down to unhook Zachary's belt, then lifted the baby from his stroller. He looked so much like her own father—actually both of her children favored the Garrett side—but the deep blue eyes that he shared with his sister were undoubtedly inherited from their dad. Would Rob recognize that fact? Would he feel anything when he looked at his son for the first time?

He crouched down in front of his daughter. "Hello, Kylie."

She smiled a little shyly. "Hi, Daddy."

"You've grown about six inches since I last saw you," he told her.

"I'm in pweschool now."

"Preschool already?" he said, sounding impressed.

"I'm fwee," she said, holding up three fingers.

He nodded. "I know. You had a birthday in April."

"Wif balloons an' choc'ate cupcakes."

"I'm sorry I missed it," he told her.

"You missed Zach's birfday, too. When he was borned."

He nodded again. "I've missed a lot."

"You were in Califownia," she said, as if that was a perfectly reasonable explanation for everything. Then she turned to Lauryn. "Can I go on the swings now, Mama?"

"Go ahead."

"You come push?" Kylie asked her.

"I'll be there in a minute," she promised.

"I wasn't kidding about how big she is," Rob remarked.

"You've been gone almost a year," she reminded him. "And kids grow up fast."

His gaze shifted to the baby. "Kylie was so little when she was born."

"And Zachary was just a little bigger than her, but he was sixteen pounds at his last checkup."

"Can I...hold him?"

"Of course," she agreed. He'd been so hesitant with Kylie when she was a baby, but at almost nine months, Zachary was solid and sturdy.

Rob took the baby from her. He didn't look entirely comfortable holding his son, but she couldn't deny that he was making an effort.

"He has your eyes," Lauryn pointed out to him.

"Do you think so?" Rob sounded pleased by this revelation and took a closer look at the baby now. "And your ears and your dad's chin."

She nodded.

"We might have made some mistakes in our marriage," he noted, "but we made beautiful babies together."

"And you took their education savings along with all of the money from our joint accounts," she reminded him. "What did you do with it?"

He couldn't meet her gaze as he admitted, "I invested in Roxi's yoga studio."

"And ran that business into the ground, too?" she guessed.

"Actually, she's doing very well in California," he told her. "Of course, it helps that more than one Hollywood A-lister has been seen entering and exiting 'Yoga Rox.'"

"Yoga Rocks?" she echoed dubiously.

"Rox with an *x*—like Roxi," he said.

And she'd worried that the Sports Destination's slogan was cheesy. "But if everything is going so well in California, why are you here?"

He sighed. "I didn't know where else to go."

"She kicked you out, didn't she?"

"We decided that we wanted different things," he hedged.

"What different things?"

"For starters, she wanted a baby," he admitted. "And I decided that if I was going to be a father, it should be to the kids I already had."

"How very noble," she said dryly.

He shrugged. "And maybe I panicked a little."

Again.

"Do you love her?" Lauryn asked him.

"I think I do," he confided. "But I loved you, too, and I still screwed up. How do I know I won't do the same with Roxi?"

"You don't," she said. "Love isn't perfect and relationships don't come with guarantees. You just have to be willing to open your heart and follow where it leads." An important lesson that she was only starting to learn herself and only because of Ryder's presence in her life.

"Mama!" Kylie called, clearly growing impatient with waiting.

So Lauryn turned toward the swings, and her ex-husband, with their baby in his arms, walked beside her.

The first visit between Rob and the kids went well enough that her ex-husband asked if he could see them again the next day. While Lauryn intended to accommodate reasonable visitation, she didn't think two days in a row was either reasonable or in the best interests of her children, especially Kylie, who was as confused by her father's reappearance in her life as she'd been by his disappearance eleven months earlier. But she did agree to the day after that, and then two days after that again.

Ryder found Lauryn in her office, doing something on the computer, when he stopped by the store a few days later.

"You look busy," he noted.

She glanced up and smiled, and he felt the now-familiar

tug at his heart that warned he was well and truly hooked. The bigger surprise was that he didn't mind at all.

"Not too busy for you," she promised. "What's up?"

"I had to make a trip to the hardware store to pick up grout for the bathroom and I thought I'd stop by to say hi."

She clicked the mouse to save the updates, then pushed her chair away from the desk and crossed the room to kiss him. "Hi."

He slid his arms around her and kissed her again, longer and deeper. "Hello."

"Do you have time for lunch?" she asked him.

"Unfortunately not," he said, sincerely regretful. "But we've been invited to dinner at Avery and Justin's tonight."

"Oh, um, tonight?"

"Is there a problem with tonight?" he asked, surprised by her reluctance.

She nodded slowly. "I'm sorry, but I told Rob that he could take the kids out for pizza tonight."

"He's not taking them on his own," Ryder guessed.

"Of course not."

"So you made plans to go out with your ex-husband and didn't tell me?" he noted.

"Because it has nothing to do with you."

The matter-of-fact tone sliced into him as effectively as the words. And though he didn't respond, the flexing of the muscle in his jaw must have given away his feelings.

"And now you're mad," she realized.

"Why would I be mad? I'm just the guy you're currently sleeping with—why would I care that you're having dinner with your ex-husband? *It has nothing to do with me.*"

She winced as he tossed the words back at her. "I didn't mean it like that."

"I think you did mean it exactly like that." And that truth was like a sucker punch to his gut. He turned toward the door.

Lauryn grabbed his arm, attempting to halt his retreat. "Ryder, please don't do this. Don't walk away mad."

"Mad is the least of what I'm feeling right now," he told her, his tone quiet and remarkably controlled despite the emotions churning inside him.

Her eyes filled with tears. "I'm sorry."

He just shook his head.

"None of this has been easy for me," she told him. "I'm trying to do what's best for my children. And as much as I wish Rob had never come back to Charisma, I can't pretend that he's not here. And I can't deny Kylie and Zachary the chance to know their father."

"It takes a lot more than biology to be a father," he said bluntly. "And a man who walked out on them once already doesn't deserve the title."

"Maybe not," she acknowledged. "But he's the only one they've got."

"If you really believe that—" He shook his head, unable to speak aloud the words that would completely destroy what he'd thought they were building together.

Instead, he walked away.

His mood didn't change at all throughout the rest of the day, so he went home in a pissy mood and woke up Saturday morning the same way. But he was okay with that—he knew his anger and frustration were justified. What bothered him more, what churned inside his gut, was the hurt she'd so easily caused with a few casual and careless words.

His anger was manageable—he could pick up a sledgehammer and pound something until he'd taken the edge off. The hurt made him feel like a teenage girl dumped on prom night. And the two emotions tangled up together ensured that he was less than welcoming when he responded to the knock at his door.

"What are you doing here?" he asked his sister.

Avery held up the plate she carried. "Leftover coconut cream pie from the dinner you didn't show up for last night—I've eaten too much of it already and wanted to get it out of the house."

Ryder stood back to allow her to enter, then he opened the kitchen drawer for a fork, peeled back the plastic wrap and dug into the pie.

"I didn't expect you to eat it now," she said.

"I'm hungry now," he told her.

"And grumpy," she deduced. "Do you want to tell me what caused this particular mood you're in?"

"Nope."

"Then I'll guess," she warned.

"Don't."

Avery sighed. "Does it have anything to do with Lauryn's ex-husband being back in town?"

He scowled. "How do you know about that?"

"My husband's a Garrett, too," she reminded him. "And I'm sorry if it seems like I'm butting in, but I don't want you to get hurt."

While he appreciated the sentiment, it was already too late.

"She's got a lot of baggage," she said gently.

"Don't we all?"

"Not in the form of an ex-husband and two kids," she pointed out. "And now that their father is back..."

"What?"

His sister sighed. "You need to understand that it's natural for most mothers to put the needs of their children ahead of their own."

"You think I don't understand that?"

"I don't think you're prepared for the possibility that Lauryn might decide to give her ex-husband a second chance, to give her children back their father, and I'm afraid it will break your heart if she does."

He couldn't deny that it would—or that his heart was already battered and bruised. And as uncomfortable as the feeling was, it was also a revelation.

"Did you know," he said to his sister now, "that for a long time, I thought my legacy from our dear mom was to be as closed off and detached as she is?"

She looked at him, stunned. "Why would you ever believe such a thing?"

Ryder just shrugged. "How many guys get to be my age without having had their hearts broken at least once?"

"So why Lauryn?" she asked.

"I don't know," he admitted. "There was just something there from the first time I set eyes on her. And I know this is going to sound corny as hell, but it's like my heart was locked up and she was the only one who had the key."

His sister's eyes misted. "Damn, you really do love her, don't you?"

"I really do," he said.

"Have you told her?" she asked.

He shook his head.

"Don't you think you should?"

"Not right now," he decided. "Not when everything is so up in the air with her ex-husband."

"But that's exactly when—and why—she needs to know how you feel," Avery told him. "If he is making a play for Lauryn, she's going to be forced to make a choice—the father of her children who claims he made a mistake and still loves her? Or the fun-loving guy who's promised her nothing more than a good time?"

He scowled at that. "She knows how much I care about her."

Avery gave him a pointed look. "You better hope she does."

Chapter Seventeen

A few days after Ryder walked out of her office, on another day that Rob was scheduled to visit with Kylie and Zachary, a rainstorm eliminated the possibility of a meeting at the park. Lauryn didn't want to invite her ex-husband into her home because she was finally starting to feel as if it was *hers*, but she knew he didn't have any other place to take them.

She'd asked him about job prospects, because she was curious to know if he was serious about staying in Charisma or just putting in time until he figured things out. He told her, not very convincingly, that he'd been looking, then had the nerve to suggest that she could hire him to work at Sports Destination. She turned him down, clearly and unequivocally, and mentally crossed her fingers that he'd decide his options were better in California.

With other parts of the house under construction, she asked him to try to confine the kids to the living room, and then she left to run some errands. When she returned from her grocery shopping, she was relieved that he'd managed to do so, because the room was a disaster but at least it was the only room that was a disaster.

Kylie was on the floor, putting together a puzzle, and Zachary was slowly cruising around the table—a very recent development, gaining more strength and confidence with every step.

"Did everything go okay?" she asked cautiously.

"Zach peed on Daddy," Kylie informed her eagerly.

Rob shrugged, looking sheepish. "I've never changed a baby boy's diaper before."

And not many baby girl diapers, either, but she didn't bother to remind him of that fact.

"Other than that, I think it went well," he told her. "We had a good time, didn't we, Kylie?"

The little girl nodded.

"I'm glad," Lauryn said.

"Do you mean that?"

"Of course, I do. If you really want a relationship with Kylie and Zachary, I won't stand in the way."

"What if I really want a relationship with you?"

She glanced at her daughter, who appeared to be engrossed in what she was doing but was undoubtedly absorbing every word of their conversation.

"Kylie, I got some of those fruit cups you like, if you want a snack before dinner."

Of course, her always-hungry daughter eagerly abandoned her puzzle.

"Please make sure you sit at the table so you don't spill it."

"I will," Kylie promised.

"What was that about?" Rob asked.

"That was about not wanting our daughter to get any ideas about a reconciliation, because it's not going to happen. I've moved on with my life and so have you. You're just looking for the comfort of something familiar because you're feeling lost and lonely right now."

"You fell in love with me once," he reminded her. "If you give me a chance, I'm confident you'll fall in love with me again."

She shook her head. "Have you listened to a single word I've said?"

"Of course, I have. But I'm asking you to think about our children—"

"Don't you dare tell me to think about our children," she

said, her voice low but sharp. "Every single day, everything I do, I do for them."

"So tell me what I can do," he said, duly chastised.

"You're supposed to be figuring out what you really want," she reminded him. "And not using Kylie and Zachary—or me—to fill the emptiness in your life."

"I know what I want," he said.

Then he pressed his mouth to hers.

Lauryn shoved him away with both hands, shocked by his audacity. "What the—"

"Excuse me for interrupting," Ryder said coolly from the doorway.

At the sound of his voice, Zachary's attention shifted immediately from the stuffed dog he'd found to the man in the doorway. With the toy still clutched in his fist, he dropped to the ground and began crawling toward him.

"You're not interrupting," Lauryn said, mentally crossing her fingers that he hadn't witnessed her ex-husband's impulsive kiss. Since she'd declined the invitation to have dinner with his sister, Ryder had been giving her space. A lot more space than she wanted. And while she didn't know how to bridge the gap between him, she was pretty sure that kissing her ex-husband would not help her cause.

"I need your approval of the hardware for the master bathroom before the guys start to install it," he told her.

She was surprised by the request. "Didn't I already sign off on it?"

He shook his head as he glanced down at the baby, who had reached his destination and was now pulling himself up to a standing position by holding on to the leg of Ryder's pants. "What are you doing, big guy?"

Zachary responded with a droolly smile.

"No." Ryder kept his focus on the baby as he responded to her question. "The manufacturer couldn't supply your first choice—this is the alternate."

"Okay. I'll come take a look."

"We were in the middle of something here," Rob reminded her.

"No," she said bluntly. "We weren't."

Kylie, her snack apparently finished, came back to the room to finish her puzzle. When she saw Zachary with her favorite stuffed dog in his hand, she snatched the toy from him.

"Mine," she told him.

Of course, the abrupt loss of the toy caused her brother to burst into tears.

Ryder started to reach for the baby, instinctively wanting to soothe his distress. Then he glanced in Rob's direction and apparently thought better of it.

"Kylie," Lauryn admonished wearily, lifting Zachary into her arms.

"But it's mine," Kylie said, her own eyes filling with tears as she hugged the toy to her chest. "He always takes what's mine."

"Come here, baby," Rob said, holding out his arms to his daughter.

But Kylie turned away from him and threw herself at Ryder, wrapping her arms around his legs and sobbing dramatically, which did not please her father.

Ryder lowered his head to whisper something to Kylie, who drew in a deep, shuddery breath and relinquished her viselike grip on him.

"I'll be there in just a minute," Lauryn told him.

He nodded and turned to head back up the stairs.

"Well, that was…enlightening," Rob said.

Lauryn wasn't quite sure how to respond. While she would have preferred if her ex-husband had stayed gone, he had been making an effort to get to know his children, and it had to hurt to see how attached they were to the other man.

"They've seen Ryder almost every day for the past six weeks," she told him.

"Are you really trying to make me feel better?" Rob mocked her effort. "Isn't it my own fault that my kids don't know me?"

"It's a simple fact," she said. "Fault doesn't matter."

"I guess it's like the song says—you don't know what you've got until it's gone. And it is gone, isn't it?"

She nodded.

And when he was finally gone, too, she called Tristyn again. "I need a favor."

Ryder didn't stick around to see how long Lauryn's ex-husband stayed. He took a list of supplies that were required and headed to the hardware store.

He'd been right about the ex. The guy had come back to make another play for the woman he'd been foolish enough to walk away from, and while Ryder had been tempted to punch him in the face when he saw his hands on Lauryn, he'd held himself back. After all, it had nothing to do with him.

But several hours later, when he was staring at but not really watching the football game on television, she showed up at his door.

"Do you remember when I said that Kylie and Zachary were my world and you wanted to know what you were to me?" she asked him.

He tucked his hands in his pockets to prevent himself from reaching for her. "I remember that you didn't really answer the question."

"Well, I'm ready to answer it now."

"Okay," he said cautiously.

"You are my gravity," she said.

He wasn't quite sure how to interpret that. "I weigh you down?"

She shook her head, the corners of her mouth lifting just a little. "You keep me grounded. And—" she lifted her arms to link them behind his neck "—you are the force that attracts my body."

"Am I?" His hands came out of his pockets and went around her, so that she was in his embrace.

"Yes." She drew his mouth down to hers. "For the past four days, I feel as if I've been floating without any direction or purpose." She brushed her lips against his. "I've missed you, Ryder."

He kissed her back, savoring the sweet softness of her mouth. He'd missed her, too. He'd missed this. "You're making it hard for me to stay mad at you," he admitted.

"Good, because I don't want you to be mad at me." She pressed closer to him. "I'm sorry I hurt you. To be honest, I didn't know that I could. I didn't know what any of this meant to you."

"Then let me make it clear—I love you, Lauryn." He sucked in a breath and blew it out again, a little unsteadily. "And that's the first time I've ever said those words to a woman who isn't related to me," he confided, "so let me try it again. I love you, Lauryn." This time he smiled afterward. "And I love Kylie and Zachary, too. I understand that you have to figure out what's best for them, but I want to be a factor in that equation, too."

She hugged him tight. "You are an essential factor in that equation." And began to unfasten his shirt. "Let me show you how essential."

"You don't fight fair," he protested.

"I don't want to fight at all." Parting the fabric, she pressed her lips to his skin, where his heart was beating for her.

He didn't want to fight, either. Not when the alternative was so tantalizing. But he held her at arm's length long enough to ask, "Who's with the kids now?"

"Tristyn."

He lifted her sweater over her head, tossed it aside. "What time is she expecting you home?"

"I warned her I might be late."

"You're going to be very late," he confirmed.

Then he lifted her into his arms and carried her to his bed.

He'd told her he loved her.

Several days later, Lauryn was still marveling over that fact—and wondering if he'd noticed that she'd never said the words back. Not because she didn't feel the same way, but because she was determined to take their relationship one day at a time. With her ex-husband still in town, his presence an almost-daily reminder of that failed relationship, it seemed wise.

She was putting more hours in at the store again as the community embraced Sports Destination and business continued to pick up. Adam wanted to hire another part-time employee in anticipation of the holiday rush, and she was giddy anticipating that there might actually *be* a holiday rush. In fact, she was so caught up in preparations for the post-Thanksgiving sales she nearly forgot about Thanksgiving itself and might have done so if Ryder hadn't asked about her plans.

"My mom and my aunts play hostess on a rotating schedule for major holidays," she told him. "I think we're at my Aunt Jane's house this time."

"Thanksgiving is in five days and you *think* it's at your Aunt Jane's?"

She opened the calendar app on her phone and scrolled to the date, then nodded. "Aunt Jane's at four o'clock."

"Were you planning to invite me to go with you?" he asked.

"I didn't think you'd be interested in that kind of thing," she admitted. "And it's usually pretty chaotic. With all of my aunts, uncles and cousins, there will probably be thirty people there."

"I like people," he assured her. "And I really like turkey."

"Then I guess there's no reason you can't come with us," she decided.

"So why does it sound as if you're looking for a reason?"

"I'm not," she said. "I'm just wondering what to tell people... How to explain our...situation."

"Our situation?" he echoed, amused. "I believe it's called a relationship. And one of the basic rules of a relationship is that the people involved usually make an effort to be together on national holidays and other special occasions."

"That's a rule?" she asked.

He nodded solemnly. "One of the big ones."

"All right. Would you like to spend Thanksgiving with me and the kids and the rest of my family?"

"I'd love to," he told her.

"Okay," she agreed. "But if you get the third degree from my dad and my uncles and half of my cousins, don't say I didn't warn you."

Two days before Thanksgiving, Lauryn was in her office with Adam, reviewing purchase orders for the summer retail season, when there was a knock on the open door.

"Hey, Lauryn. Do you have a minute?" Rob asked.

She looked questioningly at her manager.

"I'll go help Bree unpack the shipment that came in yesterday afternoon," he offered.

"Thank you." She turned her attention to her ex-husband, waiting for him to tell her why he'd stopped by—because she knew there had to be a reason.

"I talked to Roxi this morning," he finally said. "She's pregnant."

Lauryn took a minute to digest the information. "Yours?"

He nodded.

"Congratulations."

"Thanks."

"You don't sound very excited," she noted.

"I'm not sure how I'm supposed to feel," he admitted. "I know I haven't been a very good father to Kylie—or a father at all to Zachary."

"Maybe the third time's the charm," she suggested.

"Maybe," he said a little dubiously.

"How does this affect your plans here?" she asked. Because she really didn't care that he'd knocked up his girlfriend except insofar as it affected her children.

"She's willing to give me another chance," he told her. "And to put me in charge of the retail side of her business."

"So you're going back to California?"

He nodded, and she slowly released the breath she'd been holding.

"Are you going to marry her?"

"Roxi doesn't believe that a relationship needs to be sanctioned by religious or government authorities," he said, obviously quoting his girlfriend.

"The baby might change her mind about that," Lauryn told him.

"Maybe," he said again, with little enthusiasm. "You know, when we got married, I really thought we'd be together forever."

"So did I."

"I don't know when that changed," he admitted. "But somewhere along the line, I started to realize that I was letting you down. And that was the beginning of a vicious cycle—I felt like a terrible husband, so I acted like a terrible husband."

"I never had any grand ideals or expectations," she said. "I just wanted us to be partners in our marriage, to work together and build a family."

"And when I failed to do my part, you managed everything without me. You never needed me."

"That's not true," she denied.

"Maybe you wanted me," he allowed, "but you didn't

really need me. I failed you in so many ways, and you just did whatever needed to be done. You took care of the house, the baby, everything, and so competently I couldn't help but feel extraneous.

"Roxi isn't like you," he said now. "Being on her own for the past couple of weeks has made her realize that she needs me—and I think, maybe, I need to be needed."

"Your children need you." As much as she would like to see the back of him, she had to think about Kylie and Zachary and what was best for them. And she couldn't help but worry about the void his absence would again leave in the lives of their children—especially Kylie's.

"No, they don't. Not really. They're already more bonded to your new boyfriend than they are to me."

She couldn't deny that was true and she refused to feel guilty about it. If she felt guilty for anything, it was telling Ryder that her ex-husband was the only father her children had, because she knew now that wasn't true. Ryder had been there for both Kylie and Zachary in so many ways, proving that actions were a stronger measure than biology when it came to parenting.

"If I had any doubts about that, they were put to rest that day at your house—when Kylie and Zachary both turned to him instead of me. That's when I realized that I either needed to figure out how to be the full-time father my kids deserve or let them get on with their lives without me. But if I stay here, I'm abandoning another kid—Roxi's baby."

"Go back to California," she advised. "Take this second chance to be a dad—and do it right this time."

He seemed surprised—and grateful—that she was letting him off the hook, then he nodded. "I'm going to try." He stood up and hugged her. "Have a good life, Lauryn."

"I will," she said. "Good luck to you."

As Rob was on his way out, he passed Ryder on his way in. "How long were you standing there?" Lauryn asked.

"Long enough," he said. "But I had no intention of interrupting what looked like a goodbye."

"It *was* a goodbye," she assured him. "Rob's going back to the west coast."

"How do you feel about that?" he asked cautiously.

"A lot relieved and a little sad—not that he's leaving but that he couldn't be the father Kylie and Zachary deserve."

"Lucky for them, they've got a really awesome mom."

And you, she wanted to tell him. Because she'd finally recognized the truth he'd alluded to that day in her office. And although he seemed to have forgiven her thoughtlessly cruel words, Lauryn was determined to make it up to him by loving him for as long as he would let her.

Lauryn had always enjoyed celebrating the holidays with her extended family. She considered herself fortunate that she'd grown up with not just two sisters but a whole bunch of cousins, and as those cousins married and had babies, she was happy to see the next generation hanging out together.

She was even happier to see Braden sitting on the sofa in Aunt Jane's living room with Vanessa in his arms. It was no secret that her cousin loved kids—or that he and his wife had been trying for several years to have one of their own. During that time, they'd skipped a lot of family gatherings. Lauryn knew it had to be difficult for both of them to be surrounded by other people's babies, so she was thrilled to see that they were here today—and that Braden was playing the doting uncle.

Lauryn took her glass of wine and settled onto the sofa beside him. "She's gorgeous, isn't she?"

"Of course, she's a Garrett," Braden said immodestly. Then he glanced across the room to where Justin's wife was in conversation with his own. "Although her mom's got pretty good genes, too."

"Speaking of her mom—how did you manage to wrestle Vanessa away from Avery?"

"No wrestling required," he said. "I just told her that I needed practice for when our baby comes."

Lauryn's gaze immediately shifted from his smiling face to that of his not obviously pregnant wife across the room. "Are you... I mean, is Dana..."

He shook his head. "No, she's not pregnant. But if all goes according to plan, we'll have our own bundle of joy before the end of the year."

"What's the plan?" she asked cautiously.

"A private adoption. We've already signed the papers, we're just waiting for the baby to be born."

"Oh, Braden, that's wonderful," she said, sincerely thrilled for her cousin and his wife.

"It is," he agreed. "Although we're trying not to get too excited about it. Even though we've met with the birth mother and she's adamant that this is what she wants, there's always a possibility that she'll change her mind when she holds her baby in her arms."

Lauryn nodded, already praying that Braden and Dana wouldn't suffer such a heartbreaking disappointment. They'd both been through so much already.

"The way this family's been growing, we're going to need another table for holiday meals pretty soon," she said, focusing on the positive.

"Speaking of additions to the family," Braden said, grinning, "tell me about the new guy in your life."

While Lauryn was catching up with Braden in the family room, Ryder had been cornered by Jordyn in the den. Over the past couple of months, he'd gotten to know both of Lauryn's sisters pretty well—and he knew that none of them had any secrets from the others. And while Tristyn had given an enthusiastic thumbs-up to Lauryn's relationship with him, he sensed that Jordyn was still reserving judgment.

"You must be getting close to finishing up the renovations at Lauryn's house," she noted.

"It won't be too much longer," he confirmed.

"And then what happens?" she prompted.

"Are you inquiring about the schedule for my crew or asking about my personal plans?"

"I shouldn't be asking about anything," she admitted. "Lauryn would be the first to tell me that your relationship is none of my business, but she's had a rough year and I'm a little concerned that her feelings for you aren't reciprocated to the same degree."

"You're right—our relationship isn't any of your business," he agreed. "But I know you're motivated by concern, so I'll tell you—I'm in love with your sister."

The furrow between Jordyn's brows eased a little. "The ring-on-her-finger, forever-after kind of love?"

"Do you want to see the ring?" he asked. He'd bought a diamond solitaire a few days earlier, when he'd realized that he couldn't imagine his future without Lauryn in it. He still had a lot to learn about family, but he was confident that she could teach him everything he needed to know.

"You have a ring?" Jordyn asked, surprised excitement successfully pushing aside any lingering apprehension.

"I have a ring," he confirmed. "But I'd appreciate it if you kept that bit of information between us for now."

"I'll keep your secret," she said. "But don't wait too long to ask her—I'd like to be a bridesmaid before next summer."

He grinned. "I'll see what I can do."

Chapter Eighteen

The day after Thanksgiving, while most people were either sleeping off their overindulgence or racing for Black Friday sales, Ryder's crew was back on the job, eager to finish up so that they might enjoy an extended break over the Christmas holiday. And Lauryn was continuing to celebrate all the reasons she had to be thankful, because Kylie didn't seem bothered at all by the news that her father had gone back to California. Of course, Ryder's presence more than filled the void, and watching the sexy handyman with her children, Lauryn found herself starting to believe that maybe her real Prince Charming did wear a tool belt.

She was smiling at the thought as she carried a basket of clothes up to Kylie's room, the sounds of the men working almost like background music to her now. She'd thought she would hate the noise and debris and especially the intrusion into her home and her life, but over the past couple of months, she'd grown accustomed to the high-pitched buzz of saws and rhythmic *thunk* of nail guns that somehow blended together to create a not-unpleasant melody. In fact, she was beginning to suspect that she might miss the crew when they packed up and cleared out after the last stage of the renovation was complete.

Across the hall in the master bedroom, Stan and Brody were completing what Ryder referred to as punch-out work—the last-minute small details that needed to be taken care of before a job was done. She was eager to see the finished project—and excited to sleep in an actual bed again rather than the futon in the den that had been her temporary quarters while the renovations in her bedroom were underway.

She could hear the men talking, but she wasn't really listening until she heard them mention Watkinsville. The name snagged her attention because she remembered Ryder telling her that was the location of the antebellum mansion he was hoping to restore. She paused in the doorway of Kylie's room, hugging the laundry basket close to her chest as she shamelessly eavesdropped on their conversation.

"Are you planning to go?" Stan asked his coworker.

"I'd love to," Brody said. "But Melanie would have my hide. She's due the beginning of March and if I'm not here when the baby's born, there will be hell to pay."

"Maybe you can join the crew afterward," Stan suggested. "The boss seems to think we'll be there fifteen to eighteen months."

"Which is pretty much the first year and more of my son's life," Brody pointed out.

"It's a boy, huh?"

"Yeah," Brody confirmed, and she could hear the pride and pleasure in his voice. "The latest ultrasound confirmed it."

The conversation continued on that topic and Lauryn continued on her way to Kylie's room. But the whole time she was putting her daughter's clothes away, the workers' voices echoed in her head. *Watkinsville. Fifteen to eighteen months. Watkinsville...*

She dumped the dirty laundry from the bathroom hamper into the basket and had turned to head back downstairs, almost colliding with Brody when he stepped out of the master bedroom.

"Let me take that for you," he offered.

"Thanks," she said, relinquishing her hold on the basket, though the weight of it was insignificant compared to the heaviness in her heart.

"Do you like the new main floor laundry?" he asked, as they headed in that direction.

"I love it," she told him. "It's a relief not having to carry everything down to the basement and back up again."

"I imagine, with two little ones, you're doing a lot of laundry."

"Constantly," she agreed, marveling at the ease with which she was managing to make conversation despite the fact that her heart was breaking. "I hear you're going to have a little one soon, too."

The expectant father nodded. "Early March, if the baby comes on schedule."

"Babies come on their own schedules," she told him.

He grinned. "Yeah, I've already been warned."

As she followed Brody to the new laundry room, she realized that, with two exceptions, Ryder had left his mark in every single room of her house. In addition to the complete overhaul of the kitchen, his crew had patched and painted most of the other rooms, added new crown moldings and trim and updated the lighting. They'd refinished the fireplace and added built-in bookcases in the den, replaced all of the bathroom fixtures, vanities and tile. She had yet to see what they'd done in the master bedroom, but she didn't doubt that it would be equally fabulous. The only two rooms that hadn't been touched were Kylie's and Zachary's rooms. But there, Ryder had left his stamp on their hearts.

This house hadn't been her first choice when she and Rob were looking to buy, but she'd seen the potential in it and believed he would help with the necessary work to make it more distinctly their own. After her husband left, she'd hated the house and viewed every room as just another promise unfulfilled.

Ryder had given her back her home. When she looked around now, she loved everything about it because it felt as if it was truly hers. But not exclusively, because Ryder was everywhere. In every room, she saw not just the changes he'd made but the light of his smile and the sparkle in his eyes; she heard the echo of his voice and the sound of his laughter in the walls. It wasn't just her house—it was the house that Ryder built for her, and she really wished he could stay and share it with her and Kylie and Zachary. But that, she realized now, was a foolish wish.

She'd become so accustomed to having him around she hadn't let herself think about what would happen when the renovations were complete. Of course, he would move on to other projects—she'd always known that. But she hadn't anticipated that moving on would mean moving away.

And far more troubling to her than the realization that he was leaving was his complete silence on the subject. He'd told her about the Georgia project almost two months earlier, lamenting the delays and questioning whether the owners would ever get the necessary approvals to proceed with the work. But he hadn't mentioned it again since then.

The way Stan and Brody had been talking upstairs, the project was a go, with the team heading to Georgia early in the New Year. And Ryder hadn't said one word.

The only explanation she could imagine to explain his silence was that he'd never intended for their relationship to last beyond the completion of this project. When he was finished with her renovations, he would be finished with her, too.

She sorted through the laundry, tossing the darks into the washing machine and fighting back the tears that burned her eyes. After everything she'd been through in the past year, she wasn't going to fall apart over the end of a short-term relationship.

Except that she hadn't thought of it as a short-term relationship. Even in the beginning, when she'd tried to convince herself that she didn't want anything more than a casual fling, her heart had never believed it. And as the days had turned into weeks, she'd thought they were building something together. Or had she misread his signals?

But he was the one who'd convinced her to introduce him to her family at Thanksgiving. He was the one who'd told her that he loved her. And he'd made her fall all the way, head over heels in love with him in return. Even more damning, he'd made her children fall in love with him. Kylie and Zachary lit up whenever he walked into a room. They looked forward to seeing him every day—and they were going to be devastated when he was gone.

And once again she would be left behind to pick up the broken pieces of all of their hearts. It was her own fault. She'd known it was too soon, too risky. But her foolish heart had refused to be dissuaded.

And what was she supposed to do now? How could she continue to pretend that everything was okay when it was only a matter of time before he walked away from them?

The answer was simple—she couldn't. And since he hadn't told her about the Watkinsville project, she attempted to broach the subject herself.

"When do you think your crew is going to finish up here?" she asked Ryder later that night.

"If everything goes according to schedule, we should be done by the end of next week," he told her.

"And what are your plans after that?"

"After that, we'll take a few weeks off so everyone can enjoy the holidays with their families."

"Do you have any special plans?" she prompted.

He put his arms around her and brushed his lips against hers. "To spend as much time as possible with you."

Then he kissed her again until she forgot about pressing him for more details. Until she forgot about everything but how wonderful it felt to be in his arms.

* * *

She tried again the next morning, but his answers continued to be noncommittal and evasive. Even when she asked him point-blank about the Georgia restoration, he only said that Owen was working on it.

She gave up asking and decided just to enjoy the time they had together now and store up all the memories she could for the lonely days and nights after he was gone.

But apparently she wasn't as successful at hiding her true feelings as she thought. While Christmas shopping with her sisters, they decided to take a break and indulge in peppermint mochas.

"What's going on with you?" Jordyn asked her, when they'd settled at a table with their beverages. "Physically you're here, but your mind is obviously somewhere else."

"I'm guessing it's with Ryder," Tristyn teased.

"I'm sorry. I was thinking about Ryder," she admitted. "And the expiration date on our relationship."

Jordyn frowned. "What are you talking about?"

"He's packing up his tools and moving to Watkinsville in the New Year," she said miserably.

"Watkinsville, Georgia?" Tristyn asked.

She nodded.

"Why would he be going there?"

"For the next *Ryder to the Rescue* project."

"So he'll be gone a few weeks," her youngest sister said, unconcerned. "And then he'll be back."

But Lauryn shook her head. "It's a major restoration that will take months, maybe more than a year."

"Well, Watkinsville isn't that far," Jordyn pointed out.

"No," she agreed. "But he hasn't said anything to me about what's going to happen when he's gone. He hasn't even told me about the project."

"Then how do you know he's going?" Tristyn asked.

"I heard a couple of the guys talking about it, but Ryder

hasn't said a word. Doesn't that tell me everything I need to know?"

"I don't think it does," Jordyn denied.

"And I don't think you should jump to any conclusions without talking to him," Tristyn added.

"I've tried talking to him," she admitted. "And his answers to my questions are all deliberately vague."

"That doesn't sound like him."

"I didn't think so, either. And as incredible as the past two months have been with him, I have to accept that there's not going to be a storybook ending for us."

"We know you're wary of being hurt again," Tristyn said gently. "But I think, if you give him a chance, you'll discover that Ryder is your Prince Charming."

Lauryn shook her head. "It's long past time for me to stop believing in fairy tales."

"Just be careful not to close the book before the last page is written," Jordyn cautioned.

A few days later, when Lauryn found herself still mulling over her middle sister's cryptic remark, she decided that she was making too much of it. As the illustrator of AK Channing's stories, Jordyn lived in a world of science fiction and fantasy, but Lauryn had to face the realities of her current situation.

And then, one night early in December when she was tucking the kids into bed, Ryder slipped out of the house to get something from his truck.

Lauryn finished reading Kylie's bedtime story, then made her way back down the stairs just as Ryder was setting an enormous dollhouse down in the middle of the living room.

No, not a dollhouse, she realized. An absolutely breathtaking fairy-tale castle.

"Did you make this?" she asked, seriously amazed by the magnitude of the project.

He nodded. "It's for Kylie. For Christmas."

"Christmas is still three weeks away," she pointed out.

"I know, but I wanted to show it to you." He opened it up so that she could see the inside. "What do you think?"

"It's stunning," she told him, kneeling to more closely inspect the details.

"I didn't make the furniture and accessories," he admitted. "Those were beyond my skills—or at least my patience."

But every room was immaculately decorated and beautifully furnished. The windows had lace curtains, the floors had wool rugs and there were miniature portraits and paintings on the walls. The bedrooms had fancy beds with quilted covers, wardrobes and dressers; the nursery had a cradle, a change table and rocking chair; the bathroom had a toilet, a claw-foot tub and even an oval mirror above the pedestal sink. There were dishes in the kitchen cabinets, books on the shelves in the library and even a laundry room with a washer, dryer, iron and board.

"So who did the decorating?" she wondered.

"Monica Snyder—the show's interior designer. She was desperate for something to do while her leg is healing."

"This is amazing," she said.

"And check this out." He knelt beside her and touched a button beside the center door, illuminating all of the chandeliers and lamps—even the flames in the fireplace flickered.

"Kylie's going to love it," she told him. "Unfortunately, you've set the bar a little high for Santa now."

"What do you mean?"

"No other Christmas gift is ever going to top that."

"We'll see," he said vaguely.

"Don't you dare give her a puppy," she warned.

He chuckled. "I'm not going to give her a puppy—at least not this year."

Not this year. The implication being that there would be other years, other Christmases. But how could that be?

He was leaving in the New Year, and he still hadn't told her about his plans.

He tipped her chin up, forcing her to look at him. She swallowed the lump in her throat.

"That's the problem, isn't it?" he asked softly. "You don't want to think about future Christmases because you don't think I'm planning to stick around."

"I know you're going to Georgia after the holidays," she told him.

"And how do you know that?"

"I heard Brody and Stan talking about it," she admitted.

"They shouldn't have been discussing future projects that haven't been finalized."

"Fifteen to eighteen months in Watkinsville sounds pretty final to me."

"It's not quite a done deal," he told her. "We're still waiting for one last approval."

"What's holding things up?"

"I am."

Of all the responses he could have given to her question, Lauryn hadn't anticipated that one. "What? *Why?*"

"Because I wasn't going to say yes without talking to you first."

"I know how excited you are about this restoration," she told him. "I wouldn't ever ask you not to go."

He took her hands in his. "The question is—will you go with me?"

He wasn't planning to leave her; he wanted her to go to Georgia with him. And while that realization lessened the ache in her heart, it didn't change the reality of the situation. "I want to say yes," she admitted.

"Then say yes," he urged.

But she shook her head. "I can't walk away from my life for a whole year, maybe a year and a half, to be with you in Georgia."

"I'm not asking you to walk away from your life," he explained patiently. "I'm asking you to start a new life, a new family, with me."

Every beat of her heart was a yes, but her heart was often impulsive and foolish. She needed to think about this logically rather than emotionally. "I have responsibilities here," she reminded him. "The business—"

"Adam is more than capable of handling the business. That's why you hired him."

"And Kylie's going to start kindergarten next September."

"There are schools in Georgia," he pointed out. "In fact, there's an excellent primary school only a five-minute walk from the guesthouse on the property, where we could live while the renovations are happening."

"You've already looked at schools," she realized.

"I even have the registration forms."

"But…why?"

He squeezed her hands gently. "Because I know that you don't make any decisions without considering your children. Because I understand that you and Kylie and Zachary are a package deal. And because I want the whole package, Lauryn. Because I love you—all of you."

She had to swallow around the lump in her throat before she could reply. "I never wanted to fall in love again," she said softly, looking deep into his eyes. "But you didn't give me a choice. You barged into my life without invitation and started knocking down walls—" she smiled a little "—literally and metaphorically—and you made me see how much better my life could be with you in it. How much better my children's lives could be. And you made all of us fall in love with you. And I do love you, Ryder. With my whole heart," she finally admitted.

"Then say yes," he urged, releasing one of her hands to take a ring out of his pocket and offer it to her. "Not just to coming to Georgia, but making a life with me. Let me be your husband and Kylie and Zachary's stepfather. Let us be a family."

She was dazzled by his proposal even more than the diamond in his hand, but... "You said you weren't the forever-after type," she reminded him.

"Because I wasn't...until I met you."

"You also said love was a gamble."

"And I'm willing to go for broke," he told her. "Because I know that as long as you're by my side, I can't lose."

She saw the conviction in his eyes, felt it in her heart. They could make this work—they *would* make this work. "You have all the answers, don't you?"

"Not quite," he said. "I'm still waiting for yours."

She didn't make him wait any longer. "My answer is yes. With one minor amendment."

"Anything," he promised.

"I want you to be my husband," she told him. "But I'm not looking for a stepfather for my children. They need a real father. They deserve a full-time, forever-after kind of dad."

"Do you think I could be that kind of dad?" he asked, a little cautiously.

She lifted her free hand to his cheek. "You already are."

He slid the ring on her hand, and it was as perfect a fit for her finger as he was for her life. And then he kissed her, and it was a perfect kiss, too.

"I think my sister was right," she murmured.

"What was she right about?"

"I should never have tried to guess our ending—or given up hope that it would be a happy one."

"She was only partly right," he said. "This isn't an ending—it's our happy beginning."

Epilogue

On Christmas morning, Kylie awoke early, excited to discover what presents Santa had left for her and Zachary. 'Cept Mama had one very strict rule—no presents could be opened until everyone was awake. But that didn't mean she couldn't sneak downstairs and just *peek* at what was under the tree, did it?

She climbed out of bed and stuffed her feet into her slippers, then tiptoed to the stairs. She held tight on to the handrail as she made her way down. Some of the steps used to make a scary sound when she stepped on them. Mama said they groaned like an old man, but Ryder fixed that. Ryder fixed a lot of things that used to be broken—like the roof. Now even when it rained really, really hard, with thunder and lightning and everything, it didn't rain in her castle.

She was going to miss her castle when they went to… Watkin-something. She scrunched up her face and tried real hard but she couldn't 'member the name. But Mama showed it to her on a map, and it didn't look very far away. Her tummy felt a little funny when she thought about moving, but Mama said it wasn't forever. Just till Ryder fixed all the things that needed fixing in some old house there; then they would come back here.

She reached the last step and tiptoed into the living room. There were lots of presents wrapped in bright paper, but it was the castle in front of the tree that made her breath stop inside her.

She took another step closer and dropped to her knees

for a better look. She reached out, wanting to touch it, but snatched her hand back. She was only s'posed to peek, but now she really wanted to see what was inside.

She heard footsteps on the stairs and quickly backed away from the castle, climbing up onto the sofa so that she wouldn't get in trouble for peeking.

Ryder smiled at her from the doorway. "I thought I heard someone tiptoeing around down here."

"I twied to be quiet," Kylie whispered.

"Why did you try to be quiet?" he asked. "Don't you want to open your presents?"

She nodded. "But Mama said no pwesents till everyone is awake."

"Then we need to go back upstairs, stomping our feet the whole way, to wake them up, don't we?"

Kylie giggled. "Will Mama get mad?"

"Nah. Not on Christmas," he promised.

She slid off the edge of the sofa again but couldn't resist another peek at the presents under the tree.

"You're looking at that castle," he guessed.

She nodded. "Do you think it's for me?" she whispered the question.

"Let's find out," he said, taking her hand and guiding her closer. "Is your name on the tag?"

She couldn't print her name yet but she knew how to read it. She nodded as her finger pointed to each letter. "K-Y-L-I-E."

"That's right—it says 'To Kylie, From Santa.'"

She felt her mouth smile but she couldn't find any words to say.

He crouched down beside her. "Do you want to look inside?"

She nodded her head up and down.

So Ryder showed her the latch on the side, then helped her open it up. Her breath stopped again as the castle unfolded. She didn't know where to look—there was so much to see, so many rooms with lots of stuff inside.

"Did Santa do pretty good with this present then?" he asked, after she'd looked it all over.

"It's—" she need a second to 'member the word "—awesome."

He smiled. "The bestest present ever?"

She didn't have to think about the question long before she shook her head. "The bestest present ever is my new daddy."

His eyes were shiny when he hugged her. "I'm glad," he said. "Because your mom and you and Zachary are my bestest presents ever, too."

Kylie put her arms around his neck and kissed his scratchy cheek. "Can we wake Mama an' Zack now?" she asked him.

Ryder smiled. "Absolutely."

Then he took her hand and they stomped up the stairs together.

* * * * *

Don't miss Braden Garrett's story,
BABY TALK & WEDDING BELLS
the next installment in award-winning author
Brenda Harlen's series
THOSE ENGAGING GARRETTS!
On sale February 2017.

And catch up with Lauryn's and Ryder's siblings
by reading the previous books in the
THOSE ENGAGING GARRETTS! *series*
for Mills & Boon Cherish:
TWO DOCTORS & A BABY
THE BACHELOR TAKES A BRIDE.

MILLS & BOON®

Cherish™

EXPERIENCE THE ULTIMATE RUSH OF FALLING IN LOVE

MILLS & BOON®

EXCLUSIVE EXCERPT

When Dea Caracciolo agrees to attend a sporting
event as tycoon Guido Rossano's date, sparks fly!

Read on for a sneak preview of
THE BILLIONAIRE'S PRIZE
the final instalment of Rebecca Winters'
thrilling Cherish trilogy
THE MONTINARI MARRIAGES

The dark blue short-sleeved dress with small red
poppies Dea was wearing hugged her figure, then flared
from the waist to the knee. With every step the material danced around her beautiful legs, imitating the
flounce of her hair she wore down the way he liked it.
Talk about his heart failing him!

"Dea—"

Her searching gaze fused with his. "I hope it's all
right." The slight tremor in her voice betrayed her fear
that she wasn't welcome. If she only knew...

"You've had an open invitation since we met."
Nodding his thanks to Mario, he put his arm around
her shoulders and drew her inside the suite.

He slid his hands in her hair. "You're the most
beautiful sight this man has ever seen." With uncon-
trolled hunger he lowered his mouth to hers and began
to devour her. Over the announcer's voice and the roar
of the crowd, he heard her little moans of pleasure as
their bodies merged and they drank deeply.

When she swayed in his arms, he half carried her over to the couch where they could give in to their frenzied needs. She smelled heavenly. One kiss grew into another until she became his entire world. He'd never known a feeling like this and lost track of time and place.

"Do you know what you do to me?" he whispered against her lips with feverish intensity.

"I came for the same reason."

Her admission pulled him all the way under. Once in a while the roar of the crowd filled the room, but that didn't stop him from twining his legs with hers. He desired a closeness they couldn't achieve as long as their clothes separated them.

"I want you, *bellissima*. I want you all night long. Do you understand what I'm saying?"

Don't miss
THE BILLIONAIRE'S PRIZE
by Rebecca Winters

Available November 2016

www.millsandboon.co.uk

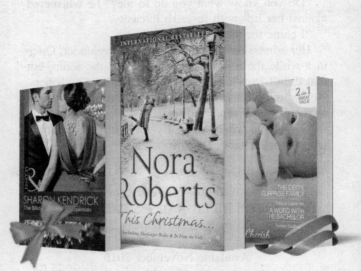

MILLS & BOON®

Why shop at millsandboon.co.uk?

Each year, thousands of romance readers find their perfect read at millsandboon.co.uk. That's because we're passionate about bringing you the very best romantic fiction. Here are some of the advantages of shopping at www.millsandboon.co.uk:

* **Get new books first**—you'll be able to buy your favourite books one month before they hit the shops

* **Get exclusive discounts**—you'll also be able to buy our specially created monthly collections, with up to 50% off the RRP

* **Find your favourite authors**—latest news, interviews and new releases for all your favourite authors and series on our website, plus ideas for what to try next

* **Join in**—once you've bought your favourite books, don't forget to register with us to rate, review and join in the discussions

Visit **www.millsandboon.co.uk**
for all this and more today!